Pamela Jooste was born in Cape Town, where she still lives. Her first novel, *Dance with a Poor Man's Daughter*, won the Commonwealth Best First Book Award for the African Region; the Samlam Literary Award and the Book Data South African Booksellers' Choice Award. Her other novels, *Frieda and Min*, *Like Water in Wild Places* and *People Like Ourselves*, were equally well received and are all published by Black Swan.

www.**rbooks**.co.uk

Also by Pamela Jooste

DANCE WITH A POOR MAN'S DAUGHTER
FRIEDA AND MIN
LIKE WATER IN WILD PLACES
PEOPLE LIKE OURSELVES

and published by Black Swan

STAR OF THE MORNING

Pamela Jooste

BLACK SWAN

TRANSWORLD PUBLISHERS
61-63 Uxbridge Road, London W5 5SA
A Random House Group Company
www.rbooks.co.uk

STAR OF THE MORNING
A BLACK SWAN BOOK: 9780552773607

First published in Great Britain
in 2007 by Doubleday
a division of Transworld Publishers
Black Swan edition published 2008

Addresses for Random House Group Ltd companies outside the UK
can be found at: www.randomhouse.co.uk
The Random House Group Ltd Reg. No. 954009

The Random House Group Limited supports The Forest Stewardship
Council (FSC), the leading international forest certification organisation.
All our titles that are printed on Greenpeace approved FSC certified paper
carry the FSC logo. Our paper procurement policy can be found at:
www.rbooks.co.uk/environment.

Mixed Sources
Product group from well-managed
forests and other controlled sources
www.fsc.org Cert no. TT-COC-2139
© 1996 Forest Stewardship Council
FSC

Typeset in 12.5/15pt Garamond 3 by
Falcon Oast Graphic Art Ltd.

Printed in the UK by CPI Cox & Wyman, Reading, RG1 8EX.

2 4 6 8 10 9 7 5 3 1

For Theo

STAR OF THE MORNING

PROLOGUE

These days they are giving Cape Town away in bits and pieces and you can take your pick, just whatever you fancy. Everyone wants to go up Table Mountain and when that's done they want to go down to the Waterfront. Then it's Cape Point and as far as I'm concerned they're welcome to that because the wind always blows there and the baboons walk around as if they own the place. After that it's the Company Gardens, especially when the hydrangeas are blooming and you can't tell the rats from the squirrels any more but no one seems to mind. Then it's the District Six Museum and when that's done you can jump on a boat and see the exact cell where Nelson Mandela was imprisoned on Robben Island. Then, if you're not burned to a crisp by the sun or half dead after all the running around, it's out to the winelands, a quick tour of the old Cape Quarter and a sunset sail on Table Bay.

It's hard to imagine that there are people who've lived here all their lives without seeing any of these things. Kogel Bay was as far as I ever got. That was in 1978 and I got there sitting on the top deck of a bus on a children's outing. I was ten years old and it put me off for life although it wasn't meant to be like that. It was meant to be a treat and an opportunity to discover the world around us for ourselves. In any case, that's what we were told. All I can say is that if I knew then what I know now I would have stayed where I was and spent the day lying on my bed reading *Superman* comics and enjoying the peace and quiet.

Ruby said that I would always remember that day and that was almost thirty years ago now and in a way, although not in the way she meant, she was right.

LIFE IN THE ORPHANAGE

I think how different my sister Rose is from me and wonder what I'm going to do about it. If I don't stop it now, the older she gets the worse it will get and I don't think the world will be kind to an orphan coloured girl who thinks she's in any position to do things her own way.

It's not my fault we're at Sacred Heart with all the other people the world has no time for. I wouldn't say it to Rose but if you ask anyone they'll tell you this for a fact, besides which I know it in my heart. I knew it the first minute I walked through the door. It's not just the orphans or children whose parents can't care for them who are here. There are old people too and some that are slow and not as bright as they could be. Even the little burn babies come here, the ones who need special care and take such a long time to heal. Once I knew about them, I couldn't stop thinking about them. I couldn't help it because I knew that even after they were well again they would never be perfect the way God first made them and intended them to be.

For a long time I blamed myself. It was as if I'd done something wrong and we were both being punished for it, but then I realized that it wasn't my fault at all. But if I had my life over again I would never choose life as an orphan. No one would. You have a safe place and people to look after you. You have a bed to sleep in and an extra blanket in winter. There's food on the table, porridge, milk and bread for breakfast. There are sandwiches for lunch, soup for supper and on Sundays there's 'resurrection food', leftovers that whoever's on duty puts together for us from whatever wasn't eaten in the week.

Sometimes our name comes up and one of the charities brings us cakes or gives us a Christmas party. Now there's a new thing. Round Table has organized it and once a year City Tramways are going to send a bus to take us children on an outing so we can see for ourselves what a beautiful part of the world we live in. I think it's the most wonderful thing that ever happened to Rose and me since we first came here. I would like to see a bit more of the world around me and judge for myself because I think there must be more beautiful places than the ones I've seen so far.

Our first outing is to Kogel Bay, a beach in the middle of nowhere where coloured people are allowed. One of the

older girls says that this is because the tides are so
dangerous we might all be washed away and drowned.
Then no one will have to worry about us any more. You
can't believe everything people tell you and I don't
believe that. I like the idea of Kogel Bay. I think it will
be like something out of a picture book with white sand
and blue sea, with shells to pick up off the beach and
maybe even small fish that would swim around your feet
while you paddled. I was hopeful but as it turned out
Kogel Bay wasn't like that at all. The bus stopped, the
engine was switched off and you could still hear a funny
noise all around you and feel the bus rattling and shaking
and that was the wind.

'It's not so bad,' I say to Rose and she's sitting next to
me like she always is. Her cotton pull-on sunhat lies on
the skirt of her dress and her hands are folded on top of
the hat. The bus shakes and rattles and outside on the
slope of the hill the top branches of the bushes are bending down to the ground as if they're praying or hanging
on for dear life and Rose is younger than me but even so
she's nobody's fool. You only have to look out of the
window at the empty car park and the empty beach and
the sand swirling everywhere and the sea being whipped
up into small choppy waves. It may be a day for everything wonderful but it isn't a day for the beach.

'You must stand up now,' I tell Rose. 'Pick up your hat
and check that your sandals are fastened and get ready to
go with the others.'

'No, thank you,' she says.

'I'll leave you here,' I say. 'Do you know how hot it's

going to be inside this bus? You can cook to death in the bus and see if I care.'

But her expression doesn't change. She sits in her seat with her hands holding on to each side of it, holding on for dear life as if it might fly away with her still sitting on it if she didn't hold on hard enough.

'Say something, Rose,' I say but she just sits there, silent, with her face turned to the window. 'You might try thinking of someone else and not just yourself for a change,' I say. 'In case you've forgotten, this is my day too and I want to enjoy it.'

Even so, she doesn't say anything and what can you do with someone when they get in that kind of mood? I've tried everything and nothing's worked. My beautiful day is sliding away from me right out of my hands, my sister won't budge and I burst into tears.

The bus is parked in the big parking lot right up against the side of the mountain. Rose can stare out of the bus window as much as she likes, there'll still be nothing to look at except the blue sky and the bushes bending to the will of the wind.

'What exactly is the matter with you?' I say for the one hundredth time.

'I don't like it here,' Rose says. 'I can't swim.'

'Nor can I and nor can the others. It doesn't matter, we can splash in the water.'

'The water's ice cold,' Rose says.

'You liked it last time,' I say. Last time we went to Camps Bay beach. It was our first outing and Friends of Sacred Heart arranged it for us. We bathed in the seawater pool and it was a lovely day and we all liked it then.

'I didn't like it,' Rose says. 'I only said I liked it because that's what you wanted me to say. The water was ice cold then too and there was seaweed wherever you looked and it stank.'

'Why didn't you say so before we left?' I say. 'You needn't have come today. We could have left you behind.'

The chance of an outing away from Sacred Heart doesn't come up every day. When one comes your way you grab it with both hands. Everyone does, but now all of a sudden, out of the blue, it doesn't suit Rose. Why does she have to be different? Why does she choose this day to be different on? There's not a single child who hasn't been longing for this day to arrive even if it's only for a chance to sit on the top of the bus and look down at the world while the bus rolls out of the gates.

The nuns don't go with us. Matron and Housemother do and even they are nicer on these days. They boss us but that's their job after all and they don't seem to mean it quite so much and I love these outings. I look forward to them. I don't say so out loud because that's the way it is where we are now. If you let on that something's important to you there's always someone who'll get hold of it and tease you about it and go on and on until it's all spoiled.

But I do love these days. It doesn't matter if they turn out good or bad, they still stand out from all the ordinary days and to me, although I'd never tell anyone, it's as if they're made out of gold. When they end I can take them back with me and turn them over again in my mind.

They're mine, they belong to me and no one can take them away and now Rose is spoiling this one by not joining in.

'The baboons will come and get you,' I say.

There are baboons. We saw them and they were frightening and they looked strong. They were ugly and they made horrible, chattering sounds like people do when they've done something they know is wrong and try to laugh it off afterwards to show they don't really care anyway. Some of the other children like the baboons. They think they're funny. 'There's the troop leader,' they say, pointing from the safety of inside the bus. 'He's just like P. W. You can see he's the boss.' It's the biggest, the ugliest, the one that sits a little apart from the others with the smallest, closest eyes that miss nothing, that's always the boss.

We're safe in the bus and can laugh at the baboon babies who haven't quite got the hang of life yet. They climb two steps up and tumble three steps down, then they pick themselves up as if they know they've made fools of themselves and look around quickly to see if anyone's watching them. Just like children do when they show off and think they can do something and then find that they can't.

Some people think baboons are funny because they're so much like people. Rose says she could watch them all day and laugh her head off but she wouldn't be laughing nearly so hard if one of them came up close to her. I also think that baboons are like people, only I don't think they're funny at all.

Baboons are moody animals. They can prance and play one minute and turn vicious the next, especially the old ones, and they're thieves. If you leave a piece of fruit or a sandwich lying around they'll clamber down screeching and chattering and snatch it away. The bus driver warned us about it. He said that sometimes they snatch human children away too and when you see them again, if you ever do, they've grown fur and long tails and they're swinging from tree branches and walking baboon-walk with their knuckles dragging along the ground next to them. I don't believe it but I'm willing to try the baboon threat to get Rose off the bus.

'They can come and fetch me if they like,' Rose says. 'I don't care. I'm not going anywhere.'

'Why?' I say. 'What's the matter?'

I have walked backwards and forwards from the beach to the bus at least three times. I have been nearly knocked over by the wind, the sun is hot, I have been stung half to pieces by the sand and the other children are giving me funny looks.

'Will you please go and see what's wrong with your sister?' Matron says. 'If she wants to be taken notice of, she's going the wrong way about it. Everyone's here to have a nice time. No one's interested in one girl who's decided to sulk. You can go back to the bus and tell her that from us if you don't mind.'

I have been to the bus and back and I have nothing to tell Matron that she would like to hear.

'She won't come,' I say.

'Then try again,' Matron says. 'Tell her that if she goes

on like this she can forget about any chance of a "next time". You can tell her that treats are for children who know how to appreciate them.'

I don't think a 'next time' is what Rose wants but I try anyway. I've sweet-talked and cried and I've threatened and still my sister won't talk to me and I don't know what I can do and at last Rose turns her head away from the nothingness that's all she can see through the bus window.

'If this is their idea of a nice time they can keep it,' she says.

'Next time will be better,' I say. 'Maybe next time the wind won't blow and it'll be a beautiful day and you'd be sad if you missed it.'

'I'm not going next time either,' she says. 'And you can tell Matron that if you like because I won't change my mind.'

'How can you say that now?' I say.

'Because next time I'll be even bigger and they'll still expect me to swim in my vest and my *broeks*,' she says.

After all the to-ing and fro-ing from the beach to the bus and all the 'Matron says' and 'Rose won't come', it is as if something strange happens to me and it is nothing to do with the day or the wind or discovering the world around us for ourselves. It is as if suddenly I can see inside my sister's heart and I see now that sitting inside the bus the way she is has nothing to do with any of these things.

'Other children have proper swimming costumes to swim in,' Rose says. 'And I'm getting to be a big girl now, too big for vest and *broeks* and it isn't right.'

Say something to that, her expression is saying. Do you have an answer, her eyes ask mine, and because I have no answer I start crying again. At first I don't even know that I am crying. The tears just spill out of my eyes and there's nothing I can do to stop them.

'I'm sorry,' I say.

What else is there to say?

Every last Sunday of the month we go to our aunt's house at number seventeen Steenbras Street, Athlone. Auntie Olive will be happy to tell you all about Athlone. At Sacred Heart we are coloured girls but in our aunt's house we are non-Europeans and Athlone is a garden suburb for non-Europeans and it suits Auntie Olive right down to the ground. Some houses in Athlone have names on brass plates on their gates. When we first used to go down Steenbras Street, I used to read them out loud to pass the time and try to take Rose's mind off things. The Williams house, next door to Auntie Olive, is called Costa Plenti. It's supposed to be a joke, just in case we didn't know. Auntie Olive doesn't care for names herself. Her house doesn't need a name. Number seventeen on the letterbox next to the gate is more than good enough for her. Everyone knows where our auntie Olive and her family live.

We don't come from Athlone ourselves. When we were still a family we lived in Woodstock. We are ordinary people and don't need to go around bragging that we live in a garden suburb. Woodstock suited us but it didn't suit our auntie Olive.

'You must bear in mind, Kathleen,' our auntie says to our mother, 'no matter what the mayor may say about up-grading, Woodstock isn't Athlone and is never going to be.'

She says this straight out while she's sitting at the kitchen table in our house in Woodstock drinking our tea and eating our biscuits.

It said in the newspaper that District Six, Woodstock and Salt River are going to be redeveloped.

'Not in our lifetime,' says my father. 'You see if I'm not right. We'll get old and grey and still there'll be no improvements and no one will have gone anywhere.'

'That's what it says in the newspaper,' my mother says.

It also says that when the redevelopment happens the mayor hopes that the 'coloured residents', which is us, won't all have to move out in one go and that if we do have to move it won't inconvenience us too much.

The trouble is that no one has asked us yet what our feelings are. If they were to ask me I would tell them that Woodstock might not be the grandest suburb in the world, it might not be Athlone but we are happy here right where we are. We don't want to go anywhere.

I don't know what our mother thought. Whatever it was, she kept it to herself and never said a word.

It's each to his own and the government puts us in suburbs according to colour and then it's every man for himself and rich people like our auntie Olive live in Athlone in paid-for houses, not rented like our house in Woodstock. In Woodstock, if you don't have the rent money ready on the front table in an envelope at the end of the month, when the landlord comes you're out on your ear and all your worldly goods with you, sitting out in the street. That is not the type of thing that would ever happen in Athlone.

In Athlone the houses may all look alike but everyone has their own front gate and their own piece of ground. 'Our little bit of garden' is what Auntie Olive calls it and Auntie Olive's house also has 'our garage' for one day 'when we decide it's time for a car' and a back 'stoep' and a concrete back yard where you can hang your washing, 'privately', Auntie Olive says, with a decent height wall between you and your neighbours so there's no possibility of your *broekies* and your bras hanging out for all to see.

Athlone may be grand, much grander than Woodstock, but all the same I never had much time for it. But then things changed and I have plenty of time for it now. I have all the time Athlone will ever need because Athlone is all we have now and it puts us one up on the other children at Sacred Heart.

Even before we walk out of the Sacred Heart gate, while we're still getting ready to go, I'm talking to Rose, making sure that she understands.

'They only do it because they have to,' Rose says.

'That's not true,' I say, although I know it is.

Rose doesn't like Auntie Olive. Uncle Bertie is worse because he never says a word but you can see what he thinks about our being there just by looking in his eyes. Then there's 'our cousin Patsy' who thinks she's better than any-one else in the world and she's the worst of the lot.

'The only reason I go is because you make such a big thing out of it,' Rose says.

'She's our blood aunt,' I say, pulling Rose's best dress over her head. 'You should be grateful. You should think of the other children who have nowhere to go.'

Rose does think of the other children. What she thinks is that if there are other children who'd like to go in her place she wouldn't mind not going at all.

I put a white pillowcase on my lap and make Rose bend over it, then I pull and tug a lice comb through her hair even though I know there aren't any lice and when I've finished I say, turn round, let me look at you.

I think she hopes that one day I'll say she won't do and let her stay behind but I won't. I always say she'll do just fine and then she has no choice, she has to come with me.

She sulks all the way on the bus and when we come to our stop and it's time to get off I grab her hand and pull her along and that's how we go the first part, with me nearly running and Rose being pulled hard behind.

Past the Main Road shops we go and I'm tugging and pulling and Rose is holding back and I don't care. I'm older than she is and bigger and I can pull hard. There's the café and the fruit and vegetable vendor. In Woodstock we used to buy rand-a-bag and you get what you're given. Here the ladies point out what they want and check every potato, onion and tomato as if they're buying diamonds and you won't see their purses until they're quite satisfied. There's the hardware shop with cut-price, green-stripe fold-up deck chairs on display outside tied up with lock and chain to a railing. Athlone is respectable but even Athlone's not so respectable that they don't have a lock and chain for 'in case'. The deck chairs are for looking at; they're not for 'help yourself'. At the 'home industry' shop they sell chocolate cake and crochet covers to put round spare toilet rolls and at the corner there's the BP garage and we make our turn and Rose gets yanked down into Steenbras Street and things change because people know us here. We slow down and I take Rose's hand properly in mine and I hold on to it hard so she can't pull away.

I've made up a game especially to get us down Steenbras Street. The game has to do with not stepping on cracks in the pavement. I suppose I look a fool dancing and hop-scotching my way down the street but I couldn't care less. I just wish it would rub off on Rose. If I could wring just one smile out of her I would be happy and goodness knows I've asked her often enough and she won't but that doesn't matter.

I can smile for both of us if I have to and I do to make up for Rose because I want Auntie Olive to see for herself how happy we both are to be there on last Sundays.

The neighbours can look at me happy and dancing from one perfect paving stone to the next if they like. Auntie Olive sets great store by the neighbours and I know what they say when they see us.

'Those are Olive's sister's girls,' they say. 'On their way to their auntie. They come from Sacred Heart, you know, poor little things, and every last Sunday of the month, every month God gives, they go to their aunt, Olive Fredericks, and at Christmastime too. Olive Fredericks is a wonderful woman. It's not everyone who'd be willing to give up a Sunday.'

Our mother's not known here in the same way our aunt is. Here, she's just Olive's poor sister, the one who fell into hard times and died. Here our mother doesn't even have a name.

I know Rose hates coming here and I know why. I don't like it all that much myself. Last Sundays at Steenbras Street are a poor 'best thing' to offer. I would give Rose the world on a plate if I could but I can't and that's that. In the meantime, she'll have to make do with last Sundays because that's all I have to give.

THE PINK HOTEL

When I think back now I wonder why, when Ruby and I were children, we always had to skip and run and half dance down Steenbras Street every last Sunday of the month. We didn't want to be there and Auntie Olive didn't want us. I don't know why Ruby could never just say it out loud and get it over with. It isn't the worst thing in the world to stay behind at Sacred Heart on a Sunday. If you can do it for three Sundays in a row, you can do it for four and I wouldn't have minded. I told Ruby a hundred times but she wouldn't listen to me.

'Auntie Olive doesn't want us,' I said, and Ruby said that the way I kept saying this over and over again was driving her crazy and she didn't think she could stand it for one minute more. If I said it again she was going to put Elastoplast across my mouth.

'Don't make me do that,' she said. 'Because I promise you, I really will do it.' Then she pulled me over the white pillowcase laid out on her lap so she could comb my hair for lice but I could still say it without saying it out loud. I said it with my mouth only and no words coming out while I was bent in half over my sister's lap while she pulled a lice comb hard through my hair and waited to see what might fall out but nothing did because I didn't have any lice.

'Try and be nice,' Ruby said to my bent head, but it was hard to be nice; it was hard to be anything while Ruby was scratching away at my head looking for something she wasn't going to find.

The way Ruby carried on you'd think that she couldn't wait to get to Auntie Olive's. By the time we told Housemother we were on our way and walked through the grounds and out of the gates Ruby was going so fast I could hardly keep up with her, even though it's down-hill and sometimes when you go fast downhill you can run away with yourself. Ruby kept looking back over her shoulder to see if I was still there and there I was no matter how badly I might have liked to be somewhere else.

Down past all the cross streets we went and the free-way was quiet because town was quiet, because anyone in their right mind stays put where they are on Sunday and enjoys the day, but not my sister and not me. There we were in our Sunday best, trotting past the low-storey blocks of flats with their stoep doors open and people beginning to enjoy their day. We went past the

Presbyterian church with its big stained-glass window and we crossed at the pedestrian crossing on Orange Street. There were hardly any cars out on the road but even so Ruby hung on to me for dear life because she thought I'd run into the road before the green man came on and a car would appear out of nowhere and knock me down flat. That was because she thought I'd do just about anything to get out of going to Auntie Olive's and I would have done just about anything but I would never do that to my sister.

Ruby didn't like it but we had to stay on our side of the road and only do zebra crossings and traffic lights and all the proper crossings. The reason she didn't like it was because if we stayed on our side of the road like we were meant to we had to go past the big, white pillars of the Mount Nelson Hotel and they were grand, like a palace, and Ruby didn't like them. They put her off and I never knew exactly why that was. She would have liked to cross over. Then she wouldn't have had to go past them at all but she'd promised Housemother and so we stayed on the same side of the road and crossed at the big traffic light in Long Street just for safety's sake.

No one but me knew how badly Ruby would have liked not to have to walk past the Mount Nelson and she didn't need to if she really didn't want to except for her promise to Housemother. I don't know why she did that. We weren't babies any more. We were more than big enough to choose our own way if that was what we really wanted to do. If we'd crossed over we could have turned our backs on the Mount Nelson pillars and taken a short cut to town all the way down Government Avenue. I would have liked that because it's the shorter way and I like the oak trees and the squirrels and the ice-cream man with his bell and how you can buy bags of peanuts to give to the squirrels, but Ruby wouldn't do it. The trouble with Ruby was that once she made a promise she'd never go back on it. I don't know why because promises are not what they used to be. Every minute of the day half the world is busy making promises with their fingers crossed behind their backs for 'in case', but not Ruby. We went the way Ruby told Housemother we'd go and I could have gone blindfold and still known when we got to the Mount Nelson Hotel because Ruby pulled my hand harder and she kept her eyes forward and she walked faster. I wondered if she thought that maybe they kept lions and tigers in the Mount Nelson garden just waiting to get us and that they might jump out at any moment? I knew that wasn't true. The only animal I ever saw there was a squirrel going quick across the road and he didn't look to me as if he was out to cause trouble. You couldn't even see the hotel from the road, just the pillars and a curved road with palm trees on either side and every last Sunday Ruby and me half running past as if our lives depended on it. You'd think the way Ruby went on that if we even dared to look back we'd be turned to pillars of salt like Lot's wife, although why we should be I really don't know.

I thought that one day I'd like to stop and have a proper look at the Mount Nelson Hotel. The people who come there are not like us. I'm sure you can see just by looking at them that they come from another world altogether. I can't say that I've ever seen anyone who stayed there except from a distance but I'm sure that they all wear bell-bottom trousers and platform shoes and are on first-name terms with Farrah Fawcett and John Travolta.

The whole idea made me fed up and that's why I did what I did. It was as if we were sitting there waiting for our lives to begin while everyone else in the world was going out disco-dancing under silver balls of light and wearing hot pants and making Bette Davis eyes at each other. It didn't seem to matter to Ruby. Once she got into a pattern she felt safe. She thought that once things were set in their place there was nothing on earth that could change them because she just couldn't imagine that, but I could. She wasn't expecting me to pull my hand loose and start walking away from her as fast as I could right between the pillars like a wind-up toy with no choice but to go forward without ever once looking back. I knew that the Mount Nelson Hotel wasn't for us, but even so I knew that nothing bad would happen to me. I thought that if Ruby came chasing after me like she usually did she would see for herself that nothing bad would happen to either of us. I knew that if I went through the pillars I would see what I'd already seen from the street, which was nothing but a road with a bend in it and palm trees on either side of it and an empty garden and a quiet early Sunday morning. But, all the same, it was a different world.

I waited for Ruby to call me back but she didn't. I kept

my back to her but she still didn't call. Then I began to slow down because I thought she would call and the joke would be over but she didn't call and I wasn't really going anywhere and in the end I had to stop and turn round and it was a silly joke anyway.

I turned round and stood where I was inside the grounds and I looked back at Ruby and she looked very neatly dressed and pretty standing where she was out in the road. We have clothes handed down to us at Sacred Heart and sometimes we get Truworth's chain-store clothes when our cousin Patsy has moved on to something new and far more in fashion. One thing's for sure, by the time we get them, whoever gives them, they're clothes no one else would want any more. Gipsy skirts and velvet jackets and corduroy pants and boots are not for us and nor is Shocking Pink lipstick, although I would like to try it. The only new dresses Ruby ever had were in those days when our mother sewed our clothes. The only new shop dress she had was her school uniform when she first went to St Agnes's School and that got handed on to me but you'd never say it. If you stood a little way up the drive that goes up to the Mount Nelson Hotel and looked back and saw Ruby standing on the pavement outside with the pillars on either side of her you'd say that she looked just like any other girl. She's so slim and neat in her hand-me-down granny print Truworth's dress that came from Patsy, with her gloves and her Bible in one hand and a hat that once belonged to Auntie Olive sitting on top of her head like a plate. We should have been in hot pants and neon colours with nice little boots to go with them but if Ruby ever thought about things like that she never said so to me.

I wouldn't have felt so bad if she'd called after me then. That would just have made the joke bigger and that was what she would usually do, but this time she didn't. I only wanted to show her that the Mount Nelson Hotel was just a place, that we could walk through the pillars if we wanted to and nothing would happen to us. There were no lions and tigers. There were no policemen with guns hiding in the bushes waiting to arrest us and drag us off to jail. I could see then that the joke was well and truly over and had fallen flat on its face. The truth is that I didn't know any more than Ruby did what would happen to me if I really was brave enough to go into some place where I wasn't allowed. For all I knew, if I did come face to face with her, Farrah Fawcett might not be so happy to see me as I would be to see her.

It took a lot longer walking back than it did marching off in the first place. I could see Ruby still as a statue between the pillars. She could have walked on without me but she stayed and I was red in the face when I got to her.

She could have asked me why I was showing off like that and what I was trying to prove but she didn't. She just looked at me and she didn't say anything. Ruby knew that there were no lions and tigers behind the pillars. She knew that there were no policemen hiding in the bushes with guns just waiting to grab hold of me and take me away and the funny thing is that there didn't need to be. I couldn't look at Ruby because something had happened to me that I didn't want her to see. Something inside me had changed and I knew then that there are some things that not even Ruby can keep from me for ever and that this was one of them.

We were coloured girls in a white world that didn't want us and if it doesn't come to you in one way it comes to you in another, and I walked back slowly and Ruby stood just where she was and she waited. When I got to her she shifted her gloves and her Bible into the crook of her arm and offered me her free hand.

'We better hurry,' she said. 'We don't want to be late.'

There was a part of me that said I should have kept my hand back. I was too old to need hand-holding but I didn't do that because I was not too old to put my hand into my sister's when she reached out to take it.

There was nothing about me that Ruby didn't know. She knew without my telling her, just by looking at me, that I'd crossed a bridge and learned a lesson that would have had to be learned sooner or later and she's right and she's wrong all at the same time. I did cross a bridge and I did learn a lesson but not the one Ruby expected me to. What shamed me wasn't what I'd done; it was the look on Ruby's face when I walked back to her. Ruby liked the ground firm under her feet. She didn't like change – but I saw then that I had my own thoughts and that my thoughts were different from my sister's. I took her hand and I held it fast to keep her by me and I thought that for the next little while I would do it her way. I would go where she took me but one day I might be the one who led the way and the way we went then would be different.

MOTHER

I would like to keep Rose safe but there are some things I can't keep her safe from. I often thought about my mother. I hated it that Auntie Olive never said her name. In Athlone she was either 'your mother' or 'my sister' or, to my cousins, 'your late auntie'. I never said anything but inside myself I said over and over again that our mother did, after all, have a name. I thought that if I wished it hard enough suddenly someone would say it out loud and in that way they would bring her back to us, but no one ever did.

Our mother's name was Kathleen and she died of stomach cancer. She was thirty-six years old and people said afterwards how young that was to die. She should have lived for a good many more years yet. She should have but she didn't.

The cancer took a long time but it seemed as if it went very fast. One minute she was with us and then, when we turned round again, she was gone.

'Not that she'd go near a doctor,' Auntie Olive said afterwards. 'But that was my sister, she always knew better.'

The way Auntie Olive went on you'd think that our mother wanted to die but that wasn't true. If my mother had had any choice in the matter she would never have left Rose and me.

My mother took medicine. She bought *rooi laventel* and *lewens essens* from the OK Bazaar in Adderley Street and carried it home like a prize in her handbag, then she took it drop by drop on a spoonful of sugar. She bought Kurra pain powders and Grandpa headache powders and herbs from the African herb sellers down on Grand Parade. She brought them home in a basket and boiled them up into tea. It's hard to imagine that someone who felt sick to her stomach for most of the time the way my mother did could possibly have managed to drink this tea and keep it down but she did because she believed in the herbs and thought that they could help her.

I can't remember my mother ever complaining but Auntie Olive said otherwise.

'She may be dead but let's at least keep the story straight,' she said. 'Your mother was lots of things but so far as I know she was never a saint. She was a very sick woman. She was dying. Of course she complained.'

My mother wouldn't go to the state hospital. She knew

too much about it, she said. You went into hospital, the doctor cut you open, had a look, said 'too far gone', 'what a pity', 'nothing we can do', 'sorry'. Then he sewed you up again and sent you home and that was that.

'I can say "what a pity" myself,' she said, 'without having to trouble anyone to look at my insides.'

When she said this she must already have known that she was going to die.

'But not yet,' she said. 'Not yet, not for a long time. You mustn't worry about that.' As if that settled the matter and we could all breathe again.

I never thought my mother would die. I believed her when she said that she loved us far too much to leave us. We were her jewels, her stars of the morning. That's what she called us and she told us that nothing in this world was strong enough ever to change that. Even death would have to stand back and wait his time in the face of so much love. The way she said it made me feel light inside myself and happy because I believed her.

'When I feel a little bit better I'm going back to work,' she said.

Before she got sick, she worked for the da Costa family at Pescanova Fisheries, in the office out in the industrial area, not in the factory. So she had something to brag about too and I wished she would remind Auntie Olive of that but she never did. The da Costas liked her because she worked hard and when she got too sick to work they were sorry to see her go.

'They always said there'd be a job there for me. They told me that and they meant it, you could see that. You girls should think about that. Not everyone is lucky enough to have a job they can step right back into.'

At night, when I lay in bed with Rose in the bed next to mine, I held my breath. Rose didn't like it because it frightened her, she thought I'd die, but I did it anyway.

'Why do you do it?' she asked.

I did it because it felt nice when I'd held my breath for as long as I could to all of a sudden let go and find that I could breathe again, but that's not what I told Rose.

'I don't know why I do it,' I said. 'Just because.'

Rose hates 'just because'. She likes straight answers she can understand but there was no straight answer to her question. I did it because I was practising, so that when things started to go better with us again I would still remember what it felt like, but I didn't tell my sister this either.

Then my mother got tired and had to lie down a lot. She was hardly up before she was down again but even so she told us that soon, just as soon as she felt a little bit better, she'd go back to her job.

'In the meantime,' she said, 'we still have Workmen's Compensation left over from Daddy's accident and I can draw sickness benefits.'

State sickness benefits aren't very much and they're less for us because we're not white but we're in no position to complain about 'less'. We must take our lesser portion and be grateful because we need the money now.

My mother's face began to change. You could see the bones sticking out from under her skin and her skin was yellow. She could only drink water in very small sips and when she showed that she would like to have some I fetched it for her.

'Don't listen to your auntie Olive,' she said. 'We aren't in the poor house, not yet.' She gave the glass back to me and put the palm of her hand against her wet mouth and her hand was very thin, you could see all the veins. 'We aren't charity cases,' she said and she didn't look at me when she said it. 'We have to be a little bit careful, that's all.'

My sister and I didn't go to state school because that would have meant a coloured school and my mother was against it.

'Not yet,' she said to my father. 'Not so soon. There'll be plenty of people later on who'll be more than happy to tell them what their place is and try to make sure that they stay in it.'

I wasn't meant to hear. I didn't know what she meant and I didn't ask.

I went to St Agnes's church school. It was near where we lived in Clive Street, Woodstock, and it was all coloureds anyway. Our school uniform was a pink dress with black lines across it that turned the pink into big pink checks. We had our black school blazer with the St Agnes's badge on it and black lace-up school shoes and white ankle socks for summer and grey woollen knee socks for winter. My mother bought big and put the hems up and made alterations so that there was room to let out when I started to grow into everything.

'You look very smart,' my mother said when she saw me all decked out, a schoolgirl for the first time. 'It's nice quality.' My mother had a sewing machine and sewed very well. She could do wonders with remnants and end-of-the-roll. She made all the clothes for my sister and me.

'You'll look after your new things, won't you, Ruby?' she said when she turned me round for a proper look after my final fit.

We had to pull in our belts to pay for my school uniform. I knew that even though I wasn't told, and I knew that when I outgrew it it would be time to pass it on to Rose. I thought it was sad that Rose wouldn't know what it felt like to go to school on her first day in clothes that still had the shop smell on them but she wouldn't be the only child in Woodstock in that position.

I went to St Agnes's Sunday school and had a gold star for attendance. There was nothing you could tell me about God that I didn't know already. The only thing that gave me any peace of mind during the time that my mother was sick was what I knew for sure about God. I thought that He would have mercy and allow my mother to stay with us. He may have needed willing servants to do His bidding in heaven but He already had my father and he was a very hard worker. I knew God had His time cut out but if He knew everything like He is supposed to then surely He knew that in heaven my father could work overtime if he had to just the same as he had upon earth. He would have done it, I knew, if it meant my mother could be spared to be with us.

I suppose I got above myself but I really thought that if only He would hear my prayers and find just a little time to think about it He would see that what I was asking wasn't really such a very big thing.

'It's not such a big thing at all,' my mother said, 'but there's something I want you to think about. God has His hands full running the world. I want you to remember that. So if something goes wrong and He doesn't have time to get round to us and our little problems you mustn't blame Him. You must promise me that.'

My mother was wearing her house overall, the one with flowers all over it that she got at Shoprite. It was the middle of the afternoon and she was resting on her bed in her room in our house in Clive Street. We were just the two of us and we'd been talking. I was sitting on the bottom of the bed with my back against the bed-end and my knees pulled right up to my chest. I could see my winter-grey school socks on my feet. I liked it when there were sometimes just the two of us and my mother was waiting for an answer and I couldn't give her one because there was no answer, at least not one that I knew.

'Whatever happens will be the right thing,' she said and her words fell like stones into my silence. I put my head down on my knees so that she couldn't see my face. 'You can always trust God, Ruby,' she said. 'He never makes mistakes. You must promise me that you won't forget that. Give me your word.'

I promised, but then I would have promised anything if I thought it would make any difference.

* * *

My mother finally gave in because she had no choice. She said the pain was too great and sent me to the neighbour to ask if I could please use her telephone to send for a doctor and she gave me a twenty-cent piece to offer for the favour.

When the doctor came the neighbour came with him and she was talking as they came in the house, whispering fast as if she was sharing a secret, telling about our mother and shaking her head. When the doctor went into the bedroom and closed the door the neighbour sat with us and I took hold of Rose's hand and we all waited together. We knew our neighbour but all the same it was a funny feeling having her in our front room with only Rose and me there, all of us waiting and no one saying anything at all.

The doctor gave our mother an injection for the pain.

'You can go in and sit with her if you like,' he said. 'She's asleep though so you must be quiet.'

In the meantime, he said, he'd just have a few words with the neighbour.

We went in and stood by the bed and our mother was sleeping, just like the doctor said. Her eyes were closed and she didn't even know we were there. It was very quiet. For a long time I was not quite sure where all the quiet was coming from and then I knew. It came to me that for the first time in a long time the pain had gone out of our house. I thought that perhaps the doctor had taken it away in his bag.

I stood by the bed and took a deep breath and held it in and then I exhaled long and slow and relief and peace came to some part of me. But it wasn't the happy kind of peace I'd been expecting when I practised breathing in my bed at night.

'Let her have a nice long sleep,' our neighbour said. 'Just let her rest. She looks very peaceful.'

I knew then that the cancer would win after all. I could see it in the way the neighbour looked down at our mother. Peaceful, isn't that the way we speak about the dead?

We lay next to our mother on the bed, Rose and me, one on either side of her, her two favourite girls in the world, her 'stars of the morning'. We had all our clothes on but our shoes were neat side by side on the floor and our feet in grey socks pointed up at the ceiling. We weren't touching. We just lay there flat on our backs looking up at the ceiling while the last of our mother's warmth warmed us.

'You girls must stay together,' my mother said and it sounded as if she was talking not just to us but to anyone who would listen. She turned to me and held me close and I lay beside her stiff as a plank, still looking up at the ceiling because I was afraid.

'Look at me, Ruby,' she said but I couldn't. 'Please look at me,' she said. 'Because I've got a favour to ask you and it's important.'

I couldn't look at her, not if you paid me.

'You must look out for Rose,' my mother said. 'You must always keep her by you. That will be your job because you're the eldest.'

There was no power on this earth that could make me turn and face her but I could nod my head.

'Please say it. I need to hear you say it. Look at me, Ruby,' she said. 'And say you understand, then promise me.'

And so I promised and that was the second promise I made to my mother.

When our father died Auntie Olive had a lot to say.

'Maybe now you'll meet a decent God-fearing Christian man who can hold down a job for more than five minutes.'

My father did casual labouring work. That didn't suit Auntie Olive. Sometimes he was in work and sometimes there was no work but we always had enough to eat.

'You're still young enough to start again.' That's what our auntie said to my mother. 'Life's given you a second chance. There aren't many people who can say that.'

No one ever contradicted Auntie Olive but I could have told her if she'd asked me that it wasn't life that gave my mother 'a second chance', it was a truck reversing on a building site and the foreman standing on our front doorstep to give us the news.

My father was hardly dead and Auntie Olive had a whole new life all ready and waiting for my mother as if it had all been arranged.

'This time you'll find someone who looks after you and treats you like a lady,' she said and I knew what that meant. It meant a man just like Uncle Bertie already sitting at our table. I never asked to have Uncle Bertie for an uncle. By the time I arrived he was already married to Auntie Olive and had his same place in my life that he would always have. In those days when they came to our house he said, 'Hello,' and after spending most of the visit with his eyes glued to his watch he'd say, 'It's time to go, Olive,' and stand up.

When we went to Athlone he spent the whole time sitting in the garage with his budgies and Auntie Olive took his tea out to him.

'He's very proud of those birds,' she'd say when she came back and my mother said nothing. In my own mind I thought he spent too much time with those birds because he was beginning to look like one. He had round budgie eyes that didn't like anything they saw, not his wife or his own house or even his own daughter and especially not a poor relation sister coming to visit with her two little girls.

That is the kind of man Uncle Bertie was and if that was the first prize according to Auntie Olive and what she had in mind for a husband for my mother then I, for one, would say, 'No, thank you.' But it might not be that easy. Even Auntie Olive could see that.

'Of course, it isn't every man who'd be prepared to raise another man's children.' She said that more than once and I felt so light I almost rose up off the floor with relief and then I felt terrible because I thought it must be our fault, Rose's and mine. If it weren't for us perhaps our mother would have been able to step out of her life altogether and leave it far behind her and go to a house in Athlone, exactly like Auntie Olive's, with a three-piece lounge suite, fully paid for, and a television and a fridge-freezer.

Before she got sick my mother was pretty, much prettier than Auntie Olive, who always seemed to find something to blame someone for and probably blamed my mother for that, as if there was anything she could do about it. My mother had black hair. When you put your hand on it it was smooth as fur and sometimes she sat down low on a kitchen stool and handed me her hairbrush.

'You give my hair a good brush,' she'd say. 'Would you do that for me, Ruby? It always makes me feel better and there's no one in the world who can do it quite like you do.'

I liked to do things for my mother. I liked it when it was just her and me.

'Sing "Star of the Morning",' she'd say. 'You know it, you always remember all of the words. I don't know how you do that. You're such a clever girl to do that. It's always a wonder to me.'

I pulled the brush down and down again through my mother's dark hair and felt happy to be me because I could sing 'Star of the Morning' or any other children's hymn you cared to name. I was one of the little children who loved their Redeemer and I knew from Sunday school that I would be 'Star of the Morning', His bright crown adorning, I would shine in my beauty, bright jewels for His crown. That was what had been promised to me. That was what my mother liked to hear.

'You will be, Ruby,' she'd say. 'You'll be all of those things. You just wait and see if I'm not right.'

Hymns are all very well as far as they go but when it came to the concert to help raise money for St Agnes's Roof Appeal, Woodstock parents weren't going to pay out their hard-earned money to hear what they could hear every Sunday for nothing. On concert night we had to show what we could do and everyone was doing something and the big girls were going to do *Flashdance* and I was one of those chosen to be in front singing and dancing and doing a solo. I was so happy I could hardly wait. I was singing and dancing round the house all day long.

'Making a noise,' my mother said.

'Practising,' I said. We 'rehearsed' at school and 'practised' at home to make sure that on the night we'd be perfect. At home Rose was everywhere I was, dancing like I danced and clapping when I clapped and doing all the movements and trying to keep up with me the way I was singing.

'You just remember,' my mother said, 'concert night's Ruby's night. She'll be the one on the stage and you'll be down in the audience with the rest of us and you'll have to stay in your place.'

We're going to have a proper stage and a record player behind to sing along to. The parents are helping and every child has a part to play so I'll have to wait my turn and that won't be easy, which is why they let the small children go on first. It was the big girls who were doing the finale, 'Flashdance ... What A Feeling', and the big girls were big enough to wait their turn.

I'm always happy to sing my head off, you never have to ask me twice and anyone who knows me will tell you that since I began to dance, I can't keep my feet still. I wake up in the morning with my toes twitching and all I want to do now is practise.

My mother said that the sooner this concert was over and we could all get back to normal, the better it would be. 'It'll be time to come back to earth for us all,' she said.

She didn't mean it. She was happy that I was so taken up with it all and so was my father. He said he told everyone that since I got involved in the concert he'd become the father of Miss Ruby Jacobs, the star of the show. I pretended to be cross and embarrassed when he said so and that made him laugh because he knew it wasn't true. The truth was that I liked the idea of being a star and wasn't embarrassed about it. If you're asked to stand in the middle of the front row and sing and dance to the last number and even have a solo part right at the end, in my opinion that makes you a star, and if it is so you may just as well say so.

We didn't have a curtain in St Agnes's Hall but on concert night we had double sheets tacked on to a washline. One of the fathers had put up special lights to shine on the singers and dancers and there were big speakers that Hi Fi for All had loaned for the evening. There were children everywhere, dressed up for their item, and mothers putting make-up on them, foundation and big lipstick mouths and rouged cheeks and all colours of eyeshadow and eyelashes painted right down on the cheeks. I was so excited I could have burst and when my moment came and 'Flashdance' started to rumble out of the speakers my feet began dancing before I'd even had a chance to tell them that it was time to begin.

If I could have my life over again and live to be a hundred and eighty-five years old and have many nights, more nights than I could possibly remember, I would still choose to have that night over again. I would never want to forget it and how it was. If I think of it now I can feel my feet dancing as if nothing could stop them and sweat pouring down my face and smudging my make-up. The music is top volume and I don't think anyone can even hear our singing but it doesn't matter. The audience are on their feet and clapping and singing along and my father and his friend Leroy Holmes have planned a surprise for me. I'm standing in the middle of the front row, shouting out the words and stamping my feet, and it seems to me that the hall is filled up and shaking with music and dancing. I step to the front for my solo part just like my teacher showed me and my father and Leroy Holmes have brought flashlights with them. They stand up on their chairs and switch the flashlights on me and there I stand singled out in the light and I sing and dance even harder and everyone claps.

I don't know how much money was raised for the Roof Appeal although I'm sure something was, something always is with all the events, and when it's all counted up the priest says it's still not quite enough. We'll have to do it all over again, he says, or something similar, if we are ever going to have a church roof that doesn't leak, but I don't care. We had a wonderful time and my feet hurt for days afterwards but I was the star of that show and I danced in the spotlight and I will have that for ever and it was worth it.

We knew how to live in Woodstock and that's something people like my auntie Olive could never understand. My mother told her about the concert and she had her opinion just like she always did.

'If that's what you call a good time,' she said, 'then I suppose that's what it must have been.'

My mother looked at me and I looked at her and it was something special between us. No one was even going to take the trouble to try and explain to Auntie Olive. The *Flashdance* night was one of those nights when you had to be there and be part of it to understand, because if you weren't there you'd never know.

I look at Auntie Olive sometimes and think what good sense God has in sorting out the right children for the right parents. If there'd been a mix-up and Rose and I had got Auntie Olive instead of our own mother, we might never have known it but in some part of ourselves, I'm sure, we would have known it and it would have been like the end of the world.

My mother had soft hands and a nice laugh and she smelled nice, like soap and fresh bread. When my father was still with us, before the truck, when I was still singing and dancing and we were still a family, he'd come up behind her and put his arms round her and press his face up against her neck and breathe her in. Rose said that you couldn't breathe people in but she was wrong, you can. I had breathed in my mother and whether Rose believed in it or not, I had breathed her in too.

'That's enough of that,' my mother said and she turned round with her eyes shining and her face flushed, not from the washing-up water but because she was happy, even though she kept saying that he mustn't because it wasn't something for children to see.

I could understand how a man would want my mother and since my father died Auntie Olive kept going on about some new man coming into my mother's life as if we should expect it any minute. What I didn't see was how Rose and I could fit into the picture.

'You know your auntie,' my mother said. 'Just let her talk, you don't have to listen.'

But I did listen and what I heard got stuck in my head and unsettled me and made my whole world unsteady.

While Auntie Olive was talking I kept thinking that if my mother stepped out of the life that we had in Clive Street into some far better life that lay waiting for her, Rose and I would vanish. Our mother would forget that we ever existed, and if that happened how would she know to come back and look for us?

I lay awake at night and thought about Rose and me in some grey place without our mother and no one knowing where we were and no one willing even to come out and look for us. I made myself so frightened that I'd start shaking and then my mother got sick and things changed and that was when I began practising my breathing again.

It's a hard thing to watch someone die and Auntie Olive came to sit out the last time with us.

'Well, who else do you think will do it?'

My mother was sick all the time, all skin and bone and vomiting. What we didn't see we could hear and she smelled funny and Auntie Olive hated every minute of it, you could see that. She came and went from the bedroom to the bathroom with dishes covered over with towels and she turned her head when she emptied them down the toilet.

'Thank you, Olive,' my mother said.

It came out small, like a whisper, but all the same it cost a lot of breath to say that. My mother kept saying it over and over all the time and she didn't have much breath to spare.

Auntie Olive made a pot of soup and we had soup for supper all the time and she sat with us at the table and she looked at us, first long and hard at me and then at Rose. If I could have grown up right there and then, I would have. I would have grown up and taken care of my mother and made things better for Rose and there would have been no need for 'Thank you, Olive' every five minutes and love would have come back into our house.

'So like Kathleen,' my auntie said, as if Rose and I were both stone deaf. As if she couldn't have cared less what we heard, as if somehow it was our mother's fault.

I knew my mother was dying. There wasn't much

time, I knew that too, but time is nothing to God and I prayed for a miracle. God can do miracles if He sets His mind to it but no matter how hard I prayed there were no miracles that day.

I wonder what my mother thought when, after everything, she was still called to go. Love is stronger than death; it says so in the Bible. Did she think that if God paused in His labours and looked down and saw how much she still had to do He'd find it in his heart to spare Kathleen Jacobs?

In that last moment of her going did my mother feel what I did, which was that God knew all the time what was happening, that He was there and He stood by and let it happen anyway? He was never going to help us. He'd turned His back on us and forsaken us and we'd done nothing to deserve that.

GOD GIVES THE SHOULDER

Auntie Olive won't be taking us in. It took her five days before she told us but when she did it came as no great surprise to me. I knew from the minute we walked in the door at number seventeen Steenbras Street with our suitcases in our hands that we wouldn't be wanted there.

Breaking the news was Auntie Olive's job. She thought the priest would do it but he wouldn't and that was all right too. If Auntie Olive couldn't find room for us in her house or in her heart then she had to tell us this herself. I wondered why it was such a hard thing for them, for those grown-ups, between all of them, to tell us something that I already knew.

'You girls come here and sit down,' Auntie Olive said. 'There are some things we have to sort out.'

We were in the front room, Sunday and special

occasions only, so we knew that whatever it was must be important. I knew that it was going to be what I'd been expecting to hear. We sat side by side on the settee of the famous, paid-for, three-piece lounge suite from Bradlow's stores. They'd had it for as long as I could remember but it still had its plastic on to keep it clean and if you got the bare part of the back of your legs on it you squeaked when you moved.

I sat up straight and pulled Rose close to me and we both sat very still and there would be no squeaking from either of us while our lives were being rearranged.

You have to be brave to do what Auntie Olive had to do and in her way Auntie Olive must have been brave because she was more than up to the job. She'd discussed it with Uncle Bertie, she said.

'What it comes down to is it's not what we'd like or what we wouldn't like to see happen. What we want is what's best for you.'

She looked right in my face when she said this but she wouldn't have seen anything at all by looking at me.

'The truth is that we just can't take it on. We've already got far too much on our plate.'

We'd been five nights in her house, Rose and me, in one bed set up in the little spare room that Uncle Bertie built on at the back to use as a pantry.

People we'd never seen before had come to look at us because we'd suddenly become special, the two little girls whose mother had died and left them behind.

'How long do we have to stay for?' whispered Rose.

She hated being called for and pushed forward so strangers could take a look at her.

'I don't know,' I said. 'I don't think very long.'

There were cars drawing up outside all the time and plenty for the neighbours to look at and out of the cars stepped all kinds of people, people from the Church and people from social services. There was so much coming and going that the teapot never went cold and it felt like a party. Sometimes we were told to go into the kitchen and wait there until we were called. Other times Auntie Olive came to fetch us and take us into the front room to be 'shown' and talked about us as if we weren't there.

'This is Ruby,' she said, pushing me forward. 'She's the eldest and the small one is Rose.'

Auntie Olive was busy in those days. Even when we were just the two of us in the kitchen or sitting on the bed with the boxes of potatoes and onions next to us and a shelf of tinned fruit and vegetables over our heads, we could still hear the whispering. I closed my eyes and I could still hear it. The room was filled with the smell of apples and onions and I put my hands over my ears but I could still hear.

Our mother's death was 'untimely' and 'unfortunate'. She'd made 'no provision'. 'Living on love and fresh air from the look of it.' 'Too proud to ask for help.'

'I don't know what she was thinking,' Auntie Olive said. 'I don't know what she expected.'

They didn't need to speak in that whisper that finds its way in everywhere. If asked, I could have told all of them that what my mother expected was to live.

' "God gives the shoulder",' Auntie Olive said when everyone else had finished having their say. 'And I was ready just like I always am. I would have done it if your uncle Bertie hadn't sat me down and talked some sense into me.'

It was the first I heard of Uncle Bertie being in the least bit interested in us. As far as he was concerned, we were the poor relations and having poor relations visit you at your house in Athlone while you sit in the garage with your budgies is one thing. When they arrive on your doorstep with their suitcases and look as if they might be moving in, that's another thing altogether.

I didn't know if our well-being ever worried him, I didn't know if he'd even been asked or said what he thought but I did know one thing. If anyone was going to sit Auntie Olive down and talk some sense into her it definitely wasn't going to be Uncle Bertie. When Auntie Olive made one of her announcements, like how they wouldn't be coming to visit us in Woodstock any more, she would have decided it all by herself and then when she opened her mouth she would talk for them both. Perhaps I was wrong but I don't think so. Perhaps there was a whole side to Uncle Bertie that I'd never seen but now we'd lived with him in the same house and he was just the same as he'd always been. I suppose I should have believed Auntie Olive but it was hard for me to know when all this sense-talking went on because I never heard it.

It wasn't easy to find a place for us. White children who needed care got first pick. There was always a plan to see that a white child was taken care of but we weren't white children. That was never a problem before, we didn't even know the difference. We lived our own life and we were happy. We didn't know that all the time the rest of the world was already out there, just waiting for the day when it could come in and claim us and give us ID papers to put us in our proper place. Our mother knew that sooner or later it was bound to happen and I know that she would have taken this cup from us if she could.

It wasn't easy but there was some good news as well. We were Catholic and the Catholics had a place that would take us. There was space for us at Sacred Heart and nuns who were willing to look after us. Sacred Heart took people who had nowhere else to go. On Sundays when we went to St Agnes's we remembered the children at Sacred Heart in our prayers while we gave thanks for our own families and for being so bounteously blessed.

'If the Church can't take proper care of you, then who can?' Auntie Olive said. 'That's what I said to Uncle Bertie and he agreed. Your mother was a good Catholic and it's the Church's turn now to do something for her.'

I understood. I understood much more than they realized.

'But every last Sunday you'll have lunch with us,' Auntie Olive said. 'That's arranged. When you think about it, even when your mother was alive, we didn't see each other every day anyway, so in that respect things won't have changed all that much. We'll still be a family.'

I looked at Auntie Olive, puffed up, knowing that what she was doing was wrong and all the time trying to talk it right again, but if Auntie Olive had known what was in my head she'd have known that she didn't have to try quite so hard. I may not have wanted Sacred Heart but I didn't want to live with Auntie Olive either. I didn't want it for myself and I didn't want it for Rose. I didn't want to live with someone who didn't really want either of us.

There was one good thing about number seventeen and that was our cousin Godfrey. Godfrey was three years older than me and six years older than Rose.

We didn't really know our cousins before my mother died because although we were family we weren't on visiting terms. Sometimes in families it just happens like that.

In the early days our mother and father and Auntie Olive and Uncle Bertie used to get together for Sunday lunch sometimes and sometimes at Christmas, but I didn't really remember those days and it didn't work out anyway. My father was the problem.

'He's not our type,' Auntie Olive said to my mother. 'Which is something you should have thought about, Kathleen, when you made up your mind to get married.'

My mother passed this on to my father and he didn't mind and they made a joke of it.

'That's fine by me,' he said and Ma and Auntie Olive still kept in touch. My mother sometimes did sewing for her and made alterations to her dresses when she began to get fat. Getting your sister to do something for nothing is cheaper than going down to the tailor on the corner, and Athlone and Woodstock mixed very well on those occasions.

'Married life agrees with me,' Auntie Olive said when she handed my mother the packets of clothes for alteration because Woodstock may not have been good for much but it was good enough for that. Auntie Olive was more than willing to come 'out of her way' to drop off her one-size-too-small dresses and then come back to collect.

'Thank you, Kathleen. Yes, I must say that doesn't look too bad.'

Then she looked at her watch and said there was just time for a quick cup of tea and maybe something sweet to go with it and then she'd have to get back.

'I hope you understand, Kathleen,' she said while she sat on one side of our kitchen table and my mother on the other. 'Things could be very different. If it was just you and me it wouldn't have to be like this at all. But then you know that without saying.'

'I know that, Olive,' my mother said.

'But that's not the way it is when you have a family to consider. Bertie also has something to say and then there's Godfrey and Patsy. I have to think about them. You can't expect children who have a back yard of their own and a park just down the road to go out and play in the street.'

This was not meant for my ears but I heard it anyway and it wasn't as if it was just like water that washed right over me. I knew exactly what Auntie Olive thought of us and Woodstock where we lived and my father and our family. It was just strange to me that she could say these things while she was sitting at our kitchen table in our house. The big brown teapot with the Five Roses tags hanging out of it was in the middle of the table, one teabag for Auntie Olive, one for my mother and one for the pot. It was our teacup that was in front of her and the two Truworth's carrier bags of dresses that my mother had altered for her were on the floor next to her handbag. There were three Baker's Choice Assorted biscuits, the ones in the Alice in Wonderland tin that we kept for special, on the side plate in front of her. Auntie Olive had told us often enough that she shopped at the new Pick 'n' Pay Cookie Matic where the biscuits were fresh every day but she knew that we couldn't afford that. Auntie Olive was very fond of a nice fresh biscuit and Cookie Matic biscuits, Melting Moments, Cocoa Rings and Peanut Crunch were all the fashion, but if you could judge by the way she was eating them our biscuits were more than good enough for her.

Auntie Olive lifted up her cup and then put it down again. Then she lifted it again and put it to her mouth. You'd think, the way she went on, that a cup from our house couldn't possibly have been decently washed but if she was forced to drink out of it then she would, for the sake of peace and the family.

There was never any mistake about how Auntie Olive felt about anything and when she ran out of words she found other ways.

'It's how she is,' my mother said. 'She's always been like that and if I don't mind it, then I don't know why you should.'

I had never said anything and I never knew my mother

had even seen me there looking, and I won't say that I never knew how much she understood because when I was with my mother I never had to say anything, she always knew my heart.

Those times when she went to Athlone, which was two buses and far, but never so far that it was out of her way, she didn't take me with her. She left me with my father and my friends playing out in Clive Street because there was always a game going on and we were happy.

That's the reason I never really got to know my cousin Godfrey but he came to my father's funeral with his parents although his sister didn't.

'I kept her behind,' Auntie Olive said, 'because a funeral's no place for a child.'

Rose and I were there. We were wearing our white Sunday school dresses and black satin sashes round our waists that our mother had made for us on her sewing machine in the night. That had been the last night our father was still in the world with us. He was down at Goodall and Williams's Funeral Parlour, not in our house, but he was still in the world. The next day, we were all at the graveside at Maitland Cemetery, my mother and Auntie Olive and Uncle Bertie and Godfrey and me and Rose. We stood by the graveside and bent our heads and prayed and when it was over a coffin was lowered in the ground and we knew that our father had been truly taken from us and was gone.

* * *

I like Godfrey because he always treats me as if I am a normal person. As far as Rose and I are concerned, you can keep Patsy.

'She's still got her puppy fat,' Auntie Olive says.

'She wouldn't have so much puppy fat if she didn't eat like she does,' says Rose and I tell her to be quiet. We aren't in a position to say what we like about our cousin, not if we want to stay in her mother's good books. If Auntie Olive's opinion is that her daughter's growing up into a beauty, then that's how it will be and it isn't for Rose or me to say otherwise.

Godfrey's good-looking though, or at least I think so.

'It's no use looking goo-goo eyes at him,' Rose says. 'You can't marry him. He's your cousin.'

As if I don't know that, but I like him just the same because he teases me.

'You're a quiet one,' he says. 'You always listen to what we have to say and never speak up for yourself. You never tell us what Sacred Heart is like or what you do with yourself there. You never say what you do between Sundays.'

I wouldn't mind telling him if I was ever given the chance but I know I won't be because Auntie Olive will always chip in, and perhaps it's just as well because what I have to tell him would be a very short story.

'You mustn't waste Godfrey's time,' Auntie Olive says. 'He's a big boy with a life of his own outside the house. He goes places you wouldn't know anything about.'

We may not go to the places that our cousin Godfrey

goes but we know all about him just the same; his mother makes sure of that. He's very popular. He has a wide circle of friends. He's so busy that he hardly has time for his own family, never mind any spare time to entertain his little girl cousins.

'He'll get himself a good trade,' Auntie Olive says. 'He'll be a motor mechanic. There's good money there and when he's finished his apprenticeship, he's going to save up for the deposit on a car. He'll show his father up and get the first car in the family.'

'Uncle Bertie's budgies won't like that,' Rose says. 'They'll get a bit of a shock if they see a car in their garage.'

But if it comes to a choice between Godfrey having somewhere to put his car and the budgies there will be no contest at all. Uncle Bertie's got more time for the budgies than just about anything else in life but they don't even get a look-in when Godfrey's around.

The one time you see Uncle Bertie really happy is when he's outside telling people about Godfrey.

Godfrey's so busy just being Godfrey and doing so well in his schoolwork and with his soccer and with his church duties as a server at Good Shepherd that he doesn't have time for anything else. His mother says so.

The story changes as the years go by but it never really changes at all. Godfrey is the shining light at the centre of that house. He's the light around which everything moves and Godfrey may be our cousin and we can look at him and wonder at him just like everyone else does but he isn't for us. He moves in a superior world altogether.

* * *

We aren't like our cousins. We have plenty of other children around us all the time but they're not children who invite us to their houses because, like us, they have no house to invite us into. Auntie Olive's is the only house we know. We know the famous three-piece suite that she bought for cash at Bradlow's that she used to like bragging to our mother about when our mother was still with us, but we're family and it's for visitors and so we aren't asked if we'd like to sit on it. We know the ferns out on the stoep. They're like a jungle blocking out the light, but next to the roses in the front garden the ferns are Auntie Olive's pride and joy and the neighbours say how fine they are and so the ferns are safe. They can stay right where they are and keep on growing to their hearts' content.

Patsy's piano barely fits in but it's there, and there's a sideboard with a display cabinet in the middle and cupboards on either side where the china's kept on one side and the glassware on the other. On top of the sideboard there's a photograph of Uncle Bertie in overalls in front of a Cleansing Department truck down at the yard, clipboard in hand. There's a picture of Godfrey's soccer team and one of Patsy in her first communion dress.

'We should get photographs done of you,' Auntie Olive says one day out of the blue when she's in a good mood. 'There should be a picture of all of us together. We'll have a snap taken.'

One Sunday we do have a snap taken, so there's a photograph of all of us together taken by Clarence-next-door. Auntie Olive tells him that he must have an extra copy made when the picture's printed.

'For you and Rose for a keepsake,' she says to me. 'One day you'll look back and you'll be pleased to have it. It will be something to remind you of the times you've spent here, with us, in Steenbras Street.'

We stand in front of the house with bright for-the-birdie smiles on our faces, except for Uncle Bertie who doesn't smile at all.

He said from the start that he didn't really want to be in the picture. He says we should go on without him, he'd rather be with his budgies. How many times does he have to say it? he says. They're the only 'birdies' he's interested in.

'Count me out,' he says.

'You're being in the picture or there won't be any picture at all,' Auntie Olive says and there's no way out.

Rose is pushed to the front next to Auntie Olive because she's so small if she doesn't go in the front you might not see her at all. Godfrey has an arm around his sister's shoulder and an arm around me and he's the only one who looks as if he's really enjoying himself.

No matter what his mother says or how much she brags about him, you have to like Godfrey because he's always nice and always the same. Sometimes, when his mother's having her say, he'll stand behind her where he knows she can't see him and point at her and wink at me and it's all I can do not to smile but I don't because I know exactly where it is I stand with Auntie Olive. I've been put in my place too often not to know, but even so Godfrey can make it better. In that house, just out of the niceness that was God's gift to him, he has that much power.

When he goes off after lunch to be with his friends he'll say goodbye to me in a way that makes me think he really enjoyed me being there.

'One day soon I'll take you down to the soccer field with me,' he says. 'I'll show you some of the finer points of the game.'

I'd have liked to go but I know that Auntie Olive would never allow it.

'You're here to spend time with me, not to run around with boys. That's what I told Sister Angelica. That's our understanding.'

What's being offered is morning service at Good Shepherd and lunch and then sitting with Auntie Olive, then afternoon tea and it's over and that's all there is and all we may expect. If there's anyone who understands that quite perfectly, then I am that person.

GOING OUT IN THE WORLD

Sacred Heart is a place where you stay while you're waiting to grow and be able to look out for yourself. It's not your home and you can't stay for ever. From the minute you arrive you know it's only temporary. Just as soon as you're ready, you have to go out and make your own way in the world and when that happens there's no going back. There's a long list of other children just waiting to step into your place and even if you'd like sometimes to forget it, you'd never be allowed to.

When the time comes you have a 'goodbye' tea, just the two of you, Sister Angelica and the 'leaver', and when your tea's finished, before the cup's even going cold, you have your last word with Matron. By that time someone else will already have moved into your cubicle. It's not your place any more and you can't go back there. Your suitcase packed with your worldly goods is waiting in the hall, closed and ready to go. House Superintendent comes into Matron's office and gives the nod. This means that as far as she can see, you'll be leaving with just what you came in with, which, when you come to think of it is not so very different from how life itself is. Once it's quite certain that there are no sheets or towels or anything else that isn't yours going out into the world with you, you get that final nod and that part of your life is over and done with for good.

Sister Angelica says, 'I'll pray for you, Ruby.'

Matron shakes your hand. 'All the very best,' she says, and that's it and then you're on your way.

It's hard to remember when you're leaving how small and scared you were when you first came, but I remembered. I remembered just how scared I was and how hard I tried not to let it show in case Rose got upset.

'We'll stay together, won't we?' Rose had said and I said yes and I lied because how would I know? I didn't think that we would stay together like we'd always been before. I knew it would be strange and I didn't think that it would all be good, but however it turned out I thought that I could manage just as long as I had Rose with me, but it wasn't going to be like that because Sacred Heart had rules.

'Rose will be with girls her own age,' Sister Angelica said. 'She'll soon make friends.'

What Rose needed right that minute wasn't 'friends'. What Rose needed was me.

The entrance hall at Sacred Heart was big and dark and quiet like a church and Sister Angelica spoke softly as if it was a church and she was big and white like a whispering ghost and I never liked her. I didn't like the way she whispered because I thought that if you didn't do what she told you her whisper would pretty soon turn into a hiss, and that when she did speak you wouldn't like to hear what she had to say.

It had taken all of my courage but there was only one thing I could have done and I had no choice, I had to do it. I had to tell her that no matter what the rules were in this new place, there were other more important rules that pushed all the rest right out the window.

'I must stay with my sister,' I said and it came out bigger than I meant.

She seemed surprised to find I had a voice but I did and I'd made a promise to my mother, and remembering that made me strong because that was what counted with me.

The place was new to us and big and Rose was holding on to my hand. She was afraid to let go because she thought that if we parted and lost one another that would be the end of it because how would we ever find each other again?

'I never thought you'd do it,' she said afterwards and I didn't think so either but I found the courage from somewhere and I did it.

'But just you remember, Rose, it's not for always, just for now, while we're still strange.'

I couldn't make it for 'always'. I wasn't strong enough for that but I could make it for 'now' and for the next little while until things weren't quite so strange, but that was the best I could do.

'We make rules for a reason,' Sister Angelica told me. 'That's one of the things you'll learn while you're here with us but I'm sure you can see that, Ruby. You're a clever girl, I can see that, and I'm quite sure that you really do understand.'

'Jesus wouldn't mind,' I said and I said it as if I'd got it direct and that all I was doing was passing on a message.

I had by now given up on God but I asked Jesus one last favour and whether He would help me or not I was never going to trouble Him again.

For a long time I tried to talk myself into believing that my mother wasn't dead at all. I thought that if I tried hard enough I could make myself believe that when my mother left this life we'd shared with her she'd stepped into the life that Auntie Olive said was her rightful place, the life where there was no room for Rose or for me.

It could make you afraid if you thought too much about it but I wasn't afraid. There were things I was afraid of but this was not one of them. I knew my mother wouldn't forget us. If there was one thing I knew for sure, I knew this and I could hold on to it. One day, in that other life, she'd remember us. Love would remind her and love would bring her back to us and she'd walk through the gates of Sacred Heart and I would hear her voice calling to me to say it was getting late and time to go home.

When that hope began to fade, when my faith wasn't

strong enough to hold on to it, I thought that perhaps Auntie Olive would change her mind. I thought she'd know that what she'd done was wrong and that it would worry her. I didn't understand how she could have the two of us in her house every last Sunday, then send us back again for another month and never once think that maybe, after all, there could be a place for us in Steenbras Street.

But she could do it and it didn't seem to worry her.

'You're a big fool,' Rose said to me one Sunday.

'And why is that?' I asked.

'Because I know what you're thinking. Whenever we walk down this road you think that maybe Auntie Olive will all of a sudden send someone to call us back again and say it's all been a mistake and she'll have us.'

'I do not,' I said.

'Yes, you do,' said Rose.

'You should stop thinking about it,' Rose said. 'Because it's not going to happen.'

I turned away from Rose and I stood still where I was and I put my head down and I cried.

'I wouldn't cry about it if I were you,' Rose said. 'I don't know about you but I don't need Auntie Olive. She's not even worth crying about.'

'It isn't that,' I said.

'What is it then?' Rose said and I said, 'Nothing,' even though it wasn't nothing, at least it wasn't to me.

It was a sad thing, that's all, to realize that in the entire world there was no one to whom you could offer your love because there was no one who had any use for it.

* * *

When it's your time to leave, Sacred Heart finds a 'place' for you. You're meant to go when you're sixteen and I stay two years over my time, child-minding and helping to take care of the burn babies.

The burn babies come to us from Red Cross Hospital and their stories are always the same. They come from squatter camps or out of huts in the rural areas where people cook on paraffin stoves. One mistake and a shack can burn down or maybe two or three or even more. One mistake, one overtired mother or a child who gets too curious, and a life can change for ever.

The burn babies stay in their own section on the Sacred Heart property, separate from the orphans and the old and the ill. Helping take care of them is not a job for everyone but I can do it even if it means that I cry myself to sleep at night out of the sadness of it. It's love and loss I feel and I know this place before I even enter it and I don't think it's a place for me but I go anyway. I'm afraid to love these babies but I do because I can't stop myself. Love flows into me and sometimes it's so strong it feels more like pain but there's nothing I can do about it. I once loved God but I love these babies more and there's no one now that I know who will suffer little children and I think that this will surely break my heart, but even so, it can be done and I can do it. I can do anything if it means I can stay close by my sister.

'I suppose Jesus gave his approval?' Sister Angelica says when I ask if I can stay on past my time and she says yes but it will have to be the burn babies.

They're very small and very sick and they need a lot of care. She didn't say anything about love, although she could have said it and I would have understood. I am a girl with love in me and I think that if she knew me better perhaps she might have known that.

I have been grateful many times in my life. I can be grateful just this once more because I'm grown now and Sister Angelica is just another old woman in white hiding away from the world, and why should I talk to Jesus when I can talk to her?

'Eventually you'll need to get a proper job, Ruby,' Auntie Olive says. 'Just so long as you realize that. Just remember that there's nothing so special about you.'

Patsy was going to be a schoolteacher but that didn't work out and Godfrey is an apprentice motor mechanic and for as long as I can be I'm a temporary baby-minder, the one who watches powerless while little children suffer.

'That's not going to get you very far in life,' Auntie Olive says.

'That should suit her then,' says Rose the minute Auntie Olive's out of earshot. 'She doesn't expect you to go "very far" in life. She doesn't expect either of us to. So what's she complaining about? She should be happy.'

The child-minding can't last for ever; I know that while I'm doing it. We go to Sacred Heart to be sent out into the world, not to stay for ever. That's for the nuns, it's not for us. We have to get real jobs and Sacred Heart helps us find them.

Matron always says what wonderful employers we're all going to have. Why do we think someone comes to Sacred Heart looking for an untrained girl in the first place? They come because they want to do some good and give some girl a better chance in life and Rose is banking on it. She's made up her mind that what she wants to do when she's ready is leave for London and find a job working for the Princess of Wales.

'Why not?' she says when she keeps going on about it and I don't say anything.

I could give her a lot of reasons why not but I won't. She thinks that once the honeymoon is over and Lady Di has got used to being Princess of Wales, she'll arrive at the door of Sacred Heart on a royal visit.

It is no good trying to say anything to Rose about this. It used to be models and film stars and Princess Caroline but that was all over the day she discovered Lady Di. I don't like to tell her that Lady Di has plenty of other things to do with her time than worry about Rose Jacobs, so I don't. I don't tell her that there is a world full of places Lady Di would go to before she would ever come here. Not with things as they are. I can get through my life without commenting on the cut-out pictures from *Fair Lady* stuck all over Rose's room or the way she talks about her as if they're on first-name terms.

'Maybe when my time comes she'll want to give some girl a better chance in life and maybe that girl could be me,' Rose says. 'That's what Matron said, isn't it? Maybe one day the person who's looking for a good hard-working girl could be Lady Di and the person she finds could be me.'

Maybe, but I don't think so. What Matron says about all these wonderful people who want to give Sacred Heart girls a job and a chance is one thing, what the girls say among themselves is another. What they say is that once you leave Sacred Heart the best thing is to expect the worst, keep your eyes and ears open and learn to stand up for yourself just as fast as you can, and I accept that. After all, not all of us are English and a 'Lady' and destined to marry a prince.

A LIFE OF SERVICE

For all of our lives together Ruby and I had lived under
one roof. Not always in the same room like we did at
Clive Street or that terrible time we stayed at Auntie
Olive's house sharing a camp cot in the pantry with
everything smelling of apples and onions. Everyone says
how much together we always are but like everyone else
we had our differences. Ruby was very quick to pick me
out if she spotted me in the playground with my friends
or being noisy in the Sacred Heart corridors, where we
were supposed to go about our business quickly and
quietly with our eyes on the floor. I was never a quickly
and quietly kind of person and never would be but if I
stepped out of line I didn't have to worry about the nuns
or one of Matron's staff spotting me because my sister was
always one step ahead of them.

'I've got my eye on you,' she'd say. 'You just behave yourself or else and remember that wherever you are I'm only one step behind you.'

I never found out what 'or else' meant but I was careful of Ruby. I acted big, as if I could do as I pleased, and sometimes I tried my luck but I didn't want to upset Ruby because when I was cheeky to my sister I was always the one who came off worst. It wouldn't be five minutes before I'd be running after her telling her that I hadn't really meant it and how sorry I was. If Sacred Heart taught me anything at all it was how to count my blessings because it wasn't everyone at Sacred Heart who had a sister, and no one had a sister like mine. Ruby could have gone off with her own friends and not bothered about me but she never did, and then she asked to stay on for two more years looking after the burn babies so that she could be near me. Not everyone would have done that. I wouldn't have, but she knew better than anyone that all it was doing was buying us some extra time before we were parted. We both knew the time would come when Ruby would be offered a proper, paying job. That was the last thing that Sacred Heart did for the girls in their care. If a girl was offered a job and she wouldn't take it, then it was on her own head because, as Matron would be quick enough to tell you, Sacred Heart was a place of safety, not a hotel.

'Just you remember, you get in first and talk fast,' I said when Ruby's turn came to be called to Matron's office.

'Maybe I should hear her out first,' Ruby said.

'No, you shouldn't,' I said. 'Remember what we talked about? Remember all we said? Well, this is the time, Ruby. You speak up for yourself. It's not as if you're asking for the moon, you know.'

That seemed to give her courage and we did what we used to do when we were little girls and clapped our hands quickly for luck. Hands together, then my right hand on her left hand and my left hand on her right hand. Then she straightened her dress and smoothed down her hair and went to stand on the small piece of tiled floor outside Matron's office and waited to be told that she could come in.

Ruby was eighteen years old then and a clever girl. It was all there in her school reports for anyone to see. If circumstances had been different she would have gone on to matric but girls put in care were only looked out for until they turned sixteen or reached standard eight, which was the State Minimum education. There was not very much that you could do with State Minimum. If you were lucky you could get a job standing behind a shop counter, and the places where white people shopped liked to have white girls serving, and so long as there were still white girls prepared to do jobs like that Ruby wouldn't get a look-in. Besides which, it wasn't what Ruby wanted.

We all knew that Sacred Heart girls usually ended up working in factories, or child-minding or cleaning or doing rough work in a kitchen. If you were lucky then you were lucky, but no one was encouraged to think higher than that because they were almost certain to be disappointed. Most of the girls didn't think about it at all because they were too scared to. So they made the most of their safe place while they had it and hoped that, when their turn came to stand on the little piece of tile outside Matron's office, wherever they were sent wouldn't be too bad. But Ruby had other ideas. She thought that if she asked Matron perhaps she could find some place that would be prepared to take her on and help her learn to be a bookkeeper. She didn't expect to sit out in the front office on display. She didn't mind sitting in a back room somewhere if only there was someone willing to take her as she was and to teach her.

I suppose that in a way I was to blame because Ruby confided in me and I egged her on.

'Matron can talk to Mother Superior and she can talk to the bishop,' I said. 'I'd like to see the person who'd look a bishop in the face and have him tell her he can't find a place for you.'

But that wasn't what Ruby wanted either.

'I'm looking for a job,' she said, 'just the same as anyone else would be. I know the Church by now and it's done quite enough for me, thank you. I'd like to stand on my own feet now.'

She said it as if it was much more than Sacred Heart she meant.

In my own heart I thought she was a fool. I thought that if she asked nicely and said that she happened to know that what Jesus needed now was for her to be a bookkeeper, perhaps Matron would listen to her like she did once before and things would work out as she wanted them to.

I never said anything because I knew the kind of look I'd get for my trouble but perhaps I should have because when her interview with Matron was over and she stepped out of the office something in Ruby seemed to have changed. It was as if something in her had died. You could tell just by looking at her that she was a different person altogether from the confident, shoulders-back girl she'd been when she walked in.

I was sitting on the bottom step of the main staircase and I heard the door open and I saw Ruby but she didn't see me. I don't think she would have seen anyone, not even if there'd been a whole crowd of people. It seemed to me that even among hundreds of others she would still have looked as if she was quite alone in the world.

I knew what Ruby's plan was when she was called in to Matron. I knew what she was going to say and I knew that Matron could help her if she really wanted to. So could Mother Superior if Ruby could only have spoken to her directly. So could any one of a number of people if they really wanted to, but I could see just by looking at her that Matron had not seen fit to help my sister. Perhaps there is such a thing as being too clever, like Ruby was, that makes people turn against you. Or maybe there was something about us that made people feel it was their job to make sure we were always kept in our place.

All I knew was that I sat on that step and wished I could stay invisible and that Ruby would never know I'd been there at all because I learned something that day. There are some moments in life that can't be shared, even by Ruby and me, and that was one of them.

Ruby was going to be a maid of all work in a hotel called the Queen's down in Dock Road. You could have dressed it up any way you liked but that's what it was and it was as if her other, greater expectations didn't matter at all.

'I did tell Matron,' she said. 'Or, at least, I tried to tell her but I only got halfway and she wouldn't listen any more.'

'Was it the teachers who put these ideas in your head?' Matron asked her. 'Because if it was, then I have to say again what I've said to other girls before you, which is that they shouldn't do it because all it does is give you expectations.'

It was that last part that made Ruby so angry. At Sacred Heart we didn't have much to call our own. What we did have were our 'expectations' and our 'expectations' were so precious to us that sometimes we didn't talk about them, not even to each other. Ruby thought that among all those people who were supposed to be looking after us there would have been someone who would have known this and been prepared to give her a helping hand, but she was wrong.

Perhaps she would have done better to listen to me and forget about Matron and put her trust in Jesus instead, because in in my opinion He owed her something for all that He'd taken from her. She had come so far from the little girl she'd once been who could tell Jesus anything, any time. I thought she still could and if she would only open her mouth and remind Him that she was still there, He'd do something to put it all right again. I wouldn't have said this to her though because it was the last thing in the world that she wanted to hear.

'You could do something else,' I said as I stood behind the curtains in her cubicle and watched her pack her clothes into the same brown cardboard suitcase she'd carried in with her when she first came.

'No, I couldn't,' she said. 'I not only need work, I need a place to stay.'

Ruby's place to stay was in a room above the kitchen. Matron had told her at least that much.

I watched Ruby as she packed to leave Sacred Heart. She packed like she always did, neatly and tidily, but her head was down so I couldn't see her face. The suitcase was on the chair and the bed was neatly made with fresh Sacred Heart linen for whoever came to sleep in it next. I think I'd begun to believe that the cubicle with its bed and chair and the locker next to the bed with Ruby's books and the picture taken that day of all of us outside Auntie Olive's place really was hers. It wasn't different from any of the other girls' cubicles but it was Ruby's place and that made it different to me, and I stood by and watched as piece by piece she packed it away until it was just an ordinary place and nothing special any more.

'That's that then,' she said, and she closed the fasteners on the suitcase and lifted it down off the chair on to the floor.

She had her bus fare to get to the Queen's and an

envelope with some extra money in it to 'tide her over' until her first payday. She was wearing her 'going out' shoes and tights and she had her handbag over her shoulder and was carrying her cardigan separate.

'Don't look like that,' she said to me. 'I'm not leaving you, you know that, and I'm not going to be very far away. If anyone gives you a hard time or if you get into trouble, you phone me and I'll be here before even you know it.'

She put her hand into her dress skirt pocket and took out three twenty-cent pieces.

'For the phone box, for in case,' she said, taking my hand palm up, putting the money in it and curling my fingers round it.

'I can come and visit you, can't I?' I said.

'We'll see,' she said but she'd turned away from me again.

We'd talked about it before, especially lately. She was the eldest and no matter what we both might have liked she had to go ahead. When I was old enough I'd be able to be with her again and by that time she'd be sure to have made a proper place for us. I knew all of that but it's one thing talking about it and another thing altogether when the moment finally arrives.

I wanted to ask her to take me with her but I didn't. I knew how things worked and I knew it would just make things even harder for her because however I was feeling she was feeling the same, and so I kept quiet and picked up her suitcase.

'Leave it,' she said. 'Just put it down.' And she gave me

a funny look. 'Didn't you know? After we've packed someone comes to check to make sure we don't walk out with half of Sacred Heart's stuff with us and we don't see our suitcase again until we get to the front door.'

I didn't know. I thought about our life at Sacred Heart and what exactly Sacred Heart 'stuff' was and I looked at Ruby and I looked at the suitcase, which was a child's suitcase, and not very big, and I started to laugh. I could just see Matron and her staff going through Ruby's few things in her neatly packed suitcase, her clothes and her undies and her second-best shoes. I wondered where she was supposed to find space to hide all the wonderful Sacred Heart 'stuff' she was supposed to be taking off the premises with her. I would have thought that all the years she'd had in the Sacred Heart would have been enough to put her off Sacred Heart 'stuff' for life. If you thought about it, it was enough to make anyone laugh. When I looked at Ruby I could see she knew what I was laughing about because at least she was smiling.

Usually Ruby and I walked down to town but that day when Ruby left to take up her job at the Queen's wasn't a usual sort of day because we were not going together. Ruby had her suitcase and her bus fares and I had permission to walk with her as far as the bus stop and wait until the bus arrived and then come straight back.

'You don't have to make a big thing out of it,' she said. 'I'm not going far and I'll be back to see you the first chance I get.'

'I know that,' I said. 'And just so you know, I wasn't

going to make a big thing out of it.' Which was a lie.

'Good,' she said and we stood side by side at the bus stop, Ruby with her case at her feet and her handbag over her shoulder and then lifted up and tucked under her armpit for safety's sake and her cardigan over her arm.

'You'll be surprised how fast time will go,' she said.

'I know,' I said and because I didn't want my sister to go I was in a frame of mind when I'd act as if anything she told me was nothing new but something I'd already known for a long, long time.

One part of me wanted the bus to come that minute and put an end to the waiting but another part of me wished that the bus would never arrive. I had never felt apart from my sister but we were the only two people at the bus stop and we were quite separate that day, each in our own world and each with our own thoughts, and I am not usually tongue-tied but that day I was. There were things I needed to say and things I wanted to tell her that I'd wanted to tell her for a very long time but I couldn't find the words and then the bus came and we'd run out of time. The only thing I could think of to do was what I hadn't done since we were children together in Clive Street. As she picked up her suitcase I gave her a quick pat on the shoulder.

'Last touch,' I said, but she was in such a hurry that I didn't think she'd even heard me. She pushed her suitcase on to the bus and climbed up behind it with the bus fare ready in her hand just like she always did. I stood in the road and watched and it was one of those buses with the two sideways seats that face one another in front and over the seats the sign that said non-white. I saw her pay the driver and take her seat under the sign while the driver counted her money. If he'd asked me I could have told him that it would be exactly the right amount because that's how my sister is. I thought that was the end of it and the way we would part, but I was wrong. I thought Ruby had forgotten but she never forgets anything. As the bus pulled away she stood up and held on to the overhead strap, which is not allowed on a moving bus, and she held up her other hand for goodbye and she looked at me.

'Last look, Ruby,' I mouthed and hoped that she could read my lips. I would have cried then for the loss of her because I'd felt like crying all day but in the end I didn't because I realized that there was nothing to cry about. I could never lose Ruby and she could never lose me. On her first day off she'd be back, she'd said so, and if you knew my sister you'd know she'd never break her word once she'd promised, not to me, not to anyone.

THE QUEEN'S

My place in life has been decided and whether I like it or not, the world still goes on turning.

When Rose asked me what the Queen's was like I told her that it wasn't Kensington Palace but it wasn't Sacred Heart either. It was just a building across the road from the main dock gate with a red postbox outside it and a hawker selling fruit off a cart to the people coming in and out of the docks.

There were rooms on top and two bottle stores below. One for whites only and another, smaller one for non-whites and that one did good business. Everything was double here. There were two bars, one for whites only and one for non-whites, and the front entrance of the hotel was so small you had to look twice otherwise you'd miss it. It was just a small wooden door that opened up on to

a black-and-white-tiled hall and I would not be using it.
Once the job was mine this was the first thing I was told.
The staff entrance is at the back, through a back door,
down a lane into a yard.

'And you're to use it if you don't mind,' Mrs Christie,
the housekeeper, said. 'Otherwise there'll be complaints.'

I had a room in the staff quarters. I was to be 'live-in',
that went with the job, and my room was next to Joycie.
'If there's anything you need to know just speak to
Joycie.'

Mrs Christie was the manager's wife. The Christies
lived 'in' too, in a small flat at the back.

The staff quarters were above the kitchen and my room
was the middle one. At the top of the stairs was Cook's
room. The room next to that was Joycie's. Stuck between
them was my room. They called it a room because a room
is what 'live-ins' get and you saw it come out of your pay
packet each week, but my room wasn't a proper room at
all. When you looked at it closely you could see that it
was really a part of Cook's room next door, which was
once bigger. It had been partitioned off with plywood;
the plywood had been painted over and someone hadn't
done a very good job. There was a single bed, a table and
chair and a small cupboard. There was a mat on the floor
but it was a poor excuse for a mat and underneath it were
wooden floorboards so brown that they were almost
black. There was a window. Joycie had the biggest room
but there was a catch. The ironing board was in there and
a table, a sofa and two chairs and a black-and-white
television set, so at least we could watch *Liewe Lulu*. This

section of Joycie's room was the 'lounge'. It was a place to relax when we were 'off duty'.

The first time I saw my room, before I was even officially told I had the job, I asked if I could step inside and look, and I walked into that room and pulled up the window and all the sounds of my new life poured in. The window looked down on the yard that backed on to the bar and it was filled with empty beer crates with Castle Lager painted on their sides and empty liquor bottles stacked up high, ready to be taken away so a new lot could be brought in. The smell of sour Multana muscatel wine rose up. It was mid-afternoon and quiet enough but at night, when business picked up, I knew it would be different.

I stood with my back to the room, thinking that this wouldn't be a quiet place, but then if what I wanted was peace and quiet I could have asked to be sent to a nunnery. Opposite the room that still might or might not be mine was the bathroom, which would be shared by all.

'Provided that's acceptable,' Mrs Christie said.

She kept saying that all the time she was showing me round. I knew she didn't mean to be funny but in a way she was funny, although she didn't realize it. Would it be acceptable? Of course it would be acceptable. It would be perfectly acceptable. Anything can be acceptable when it has to be and you have no choice.

My work clothes were laid out on the bed in 'my' room. Green Sweet-Orr overalls for rough work and a scarf to tie round my head.

'Fresh every day, if you don't mind,' Mrs Christie said. 'There's a sink and a washline in the back yard. You do your own laundry in your own time. The rest's up to you.'

There were black waitress dresses and white aprons for waiting at table and a silly white cap to go with them. I could hardly bring myself to look at it.

'Don't look at it like that,' Mrs Christie said. 'It won't bite you. I don't know what they told you at Sacred Heart but here our guests have their standards.'

I didn't say anything. There was nothing to say. All I knew was that Sacred Heart might have been an institution but at least it was in the twentieth century. I knew one thing for certain. If the Sacred Heart girls could have seen me dressed to the standard of the Queen's Hotel, Dock Road, they'd have fallen over laughing, and I was so ashamed I could have died.

'We turn our hand to everything here,' Mrs Christie said. 'Everyone's expected to do her fair share. By that I mean you do what I set out on your weekly roster for you to do. You'll make beds, sort laundry, clean rooms and bathrooms, set up the dining room for meals and wait tables, but you won't have any problem with that, I'm sure.'

That was why some 'establishments', as Sister Angelica liked to call them, prefer decently brought up girls who've been taught by nuns. They know how to do their fair share. As far as that goes, there will be no problem at all.

Joycie will 'train' me. Joycie's small, much smaller than I am, and plump like a small juicy fruit, but that doesn't stop her being in fashion. Her skirt's so tight it's a wonder she can sit down without splitting something. She has big breasts for such a tiny girl and she wears a short-sleeve jersey that clings just in case you miss them. She smells of Californian Poppy perfume. The whole room smells of it.

'It's nice, isn't it?' she says. 'Californian Poppy.'

I wouldn't know if she hadn't told me. You don't learn much about perfuming yourself at Sacred Heart. Sunlight soap is what you get there, and sometimes on hot Sundays Auntie Olive would ask me to go to her dressing table and fetch some Mitchum's Lavender Water so she could put it on her hanky. The only person I know who wears perfume is my cousin Patsy and she doesn't easily share, although she let Rose try some once.

'How about you, Ruby?' she said but I said no, thank you and got a look from her as if I thought I was too good to go out splashed with Intimate or You're the Fire. They may be very nice for all I know.

'You could catch yourself a man,' Patsy said, and maybe I could, but before I go out smelling like the perfume counter at OK Bazaar I'd like to see exactly the kind of man you could expect to get just by going out splashed all over with You're the Fire.

'So?' Joycie says. 'What brings you here?'

The answer's simple although I'm not going to give it. Nothing brought me. I was sent, and if I wanted to go further I could tell her that it was life itself that sent me.

'It's a job,' Auntie Olive says one Sunday. What she doesn't say is that it's a good enough job for me but it's not the kind of work she'd like for her own daughter.

When Patsy being a schoolteacher didn't work out she was going to do a typing course. Being able to type can be useful but Patsy doesn't want to type. Patsy wants to be Krystle Carrington in *Dynasty*. She's already got the big shoulders in all her jackets and the big hair to match and not all of it's her own.

'It's hairpieces,' Rose says. 'Imported from China.'

I don't know if I would like to have a big 'bouffe' of some poor Chinese woman's hair pinned on my head. I'd feel a fool. In any case, as far as I'm concerned that hair should stay just where it belongs, back in China, but Rose is full of such information these days.

'Yes, I think she's found her place at last,' Auntie Olive says, very satisfied with herself. 'She's finally made up her mind and settled on the beauty business.' As if it's Patsy that's doing the beauty business a favour.

'She's washing hair at a shop down at the shopping centre,' says Rose. 'That's not what I would call the beauty business. You won't be falling over Linda Evans or Victoria Principal down there, not down at the Athlone shopping centre between the butcher shop and the dentist.'

'It doesn't matter,' I say. If it's beautiful enough to be the 'beauty business' for Auntie Olive then it's more than beautiful enough for us. We can look at our cousin Patsy's Barely Black all-in-the-fashion tights with the embroidered diamanté on the ankle and think what we like about them. I think Rose would like to pick them up and feel them but I give her a look to remind her that, no matter what we may think, in the Frederickses' house we keep our opinions to ourselves.

I'm out in the world now and so I must make the world my business and the first thing I see is that so far my world has been a small place. I don't know very much and I haven't learned much from the Frederickses. The Frederickses are not 'political' so we never talk about what's happening all around us when we're at Steenbras Street. Auntie Olive says there's no point.

'People don't like the government,' she says. 'That's their business. We never got our say when it came to voting them in and that's fine too. We know where we fit in, it suits us and we're happy to just stay in our place and mind our own business.'

'Fine for her to say,' Rose says. 'I could also like a place where I could lay down the law and do just what I like.'

We all know Auntie Olive's views by now and I have views of my own. I could like a place where I didn't have to wear a maid's scarf on my head and move out of the way with my head down when one of the permanent residents decides it's time to come out of his room.

'I see that there are bombs out on the streets now and cars being blown up,' Auntie Olive says, so at least she knows that much. 'The government should sort that out. It's a sad day when you can't even go to town to do a bit of shopping in case you don't ever come home again, but that's the government's affair and in the meantime the man in the street just gets on with his life.'

Auntie Olive always likes to say that she 'hears things'.

I hear things too now and what I hear makes me think that, no matter what you read in the newspapers and no matter what the government would like us to believe, things are changing. But Auntie Olive has her eye on me, I can feel it.

'You can get on with your meal, Ruby, you don't have to hold your breath,' Auntie Olive says. 'If anything changes it won't happen before you finish your lunch. Curry mince doesn't stay warm for ever and you can eat your vegetables as well if you don't mind. No politics at the table.'

But I only have one lifetime and I would like to know what to expect and Godfrey's young like me so I ask him what he thinks about all the big changes that are meant to be coming.

'What do you think it'll mean to us?' I say. 'Will things really change or is it all just talk?'

'You're always so serious about everything,' he says.

'I'm not serious,' I say. 'I'm only asking.'

'If anyone's going to go out throwing bombs down in Adderley Street, it won't be me, I can promise you that,' he says. 'I've got my game and I've got my friends. You know I'm not political, that's up to other people, so I don't know why you asked me.'

It's his mother's voice coming out of his mouth and I wonder if he even knows it.

'At least they put signs out,' he says, trying to make a joke of it. 'All you have to do is read. If a bench says "Whites Only", don't sit on it and how much can that hurt you?'

His opinion is that life's too short to worry about it. A bench is only a bench after all. A 'Whites Only' train carriage is only a train carriage. Further down the train closer to the engine there'll be another one with no sign on it where anyone can sit, and so what? We all still end up sitting on the same train going in the same direction.

'As far as I'm concerned, it's like soccer,' he says. 'There are rules. You know what they are and you stick to them, otherwise you get the whistle and maybe a yellow card.'

I remember those Sundays when we first started going to Steenbras Street, when Godfrey promised to take me down to the soccer field with him to show me the finer points of the game. He never did and I knew he never would because Auntie Olive would never have allowed it, so perhaps Godfrey knows something I don't know – but I don't think so.

There may be parcel bombs at the railway station and people coughing their way through police tear gas in Wale Street and other people holding up placards outside St George's Cathedral. There still isn't a problem in the world that can't be put to one side while we all bend our heads over our Sunday lunch and keep silent as Auntie Olive gives thanks.

A MAN IN HIS PRIME

I met Mr Silver my first day on the job. Joycie took me to his table and introduced me.

'This is Ruby,' she said. 'She'll be serving you from now on.'

'Hello, Ruby,' the others said. 'A new one,' said someone, making it sound like a nuisance. 'What happened to the other girl? That one, you know, what's her name?' Then that one sat down and shook out his serviette and as far as he was concerned I'd already vanished and all that was left was another pair of hands.

I was in my black waitress uniform with the white apron tied round the waist and the stupid white cap on my head. I had a badge, white plastic with my name on it in black. It was pinned to the lapel of my dress and for what seemed like a long time Mr Silver didn't say anything and I stood looking down at the ground. He was supposed to say something similar to the others and then I could move on but he didn't. He could read a name tag; it was only one word after all. The 'new' one, the 'old' one, what difference is that to him? Someone invisible doesn't need a name. But it isn't like that. Mr Silver looked at the name tag. He looked at my face. His eyes looked into my eyes just for a moment and it was as if he was taking a snap of me, and that was the first thing I noticed about Mr Silver that set him apart from the others. He saw me and I was grateful for it.

'Of course he "saw" you,' Joycie said afterwards when I said this to her. 'Goodness me, Ruby, where have you been all this time? Mars? Of course he saw you. You're a woman after all and Mr Silver's not old. When you look at him closely you can see that he's a man in his prime.'

I didn't know about 'prime' but Mr Silver was certainly younger than the others were. He kept himself even more apart than the rest of them did and it didn't take long to work out that all his great apartness had done for him was to make him more interesting to the kitchen.

'A very sad past,' Joycie said. 'But if you take a good look at him you can see that he's not like the others and he's actually not so bad-looking. Not if you like the type.'

A fountain of information, that's what Joycie was, and you might just as well not have been there at all and that suited me. The more Joycie talked about other people the less she could ask about me, but if she had asked I'd have told her that I didn't have a 'type' and I'm not on the lookout for one either.

'He was a boxer in his day,' Joycie said. 'He may still be for all I know but I don't think so.'

Mr Silver was a peculiar kind of man. He had arrived one day out of the blue, walked into the bar and asked for a room.

'The whole bar was looking at him trying to pretend that they weren't looking, and Mr Christie asked him if he was quite sure he'd come to the right place.'

The men who stayed at the Queen's were tally clerks down in the docks. There was one who was a driver for a big firm of ship chandlers. There was Mr Duncan McDermott, who was a night-club bouncer at the Navigator's Den and worked odd hours. Mr Rudolph went out to work too but he was a man in a wheelchair. The bar boys got him up and down from his room but once he was in for the night he was in. He whistled all night even though he couldn't keep a tune and drove everyone round the bend.

'Now, ask yourself,' Mr Christie had said very politely to Mr Silver and everyone was just waiting to hear what the answer would be. 'Do you really think this is a place for you?'

'If I didn't want a place here I wouldn't be asking for one,' he said.

'And how long were you thinking of staying?' Mr Christie asked and Mr Silver didn't answer. He just took out his wallet.

I didn't know Mr Silver but even so I felt sorry for him. Even boxers can get tired and people came to the Queen's for all kinds of reasons and Mr Silver paid cash in advance.

'It's because he had a tragedy,' Joycie said.

I didn't want to hear but even so she was going to tell me, and Mr Silver's story when it came was very short. He had a wife and daughter and they were both killed in a car hijack.

Mr Silver, his wife and his daughter had lived in a house in the Avenues, Joycie tells me. I don't know the Avenues but Joycie does. They are on the Sea Point side, on the backside of Lion's Head. They run all along the lower slopes and stretch down towards the Sea Point beachfront and to the Pavilion and Robben Island beyond, and its streets are steep and lined with palms. You don't see many people out on the streets, just big cars coming and going and delivery vans that look into a TV camera to say who they are and security gates that slide open and closed when you enter a pin code.

The Avenues is where rich people live. People who would laugh about Athlone and Costa Plenti and the rose bushes in the front and the back yard where no one can see your *broekies* hanging out to dry. That may be the world to Auntie Olive but it would be very small fry if you'd ever seen the Avenues.

'It's film star houses,' Joycie said and I'm sure that my sister Rose would agree with her. Rose knows everything about film stars these days. She's danced along with Irene Cara in *Flashdance* and although she hasn't lost faith that

Princess Diana will come and fetch her one day, if that doesn't happen then she'll settle for Michael Caine. That's ever since she saw *Educating Rita* and thought that Rita was a lot like she was.

'You saw what he did for Rita,' she said. 'And she was just an ordinary girl. She was a hairdresser just like Patsy is so why shouldn't he do the same for me?'

Rose knows about the Avenues.

In the Avenues everyone had exactly what they pleased and every house was different and each one was bigger and better than the one next door. Some were in the old style with high white walls and wrought-iron gates and some of the new ones were like palaces made of glass and steel and so many windows for the views that you wondered what had happened to the walls.

According to Rose, film star houses had gardens that went on for ever and air-conditioning and live-in staff and guest cottages and swimming pools. There were statues in the garden and outside jacuzzi bubble pools and tennis courts and everything your heart could desire, but if I'd chosen to tell Rose what Joycie told me I would have had news for my sister about something that film star houses did not have.

'The hijackers were waiting for them when their car came in the gate,' Joycie said. 'They should have been on the lookout but they weren't, but I suppose that's just the way rich people are.'

I don't know how rich people are. If you believed Joycie then you'd believe that rich people spent all their lives being taken care of by people like us.

'I suppose we should be grateful then,' I said, 'if it keeps people in work.' It's not a nice thing to say but Joycie doesn't even seem to notice, she goes right on.

'Rich people always think that this is the kind of thing that will never happen to them but they're wrong. After all, they're the ones driving the latest model Mercedes Benz, not the "one lucky shopper" who won his Toyota in the draw at Pick 'n' Pay Mitchell's Plain, and why do they think Mercedes Benz are called "German takeaways" anyway?'

They found the Silvers' car out in the township, with the tank empty and the tyres off and the seats taken out to be a three-piece suite in a squatter camp house and the rest stripped down for spare parts.

The stories are all different but they always have the same ending so that one way and another everyone already knows what comes next. I would have liked to stop Joycie but nothing could stop her once she got going. So I tried to close off my mind and not think about Mr Silver and a story about a woman and child that ends in a ditch by the side of the road at Monwabisi Beach.

'Three or four days they must have been there before the police found them and the girl was wearing ballet clothes. Shame, she must have come from a class.'

After that, Mr Silver went right off his head and then, eventually, he ended up here.

Even though I'm working, Rose and I still go to Steenbras Street every last Sunday just like we used to and

I try to make conversation when we get there to make the time pass faster.

'I don't know why you waste your time,' Rose says but I do.

'I saw Patsy on the way down the road,' I say. 'She looks very well.' I don't say that she was with her friends and could barely bring herself to say hello to us.

'I'm glad you think she looks well, Ruby,' Auntie Olive says. 'If you want my opinion, I think with all that paint on her face she looks like a circus clown but then I'm only her mother. Why should anyone pay any attention to me?'

'I wouldn't like to be the person sitting behind her in the bioscope,' Rose says, 'not with all that false Chinese hair pinned on top of her head. You wouldn't be able to see a thing.'

'How's Godfrey?' I say to change the subject.

'If you see him ask him,' she says. 'Then you can do me a favour and let me know and while you're at it you can tell his father as well. He'd be just as interested as I am, I'm sure.'

Even when the cousins are at home for Sunday lunch it's not how it used to be.

Godfrey keeps the door of his room closed. If you want to go in you have to knock and wait until he says, 'Come in,' and even though you know he's in there sometimes you think he's not going to answer.

He's got a locked tin that he keeps under the bed. Patsy, who knows everything, says he keeps letters and photographs in it and used torn-in-half cinema tickets and even old bus tickets. He smells of Tabac these days and he wears a silver St Christopher medal round his neck that he won't take off even in the bath and that's something new too.

'Where'd you get it?' Patsy asks.

'Bought it,' he says, 'if you want to know.'

'Leave the boy alone,' says Uncle Bertie and gives her a glare.

'Why does it have to be such a state secret?' Auntie Olive says loudly.

Uncle Bertie lifts up his knife and fork.

'Grace,' Auntie Olive says but you can see just by looking at Uncle Bertie that he's not in a 'grace' state of mind.

'I wish that just for five minutes you'd give Godfrey a bit of peace,' he says.

'I wish that you'd sit him down and ask what's going on with him,' says Auntie Olive.

You'd think Godfrey had gone invisible the way his parents are talking about him as if he isn't even there. He's sitting right there with us and you can see just by looking at him that something isn't right because his face is pale and he looks miserable. It looks to me as if any minute he could burst into tears.

'I wish you'd both stop going on about it,' Patsy says, fed up. 'Godfrey's lovesick, OK? Big deal, so now can we please just leave it? It's gone twelve o'clock. Can we please have our lunch now and just get it over with?'

'Stop this "love" business,' says Auntie Olive turning

on Patsy. 'Godfrey's twenty-one years old. He's got his whole life in front of him. He's a decent Christian boy. He's too young to know about love.'

'Suit yourself,' says Patsy, shrugging her shoulders. 'You can believe it or not but if you knew what I knew you'd know that I know what I'm talking about.'

'Shut up, all of you,' Godfrey says, standing up from the table. He pushes back his chair so hard that the condiments rattle and suddenly everyone's gone quiet. Godfrey's red in the face and then pale and all the light has gone out of him.

'What do we say?' Auntie Olive says, steadying her knife and fork, looking up from the plate, trying to work out exactly how much or how little of her power she has left.

'Please may I be excused?' mutters Godfrey, giving in to her like he always does, and he storms away from the table and we wait for the slamming of the door.

'And what would you like to say now?' Auntie Olive says to Uncle Bertie and because Uncle Bertie doesn't usually backchat her we're wondering exactly what there is he can say.

'Shut your face,' Uncle Bertie says. 'That goes for you too, Patsy. Why can't the two of you just leave it alone?'

It's so unexpected that everyone stops eating and looks up, wondering what might happen next.

'Just do us a favour, both of you,' Uncle Bertie says and it's Patsy and Auntie Olive he's looking at and then it's

no longer both of them. He turns right on Auntie Olive.
'Just for once in your life give it a break and keep your
mouth shut. I can't speak for any of the others but I, for
one, have had a guts-ful.'

A STAIN ON THE HEART

I'm walking down Dock Road, along near the dock gate by the Imperial Café where the fishermen shop, and I see two Railway and Harbour Police, men who come to the Queen's white bar for a drink when they're in plain clothes, and they're beating a black man. I can see the man's face. I can look right into his eyes. There must be something I can do to help but what can I do? I'm a bit nervous of the policemen myself. When they're off duty, in plain clothes, in the Queen's bar they send to the kitchen for a plate of potato chips to eat with their double Viceroy and Coke and I have to take it to them. I don't like going into the men's bar because it smells of men and Ransom cigarettes and stale drink and I don't like these men.

That's when they're in plain clothes and when I see

them out on the street in uniform beating a black man for I don't know what I more than don't like them.

'He must have done something.' That's what people will say if I say what I saw. 'Probably had stolen goods on him.' 'Resisting arrest.' 'Refused to show his pass.' That's the big thing these days. Black people have to have their passes with them at all times so they can show them when asked but some of them don't have passes because they've made big bonfires of them out in Langa and Nyanga and burned them. 'That's foolishness, they know the laws.'

That's supposed to make you feel better and make it all right. It doesn't make me feel better and it isn't what the black man has done or hasn't done that makes my stomach turn over, it's the policemen. They're enjoying themselves. They put their whole heart and soul into it. You can see that and that's the terrible thing. The man has his hands up against a pole and they're beating him with a leather belt.

People don't get beaten if they haven't done anything. If I say that over and over again it might make me feel better but I don't feel better and I don't know this man. I don't know what he's done. I can't imagine what anyone could have done that would be bad enough for them to be beaten like this.

You can hear the bang of the belt on his back. The policeman beating him beats him so hard you can hear all the air pushing out of his own body with the effort.

I should do something to help this man but what can I do? I can do nothing and so I look away. I want to spare him the shame of being seen with his shirt pulled off and his head held by the hair wrenched back while he holds on to the pole and his trousers hanging down low on his hips. It's a thing that you don't want to see. Nobody would. I'm not on speaking terms with God; I asked my last favour of Jesus on the day Rose and I went into care. That's the end of it. There are people who know a lot more about life and the world than I do. As for me, I am alone and I am as powerless as the black man who's being beaten. I have no one left to turn to for help, not for him and not for me, and I stand in Dock Road and I am as alone as any human being can possibly be.

This is how life is now. It isn't a sideshow, the blows are real, the man is real, the pain I am sure is real and where is this change that's coming and when will it ever get here? I don't see it in this place.

I walk on and walking on is one thing. Getting it out of my mind is something else altogether. The man's face won't go away. I wake up in the night and open my eyes to the darkness. If he'd been angry I wouldn't have minded so much. If he'd been angry with me for standing and looking and not lifting a finger to help I wouldn't have blamed him.

We were four people in the empty street, the two policemen, the man and me. Had it really been just the four of us? I can't be sure. I can't remember seeing anyone else but Dock Road is a busy street. At that time of day there are always lots of people and there are cars and lorries going up and down, in and out of the dock gate. There's the hawker who's always at the same place on the corner outside the non-white bar. Surely he must have been there. There are always people sliding in and out of the bottle stores for their lunchtime bottle of Oom Tas wine and they're all working men and can look after themselves if they have to. There's a municipal cleansing truck and the council workers who come to pick up the rubbish, and they are four men on a truck and the driver. I can't believe that they all disappeared.

If there were other people they must have seen what I saw. If they did and they were many, why hadn't someone called out? If it was just the four of us, me and the black man and the two policemen, then there truly was nothing that I could have done. Surely the man would have known that?

He hadn't expected me to help him. He knew that I'd turn away. When I realized that he'd never expected anything of me it made me ashamed. I did what I did. There's no one I can blame. It is a stain on my heart and I must carry it for ever.

The last Sunday of the month, I sit in my place beside the others in the third row of Good Shepherd and when communion's offered and the congregation file up to receive it, I stay where I am.

'Come on,' says Rose. Auntie Olive has already stood up, moved forward, turned round and given me a look. I shake my head, no. 'Come on,' Rose says. 'Everyone's looking at you.'

'You go,' I say but I stay where I am.

Some of the returning communicants take a quick look at me but I hold my head high and look forward. Auntie

Olive's eyebrows are well up inside the brim of her hat when she comes back to her place and her cheeks are stained angry red. Patsy looks as if she might giggle and Godfrey smiles his nice smile and slides along the pew so that he can sit next to me.

Auntie Olive waits till lunchtime and it's chicken and pumpkin and rice and Rose is helping herself to extra potatoes and already has her eyes on the Carnation ivory pudding that's standing in a glass bowl on the sideboard.

'You'll join us giving thanks?' Auntie Olive says, looking at me while she helps herself to a big scoop of pumpkin and the smell of butter and cinnamon is heavy in the air. 'Presumably you've no objection to that.'

I say nothing but I offer my hand into the circle of hands. If I'd wanted to I could have said that I have no objection at all to giving thanks. If anyone has practice and to spare when it comes to giving thanks, then I am that person.

'And later you can tell me what all that was about,' Auntie Olive says. 'If you've got something to tell me, you better tell me now, while it's still early days.'

'It's nothing like that,' I say and I can feel my face go red.

'Leave it, Ma,' Godfrey says and Uncle Bertie says that if no one has any objection he'd like to eat before the food goes ice cold and so it's left.

'Why did you do such a thing?' Rose wants to know as we walk back down the road together.

'God knows,' I say and I shrug my shoulders and try to make light of it.

Did He know? That's what I wonder.

When Mr Silver comes in from work, before he comes down to the dining room he goes upstairs to wash and change his shirt. When he comes to the table his hair's neatly brushed. The others come in from the street just as they are and most of them make a stop in the bar. You can smell it on them. Mr Silver smells of Cuticura soap and he doesn't drink. He has a jug of water and a glass put out on his table at mealtimes. The others don't have that, but then I already knew that Mr Silver was not like the others. Mr Silver lived in a different world once but after what happened he couldn't go back there.

'I don't know,' Joycie says. 'If I was him I'd spend five minutes in this place and go back where I came from so smartly you wouldn't see me for dust.'

She can't understand how a whole world can end when the people you love die, but I can. I understand it and I understand something else too. The new life you make for yourself isn't anything like a real life at all. All it is is a place you can hide in and be alone with your pain, and the Queen's Hotel, Dock Road, may not be good for much but it's more than good enough for that.

Mr Silver's life must be a small place now compared to how it once was. He goes to work every day in casual khaki trousers and a white shirt, with Hush Puppies on his feet and a jersey thrown over his shoulder if the weather is cool. He goes to a small job to keep busy where no one knows him or cares what he once was. Someone like Auntie Olive would say that life's brought him down to size and it would make her happy to say it. It doesn't make me happy.

Every evening he goes to the gym at Mission to Seamen because people come and go there all the time and no one really wants to take the trouble to get to know anyone else. On Saturdays he gets all dressed up in a blazer, a white shirt and grey flannels and he disappears and no one knows where he goes, not even Joycie.

'Maybe he goes to visit his family,' I say but Joycie says no, his only family is a brother and he lives in England.

'A man came to see him once and you could tell just by looking that he was a brother. He came in a Mount Nelson Hotel car with the name on the side and a driver in a peaked cap and no one will forget that in a hurry.

'He didn't ask him into the hotel,' Joycie says. 'He didn't even ask him to step inside the building.'

I think I know why Mr Silver's brother came. I think he came to take him away to somewhere quiet and safe where he could put all that happened behind him and put the leftover pieces of his life back together and start over again, but whatever it was his brother asked him to do Mr Silver's still here.

Joycie said that while his brother was talking to him he just kept shaking his head, no, as if whatever it was his brother was asking just wasn't possible. All you had to do was stand back and look at them and you'd know that Mr Silver wasn't going anywhere.

* * *

If things were bad for me the way they were for Mr Silver, I would have wanted Rose. If I was so terribly alone as Mr Silver is and Rose came all the way from England just to find me I would have stepped into her arms and cried my eyes out and felt that I'd come home. I would have gone with her to wherever in the world she happened to be. The world's just a place after all, it's just dots on a map, but a brother who comes to find you and ask you to go with him is a rare thing. No matter how much the world takes from you, it gives back again when it shows that there's still that kind of love and if Mr Silver were my friend and I was in a position to, that's what I would have told him.

I don't go to Good Shepherd any more. I don't go to church at all. For a long time I only really went to keep Auntie Olive quiet, but even since I've refused we still go to Steenbras Street for lunch. Rose wants us to stop going but it's not a subject for discussion.

'Ask me,' she says as we walk to number seventeen.

'Ask you what?'

'Ask me what I think about our having to come to have lunch at Auntie Olive's every last Sunday.'

'No, thank you,' I say. I know what she thinks and the last thing I need now is a fight.

'Ask me,' Rose says.

'Why should I bother asking you, Rose?' I say. 'I can see you're going to tell me anyway but whatever it is you've got to say, say it quickly because we're almost there.'

'They can wait,' Rose says and she stops where she is and she catches me off-guard and I stop too. 'It won't kill them to wait and you can listen to me for a change. I've been listening to you all these years, now it's your turn.'

People are looking at us. In Steenbras Street there are always people going up and down to the main road or sitting out on their stoeps just looking and if there's one thing you can be sure of, you can be sure of that.

'Say what you have to say,' I say. 'Just for goodness' sake hurry up.'

I'm sure that behind the forest of ferns Auntie Olive's looking out, watching us. If I look at my watch she'll see me and know that I know what time it is. The minute we walk through the door she'll ask what was going on between us that was so private and important it couldn't be discussed in the house.

'Arrangements can be changed,' Rose says.

'I know that,' I say. 'But I don't want to change this one.'

'It's not nice coming here,' Rose says. 'And now, just lately, it's awful.'

'If anything's to change, I think Auntie Olive should be the one to change it,' I say. 'That way we'll stay in the right. If they don't want us any more now that we're grown-up, they should be the ones to say so.'

'They have said so,' Rose says. 'They said so the day they stood by while we went to the orphanage.'

If Auntie Olive is looking at us then I'm glad she'll be looking directly at me because I can keep a nice, normal face. I can keep that face I always keep for visits to Auntie

Olive's, the one that is just about ready to be dressed up with a smile. If Auntie Olive can only see me and not Rose she'll think we're talking about a small thing between sisters and nothing that has anything to do with her. If Auntie Olive could see Rose, she would be out from behind the ferns and down to the front gate like a sergeant major to ask what it is that we're so busy talking about, as if she has the right to ask us such a question.

'I'll tell you one thing,' Rose says. 'If it was you and me, if one of us was dead, our children wouldn't be standing out here in the street talking like this about their auntie.'

And what answer can I make to that?

'We'll always look out for each other,' Rose says suddenly out of the blue, as though it's something new and not something that we've both always known.

'Of course,' I say. 'And what's all this about anyway?'

'You'll find a man,' Rose says. 'You'll get married.'

'Maybe,' I say. 'So more than likely will you but not, I don't think, today.'

I look down at my watch. I just can't help myself but Rose wants to talk and won't be put off.

'I'll never leave you or speak badly of you,' Rose says. 'To your face sometimes maybe because you'd be there and know I don't mean it but never behind your back and never if you'd passed on.'

Her eyes fill up with tears.

'I know that,' I say.

'If we were parted . . .'

'. . . which we're not going to be,' I say, crossing my

arms, pretending I've had enough of such nonsense and silly talk.

'But if we were,' Rose says, 'if you ever needed me, I'd come to you. You know that. Whatever else happens in this life you will always, always and for ever have me.'

'I know that,' I say.

'And if you have children,' says Rose, 'I would never, as God is my witness, do to them what that woman did to us.'

'Rose . . .' I say but Rose is still crying. She's wiping the tears from her cheeks with the back of her hand and she couldn't care less who's looking or what it is they'll see.

'I would take them into my house and into my heart, no questions asked, even if I thought they weren't such very nice children.'

'If they weren't really such very nice children then that might not be such a clever thing to do,' I say, trying to make Rose smile, but she's not in a smiling mood, at least she's not today.

'I'd do it for you,' Rose says. 'Because you're my sister, you're all I have in the world and I love you.'

SOMETHING'S HAPPENING

Every evening Mr Silver takes his seat at his table and
then he turns round to catch my eye to show that he's
ready to order and I go over. Soup, fish, dish of the day
and sweets, that's my daily recitation. Then I wait while
he chooses. This is how it has been for what seems like
quite a long time now. Walking towards him I pass the
sideboard with its murky mirror in the middle and out of
the corner of my eye I can see a girl in a black dress and
white apron slowly sliding across the glass through the
small distance that divides me from him. Then I stand in
front of him and he looks up into my face.

I am eighteen years old turning towards nineteen and
I still have my bloom. This is what Auntie Olive says and
Auntie Olive says more.

'A young woman only blooms once and come the

117

Sunday you come to Steenbras Street with your bloom
gone don't think that I won't know it.'

'You better not tell her about your man,' Rose says. 'Or
the next time you walk through the door she'll give you
a good rub to check that your bloom's still where it
should be.'

'I don't have a man,' I say. 'That's just nonsense.'

'You better watch out all the same,' says Rose.

'There's nothing to watch out for,' I say and I can say
that because it's true.

What I can't say is that I never think about Mr Silver and
his life before he ended up where he is because that
wouldn't be true. I imagine Mr Silver with his wife and
in my mind she's tall and beautiful with a long curtain of
hair that hangs right down her back. She walks like a
dancer and she calls him Saul-darling. Saul-darling, she
says and the words are joined together and smooth
because she's used them so often they've forgotten how to
be two words any more and now they're one.

I can imagine that other life he once had in the
Avenues. A beautiful house set far apart from its nearest
neighbour with flowers in all the rooms and during the
day the sun will pour in. In the morning there'll be peace
and silence and in the afternoon there will be children
there. The little girl will be home from school with her
friends. The garden will be filled with the sound of
laughter and the thud of tennis balls and the splashing
water of the pool.

In the evenings there'll be a maid who draws the

curtains and puts on the lights. That's how it will be in that house in the Avenues. Saul-darling's wife will come home fresh from the shower after exercise class at Issy Bloomberg's gym, members only.

I tell Rose lots of things but I don't tell her this.

Imagine you're sitting in the front seat of a beautiful car. You're all dressed up for your ballet class. Ballet teachers are fussy. Even if you're not the star of the show yet, one day you will be. Your daddy says so and you know that in your heart because you already look the part. Your mother's with you. Your mother loves you. She's always there, right on time to fetch you from ballet, to fetch you from tennis, to fetch you from your extra lessons. Your mother's in the driver's seat, sitting right next to you.

'You must hurry up and change,' your mother says. 'We're running late today and Daddy will be home soon and there's homework to do and before you know it it'll be time for supper.'

Sometimes she turns her head to look at you, to smile at you, to listen more carefully to all you're telling her. You're right at your house and it's the most beautiful house in the Avenues and the roads in the Avenues are lined with palms and end high up against the mountain-side. The whole world stretches down from here, right down to the sea and on to South America if you can only think that far, and there's nothing in it you can't have. No one has a daddy who loves her as much as your daddy loves you. If you asked him he would give you the world. That's what other people think when they see you.

There's ballet to think about and a birthday party on Saturday and all the things you have to tell Daddy when Daddy gets home. You may think that politics is a very long way away but politics is right there too, waiting for you, while your mother presses the remote control and the gate slides quietly open.

I don't know why I think about Mr Silver such a lot. It doesn't make me happy but I still go on doing it because I can't stop myself and there's one thing above everything else that stays in my mind. What is worse? I wonder. To have known something wonderful and have it taken from you, or never to have known it at all?

That's what I ask myself about Mr Saul Silver and the life that he lost. It's what I ask myself about me.

I may be invisible and not even worth looking at but people can see someone like him and he makes them afraid. It's hard to know what you're supposed to do with a man who's been called on to suffer the way he has. What's happened to him is too horrible even to think about. When he's standing in front of you can you even look at him? How will you know what to say? People will say how sorry they are. They have to look into his face, into his eyes, and say that but after all the 'sorry' is finished there's something else. There's 'sorry' but 'sorry' is such a small thing. Sitting right behind 'sorry' is 'grateful' because what they're really feeling is both at the same time. They're grateful it's him and not them and if they're honest they'll know that 'grateful' is much stronger than 'sorry' is, and if they feel shame at all then that's what they're really ashamed about.

Sometimes I take him his food and put the plate down in front of him, then I step back. I can stand there for a moment if I like. No one will notice.

I look down at his bent head, at his hair, which is thick and dark and would be unruly if he didn't comb it down flat. I look at the nape of his neck. I'd like to put my hand on him, on his shoulder, just to touch him softly, the way my mother used to touch me. I'd like to ask him where it hurts most and tell him how much I'd like to share that pain with him if I could and perhaps help make it better.

I've been waiting on Mr Silver for quite a few months and it's always been the same and then suddenly it changes. One day he calls me back at the end of the meal, takes a fifty-rand note out of his shirt pocket, folds it in half and holds it out to me.

I can smell his own special smell of Cuticura soap on him. I can see his eyes. He has olive eyes with small flecks of brown in them. He has the kind of eyes that you can't see to the bottom of and fifty rand is a lot of money and the fifty-rand note is between us and it hurts me. Although we haven't talked to each other I always felt that Mr Silver 'knew' that I was out of place there and that he understood, but I was wrong. A waitress is just a waitress to him. A maid's a maid.

I stand in front of him and look into his face and there are maids with references and experience who work in mansions and then there are girls who end up at the

Queen's Hotel, Dock Road, and he looks at me and there's nothing to say.

I turn and walk away. I leave him with the folded fifty-rand note still in his hand and something is changed between us. I can feel it and whatever it is, it's not about money.

'He's just a man.' That's what I said to Rose when I first told her a little bit about Mr Silver. 'He's someone who's had a sad life and I feel sorry for him, that's all.'

You'd think you could feel sorry for anyone you liked. There wasn't any law that said you couldn't, but even so, it wasn't quite so easy. Rose may not have known this but Auntie Olive did.

'Ruby's met a man down at the Queen's,' Rose said.

'That's very nice,' said Auntie Olive. 'And are we allowed to know who this man of Ruby's might be? Does he have a name? Are we at least allowed to ask that?'

'He's no one,' I said and I would have liked that to be the end of it but it wasn't.

' "No one" has a name,' Rose said, her look telling me to speak up for myself.

'His name's Mr Saul Silver,' I said and I held out my plate towards Auntie Olive, who was offering yellow *borrie* rice with raisins today to go with the *bobotie*, and I kept my eyes on the tomato and onion salad because that was what would be offered next. I didn't have to tell them. The name was enough. They already knew that Mr Silver was a white man and I thought that was the first thing Auntie Olive would jump on but I was wrong.

'Are you involved with a Jew now?' she said and she held the spoon of *borrie* rice studded with raisins over my plate as if it was the last thing in the world she had ever expected to hear.

'I'm not "involved" with anyone,' I said.

'They only want girls like you for one thing,' Auntie Olive said, handing my plate back to me. 'And it's not only the Jews that I'm talking about. You can look at me all you like. Maybe you don't want to hear it but it's true all the same.'

That was the kind of thing Auntie Olive did best. She might not have known the wider world but she still knew how the world worked and it could only work one way and that was Athlone style.

'If you're wise, you'll listen to me when I talk to you,' Auntie Olive said. 'It could save you a lot of trouble in the long run if you learn your lesson right now.'

White men and brown girls are not for each other. That's the law and the Frederickses may not be a 'political' family but even Auntie Olive knows about Immorality. That was what she was really talking about when she talked about Mr Silver and me.

Of all the laws, the off-duty policemen who came into the bar at the Queen's said they liked that one the best. Sometimes they said they went along, just for the fun of it, off duty, straight from the bar, to catch out some couple that someone had reported. They took flashlights and they'd let the couple carry on for a while and get down to business, then at a signal they'd turn all the flashlights on at the same time. They said it was like blinding rabbits with car headlights and very funny to watch. There was always something laughable about a man scrabbling for his pants. They're men themselves so they know, and in their opinion there isn't a man any- where, any colour, caught out with a woman he's got no business being with, scrabbling for his pants, who manages to look dignified. You want to laugh out loud but you can't laugh because Immorality's a serious business.

'Why didn't you take it?' he asks me the next day, which is the next time he sees me. It's the first thing he says and he says it even before I've asked him for his order. I know what will be said in the kitchen. They'll have got a big surprise because it's the first time he's actually asked me to stay and talk to him.

'I want to show my appreciation, that's all.'

He says it so nicely that I feel as if I've taken him up the wrong way and done something wrong out of not knowing any better, but how could I know better? I didn't know there were people who spoke to waitresses as if they were ladies who'd misunderstood.

There are other tables to be served. Mr Silver isn't the only one in the room. A good waitress is an invisible one. When she leaves the table where she's served you shouldn't even remember her face, but it isn't like that between Mr Silver and me. The first time when Joycie introduced me to him I thought that he 'saw' me. I thought that if he saw me out on the street he'd know who I was and even remember my name, and I know that

I see him. I can see the sadness of him and his pain vibrating around him like a living thing and him trapped inside it, with no way to be free.

I wonder if he knows what it feels like to be me standing in front of him with my back to the rest of the room, having been told a hundred times not to 'waste time' 'making conversation' with any of the 'permanents'. Those are my instructions and they might just as well be my instructions for the rest of my life inside and outside the hotel, while he's free to say just what he likes.

'If I were you, I'd take it and save it,' he says. 'This place isn't for you. You don't belong here.'

'Neither do you,' I say.

It just comes out and it hangs there in the air between us, something that neither of us expected.

When I'm 'off duty' my time's my own and I can do what I like with it. What I can't do is spend it with a permanent, and after saying that he thinks I should have taken the money and saved it Mr Silver then says that he would like to apologize to me.

'I never meant to offend you,' he says. 'And I realized afterwards how very offensive it must have seemed. It wasn't meant like that, I'm sorry.' I can see just by looking at him that he does feel badly.

'I'd like to talk to you about it,' he says. 'To clear it up, if you like. Would you let me? Could we do that?'

I know that whatever the world was like that he came from he isn't used to sitting down to chat with a maid. It doesn't work like that. Usually, if there's anything good or bad to be said, the madam says it and she'll say it in the kitchen or the maid may be specially called into the living room. The madam will say what she has to say, good or bad, and one thing's sure, it will be a one-way conversation and the maid will stay standing while she listens.

This may be Dock Road and very far from the Avenues but surely Mr Silver must know that there are things that a white man and a coloured woman can't do together?

He can't come to the 'off-duty' section of Joycie's room and say what he has to say while *Kojak* is blasting out of the television in the background, and I can't go into the residents' lounge. I suppose there must be a place we could go where no one could care less and we could sit there and talk to our hearts' content, and what will I do if he suggests we do that? If I say I'm agreeable even though I've never been to such a place in my life, what will he think of me?

A man like him and a woman like me are not for each other. I don't need Auntie Olive or anyone else to tell me what I already know. If he says let's go somewhere and I say yes I'll be sitting right next to him instead of serving him and everything will be different, and who knows better than I do that once things are different it's very hard to get them back to how they once were.

Outside the hotel dining room, I can't see Mr Silver; it's that simple. All I have to do is tell him that.

A DEATH IN THE FAMILY

We aren't allowed private calls in work time but this time
it's different and Mrs Christie sends a bar boy to call me
from where I'm working upstairs.

I think it must be Rose because who else would be
phoning? Then my heart contracts because maybe it's not
Rose. Maybe it's Sacred Heart. Maybe something's
happened to Rose. I feel quite sick before I even pick up
the phone and when I do pick up it's a man's voice on the
other end and he asks if I'm Ruby Jacobs and I say yes I
am.

My heart's right in my throat. I can feel it beating. I
think that now this man, this stranger who has the hotel's
telephone number, is going to tell me that something
terrible has happened to my sister.

I thought that I knew 'unbearable' but I see now that

I never really knew it at all but I look it in the face right that minute as I stand there with the telephone receiver in my hand. I see it and I know it for what it is. I see its power and I know that I will be no match for it.

I am in my green overall. I have the maid's scarf that I hate tied round my head. I've come downstairs from the permanents' side, where I've been putting down polish on the linoleum that runs down the middle of the passage. I can feel the polishing in my knees and my hands. I can smell Cobra polish on my fingers where they're curled round the phone's handset right next to my nose.

The maid is having a telephone call in work time. It isn't allowed.

The man on the other end of the line gives his name, he says he's calling from Goodall and Williams's Funeral Parlour and I say yes. It can't be Rose. I won't think that. This man, whoever he is, wants to sell me funeral insurance. That's what it is. He sounds smooth, like a salesman, but no one would call me to the telephone in the middle of work just to talk to a salesman, not even if what he's selling happens to be life everlasting.

Then he says that he's phoning to tell me that my cousin, Godfrey Fredericks, is dead and I think that I will pass out for sure from the sudden rush of blood to my head. It's such a strange thing how I stand there while life reveals itself to me. It isn't us. Just for a change it's someone else's turn. I am so light with relief that I feel I could rise up like a balloon and float right away.

Then I'm ashamed of how I feel in that moment and how selfish I am when someone tells me that my cousin is dead but it's done now and can't be undone and that's another shame that I will have to bear.

That's how I hear about Godfrey, just like that, and I stand with the telephone in my hand and try to take it in.

'Are you there?' the man on the other end says and I say, 'Yes, I'm here.' He asks if I heard what he said and if I'm all right and I can hear then that he's said this more than once already because the words are tired and worn down with using.

'Yes,' I say. 'Yes, I've heard and yes, I'm quite all right thank you and yes, thank you for telephoning and thank you for telling me what's happened.'

Thank you? To the total stranger who gave me such news?

The funeral arrangements will be in the newspaper. That's what I'm told and I'm such a fool I say thank you again and then I hang up and stand with the phone in my hand and it's all been too much. The smell of polish on my fingers is making me feel so sick I think I might vomit.

I can feel my body under the overall. It feels as if there's suddenly too much hot blood rushing around in it. I want something to hold on to but there's nothing to hold. I need something to hold on to because all of a sudden there's no blood in my legs; they won't hold me up any more. I can't stay standing for one minute longer and I sit down hard on the last step at the bottom of the stairs that lead up to the 'permanent' rooms and I sit there with the telephone receiver still in my hand.

*　*　*

129

I ask Mr Christie if I can telephone my aunt because there's been a death in the family and he says yes I can but please keep it short and Patsy answers the phone. Her mother's lying down, she says, and she won't speak to anyone. The doctor's come and given her some pills that knocked her out.

'What happened?' I say.

'I can't say,' says Patsy.

'What do you mean, you can't say?'

'I was told not to say,' Patsy says. 'Godfrey's dead. The details are private. Let him rest in peace. That's the best thing to do. That's what we as a family have decided.'

If I'd had fat, painted-face Patsy right there in front of me that minute I would have shaken her by her shoulders and slapped her so hard her fake Chinese hair would have fallen right off her head. I've never felt that way about anybody, ever in my life before. It comes as quite a shock and there's something else too because I realize now that this is something I've wanted to do from almost the first moment I laid eyes on her. Now, with only silence on the other end of the phone, I wonder how I managed to hold back for so long.

'We as a family.' If 'we as a family' are such a wonderful family then where exactly is it that Rose and I fit in? What are we exactly, what have we ever been that we should be cut out in this way? This is what hurts me even though it is not the time to say so.

'I'm very sorry,' I say.

'Sorry' is what people always say. It's what you're supposed to say. It isn't nearly big enough for all that I feel but that's all right. If I had a better word I would have kept it to myself or maybe just told Rose. What I wouldn't have done is wasted it on our cousin Patsy.

'Thank you,' Patsy says. Thank you for the 'sorry' and I know from the way she says it that she's like the funeral parlour man. She's said it more than once already and I know that, family or no family, I wasn't the first person who'd been told about Godfrey.

Sometimes people do die young. There had been a girl called Molly at the orphanage who had wanted to be my best friend and she had died. I don't like to think about it because she once held out her hand to me and I didn't take hold of it. Molly Small was her name. She was playing with some of the other girls at a building site where they shouldn't have been. No one knows for sure, perhaps they were egging her on. Molly climbed up a scaffold and lost her footing and she fell. She hit her head and died, even though it wasn't very high. You get a certificate when you die, all set out in a proper way although you never see it. I suppose that Matron would have had dead Molly's papers saying 'born' and 'died' as Molly had no one to come and take her away, or 'to claim the body' as Matron called it. But that wasn't a surprise. Molly wasn't one of the children who had been 'fetched' while she was living, so no one really expected anyone to come and fetch her when she was dead. 'Born' and 'died' just like that and she never even got old enough to apply for ID, as if it mattered. Wherever she was now, God would know her, or at least that's what I would have thought in those days when I could still speak for God.

'What does she mean, she can't say?' Rose says when I phone her.

'And that's the last call if you don't mind,' Mr Christie says. 'I'm sorry for your loss but we've got a hotel to run here.'

'People don't die of "can't say",' says Rose.

'I know that,' I say.

'Then why didn't you ask?' Rose says.

'Because when they're ready, they'll tell us.'

They didn't tell us but eventually we found out. The whole world found out. Godfrey hanged himself. He went in early to the motor workshop where he was apprenticed and by the time his work friends arrived they found him hanging there dead. I can't think about it.

He was in love with a white girl, a Portuguese girl called Dolores Nuñes, and I suppose because he was light-skinned and could pass for white she never thought twice about it, and once it had started off like that when he began to get serious about her he couldn't bring himself to tell her.

His friends at work knew. They said he must have known that sooner or later he'd have to break it off even if he never said it because he knew that there could be no future for them. All they could expect was trouble, but even though he knew it he couldn't bring himself to part from her. He'd been to her house and seen how strict her parents were and never mind what colour he happened to be, she was only seventeen, and if they found out how serious things were between them they would have put a stop to it anyway and probably given her the hiding of her life and then come out looking for him, and it all got too much. Then his sister found a photo of his girlfriend hidden in his room and said that if he didn't own up and put an end to it she'd tell and by that time he was at the end of his tether, he had nowhere to turn, his nerves were all used up and he just couldn't take any more.

How long did the Frederickses think they could keep it a secret? They must have known it would come out eventually, and even if we were right at the bottom of the list the time would come when we'd hear about it just like everyone else did.

I put a death notice in the morning newspaper. You have to go to St George's Street to the big hall in Newspaper House and fill in a form. You fill it in then you take it to the desk and you pay, but while I'm filling it in I start to cry. I stand at the filling-in counter with the blank form in front of me, in a long line of other people filling in forms and they're all just going about their business. There are flats to let and cars to sell and 'want to buy' and 'want to sell' and I'm the only one who cries.

I cry because I know that if I'd been the one who died, Godfrey would have done the same for me. He'd be standing here, right where I'm standing now, in his jeans and T-shirt filling in the form, writing the words down carefully in big block letters. My heart hurts just to think about it.

I put in 'beloved'. Now that he's dead and gone for ever

I can say it and even put it in the newspaper. If I had gone before him I would have been 'beloved' too, the late Ruby, niece and beloved cousin. When I think about this I cry even more. It's a nice thing to know that, even if you do sometimes think otherwise, you do have a place in the world and people who belong to you but it's sad to think that someone has to die before you're really sure.

I can't 'do' my tables because I can't stop crying. I know the rules. No private business during working time but even so I can't stop crying. The permanents want their supper. They aren't interested in my tears. The permanents have their own problems and they're fussy. The last thing they need is a maid in a waitress dress salting the soup with her tears.

I sit on the bottom step of the flight of stairs that lead up to the staff rooms and I cry and Joycie serves my tables as well as her own and I have learned something today. I came here as a 'willing girl'; that's what it says in my Sacred Heart testimonial. But 'willing' can only take you so far, then it stops. You can be as willing as you like but some things are too big for even the most willing to bear. Crying for my cousin and myself, that's all I'm good for today.

'Your friend's asking after you,' Joycie says between the soup and the fish. 'He wants to know what's the matter. I told him if he wants to know he should ask you. I'm not the messenger service.'

I know who Joycie means. She means Mr Silver but Mr

Silver's not really my friend, he's just a man I feel sorry for. I don't have friends. If I didn't face up to it before, I see it now because my heart is full and there's no one I can talk to.

Joycie makes out that Mr Silver's so keen he takes the trouble to ask after me. Imagine if I told him? Imagine how he'd like that? I know right now what he'd think. Poor girls always have a story. That's what people like him say. There's always a dead mother, an aunt who's unkind, a life that didn't turn out the way it should have.

This time it's a cousin who died. That's how it is with 'them' and it always ends up the same, time off for the funeral and money for the expenses because there's never money and there are always expenses. In the end that's what it all boils down to.

'Are you going to tell him, or must I?' Joycie says between the main and the sweets and I turn my head away.

What's happened to me doesn't concern Mr Silver. People like me are owed nothing by people like him. What's happened to me has to stay with me because that's where it belongs.

'That's that then,' says Joycie, banging down the last plates. 'They're all finished now and so am I. I'm half dead.'

Then she looks at me sitting on the stairs with my swollen-up face.

'He's still in there,' she says and shows with her head. 'Hanging around in the dining room and I'd like to call it a day now and lock up if that's all right with you.'

'Knock-off time,' says Cook. 'It's up to you to sort out your own private time, Ruby.'

Then it's Joycie's turn.

'He wants to know what the matter is, so either you go in and tell him or he's going to come out here and ask you himself. It's up to you. Either way, he says he'd like an answer.'

I told him in the street. That was the shame of it. I had to go into the dining room, swollen face and all, and tell him that the dining room couldn't be kept open all night. It's kitchen's job to lock up and they wanted to lock up right then, that moment, so that they could knock off.

'I want to know what's wrong,' he said, and even if I were going to tell him, which I wasn't, where did he think was a proper place for me to do it? There was no private place where maids and permanents could be together. That wasn't the way the world was made.

I wished I was sassy the way Rose could be when she put her mind to it. Then I could have said, 'Why don't I just get my coat and bag and we'll pop out to the Mount Nelson.'

That's the kind of thing Rose would have said but I'm not Rose.

'We could step outside if you like,' I said.

'Let's do that,' he said and I went out, just as I was, and he walked out after me, and Joycie with a big bang of the dining-room door locked up behind us.

I stood in front of him round the corner at the side of the hotel. I was still in my black waitress dress with the

136

name tag on the lapel, which I hated because it looked like a funeral dress and it had looked that way before anyone died. I stood there in that dress and I told him all of it because it was all bottled up inside me and it had to come out somehow.

I told him about me and about Rose and our mother and the orphanage and going to Steenbras Street every last Sunday and how not even our own blood family had any time for us.

Once I start I can't stop and it wasn't hard or as bad as I thought it would be. I talked and he listened and, I thought, so what? I could say it, I could say anything I liked now because what could it matter?

I said about Godfrey and how he could make me laugh.

'If you look at me I'll make you laugh.' That was what Godfrey used to say to me in those days when he was an altar boy, before he outgrew it all. 'You will not,' I'd tell him. 'Yes, I will,' he'd say. 'You just look at me and you won't be able to stop yourself.'

I could feel my knees on the cold floor in front of the communion rail. My head was bent and my eyes were cast down in case Auntie Olive was checking on me and I was praying, 'Please, God, don't let me laugh.' Body of Christ, Blood of Christ. When the priest was right in front of me I could see myself the way Godfrey must have seen me, kneeling down with my mouth wide open, gaping like a fish, waiting for my wafer. It was the way he said it that made me want to laugh. He was like that and now he's dead and I can't take it in.

It was a strange place we had all come to where people stand out on the street to talk about death.

On the day of the funeral Auntie Olive and Uncle Bertie stood outside the church next to the priest and people came past them and took their hands and said those things that people say at funerals and Rose and I said them too.

'Sorry, Auntie Olive,' we say and she says thank you. She says thank you to everybody, one after the other. 'Thank you for coming.' As if we've all been to a party.

'Why does she keep saying thank you the whole time?' Rose says.

'Because that's what you're supposed to say when people come up to you after a funeral to tell you how sorry they are that you've lost someone.'

There's tea afterwards in the church hall and rusks and Hertzoggie coconut cookies and *koeksusters* and milk tart and date bread with butter and everyone stands around talking in funeral voices and their mouths say one thing while they're thinking something else.

'Let's get out of here,' I say, grabbing hold of Rose and Rose's mouth is full of date bread and she's reaching for a *koeksuster* as if she hasn't already had far too much to eat, as if anyone would even feel like eating at a moment like this.

'Don't pull me,' Rose says.

'There's nothing here for us,' I say and it isn't just the hall at Good Shepherd that I mean.

The funeral will end. All the *koeksusters*, every last

Hertzoggie, all of the date loaf, every bit of milk tart will be eaten. The church ladies will wash up and take their empty Tupperware back home. The Goodall and Williams car will take Auntie Olive and Uncle Bertie and Patsy back to Steenbras Street and I don't know how they'll stand it but they will.

The mourners will walk to their houses or get in their cars and they'll go home. They'll take off their funeral clothes, those tight best suits and those shirt collars that choke you half to death. They'll put on jeans and jerseys and slippers, supper will be put on the stove and the TV switched on and life will begin all over again because that's the way life is.

'You don't have to run,' says Rose. 'There's no one chasing after us, calling us back. No one's even noticed that we left.'

ARE YOU HAPPY?

Since the night out on the street Mr Silver's been different. He's still at his same table at mealtimes but I can feel him moving away. He's nice to me just as he's always been but he looks at me differently and I don't look at him at all. I've told him far too much and I wish now that I hadn't.

There are people who think there's something going on between Mr Silver and me. He's not a stupid man, so I suppose he must know that. I put up with the remarks because there's nothing I can do about it. No one's ever going to say anything to him but even so I'm quite sure he doesn't like it.

Not one word of it's true and I would put a stop to it if I could but I can't because it gives everyone round here something to pass the days with and the made-up stories are getting bigger and bigger and the other staff tease me. Joycie, for one, knows that not one word is true but even she puts her oar in.

'Have you heard the latest?' she says. Then she tells me things Mr Silver and I are supposed to be getting up to together that never happened and never will, and that's how things stand when Mr Silver tells me that he's leaving.

I don't know if the stories have anything to do with it. He asks me before I bring pudding, which is tinned guavas and custard, if I'll stay behind after supper because he has something to say to me and when I do stay he doesn't mention the stories.

I have to ask Joycie for the key because locking up's her job.

'Give it to her,' Cook says and Joycie takes the key out of her apron pocket and gives it to me and this is going to be something else to talk about, I can see that already.

You could laugh about it if it wasn't so sad. I really don't know about Joycie and what she thinks a man like Mr Silver and a girl like me might get up to in a locked-up dining room with the smell of cottage pie and guavas still in the air. At least we don't have to talk out on the street this time and that's good but it's strange to be just two people in a dining room that has fourteen tables, thirteen of which have already been reset for breakfast.

'Well, here I am,' I say and I wait.

For a long time he's quiet. He doesn't even look at me. He looks down and he looks far away and it seems to me that he's somewhere else and it's a place where I can't go and then he looks up at me right into my face.

'Tell me, Ruby,' he says, 'how do you like it here? Does it suit you? Are you happy? Is this really what you want to do with your life?'

There are twelve men here at the Queen's, each with a story, and three of us women in the kitchen. Mr Silver could ask any of us if it suits us and if we are happy. He could go out in the road and ask the first person he lays his eyes on the same question. He could stand up and go and look at himself in the sideboard mirror and ask himself how happy he is and that should give him his answer.

Then he tells me that very soon he'll be leaving the hotel and joining his brother in England.

'Just to begin with,' he says. 'After that, well, I'm not quite sure yet. I haven't made up my mind.'

The dining-room windows face out on to an outside passage that runs past the kitchen. Anyone can look in at the window and see us. There's nothing to see but a man sitting at a cleared table covered with a white damask cloth in a room filled with tables that look exactly the same. Just that and a girl in a black-and-white waitress uniform with a silly cap on her head standing in front of him and the light shining down on them.

'I want to tell you something,' he says. 'It's something I'm not in the habit of talking about.'

When Joycie first used to come to me with her titbits about Mr Silver, the first thing that came to my mind was that I didn't care what the story was, if it concerned Mr

Silver, I didn't want to hear it. All the time I was lying to myself. I wanted to hear then and I want to hear now.

He asks me if I know about his misfortune. If I say I do he'll think that people have been talking about him behind his back, taking his story and making it less by telling it as if it's for everyone to know and he'll know that I've been listening, but it isn't like that.

It doesn't matter how different we are. He's like water to me and I can see through him and he can see through me and he knows it's not like that and he has no need to tell me what I know for myself.

Then he tells me something that no one here knows. He tells me what he does on Saturdays when he goes out all neatly dressed up and is gone for almost all of the day.

'I go to be with my family,' he says. 'Can you understand that?'

I do understand it and if he can bear to speak it then I can find the courage to listen. He tells it very clear and quiet in neat sentences as if he will say it this once and never speak it out loud again and I can see it all.

Daddy is dependable. If Daddy says a time he means it to the minute and he wants you there. He likes you to be waiting for him because then he knows exactly where you are and doesn't have to worry about you. Daddy brings you presents that aren't like the presents other children have. Daddy brings you stories and although you're getting big you love his stories because the stories he tells are always about you. Children forget their small selves but Daddy will never allow you to forget. He tells you how long he and Mummy had to wait for you and how much you were wanted and how once you came he knew that when the person you're waiting for is so special you realize that you didn't really mind the wait at all.

Children forget but that's all right. As long as Daddy's there, everything, even the very smallest things, will never be forgotten. If you should wake up in the night you should remember that. Daddy keeps you in his heart and there's no place in the world that you could be safer because there's no one who can touch you while he keeps you safe in there.

He says the hardest thing is when the time comes to leave them again and return to the hotel. Every time you think your heart will break but it helps at least to be dependable. That's why he goes every Saturday. Dependable is the one last thing he has left to offer. It's something he can still do for his family.

'You understand?' he says and I do and he's a teller of stories and I take what he's told me as a gift and it's worth more to me than gold.

There's no one in the world who could understand in quite the way I do. I had a father once who loved me. People forget.

'I can help you, if you let me,' Mr Silver says, but I don't take things from people. I thought that Mr Silver of all people would know that.

'Not like that,' he says. 'Not what you think.'

He suggests that I could change jobs. He knows a lady

in Sea Point who needs a companion, someone who'll be with her and take care of her.

'I've spoken to her,' he says. 'I hope you don't mind my doing that but I didn't want to waste your time. It isn't like this there. I think that you might like it.'

I don't know Sea Point. Mr Silver may think that's funny because I've lived here all my life but if that's what he thinks he doesn't show it.

'Sea Point has lots of blocks of flats where older people live,' he says. 'You don't mind the idea of older people, do you? Some of them have had very interesting lives. If you go there, you'll find out for yourself.'

I ask if I'll be able to hear the sea there. I would be shy about saying that to anyone else but I don't mind saying it to him.

'You'll be able to hear it and see it,' he says. 'And the work won't be hard work like here and I think you could find it pleasant.'

The dining room is half dark. The lights in the kitchen have been switched off for the night and it's very quiet. I think that if I look into the sideboard mirror now I will see myself in a flat in Sea Point with only one person to take care of. I took care of my mother when she was sick and I've looked out for my sister and myself. I've cared for the burn babies and I don't know older people with lives like streamers flowing out behind them but I think I could like that.

'Go and have a look and decide for yourself,' Mr Silver says and he takes a little piece of paper out of his pocket. 'Here, I've written down the number and the name.

She's Mrs Margolis and she expects a call from you.'

I reach out to take the paper but even as it passes from his hand into mine I know that I can't go, no matter how much I may want to, because I can't leave my sister. To think that is like having something you want really badly offered to you and then snatched away. The idea of losing this chance makes me brave.

'Will it be live-in?' I say, and he says that it will.

'All those big blocks have staff accommodation. You should ask to see it and see if it'll do.'

He doesn't say it but we all know about staff accommodation. Wherever there are full-time maids or caregivers or companions or housekeepers or any other name you choose to give them, there are rooms. Sometimes nice and sometimes not so nice but there are always rooms. 'Indispensable', that's what they call the people who live there. 'Part of the family.' 'Can't imagine life without her.' All the same there must be rooms, some place close by that you're meant to vanish into when it suits, and I don't mind. I can work and I can vanish. I can do anything life asks of me as long as I can have my sister with me.

It's hard to have to ask for things. I've had to ask for things all my life and so I know. You have to want something very badly to ask straight out for it and there isn't much that I could bring myself to ask for but I can ask for this.

ANOTHER COUNTRY

Mrs Margolis's telephone number is in my apron pocket on the slip of paper where Mr Silver wrote it down. I keep it on me wherever I go. I've written it down myself and put it under the newspaper lining of the drawer in my room and in my handbag in the zip section inside at the back so there's no chance I'll lose it. It's the actual number Mr Silver wrote down for me in his own handwriting that I keep on me all the time, for good luck. I move it from my cleaning overall pocket to my apron pocket and at night I put it under my pillow to bring me luck so that I can get this new job. I don't want to be here when Mr Silver's gone.

I look at his table in the empty dining room. The only table where we put a jug of water and a glass behind and to the left of the table setting. Soon there'll be no more need for that but if I were to stay I think I would always see it there. I could never go past that table without thinking of him. I look at it now and it's as if I can see our two ghost selves there, him sitting in his place and me standing in front of him, just talking quietly about his life and where it's taken him and my life and where it might take me.

'Ruby's boyfriend's left her.' That's what people will say but it wasn't like that, and there's something else too. It's not his fault and it isn't mine either but other men will also have that impression and this is a place of men and that will not make my life any easier.

I don't want the people at the hotel to know that I'm looking to make a change. If they know and I don't get the job I'll be back in my same old boat of being with people who think I want to leave them because I think I'm too good to be where I am. That can be difficult too, so I take a deep breath and all my courage and go out to the phone booth on the corner that I use in my 'off' time to telephone Mrs Margolis.

It doesn't smell very nice in the phone booth and the phone directory is pulled to pieces like they always are in phone booths but at least the phone's working. I stand there in my cleaning overall with my scarf pulled off my head. That scarf all by itself is enough to take away every piece of courage I ever had. With that scarf on my head what I will be, for ever and always, is a cleaning girl. I will act like a cleaning girl, think like a cleaning girl and one day I'll wake up and discover that I've even begun to dream like a cleaning girl, and when that happens my whole life will be cast. I'll turn round and I'll see that while I wasn't minding out, that's what happened to me, and that's my big fear. It's not the scarf's fault but I pull it off my head as if someone had set it on fire and if I didn't get rid of it I'd burn up and die. I roll it up and push it in my pocket and then I dial the number that Mr Silver wrote down for me in his neat writing in fountain-pen ink.

The phone rings for a long time and I almost put it down out of nerves and in the end I don't think that I can stand it any longer. Every change I've had in my life has been bad for me. Yet here I am in a phone booth in Dock Road looking for more. The phone is ringing in my ear and I'm waiting for a woman I don't know to pick up on the other side so I can walk straight into change again, as if life hasn't taught me anything at all. Then just when I think I'll hang up the phone's picked up and it's Mrs Margolis herself who answers and she says her name and I get a fright.

Mr Silver told me that Mrs Margolis was an old lady who'd need looking after but I don't think this can be the same Mrs Margolis who answers the phone. This Mrs Margolis has a big voice. I think she must be a big, strong woman used to giving orders and having people jump to attention when they hear her. I pull the phone-booth door closed without even thinking, as if to stop the whole street from hearing, and that makes the smell inside the booth even worse but I've made the call now and so I have no choice. I have to speak and say in what connection I'm calling and she doesn't sound one bit small or uncertain the way old ladies are supposed to sound. She doesn't sound as if she needs looking after but at least she knows who I am, she remembers being told about me and she's willing to see me and my afternoon off will suit her just fine.

'Do you know your way around Sea Point?' she says.

'Yes,' I say and I try to sound as sure of myself as she is even though it isn't true.

'Then you won't have any trouble finding Pleasant Ways,' she says. 'If you get lost anyone will direct you. It's on Beach Road at Mouille Point right near the lighthouse.'

'Yes, thank you,' I say.

I stand in the phone booth with the telephone receiver in my hand and I can't believe what's happened. It's such a big event I'm sure it'll bring rain to the desert. Ruby Jacobs has gone out to look for change.

'Out of the frying pan into the fire.' I can just hear Auntie Olive but Auntie Olive isn't the one standing in a maid's overall in a stinky phone booth with the street life of Dock Road going on through the dirty glass panes. I only have to take one look at those panes and I know. You could try any cleaning trick in the world and rub your life out with effort; you'd never get them clean, not in a million years.

I'm still holding the good luck piece of paper with the phone number in Mr Silver's handwriting in one hand and the maid's scarf pulled out of my pocket ready to put back on my head in the other. I take the paper and tuck it inside my bra and then I pull it out quickly and put it back in my pocket because my bra is maybe not the right place for it and I'm all by myself but I go blood red in the street. It's all the excitement. It's made me feel hot and the phone booth didn't help either. Being trapped inside, just you and a stranger's voice, with your heart beating a hundred miles an hour while you make an arrangement and have an address to remember is enough to make anyone hot.

When I've finished and step outside into the fresh air I stand still on the street for a moment. People come out of the Imperial Café with packets of fish and chips. You can smell the vinegar. The hawker on the corner has bananas on his cart and cabbages and bunches of carrots. There are black men coming out of the dock gate. There's no work for them today and no bread on the table in the township. There's a seagull on the open field across from the hotel. You can see it reflected in a pool of stagnant water. One of the on-duty Customs officers waves a car through the dock gate and I breathe and I hold my breath and then, when I can't hold it for one second more, I breathe out again and the world rolls off my shoulders. I look at my wristwatch, my luxury I saved up for and allowed myself after I'd put money aside for everything else. There's a few minutes left of my tea break and if I hurry I can still have tea.

'Don't tell me that you've lived in Cape Town all your life and don't know how to get to Sea Point?' Joycie says.

It's funny but I think about our old days of Rose and me and the Sacred Heart outings. That didn't last very long. First of all there was Rose's performance in the bus the day we went to Kogel Bay, and then it was decided that Kogel Bay was too far anyway and the outing was too expensive. So, after that, we stayed in our own neighbourhood and the nuns made a special arrangement and we walked two by two holding hands down to De Waal Park with our picnic. Then the treat was to be allowed to go into the park and play on the swings and roundabouts while the white children stood and looked at us with big eyes and wondered who we were and where we came from and how we got to have such a cheek.

In the end it didn't work out and perhaps it should never have been offered to us in the first place. What was the good of trying to show us a world that wasn't meant for us, and never would be? But that's all right. I may not know Hout Bay or Simon's Town or how beautiful Stellenbosch is but I know how to get to Steenbras Street, Athlone. I could get there with my eyes closed. I know the hill up the side of Devil's Peak that goes up to Sacred Heart. I can tell you every criss-cross road name on the way. Knowing these things has been useful in its way but those are the old roads of my life and knowing them like I do is not much use to me now.

'Getting to Sea Point's not hard,' Joycie says.

'Write it down anyway,' I say.

'I don't know, I give up,' says Joycie but she writes it down. 'There you are,' she says. 'Are you happy now?'

I don't know about 'happy'. After all, I'm not there yet and I would rather die than be running around Sea Point showing my piece of paper and asking strangers for directions. I don't like having to go up to strangers. I've tried to do it once or twice when I needed to ask the time or for directions but I gave up before I even spoke and found another way.

'I don't know what gets into you, Ruby,' Rose says. Rose hasn't got any fear in her at all. She'll go up to anyone and start talking to them and before the conversation is over, without even being asked, she'll have told them all our business. As for me, I could never do that.

'It's only a person. If you went right up close and gave them a pinch you'd be disappointed because you'd find out that they're only flesh and blood after all. Just like we are.'

That may be so but what I'm afraid of is the way their face might change when they saw me coming, as if I was going to ask for money. I know it's foolish but that's how I feel. I haven't even begun to move towards them and I can feel them begin to move away. I've never asked anyone for anything in my life but even so I think what strangers see when they see me is a poor, respectable-looking girl who'll sidle up and have a story and then, when the story's over, she'll ask for money. This is how I feel and even when Rose is right next to me, small and full of confidence and looking to me to say what my problem is, I won't tell her because I'm too ashamed.

I haven't told Joycie what the Sea Point visit is about.

'There's something I have to do there.' That's all I say and just for a change she doesn't ask and that's a big surprise, and I look at Joycie and she looks at me and I think she doesn't ask because she knows. I know that she knows not one word of all the teasing about Mr Silver and me's true. She never believed it for a minute and I think in one way Joycie and Mr Silver are a bit the same although she would never say it. Joycie knows I don't belong here and she likes me enough to wish me well out of this place.

I'm as neat as I can be. I've practised my face and what I will say. I've got my directions on a piece of paper and if I lose the paper it doesn't matter because I have them off by heart.

'You look very nice,' Joycie says. 'Turn around and let me have a look.'

It's the kind of thing I used to say to Rose last Sunday of the month. It's not the kind of thing anyone's ever said to me.

'Very nice,' Joycie says and then she does something I never expected. 'Come here,' she says and she steps forward and puts her arms around me and she's a small girl. Her head only comes up to my chin.

'You go and show them, Ruby,' she says and all I can do is smile and nod my head. I can feel her body against my body through my clothes. I suppose it's nerves and all the excitement but something catches at my heart and tears come to my eyes.

No one in my grown-up life has touched me easily with love like that except my sister and it's a funny feeling. It's like being allowed into some other country that was close by me all the time where I have never been before.

* * *

Mrs Margolis was an actress in her day. She was a star 'of stage not screen' and plenty of people knew her name. I'm sitting in the lounge of her top-floor flat in Pleasant Ways, Beach Road, Sea Point, near the Mouille Point lighthouse. I'm sitting with a straight back right in the middle of the sofa, right up at the very edge, with my hands folded in my lap and she's talking and I'm listening. You can't be nervous and listen properly at the same time and so I try not to be nervous. Sometimes when older people talk a lot they lose the thread and if Mrs Margolis asks me what she's just said I should be able to say it back so I have to listen hard and it isn't easy.

Mrs Margolis is the wife of the late Monty.

'You would be too young to know,' she says. 'He was a boxing promoter and a sportsman. He was a lovely man.'

I've never met anyone like Mrs Margolis before. She's old and dressed in shocking pink. Her nails are pink and there's a little dash of pink lipstick near her mouth and she has eyebrows painted on. They look like railway arches and her eyes underneath are watery. They've washed a little trail of mascara down on to her cheek but she doesn't seem to notice.

She has old lady feet. I look down and then I look away. She's wearing a loose caftan and silk scarves, all colours round her neck, pink and turquoise and bright yellow. They're so bright inside the house you should put on sunglasses before you look at them but it's not my place to say. She asks me if I'll have tea and that feels wrong to me.

I don't know what I'm meant to say. I'm here to make the tea, not to drink it.

'Olga will bring the tea,' Mrs Margolis says. 'She works for the establishment. But if I have a visitor and she's finished her rounds for the day she's kind enough to come up and make tea for me, but only if I ask her very nicely.'

Olga's a black woman in a white nurse's uniform and she doesn't seem to mind me sitting there. I want to hide my rough work-maid's hands from her. Her uniform's so white and clean. Her hands are smooth, her fingernails are neat and she looks nice and she doesn't stare.

'This is Ruby,' Mrs Margolis says and if I could I would sit on my hands. 'She's here about the job.'

It's surprising how quickly you get rough work-maid's hands. The floor polish gets stuck inside your nails and you can never get it all out, no matter how hard you brush. Blue scrubbing soap has a bite in it that can make you come out in a rash. Sometimes when the cleaning's finished your hands swell up and your fingers feel soft like sausages and they hurt, and so do your hands and your knees and your feet.

'You can bring us tea, Olga, if you don't mind,' Mrs Margolis says. 'And some of those Chocolate Vitola biscuits too, please, if you don't mind.'

Then she looks at me. In the middle of all the lines and brown spots and under the railway arches that are her eyebrows are Mrs Margolis's eyes. They're milky green and it seems to me as if they float in her face. I have a funny feeling. It feels as if she's looking at me down a long corridor of time, all the way from her time to my own. I know that

Mr Silver spoke to her about me. What I don't know is what he said but I'm here now in her flat on the top floor of Pleasant Ways and I see her looking at me but I don't know what she knows and I don't know what she sees.

'I like bright faces around me,' she says. 'That's one thing I insist on. There's enough misery in the world. If at all possible I like to leave it outside my door. My husband and I liked to entertain. We always had a house filled with people.'

She sits forward in her chair and shows with her hands for me to look around the room and everywhere you look there are photographs.

'I like to have my pictures all around me,' she says. 'I look at them and there are some stories there, I can tell you.'

It's just as well that she's the one who's doing all the talking because if she asked me if I had any pictures I'd have to tell her that I only have one. The one that Clarence-next-door took so Rose and I could have a happy memory of Steenbras Street and something to remember them all by.

'It's lovely when you're young,' Mrs Margolis says. 'Then it's parties and good times and you think it'll never end, but it's not so good when you get older. Your friends start to die. One by one they leave and then one day you realize that you're older too. It comes upon you, you know, without your expecting it and you're not coping the way you once were. You need help and some arrangement has to be made.'

She puts down her cup in its saucer and looks at me.

'Mr Margolis and I were the happiest couple in the world. Everyone said so. I was everything to him and he was everything to me.'

She lifts up her old hand and she's wearing a watch and a bangle and they slide together, and it looks as if she's trying to wave something away in front of her face or as if she might cry, but then it's over.

'Unfortunately our union wasn't blessed with children,' she says. 'Which isn't to say that we've been without younger people in our lives. We haven't and some of them have meant a great deal to us and they worry about me, even now. I suppose you could say that's why you're here today.'

There's a fireplace with an electric fire made to look like wood in it and over the fireplace is a painting of a blond woman with bare shoulders and she's wearing a red dress that can't be made of anything but satin. It shines out of the paint and her head's turned round and she's very beautiful in her frame high up on the wall looking down at the world.

'That's me,' Mrs Margolis says, and I look away as though it's something I shouldn't see. 'That's all right,' she says. 'I don't mind if you look. I was quite used to being looked at in my day but that was long ago and I accept that.'

I'm sad for her, as if she should be ashamed of not looking like that any more. She minds, I know because I can feel it. You don't expect old people to mind. They must have known that one day they'd get old and I feel that it's rude of me to keep staring at the painting but it's hard to look away and at Mrs Margolis the way she is now. When I look back I look at her face, not at her feet, because they're old lady feet that look like crooked bird's claws in sandals with straps wide enough to leave room for the bunions.

'You're very young,' she says.

I am young and there's nothing that I can do about it. She's old and there's nothing she can do either. She knows about me because Mr Silver told her. She doesn't look at my hands and I don't look at her feet.

'I think we'll get along,' she says. 'Drink your tea and I'll tell you what's required of you and you can tell me if you think that taking care of an old lady like me is the kind of job that will suit you.'

SOMETHING THAT HAPPENS TO YOU

'What suits you doesn't have to suit me,' Rose says.

'I know that,' I say.

It's a nice day and we're sitting at the end of the garden at Sacred Heart. The big wooden cross with the suffering Jesus is hanging behind us and down below it, where we are, it looks as if He's turned His back on us because His suffering is private and something He wants to keep to Himself and that suits me. I know something about life now. I know at least enough to tell me that there are plenty of people walking around with their suffering locked up inside them and no one able to take on their burdens because life just doesn't work that way.

Since Godfrey died we don't go to Steenbras Street every last Sunday any more. It just fell away. Everything changed and we didn't want to push ourselves and Auntie Olive never asked, I suppose because she had other things on her mind, and now that I was working and didn't see Rose every day I liked to spend my free time with her and so it suited me, and if you asked Rose she'd say that it suited her even better.

I've brought hamburgers from the shop at the bottom of the road and a big bag of salt and vinegar chips. I have paper serviettes and plastic straws to make a picnic and something a bit special for Rose and there's a bench where we can sit. We often sit here and I tell her that we're like two ladies having lunch at Stuttaford's, eating all those things we like the best. I don't know what the Stuttaford's ladies like but Rose and I like hot dogs or sausage rolls or hamburgers, what we want and choose for ourselves and not what Sacred Heart kitchen says we're going to have, and no white fish and white potato on white plates on Friday.

Sacred Heart's a big place. It's very old and made out of stone that the builders took from Table Mountain. You can see that it will stand for ever with the suffering Christ hanging from His cross at the end of the car park just in case we're careless and forget. Behind His back the steps go down to the garden and then on to the wild patches that lead into the pine grove.

Usually Rose likes it when we are the two of us together having a walk or a picnic or a little outing down to the shops. We shop down in Plein Street and at the Grand Parade and it's nice because we can walk there and don't need a bus and also because you hardly ever see a white face. It's the coloured part of town so at least, in that way, we belong.

Now that Rose has pocket money from me she likes to spend it and buy little things for herself, and sometimes she buys things for me like a nice bar of soap or a pair of earrings.

'Do you like them?' Rose will say. 'Why don't you buy them then? They're a good price.'

They are luxuries and I have done without luxuries for so long in my life, I can do without them for a little bit longer. Besides which, I'm saving my money for something much more important to me than earrings could ever be, but if I don't watch Rose I'll end up with more soap and earrings than any woman could ever want and I'll get fat.

Rose likes takeaway down at the Parade.

'I'll treat you,' she says. 'I never knew that one day when you had money you'd be so tight with it – but it doesn't matter, I don't mind spending my pocket money on you.'

I eat at the hotel. Rose knows that. At the hotel we eat the same as the permanents do but we only eat after they've finished and we eat in the kitchen and Cook gives us leftovers on our days off to take with us to anyone who'd like to have them. All of us will know someone who'll be glad to have them.

'This isn't for eating,' Rose says. 'It's for treats.'

Treats are one thing but waste's another.

'You buy something nice for yourself,' I say. 'Don't worry about me. I couldn't eat anything even if I wanted to, really, I couldn't.'

'Neither could I,' Rose says. 'But I'm going to anyway.'

It isn't long before the food vendors know about Rose and how she can't make up her mind between samosas and boerewors rolls and Sputnik red Viennas in cold mashed potato and mutton and vegetables wrapped up in a pancake.

I like to see her happy but this new thing, the greediness, is something I never saw in her before. It isn't hunger that makes Rose eat like she does, it's need, and it isn't a samosa or a Sputnik that she's greedy for. It's all her missed life that she's gobbling down and it isn't good for her. She'll get fat if she doesn't watch out, but even so, I don't criticize and ask what happened to all I taught her and why can't she use a serviette like a properly brought up person would. I don't make a remark when she asks if she can have another ice cream before she's even finished the one she's holding because who am I to deny my sister this pleasure?

Before the end of this year Rose will be sixteen years old and Sacred Heart will find her a place and it'll be a place looking for willing girls, to give them a chance in life, and I don't want that for Rose.

'It's not up to you to decide for me,' Rose says.

'That's true,' I say. 'But if you had to choose between me or Sister Angelica or Matron deciding what you should do next, which would you choose?'

I open up the paper around the hamburger and fold it halfway back so Rose has something to hold on to and then I pass it over to her. The air is full of the smell of it and onions and gherkin and margarine and All Gold tomato sauce oozes out from between the two halves of the roll.

'I don't want to work for a Jewish lady I don't even know,' Rose says.

'You won't be working for her,' I say. 'I will.'

'You could keep your job at the Queen's and get me a job and I could share your room there.'

'No, you couldn't,' I say.

My life at the Queen's, how it is and the version that I choose to tell my sister are very different and that's my own business.

Rose has almost finished her hamburger. She's come to that part where she has to take the last bit out of the paper wrapping to finish it off. There's grease round her mouth and grease on her fingers and I hold out a serviette and show that I would like her to use it.

'You've changed, do you know that, Ruby?' she says. 'You've changed like nobody's business since you left here.'

I know that and she'll change too when her time comes. She just doesn't know it yet.

There's something I've wanted to tell my sister for quite a long time but I was waiting for the right time to come along when she would be ready to hear it. Rose is a big girl now, she doesn't have to listen to me any more, and I know that. She's big enough now for me to say what I have to say, but even so it isn't easy. How do you tell your sister that you've given up on God, that you gave up on

Him a long time ago? That's a hard thing and in the end I just sit quietly looking out over the pine trees and I say it.

'I knew that,' Rose says. 'Just because we didn't talk about it doesn't mean I didn't know. I was just wondering when you were going to get around to telling me, that's all.'

She picks up the paper serviette and wipes her hands clean and her mouth and then she folds it up neatly with the hamburger paper and puts everything back in the bag to be thrown away when we come to a bin and I could smile at Rose. She knows how to do things properly when she tries.

'I knew you hated going to Good Shepherd every Sunday, doing pretend happy families with the Frederickses. I knew you hated it just as much as I did but you did it anyway.'

'I did it because I was so set on our having what was due to us by way of a family even if it was only Auntie Olive and I was wrong to do it and I'm sorry.'

'Is that what put you off God?' Rose says and I say no, it wasn't that.

She asks me if it was maybe to do with our mother and the way that she was taken from us.

'That always played on your mind,' she says and I say maybe that was a part of it but I don't know for sure.

'If it makes you feel any better, God didn't "take" our mother,' Rose says. 'Cancer did.'

'If you say so,' I say.

'I do say so,' she says. 'Because it is so and I think that perhaps it will help if you remember that.'

I've said what I wanted to say to my sister. I don't want to sit here with her and talk to her about how losing your faith is something that happens to you, not something you choose.

Getting old isn't an easy business. No one has time for old people any more even though they've been here longest and they know this and so they keep young and show the best face they can. If you walked past Pleasant Ways and only knew it from the outside you would think that it was just another smart beachfront block of flats. The lower floors are like a stylish hotel with lounges and a dining room and security and reception and at the back there's a nurses' surgery and a frail care centre for when you can't take care of yourself any more, which is why Mrs Margolis likes it.

You could say that in her way Mrs Margolis is the queen of Pleasant Ways because in her time she was like a film star would be today and people here remember that. Also, she has the biggest top-floor flat and she has something else too that not all the others have. The years have passed but she hasn't let them take her glamour from her. She still has that.

She's very generous with her money. She tips all the time and she tips well, so when she asks for something it's a pleasure for the people here, who know her, to do the best they can to keep Mrs Margolis happy.

A lot of the people here don't want their own live-in people because they pay good money for Pleasant Ways to see that they're looked after. There's twenty-four-hour call and an emergency button down to reception if you need anything, but Mrs Margolis wants her own person with her. So, I'm lucky and Mrs Margolis knows all about Rose and how badly I want to keep her by me and I have Mr Silver to thank for that, except that I can't thank him because he's gone.

I knew it was going to happen but I didn't think it would happen like it did.

He never said goodbye to me. He didn't shake my hand, or wish me well, or even leave a word for me to say that he was on his way. It isn't what I expected but it was what I got. One evening after my afternoon off I came back to the hotel and he'd already left. There was no one at his table. I waited and he never came and in the end I asked Joycie because I had no choice, and Joycie was waiting for me to ask because then she'd know for sure that I didn't know.

'His brother came for him,' she said. 'In a big car just like before with a driver in a peaked cap and a Mount Nelson Hotel sign on the side and Mr Silver was very nice. He was very friendly, like a different person. He came to the kitchen to say thank you to all of us for what we'd done for him and that was a first time in this place, I can tell you.

'You should have seen him,' Joycie said and she's right. I should have seen him.

'He was very smart, nicely turned out, and his brother waited in the car for him and before he left he gave each of us an envelope and I must say he was very generous.'

It's not how I wanted it and it hurt me before I could remind myself that I had no right and I couldn't do anything to stop it.

'Nothing for you,' Joycie said. 'The others are saying he must have given you yours privately.'

'He didn't give me anything,' I said, and she acted surprised but she needn't have.

I think now that perhaps I was special after all, because leaving nothing is much bigger than leaving something. The 'nothing' he left for me has made me high as if I stand beside him and am his equal. It makes me believe that if things had been different, Mr Saul Silver and I could have been friends. But that's where life put us and he's found his place again, and out of all that he lost he still has people who care for him and I must be glad for him, and I am. I like to think that somewhere, in some part of himself, he'll remember me as he moves on. I don't expect him to keep me all in one piece in my black waitress uniform sitting somewhere in the back of his mind like an old photograph. That way I would be the same for ever while life moved on and I wouldn't like him to remember me like that. I don't want to be stuck in his mind as a Queen's Hotel waitress standing stiffly with a smile pinned on her face; a smile that will say as little as the one word on the name tag does. I don't have a choice but if I did there's another way I'd like him to remember me. If he thinks of me at all, I would like him to feel what I feel. I think that we are two lives that flowed towards each other, that some strange tide brought together, and that there was a moment when we flowed through each other before we went our separate ways.

That's how I feel but I could never say it and he would have to be inside my heart to know. How could he tell just by looking at me when I stand in front of him at suppertime reciting soup, fish, mains and pudding?

A UNION NOT BLESSED WITH CHILDREN

I like Mrs Margolis and the bright pink line of lipstick in the middle of her face. It says that she's still in the world, and while she is she expects the world to remember that she's there and to sit up and take notice of her.

She has a funny way of looking at me with her old eyes. She looks at me from far away down a long passage of years, her years and my years that have brought us together to this place. I don't think that every day of her life has been as glamorous as the photos in her flat make out but I can feel goodness in her towards my sister and me. She had a sister once but only for a little while, but even so I think she must know what it feels like. Her sister died young in a flu epidemic because life was like that in the olden days. There were people dying all the time but that didn't make it any easier and in time her father died and then her mother. Then the late Monty went and she was on her own. I'm not glad for her that she has no one but I'm glad for me because now I've left Queen's Hotel, Dock Road, behind me.

I like Mrs Margolis and I like the flat. I like the old people. They're not like Sacred Heart old people, who we big girls always said were sitting in God's waiting room just waiting out their time. I'm sorry now I ever said that and I'm sorrier still that there are people who live out the last of their lives like that. There are old bodies here at Pleasant Ways and they're full of aches and pains but there's more life here than I've seen in my whole life before.

'Bring the telephone, Ruby,' Mrs Margolis says when she's ready and that's how we start the day. I carry the telephone into her bedroom with a long cord that curls along on the floor behind me like a snake. Mrs Margolis likes things like her telephone in the old style because old-style things work better and last longer. The telephone is important to Mrs Margolis and when it rings she doesn't answer it herself. She has taught me how to do that.

'Mrs Margolis's residence,' I say. 'Who shall I say is calling? Just a moment,' I say and I take the phone to Mrs Margolis wherever she is in the flat and put it down next to her and give her the receiver.

In the morning she orders her deliveries and the phone sits on the bed beside her and she has a list all ready and she dials. For whatever she needs Mrs Margolis does 'deliver' and when she's dialling it's as if she's calling friends and everybody knows her. I have never seen anything like that in my life before.

'What are you looking at, Ruby?' she says. 'I may be a hundred and fifty-four years old but I still have a house to run.'

Pleasant Ways has girls who come in to clean the flat and nurse aides like Olga who come to see to medicines and take blood pressure and test blood sugar levels and talk about the aches and pains. My job is to answer the phone and get the door when someone is buzzed up from the foyer and to lay the tea tray, make tea and take it in when asked. Sometimes Mrs Margolis goes down to the dining room to eat with the others and sometimes she eats 'in' and I set a place for her and serve her and when she's finished I take her tray back to the kitchen.

It's a new world to me and I can see Mrs Margolis looking at me sometimes and I wonder what she thinks. I'm not a big talker but I'm willing and I learn fast. I think she knows this but there's something else and I have only just discovered it. I like nice things and Mrs Margolis has some of the nicest things I've ever seen and they are my responsibility.

When she entertains I wash the glasses and the plates. I clean the Royal Doulton ornaments and the silver and all the photographs in their frames. I help her set her clothes out for the day while she's still sitting on her bed with her body full of night aches. I open up the cupboard and she chooses and then at half past nine Olga or the nurse aide on duty comes and we get Mrs Margolis ready to start her day. That is my life now and Mrs Margolis keeps reminding management to remember my sister next time a vacancy comes open for a kitchen girl. I can't wait for that to happen because then I will be able to have my sister with me and then I can do what I have to do and rest for a while because there will be nothing else to worry about. I don't think a job in the kitchen with food all around her is the best place for Rose but it's the best I can do for her for now.

'Look at her school reports, Ruby,' Sister Angelica says. 'And tell me what's the best thing we can do with that?'

No one could call Rose clever but I'm not sure that really matters very much. I was so-called clever but it didn't get me very far.

'I'll look out for my sister,' I say. 'I've found her work where I work now.'

'I see,' says Sister Angelica. 'So that's that then?' She closes up the folder in front of her and looks up at me and I know she doesn't like me. 'What kind of work, if I may ask?'

'Kitchen work,' I say. That was what I asked for and that was what was offered.

'Well, I suppose she'll be up to that,' Sister Angelica says. 'And she'll have you to look out for her. I suppose we should count that as a blessing.'

It is a blessing and we're lucky to be still together and I know what Sister Angelica sees when she looks at me. She sees the little girl who was so sure that Jesus would never part her from her sister but I've come a long way from there and that girl is gone for ever.

I don't even bother to say to Rose what Sister Angelica said about her school marks because, in my opinion, they don't count for anything, not when you know what Rose is like. Rose has a good heart and an open nature; she's friendly and she's kind. She likes to joke and people like her. I'm not like that but I don't begrudge her.

'I know that you're ambitious, Ruby,' Sister Angelica says. 'But you'd be wise to be ambitious for yourself, not for your sister. Rose isn't like you. She's a girl who'll make her way doing the simple things in life. You understand me, don't you?'

I do understand. I understand that there's always someone who has to do 'the simple things in life', otherwise how could life go on?

I want to say, 'Thank you, Sister,' but I don't. The first thing I'm going to teach myself in my new situation is to stop saying thank you all the time.

'I'll look out for Rose,' I say and I stand up and hold out my hand but Sister Angelica doesn't take it.

'I'll keep you in my prayers,' she says and she thinks that I'll say thank you but I won't.

'If Rose is ready now, I'll take her with me, if you don't mind. I need to get back to my work.'

'Why are you cross?' Rose says as we walk down the hill from Sacred Heart.

'I'm not cross,' I say.

'You could have fooled me,' Rose says.

I told her to give me her suitcase, I would carry it, but she says that she can carry it herself, thank you.

People don't go back to Sacred Heart when they leave. I went back because of Rose but there was nothing else that could have made me do it. It was our life when it needed to be our life and I wasn't happy there but I wasn't unhappy either. It was a place for us to be until we were old enough to take care of ourselves. It was never a home to us but it was never meant to be. That was the understanding and I understood it very well.

Past Bedford Street we go and Luton Street and Warwick and the freeway's on our right and cars fly by and I've walked up and down this hill more times than I can count.

'What's the matter with you?' Rose says.

'Nothing,' I say.

I can't tell her but I will not have people speak about my sister in that way. 'Simple tasks'. 'God's will'. I know Sister Angelica in the way that one person still very much in this world can see another and I walk faster.

Rose will start small in the big kitchen at Pleasant Ways. When the job was offered I went downstairs and talked about it with the head chef, because that is what they have there. She'll do scullery work and peel vegetables. She'll set trays and take them up to rooms when food is ordered up, and if she takes to it and works well she can move up through the kitchen.

'I think you'll like it,' I tell Rose.

'I suppose I will,' she says.

Rose can like anything, that's her gift, and I think about my mother. I can't stop myself. I think about Rose and me, small, sitting at my mother's table holding hands, saying grace. I don't want to think about it but now she's here I can't make my mother go away again. I love her far too much for that.

My hand is in hers, my sister holds my other hand and we are linked together and our eyes are closed. We have soup in front of us. I can smell the vegetables, celery and potato, soft old leftover tomatoes rand-a-bag from the hawker down the street and carrots and there's bread on the table. It's my turn to say grace and I say thank you, which came easily to me in those days, and because I'm speaking and not my mother I say, 'Thank you for those hands that lovingly prepare our meals,' and my mother's hand is in mine.

'What's the matter with you?' Rose says and I say nothing but I'm not running any more. I'm standing in the street and I tell my sister to put down her suitcase and I put my arms around her.

'It will be all right,' I say. 'You'll see.'

'I could like working in a kitchen,' Rose says.

'You could,' I say. 'I think that you could like it very much.'

I sleep in Mrs Margolis's spare room in case she needs something in the night. It's difficult at first but you get used to things and you get to know a person. Rose is downstairs working in the kitchen and she's happy and we have our room on the roof with our own things in it. I suppose you could say that we've never been better off. We have a door that we can close behind us. We have a Sony colour television and Rose has a portable radio that she takes downstairs with her when she works and everyone in the kitchen enjoys it.

There's no breakfast in the dining room here. Everyone eats in their own flats, except for frail care and those who place an order, and Rose takes their tray to them. After that she sets up tea for the lounges, then she does the vegetables for lunch and she listens to the DJs on the morning show while she works. They play nice music and they can make you laugh and you can phone in for requests.

They aren't nearly so strict here as they were at the Queen's and when the kitchen girls dare Rose she phones up to ask for a request for all at Pleasant Ways.

'Special request for Rose Jacobs,' comes over the radio.

'I just hope Auntie Olive was listening,' Rose says. I don't know about Auntie Olive but it seems to me that all of Pleasant Ways was listening because that whole day everyone stops me to say what a nice girl my sister is. She's young and she's new but she's not shy and she'll take a bet.

She knows exactly what song she wants to hear and the DJ asks who she is and where she works and why the song's so special for her. I'd be dead of embarrassment but not my sister.

'For Rose Jacobs then,' says the DJ and it really is for the whole world to hear or at least the Western Cape and if you come to think about it that really is our world or, at least, the bits we know of it is. 'Dionne Warwick singing "That's What Friends Are For". This is for you and your friends, Rose, enjoy it.'

What does Rose know about 'friends', I wonder? I was at Sacred Heart myself so I know that it's nothing you learn there but perhaps I'm wrong. Somewhere along the way I see that I have got my life mixed up with my sister's and actually we are two of us and we are different. When people talk about us I know exactly what they'll say. Ruby's not the one who knows about friends, that one would be Rose.

I'm on the eighth floor in Mrs Margolis's flat washing Mrs Margolis's china ornaments carefully, like I always do, with everything laid out on the table. A big bucket of soapy water, a bucket of clear hot water, towels spread out to drain the water off and soft cloths for a final dry-off. Down they go into the soapy water, 'Sweet Seventeen' like a dancer in her white dress with her petticoat fringed with yellow, 'Daydreams' sitting on a bench in a blue bonnet, and 'Jennifer' and 'Clarissa' and 'Kate'. There's the little shepherdess with her tiny crook and wide-skirted dress and the shepherd with his hard china curly hair and painted blue eyes and then the little girl standing on tiptoe looking up at a bird sitting on a branch. You've got to have all your wits about you on ornament day because the ornaments are so fragile they could easily break.

'Your sister's special request put everyone downstairs in a really good mood,' Olga says. 'I must say she settles in well. It's like she's always been here. Everybody likes her.'

'Yes,' I say. 'She's like that.'

What I don't say is that this isn't the sort of thing people would ever say about me and I think that perhaps now we're in the same place and people are comparing us I feel something different inside me, and I think that perhaps it is envy. I never used to be envious of my sister before but I'm full of spite this morning. 'Miss Wishful Thinking', that's Rose.

'Ruby,' calls Mrs Margolis and it's time to help her dress and the china figures stand side by side together on their special towel. It's a funny arrangement and it's strange to think how carefully we look after little china figures because they're so fragile they could easily be damaged. We don't treat flesh and blood like that. You can treat flesh and blood any way you like and it will just go on doing what it has to do and no damage will be done, at least not on the outside.

Mrs Margolis is 'at home' twice or three times a week between six and eight in the evenings and sometimes people phone and ask if she'll be home and if they can drop in for half an hour, and this is my time to be with Rose. If the weather's warm we take our chairs outside and sit out on the front of the roof where we can watch the people and dogs walk along the promenade and there's always the rumble of cars and sometimes a big ship moving slow and grand towards the harbour.

'You certainly got us ringside seats,' Rose says and the radio's playing loud inside our roof-room and the sound comes spilling out. I like it when there are just the two of us and we have time to spare for each other and the roof is all our own. Rose is in her green-checked kitchen over-all. It's a big size and the hem had to be lifted halfway to the waist because she's so short. I am in one of my blue 'housekeeper' dresses Mrs Margolis had delivered from Garlick's and they're neat and smart, buttoned down the front with a belt at the waist, and a very far cry from a maid's overall and scarf and I'm happy wearing them. The seagulls are coming in for the night and we sit as close to the front of the roof as we can so we can see the lighthouse light when it goes on and smell the sea and watch the first stars come out.

There's something I haven't told Rose. For a long time I didn't think about it myself and then I did and that was a long time ago, before Godfrey died and was cremated 'private' so we weren't there.

We had all been at my father's funeral service except-ing Patsy. We went to the cemetery and we saw his coffin put in the ground. Rose doesn't remember it but I do, and then our life went on and we did what our mother told us and then she got sick and died and we must have gone to her funeral but I can't remember it.

I can remember Auntie Olive telling me to stay in the kitchen when my mother was taken dead out of our house in Clive Street. There were neighbours out on the street standing looking like they do when someone dies but I wasn't there. Auntie Olive told Rose and me to stay in the kitchen and we did. We stayed in the kitchen while strange people moved through our house. I thought that when I was told we could come out I'd go to my mother's room and she'd still be there and no matter how sick she was it would be all right again, but it wasn't like that.

We did come out of the kitchen and I did go to my mother's room but she wasn't there and nor were her bed things, her sheets and pillows and her green blanket. There was only the bare mattress and the empty room and the only way you could know that she was ever there was because you could still smell her on the air, sick and all, and the mattress had stains on it. My mother would have been ashamed for people to see that. She had a white underblanket that would have hidden the stains. I wish that Auntie Olive had put that on.

It's a terrible thing to say but in those days when my mother died and we left Clive Street I couldn't think about her. I was too worried about Rose and me and thinking what would become of us. It hurt too much to think about my mother and her being in a place where she couldn't know how I felt or make it better. I knew I could never hold that hurt inside me and so I just didn't think about it. I didn't think about it for a long time and then one day after we were in Sacred Heart and we were no longer new there and beginning to settle, I thought about it again. It slid into my head before I could do anything to stop it and once it was there I had no choice but to look at it. I didn't know what had happened to my mother. I didn't know where in the world I could go and tell her what had happened to Rose and to me.

'Unhealthy,' Auntie Olive said. 'It's not a good thing for the living to think too much about the dead.'

All the same, it was my mother I was asking about and it was a fair question and I wanted to know.

'What difference can it make now, after all this time?' Auntie Olive wanted to know. 'It's nonsense, all this dwelling on the past and graves and death. You need to put all that behind you. What you need now is to get on with your life.'

That may be all right for some people but wasn't all right for me. It made a big difference to me because that's how I am and I wasn't going to let it go. Auntie Olive did her best but for once in my life I wouldn't allow myself to be put down. I knew that I risked Auntie Olive saying that if I didn't stop she might no longer be quite so willing to have Rose and me every last Sunday. Even so, I had to do it. There were times when I would have liked to be in the place where my late mother was buried and all I was asking was if there was someone who was willing to tell me exactly where that was.

'Pray for her immortal soul,' Auntie Olive said. 'That's all that's important now and it'll make you feel better. Why don't you try it and you'll find out that I'm right. You'll see.'

I wanted to know where my mother was, not for right that very second. I knew I couldn't go to her right that very second. I needed to know for 'one day' and if Auntie Olive would only realize that and tell me what I wanted to know it would make me feel better and give me peace of mind.

'I'll tell you if you really must know,' Auntie Olive said at last. 'Only remember that I didn't want to. Remember that I was the one who told you to leave it alone and never say that I didn't warn you or try and stop you because I did.'

In this matter of my mother I had become Ruby 'who always wants her own way' and Ruby 'who never knows how to leave things well alone'. I'd thought that the one good thing about being dead was that it would keep you safe and out of the reach of the living but I was wrong. Whenever my mother's name came up it gave my aunt fresh power to hurt me.

My mother was buried in a pauper's grave. That's what Auntie Olive told me and she told me straight out, just like that, and she must have been able to tell just by looking at me that I didn't really know what it meant.

'It means there was no money. Nothing, a few pennies but they don't count and funerals cost money, in case you didn't know.'

I didn't know. How could I? My father had a funeral. I was there. I saw it.

'Yes, he did,' Auntie Olive said. 'That took just about the last of the little money that was there in the first place and I told her then but of course she wouldn't listen.'

We sat there, my aunt and I, and we looked at each other. You can tell how old you are, how big you've grown, if you're tall enough for your feet to touch the floor under the kitchen table. I was grown-up enough for that but not nearly grown-up enough to be able to take in what my aunt had told me.

'It was a lovely service,' she said. 'You were there, Ruby, I'm sure you remember.'

I did remember but there were other things I remembered far more clearly.

'The body isn't important, you know that,' Auntie Olive said. 'You used to do so nicely in your Sunday school. They must have taught you that.'

I could have made it easy if I'd wanted to. I could have put a stop to it right then and there if now I'd just said, 'Yes, Auntie Olive,' but I wouldn't. I could be a peace-maker, I'd learned that much already and I had much more to learn and not everything life teaches you is easy. I'd learned that too and I could keep a lot inside me but not what my aunt was telling. I couldn't do it. It was just too much to hold.

'I don't know where your mother is, Ruby,' Auntie Olive said. 'You ask me and you want the facts and any person who knows anything about life and how it really is will tell you that facts are not always what you really want to hear.'

A pauper's grave could be anywhere. There would be a number and a record somewhere and one day, when I was older and able to, I would be free to track it down.

'I'm sure it won't be so very hard,' Auntie Olive said. 'And for goodness' sake don't start Rose off. Even if there was a grave, what difference can it make? Graves are good for five minutes and then people forget. I could take you down to the cemetery right now. If you want to see for-gotten graves there are plenty you can choose from.'

I know now and I won't tell Rose. Auntie Olive can show me as many forgotten graves as she likes. None of them will be my mother's. She thinks she can speak for the entire world but she cannot speak for me. One day I will find my mother, where she is, and I will make a fine place for her and she will not be forgotten.

After a time, while she and I were still finding our way, Mrs Margolis's visitors got to know me.

'This is Ruby,' Mrs Margolis says and if the person is someone who knows Mr Silver they'll say, 'Oh? The girl Saul recommended.'

There are no name tags at Mrs Margolis's. We are all just people here even if we're each of us in our own place. So there's no need for name tags and that's just as well because 'the girl Saul recommended' will need a very long piece of plastic name tag to put it all down on. With something like that pinned to my lapel I'd hardly be able to get in and out of the door carrying my tray or a plate of snacks.

Sometimes I'll hear something about him and sometimes Mrs Margolis will tell me something. The best news is that he's in England. He won't be walking through the flat door at Pleasant Ways one of the evenings when Mrs Margolis is 'at home' and receiving.

'That's a shame,' says Rose.

'No, it's not,' I say and I mean it.

We are each of us who we are and there's nothing that I can do for Mr Silver and he has already done more than enough for Rose and for me. You could say that what he did wasn't so very much. Mrs Margolis couldn't have gone on as she was, she'd become a woman who needed care, so you could say that we needed one another and it's a nice job and it suits me and the room on the roof comes free.

'It won't last for ever.' This is the first thing Rose says after she meets Mrs Margolis for the first time.

'What's that supposed to mean?' I say. I know what it means. It means that Mrs Margolis is old and may not be much longer for this world.

'I didn't mean it like that,' Rose says but she did. There are other girls here who talk like that but I will not allow my sister to be one of them.

'You should be grateful,' I say. 'At least you have a nice place to go.'

'I am grateful,' Rose says to make me feel better. 'Truly I am, although I really don't know why I bother when, goodness knows, you're always more than grateful enough for us both.'

While I'm still 'the girl Saul recommended', when visitors who haven't been for a while see me it seems to remind them of Mr Silver. His name comes up and floats into the conversation.

'Back on his feet again,' people say. 'Working for Nathan.' 'Some talk of him leaving London and going to San Diego.' 'Don't think we'll see him back here in a hurry. Too much went bad here. Too many memories.'

What can it matter to me? Even if I'm recommended I'm just 'the girl', but even so I know something these people who have known Mr Silver don't know. I don't even know where San Diego is but I know about memories. You can travel very light when it comes to earthly possessions, I know because I've done it. If Mrs

Margolis passed on in the night and I was without a job I could take all that I own packed into the same one suitcase. The same one that I took from Clive Street to Sacred Heart and then on to the Queen's and I could carry it quite easily myself, but memories are another thing altogether. I would have to hire a Stuttaford's van or maybe something bigger and even then they wouldn't fit and if anyone ever said memories don't weigh anything then they don't know what they're talking about. Memories can be the heaviest thing in the world to bear and happy ones, when that time for happiness is past, can weigh the most. That is how I see Mr Silver, moving around the world carrying memories with him, and sometimes it surprises me that all these clever people who come to Mrs Margolis's flat can know so much and not know this.

I 'do' the pictures. I dust and I wipe the glass carefully with glass cleaner and a special chamois and I clean the silver frames and brush away the last of the dry Silvo with a soft toothbrush. I do this while Mrs Margolis takes tea with her friends or when someone comes to fetch her to take her out for lunch. It's a peaceful job and I like doing it. The flat's very quiet with only me inside it. It may be waiting for Mrs Margolis to come back and fill it up again but when it's only me it's peaceful and I move around soft in my blue housekeeper's dress on the beautiful rugs that look like fields of flowers and it rests itself around me. I can see the sea. I never thought I would stay in a place so close to the sea. From Sacred Heart you can look down to the sea but it's a long way away and that sea is a sea for ships and shipping, not people. It seems to say, 'Look as much as you like, I'm not for you.' Here it's different. I lie in my bed in Mrs Margolis's spare room, where her light shines out into the passage for almost all the night as if it can keep away the dark. I close my eyes and hear the sea and it's like an old person. It sighs and grumbles, and when the fog rolls in the foghorn groans as if it will keep company with the sea.

Before she came to Pleasant Ways Mrs Margolis and the late Monty who was still with her then had a big house in the Avenues, but when he died and after what happened to Mrs Silver Mrs Margolis came to Pleasant Ways for safety.

'It made a lot of people think again,' she said. 'You know it all happened while it was still light, with staff in the house and panic buttons just a touch away.'

She doesn't talk about Mr Silver more than she does about anyone else and when she does talk it's more to herself than to me, but I don't mind. I wondered when I first came here why she had so many photographs, I suppose because I only have one photograph myself, but I hold people in my head. I had no choice and I thought that it was good enough but I see now I was wrong. People change when you don't see them every day, they leave you to go to other places, they die and you can't hold on to how they were for ever. I would give anything now to have a photograph of my mother and father and our family together. I lie in bed and listen to the sea and think that I have lost myself. I think that maybe if I had a photograph it would help me to remember. I try and remember that long-ago girl I once was, playing out in Clive Street and singing and dancing for my family and the neighbours. I try but I can't do it. I lost my memory of my father very quickly. I don't know why he went so fast but one day I woke up and he was gone and I couldn't bring him back again, or that's how it seemed to me. I hung on to my mother for as long as I could but in the end she left me too. I couldn't remember what she looked like, not even in dreams, no matter how hard I tried and so I understand about the photographs.

'I don't know why you keep the snap of Steenbras Street,' says Rose. 'You should throw it in a drawer.'

I won't do that because then, for better or worse, I'll lose how we were then and Godfrey would go too and that snap is the only thing I have left of him.

Mrs Margolis has a snap of Mr Silver with the late Monty. She showed it to me and it's funny about her, when she's looking in her photographs for someone she knows exactly where they are. She puts her hand out and puts it right on just the picture that she wants.

'There he is,' she says. 'That's Saul.'

She gives it to me so that I can look. I would have found him in the end but it would have taken time because the man in the picture is not anything like the Mr Silver I knew. This man is younger and he's happier. His hair is thick and dark and I think I'm supposed to look at the photograph out of politeness and hand it back but I look much longer than I should. I can see then how he was before and I remember how he was when we talked together and people say that there can never be a scale to show how much a person suffers when something really terrible happens to them. If you look in Mr Silver's eyes how he was then and how he was when I knew him, you can see that they are wrong.

I give the picture back and Mrs Margolis takes it and she does say one thing. Mr Silver was a boxer in his day, so that part was true.

'Strictly amateur,' Mrs Margolis says. 'But my late husband always said he had talent and he could have done something with it if he'd wanted to but he didn't want to.

'We knew him and his brother, Nathan, when they were just boys and making their way. They used to come and see us very often.'

I think she knew his family, the wife and the little girl who died, but she doesn't talk about them, as if the way they died blotted out all of their life before that moment so that all that's left is that one sad thing.

I know quite a lot about Mr Silver now, one way and another. I know that he was poor once and how hard he worked to pull himself up until he wasn't poor any more. He had a house in the Avenues where all the world lies at your feet and anything you want is yours for the taking and I think it's like the sea which I have come to love so much. It can be so beautiful you can hardly take your eyes off it. It can be so angry it can scare you, but all you ever know about it is what it cares to show you. It's down below in those places you can't see that it keeps its secrets.

* * *

Rose is right. I can't go on looking backwards for ever. I have to look forward as well and make some plans. In that regard I have discovered Office Management by Correspondence, Basic, Intermediate and Advanced, which is not to say that I'm about to pack up and leave Mrs Margolis in the lurch because I'm not. I've been with her for two years now. It's a three-year course and three years looks like a very long time to me but I'm going to do it anyway, so that when a time does come when Mrs Margolis is beyond my care I am ready to move on.

'It costs a lot,' Rose says but that's all right. I've been saving and I have the money. When we go to Grand Parade or to the shops on Main Road, Sea Point, Rose calls me Miss Ruby 'no luxuries' Jacobs. She can tease me as much as she likes. I've never had money in my life and now that I get a pay packet I like to hold on to as much of it as I can. Looking in my savings book and seeing the money getting a little bit more every month makes me feel a lot better than a new dress or a pair of shoes or a Three Flowers lipstick or a bottle of Cutex nail polish would. Besides which, Rose spends enough for us both. Friday is payday and by Saturday night she's broke.

'Broke but happy,' she says.

Rose has already filled up her part of our shared room with things. She has more than enough clothes to keep any other girl happy for the rest of her life and she keeps on buying more. Every Saturday she goes off with her pay packet shopping and every time she comes back with her Foschini and Truworth's and Ackermans bags the clothes she buys get brighter and brighter and every couple of weeks it's one size bigger. I think that when Rose cuts and butters bread for the trays it's one slice for the tray and one for Rose and she has bad habits. Some of the old ladies don't eat very much and Rose eats leftovers because she can't understand how you can throw food away.

Rose is getting fat and I can't find it in me to tell her to stop eating. I'm not fat myself and I don't think I ever will be because I take my meals from Mrs Margolis's kitchen and I eat how I am. I take very little and I eat slowly. That's what I learned in my mother's house because it was a good habit, she said, but that's not why I did it. I did it because it made the food seem more.

'Not finished yet, Ruby?' she used to say and slow-slow, little-bit-little-bit I would eat even though I was hungry because I could see that it made her feel better and once you've learned to do that I think you will do it for ever.

Mrs Margolis's flat and our room on the roof isn't our home and we mustn't get too comfortable.

'It's nice here,' Rose says, but then it doesn't take much to please Rose. 'Don't get too settled,' I say, 'because one day we'll have to move on.' This is what she said the day we first came here but I won't remind her of that now. I know she's right and I also know that when that day comes it will be me, not my sister, who has to be ready.

Taking care of Mrs Margolis is not a five-minute business. Days pass by very quickly and I'm getting older and growing up here. The people who come here to visit are getting to know me and I'm much braver now than I used to be. I can phone and do 'deliver' the way Mrs Margolis did when I first came here and that seems like a long time ago now. She doesn't mind. It means she can lie in bed and rest for a little bit longer before she starts her day. She needs that now and she knows she can be peaceful with me in the house and in that peaceful house I can start doing something so I'll be ready for the next part of my life, when that time comes.

Education by correspondence is expensive and you have to pay in advance and I do have some money put by but I'm saving it, a little bit each month, for something in particular. I used to say that I wouldn't touch it and would never use it for anything else but that day has come and gone.

One day I made up my mind and asked Mrs Margolis for some extra time off because there was something I wanted to do.

'Are you going to do something nice with your sister?' she said and I told her not this time and she didn't ask any questions.

'We all need time to ourselves sometimes,' she said and she didn't ask any more and I didn't tell her any more.

It was winter and a grey day and I was wearing a pencil skirt, a jersey and a tweed jacket from Lilian Salmon where quality never goes out of style, a hand-me-down from Mrs Margolis because although she likes clothes this was something she wouldn't be wearing any more. I had an orange beret on my head, a sling bag over my shoulder and dark brown tights and short boots.

I told Rose that I was going out to do some chores for Mrs Margolis. I thought she'd take one look at my face and know I was lying but she didn't.

'A little lipstick wouldn't hurt you,' she said because that's all Rose is interested in these days. 'I don't know why you always think it's all right for you to go out with no make-up on your face. You should think of those poor other people, they're the ones who have to look at you.'

Rose had more lipsticks than the whole stock of the Max Factor counter at OK Bazaar and I could have used any one of them if I'd wanted to, but I am not my sister. Rose wasn't happy unless she went out dressed up like a Christmas tree. I don't know where she got that from but she certainly didn't get it from me.

'I'm not going out dancing,' I said.

'You've never been out dancing in your life,' she said.

'Nor have you, if it comes to that.'

'But I will,' she said. 'Just as soon as someone asks me, I'll say yes straight away.'

Sometimes when there was a good song on the radio the girls danced together in the kitchen.

'Until the manager catches you,' I said.

'And then?' Rose asked. 'What difference can that make? All it does is show how happy we are in our work.'

People are cut out to do different things and even if I might once have thought otherwise I'd learned enough from life by then to know that I wasn't cut out to be a dancer. There were some things that fell to me and some things that fell to my sister. She was the one waiting for a chance to get dressed up in a dress that was so bright with spangles it could stop the traffic and go out having a good time in it. I'm the one who looks for graves. That's what I'm doing in the administration office at the main gate of Maitland.

I'd discovered that it was easy enough to find a death certificate because the government's in charge of that. Finding a grave is a different matter altogether. It's hard to keep track of old graves and it's even harder when the people are paupers. Paupers are buried at the cost of the state and the state doesn't bury them out of love, they bury them because they have to.

The young man at the administration office was white and he got up from his desk the minute he saw me. He could have made me wait for as long as he liked if he'd wanted to but he wasn't going to do that and to me that seemed like a good start. There were three desks behind the counter but the chairs of the other two desks were pulled back and whoever was supposed to be working there wasn't there and so it was just him and me and he got up and came over.

'Can I help you?' he said.

It's funny but I did what I always did and looked behind me to see if some other person had come in that I hadn't seen, but then I saw that it was me he was talking to and he was waiting for an answer. I took the envelope out of my bag and put my two pieces of paper down on the counter. Then I told him why I was there and he listened politely and he stood on his side of the counter and I stood on mine. When I'd finished he picked up the papers and looked at them and said he was very sorry but he thought it was unlikely he could help me at all.

I couldn't imagine what he had to be sorry about, how could he be sorry? All he'd done so far was tell me to show him the two pieces of paper that happened to be my parents' death certificates and I'd put them down on the counter for him to look at.

After we'd had our talk and I'd heard what Auntie Olive had done, I asked her to give the certificates to me and she did. Without saying a word, she went and fetched them and handed them over to me.

'If you want them so badly,' she said. 'Although I don't know what use you think they're going to be to you.'

All I had of my parents was their death certificates and their plastic ID cards. That's what Auntie Olive gave me and I kept them in an envelope under the wax-paper drawer liner in my private dressing-table drawer. I'd never showed them to anyone, not even Rose. That boy, with his middle fingers on the bottom of the certificates that lay on the counter, was the only person whose hands had touched them, except mine, since they came to me. I couldn't understand why he was pinning them down like that with just the tips of his fingers. They weren't going to fly away anywhere. I couldn't understand why he didn't pick them up so he could look at them properly. Perhaps he didn't like touching coloured people's things. I thought then that perhaps I'd come to the wrong place after all. Perhaps I read the sign outside the office incorrectly and he was going to say that what he was sorry about, the reason why he couldn't help me, was because I'd come to the wrong place. Coloured people go to the back door. If he'd said that I wouldn't have been surprised because that kind of thing happened. It had happened to me before.

'I don't think you're going to be able to find these people,' he said.

It was very quiet in the administration office, I suppose because there weren't all that many people interested in the dead the way I was, and I looked at him and he wasn't the handsomest boy in the world and I could find it in my heart to feel sorry for him. He was the kind of boy girls laugh about even when they know he can see he's the joke. He was young, not much older than I was, and his couldn't have been a particularly nice kind of job. It must have been boring with nothing very much going on but at least he was in state service and maybe one day the state would remember him and move him on to some place where he could be back with the living.

'It's hard to find people who are buried in paupers' graves,' he said. 'You'd need a grave number and even then it doesn't always work.'

My father isn't buried in a pauper's grave. My mother spent the last of her money burying him.

'But you don't have a grave number,' he said.

I didn't know why I needed a number. My parents had names.

I put my hand into the envelope and took out my parents' plastic ID cards and put them down on the counter. In the corner of each, smaller than a standard-size postage stamp, were the only pictures I had of my parents.

'I thought there were others,' Auntie Olive said when I asked her about it. 'I'm sure that there must have been, but in all the fuss and with us all being so upset I really don't know whatever could have happened to them.'

I never showed these pictures to Rose because although I would never have parted with them they really had nothing to do with the father and mother that I remembered. The boy looked down into their faces and what was it, I wondered, that he saw? I looked at them very often myself and I'd known for a long time that they'd moved far away from me. Death has made them like the burn babies and much too innocent to understand why the world is the way it is.

'I'll try,' the boy said. 'We've got a computer but there's a backlog getting things on to it. It's a long time ago, more than ten years, and with just names and no numbers I don't know.'

He had a poor boy's way of speaking and pimples and a big Adam's apple. He could have talked to me any way he liked but he talked to me nicely and I thought that if he could help me he would.

'The best I can tell you, from what you tell me and from the death certificates, is that they'd be in the section for non-whites. That's something, I suppose, but even so it doesn't take us very far.'

I suppose that, in its way, it was funny because it was all right to lose people put in a pauper's grave and he was quite sure that they were lost but at least they were lost in the right part of the cemetery. He was sure about that much. As for me, I felt as if I'd walked straight into a brick wall.

I felt like a fool standing there because what I wanted seemed so silly. I thought that if I could find the place where my parents were I would know that, whatever happened to me in my life, there would always be a clear pathway ahead. I wanted to know that in the end I would have a place to go and my own people waiting for me when I got there and that I could be with them again. If I'd told Rose she would have said that now she knew for sure I'd gone mad. I did want it though and I thought that if I set my mind on it I could make it come true.

I wanted a headstone too and my mother and father's names on it and their details because who is there now that still remembers them? The world is big and this wouldn't take much space but it doesn't matter now. If I can't find them, none of this will ever come about and there's nothing I can do about it.

'Are you all right?' the Adam's apple boy said. 'Is there anything more I can do for you?'

There's nothing he or anyone else can do for me as far as this goes but that's all right because, as far as it went, I think far too much had already been done and there was nothing I could do to undo it now.

'I'll advance you the money to pay for your course,' Mrs Margolis says.

Mrs Margolis believes that it's always a good thing to

try and improve oneself because it means better opportunities in the long run and that Office Management, Part One, by correspondence is a good place to start. I have to wait for the new year before I begin. If I start now and do the whole course I'll be twenty-five years old by the time I finish. Mrs Margolis, if she's spared, will be nearly ninety years old then but we don't talk about that.

'You could end up with an office job,' Rose says.

'Perhaps I will,' I say. 'But only once Mrs Margolis doesn't need me any more.'

'Why?' Rose says. 'You don't have to. Once you finish your course you can get office work. You can work nine to five. That will make a nice change. You can have week-ends off.'

Rose goes on as if it's already done but it's not so easy as that, and in any case as far as Mrs Margolis is concerned I've made up my mind.

'You can call it a day at five o'clock the way other people do and sleep in your own room for a change,' Rose says.

I know that and that time will come and when it does I'll know, but in the meantime I am happy to stay with Mrs Margolis. I have learned something from her. I see the way she holds on to her place in the world with a smile on her face and keeps the secrets of her body to herself but I don't need an advance from her to pay for my course. I have my own money put by.

'All that money that you didn't spend on luxuries,' Rose says.

'Yes,' I say. 'It'll come in handy now.'

What I don't say is that I could have borrowed if I had to. I wouldn't have liked it but I would have done it. I had other plans for my 'luxury' money that Rose didn't know about. They were plans that couldn't come off in the end. It would have taken much more than I have but that doesn't matter. I would have gone without luxuries for as long as I needed to, for all my life if I had to, if I could have had that one thing that I really wanted.

Some dreams don't come true but perhaps that's not their job. Perhaps their job is just to keep you going while you still believe they can and perhaps that is enough.

I've lived in Cape Town all my life but I only know a few places. I don't know Pinelands but when Mrs Margolis invites me to go with her to Pinelands I say that I will. It isn't every day that I go anywhere in a taxi and a taxi has been sent for from Springbok Taxis to collect us and bring us back and Mrs Margolis is all dressed up for the outing in a fur coat and Italian shoes.

The first thing I see when Mrs Margolis and I step out of the lift into the foyer is Rose and the taxi driver. I see them through the glass foyer walls and she's talking and he's smiling at her as if they've known each other for years.

Rose will talk to anyone. I've told her a hundred times not to engage in conversation with men she doesn't know because she'll begin to get a name for it.

'If I don't talk to men I don't know, I'll never get to

know any men,' she says. I know how she is but even so it gives me a shock to look out through the glass and see Rose talking to the man in the way that she is, and the man is old enough to be our father.

'Are you doing all right?' I ask Mrs Margolis because she's walking very slowly and the taxi driver may have eyes only for Rose but at least Rose has seen us. She points us out to him and he smiles at her and moves to open the door for Mrs Margolis with his head still half turned backwards.

I don't mind sitting quiet in the back of the taxi looking out of the window. I know that the taxi driver can see me in the rear-view mirror and my sister is one thing but I'm something else altogether and I'd like him to know that straight away before we've even turned out of Pleasant Ways into the traffic on Beach Road. I don't know how far Pinelands is, it may be fifteen minutes or the best part of an hour, but it's always best to get things straight from the start.

I thought we'd go to a nice house or block of flats or even a hotel. I thought the taxi driver had got it wrong and that Mrs Margolis would give him a piece of her mind and I could stand by and listen but he hadn't got it wrong. It's the anniversary of the late Monty's passing.

'Fifteen years,' says Mrs Margolis.

She always comes out for a visit at this time of year and this time she needs someone she can lean on and I don't mind if it's me.

'You wait here for us,' Mrs Margolis tells the taxi

driver and I check to see she's got her handbag safe over her elbow because we are two women alone and it's very quiet here and you can't trust anyone, not these days.

Mrs Margolis walks slowly and every now and then she stops and I stop too. She'll look at a gravestone and read the name and she'll show for me to bend down and pick up a stone for her to put down on top of it, to show someone's been. I like the way Mrs Margolis stands for a while before she asks me for a stone because I can see that in that moment these people are living inside her, in her memories, how they once were. If they were here on this earth still they would appreciate that, and the stone going down is the sign that they've been remembered.

I don't tell Rose although when I get back Rose is in a mood to hear anything that I care to tell her.

'I'm sorry to disappoint you,' I say, 'but I'm not you. I didn't spend my time making eyes at the taxi driver, who, by the way, in case you didn't notice, is just about old enough to be our father.'

'The taxi driver has a name,' Rose says. 'But his friends call him Alf.'

'And are you his friend now?' I say. 'After all, you've known him for five minutes.'

'Could be,' she says.

I'm pulling off my going-out clothes and putting on denim jeans and a jersey and slippers and I know Rose wants to talk but I don't want to listen.

'Could you make us some tea?' I say and I pick up my clothes and hang them back in the cupboard. 'Do you think you can pack your clothes away?' I say and I don't know about Rose's taste in clothes these days. They're lying all over the place, every colour of the rainbow; you need sunglasses just to look at them. 'It would be nice if I could make a space where I could sit. This is my room too, you know. Just in case you don't remember.'

I always say that Rose should be tidier. I know that she never will be. She says she was tidy enough at Sacred Heart to put her off for life because unlike some of us she wasn't born tidy and it doesn't come naturally to her.

'I'm not you, Ruby,' she says.

What is 'me', that's what I'd like to ask her. I put my clothes away neatly and it may be a joke to my sister but I don't spend my money on 'luxuries', which is something she's forever teasing me about. If she one time asked me as if she really cared why I don't spend money on luxuries, I'd be happy to tell her that it's not because I don't want to. As far as that goes I'm just like everyone else. The trouble is that I just don't know how to do it.

'Are you all right?' Rose says.

'I'm fine,' I say.

'Where did you go to then?' she says. 'You never said.'

'Mrs Margolis went to visit a friend,' I say.

'I've got chocolate digestives,' Rose says and she pours tea at the little side table where we keep our kettle and cups on a tray and she shows me the packet which is only half full, as if chocolate biscuits are the answer to everything.

No matter what Auntie Olive says about there being only Jewish people at Pleasant Ways because they're the only ones who can afford to live there, there's a Catholic priest who comes to do home visits and my sister talks to everyone and so she talks to him too.

'Just so long as you don't tell him about me,' I say.

'Why should I talk about you?' she says.

'Exactly,' I say. 'Just so long as you know.'

I don't want a priest after me, trying to bring me back into the fold. Once a priest knows about you, before you even know what's happened they'll make you their mission and you'll never be able to get rid of them.

'That's their job,' Rose says. 'I don't know what you're so cross about.'

'I'm not cross with you,' I say but I know that Rose can't tell about herself without telling about me because that's the way we are, and in any case I can see it on her face.

'Father Basil's nice,' Rose says to change the subject.

'Must you know everyone's name?' I say.

'I never asked,' Rose says. 'He said.'

Nice priests are the worst. They're the ones who don't mention anything but if they see you before you see them, before you can get away, they say, 'See you at Mass on Sunday,' but Father Basil will have to be quick if he wants to catch me. If I see him coming I turn in at the first door I come to. Once I even walked into a strange person's room and had to apologize.

'He's not interested in you,' Rose says.

Even so, if I press the lift button and the lift door opens and he's standing inside trying to go down, I say wrong floor, my mistake. I would rather walk down eight floors than get into a lift with him, and maybe he knows that and maybe he knows why but if he does you wouldn't see it on his face.

'You're acting like a fool,' Rose says.

Once when he came into the kitchen to say hello to the staff, I hid behind the dishwasher. There was nowhere else to go and only one door to get out and he was standing in the doorway. I did a slide and a quick sit-down and got hold of Rose's leg and pulled for her to stand in front of me.

I know it's not a proper way to behave towards a priest but I don't want Father Basil to get hold of me. I have nothing to say that he'd want to hear but I don't want to look him in the face either. If Father Basil has any thoughts I don't know what they are, but he's not the one hiding in the coat cupboard behind the reception desk in the entrance foyer like I did once when I saw him coming through the door. He must have seen me looking for somewhere to hide, like I always do when I see him coming, but I don't care. I stand inside the cupboard with my eyes closed and count off time. I count off enough time so that when I step out he'll be gone and while I'm counting I'm thinking what a fool I am and how much smarter he is than me. He knows there's no cupboard small enough or dark enough where you can hide from God. If He really wants to find you, He always will. I can smother to death in the dark in that coat cupboard but apart from that I'm safe. I know very well that I am not the lost lamb. There is no one who'll waste their time to come looking for me.

* * *

Father Basil's church is on Beach Road, half an hour's walk from Pleasant Ways, along the promenade past all the flats and restaurants and the Sea Point Pavilion and the swimming pool. It's called Our Lady of Good Hope.

'Thank you, Rose,' I say, 'but I won't be needing directions.'

I know my sister and Father Basil is coming into her conversation just a little bit too much these days but I don't mind. I'm waiting for the day when she tells me that she misses going to Mass and would like to go back because I know that day will come and when it does I'll be happy for her and better in myself. I never told Rose to cut herself off from the Church. She did it for me and then once she'd made up her mind it was hard for me. I just think that if someone still has their faith and has managed to hold on to it intact then that's exactly what they should do. I know that Rose can love God and there will still be plenty of love left over for me. I would accept that without question and be glad for her, but this is something that she has to find out for herself. I don't think it will take her long and I expect it any day but when it comes at last it's not in the way that I expected.

'I've been talking to Father Basil,' Rose says. 'He says that Our Lady of Good Hope is always open, all services, all times, everyone's welcome.'

'Well, there you are then,' I say.

'I said I'd given all that up and put it behind me,' she says, and it's my voice coming out of her mouth and it's on the tip of my tongue to tell her that she shouldn't lie. Not to a priest, not to me and not to herself.

'We made an arrangement,' she says. 'I'm not going to Sunday service, nothing like that.'

'What then?' I say.

'I'm going Sundays to help make the tea,' she says. 'They can always do with more hands. Father Basil says so and the other ladies don't do it professionally the way I do. So, in that respect, I'll be more than welcome.'

She wants me to say something but what can I say? Mrs Margolis is 'at home' in her flat downstairs and we are in our roof-room and Rose is sitting in the armchair, filling it up. She's still in her kitchen overall with her bare feet up on the bed and for some reason she has gold dust over the pink polish on her toenails.

'You don't have to worry,' she says. 'The teas are served in the church hall and even if I can hear the hymns being sung I won't join in.' I know that will be hard for her because she's like me, she loves to sing. 'I won't listen to the service or anything like that. I explained that to him. I told him just as far as the church hall and only the teas.'

'I see,' I say.

'If you won't, then I won't,' she says. 'So, you see, nothing's changed.'

She's right. As far as Rose was concerned, nothing had ever really changed at all. She never had to find her way back because she never really came off the path in the first place.

* * *

Mrs Margolis has had a small stroke and I spend more time with her now because she needs me. Sometimes even in what's supposed to be my time off I stay in Mrs Margolis's flat and don't go up to my room.

She speaks very slowly and the words get stuck but it's not so bad. If you put your mind to it and concentrate it's not so hard to tune in. There's still life in her eyes and she likes the comfort of another person close by her. I can't believe Rose has forgotten how she liked to crawl in next to me at night when we were first at Sacred Heart. People don't like to be alone in the dark, not when the dark is so deep that they can't see to the bottom of it.

There's something else too. Rose has taken up with the taxi driver, the one whose friends call him Alf. The one who's almost old enough to be her father.

'Well, say something,' Rose says but what is there to say? I count off in my head the kind of things our family in Steenbras Street will say when they hear. Auntie Olive always says that they may live in Athlone but that doesn't mean they ever miss anything and it's true. I found that out for myself in my days at the Queen's. She heard about Mr Silver and she will surely hear about Rose's so-called 'boyfriend' and there are a few things I can say.

In the first place, he's not a boy; he's a grown-up man. In the second place they are May and September and if Rose is going to spend time with him in other people's company she will have to get used to the idea of people asking if he's her father.

'Are you listening?' I ask my sister.

'In the third place he's a white man and on top of that

he's not even South African, he's Portuguese, so I don't know what you think you'll have in common.' I am sorry to have to say it but someone has to, plenty of other people will and it may just as well be me.

'And so?' says my sister.

'And so?' I say. 'And so, you can tell Auntie Olive this all by yourself if you want to because she's certainly not going to hear it from me. In case you've forgotten, the Portuguese have not been very good luck in our family.'

'At least I can tell her that I found him at church and not down at the shopping centre,' Rose says. Which is to say that she's not like our cousin, Patsy. From what we hear, although not from Auntie Olive, Patsy's discovered men in a big way. So Auntie Olive has her own problems, although that won't stop her when it comes to having a few things to say about Rose's choice.

'I don't care where you found him,' I say. 'You'll have to tell him thank you but no, thank you because he's not the man for you.'

'Why not?' Rose says. 'He's a good man. He's church-going, he's got a good job and before you even ask me, I'll tell you. He was the last child in the house and he lived with his mother and looked after her until she passed away and now that he has a life of his own he wants to enjoy it.'

'He's too old for you,' I say.

'Surely that's for me to decide,' she says. 'I don't mind older. Why should I? You're around old people all the time and you never complain and when you look at the people around here, Alf's like a spring chicken by comparison.'

If he'd started out young enough like some men do he could be her father, but I don't say that because I'm wondering if that isn't what she sees in him. Oh, Rose, I think but I don't say it out loud. It doesn't work like that. You didn't have Daddy when you were small but that time's over now and you can't get it back. This man's too old for you and he's not your father and he never can be, and I look at my sister and feel that in some way it's my fault and I've failed her.

'He's used to looking after people,' she says. 'He says that he'd like to look after me and I'd like that. I don't want to work in a kitchen all my life. I'm not the clever one like you. All I want is a place of my own and someone to look out for me and he can give me that.'

We're in our room on the roof. It's not very big and I'm sitting in the armchair and my sister is sitting on the edge of the bed in front of me. If I move my knee it will touch hers. She's that close to me but I don't think she sees me at all and she can be thoughtless and sometimes she can be cruel and I must tell myself that she doesn't know when she does this.

Has she not been looked out for all these years since she was a little girl? Has she not been cared for? She knows my life; she's lived it with me. She has always stood at its heart and I have always thought that she understood but I have to ask myself now if she understands anything at all.

'In a way it's really your fault, you know,' she says. 'You

were the one who sent me out to wait for the taxi that day.'

'I sent you out to wait for a taxi,' I say. 'I didn't send you out with a net to pull in the first man who looked at you.'

'Don't begrudge me, Ruby,' she says. 'You could have a boyfriend too if you wanted one.'

'I suppose I could,' I say. 'Except that I'm not like you. I'm not looking for one.'

'Just as well,' Rose says. 'Because looking back towards the past and whatever it was that went on at the Queen's isn't where you'll find him and you won't find him here either.'

'Thank you, Rose,' I say. 'I'm sure you mean well but you forget that I know you. If you decide to do something you always want everyone to join you, even if they don't want to join. Has it ever occurred to you that I'm happy like I am?'

She looks at me and thinks about it and then she shakes her head, no.

'You wouldn't know happy if you fell over it in the street,' she says.

I know she isn't saying it because she doesn't love me or want the best for me because I know that she does. The trouble is that our ideas about what's best for me aren't always the same.

I've said as much as I want to say about Mr Alfredo 'Alf' de Gouveia. You may not find a man in a retirement centre or between the pages of *Practical Accounting, Part One*, but in my opinion you don't find him when you're strolling outside in your overall one day waiting for a taxi to arrive.

'Is a taxi driver not good enough for you, Ruby?' Rose says and I can hear our auntie's voice coming out of my sister's mouth. 'It's honest work and it's hard. They work shifts, you know, and they have to put up with all kinds of people.'

There's nothing I can say to that.

'If you would join us sometimes you'd see how nice Alf is,' she says. 'I'll tell you something else for nothing, he can make you laugh until tears run down your face and you have to tell him to stop and I like that.'

'That's nice,' I say. 'Daffy Duck and Tom and Jerry on television can make you laugh as well but you don't have to go out with them. You can stay home and watch them on TV.'

'Why are you like this, Ruby?' she says.

'I'm not "like" anything,' I say.

'You're welcome to join in,' she says. 'Alf's got a big family. They would welcome you and he's got nice friends and there's always a lot going on down at the Portuguese Community Centre.'

'No, thank you,' I say. 'If it's all the same to you I think I'll give it a miss.'

'Suit yourself,' she says and it's not often that there's any coldness between Rose and me and I don't like it.

'When do you think there's any time for me to "join in" even if I wanted to?' I say and I know that I should leave it alone except I can't.

'You can make time if you really want to,' she says.

'Really?' I say. 'And how would I do that?'

I'm in my third year of Office Management by correspondence and it's hard. There were times when I thought I'd never even get this far but I have and if I'm successful I'll get my diploma and then I can start looking for a better job. Except I won't leave Mrs Margolis.

There's something I do for Mrs Margolis. I don't know why I do it but I've done it ever since the first stroke, in those days when her world got smaller. She didn't ask me, I just said that if she wanted me to, I'd do it. I knew it wouldn't be the same as if she did it herself but it would be on her behalf and in the same spirit.

I don't need Alf de Gouveia's 'free of charge off-duty for my friends' Springbok Taxi which has a *Whites Only* sign on the top but you can't tell Rose about that either. There's no one like my sister when it comes to putting her head in the sand. Rose is not a reader. When she picks something up it's *People* magazine. She likes to read about royalty and film stars. She knows who's putting on weight and who's thin. She knows who's married and who's getting a divorce. She knows who's having a baby and who's busy breaking whose heart, so you could say that Rose's convent education hasn't been entirely wasted. At least it has enabled her to keep up with world events and entertainment.

Auntie Olive would be proud of her but I've given up. If I say about whites-only sections in the bus or whites-only cinemas, which means that we can't go to the cinema closest to us, she says that she doesn't mind. It's not whites-only shops because money has no colour but it's whites only in the queue at the post office and Rose may walk past Sea Point whites-only swimming pool on her way to church on a hot day and that's fine by her.

'Just try and go back there in the afternoon with your bathing costume wrapped in a towel and your entrance money in your hand and see how far it gets you,' I say.

I have to say it just so she knows but you can't tell someone something if they don't want to know about it.

'I don't mind,' Rose says.

'You're like a cracked record with your "don't mind",' I say.

'I take you for my example,' she says. 'You make yourself sick with minding so much but where does it get you? Only as far as the non-white section. It doesn't do any good and you still go on about it but I'm not like you. It suits me to put it to the back of my mind and think of other things that aren't going to upset me.'

I want my sister to stop saying that she doesn't mind and let me talk and get some things off my chest and it may not make a difference as far as the great changes people talk about are concerned but it will make a big difference to me.

I think a lot about my cousin Godfrey. Godfrey was like Rose. It frightens me to think so but I do. Godfrey took the easy way and in the end all he found out was that there was no easy way and his 'easy' way turned out to be the hardest way of all.

Rose goes with Alf to Salt River to buy fish and chips and then they park by the sea and eat them in the car.

He's taken her to Signal Hill so that she can see the view. He waits for her at church on Sunday and after the teas are served and the washing-up's done he gives her a ride back to Pleasant Ways and they park outside and talk in the car. It can't go on but I don't know how to stop it.

'You worry too much,' Rose says.

I don't mind about the fish and chips or the lifts home from church. I don't mind the way he makes her laugh. What I worry about is that even if I put it down in writing and pulled *People* magazine out of her hands and made her read it, black and white, my sister still will not understand.

Alf can make Rose laugh just as much as they both like; he's still not for her because he's a white man.

Phoning is easy for me now and so I phone the Jewish Board of Deputies and ask if they can find a person if I give them a name, and they aren't like the state. They tell me that if I give my name and a telephone number they will do what they can to help me.

There are buses and there are trains. I don't need Alf de Gouveia's taxi. I wouldn't go in it even if he offered because besides anything else, there's something that I hold against Alf de Gouveia from the early days when he first became my sister's friend. He told Rose how he'd taken Mrs Margolis to the Jewish cemetery and how I'd gone with her, and if I'd wanted Rose to know that I would have told her myself.

'Why did you go?' she said.

'Because she wanted company,' I said. 'You remember? I told you that at the time.'

'She should have taken Olga if she wanted company,' Rose said. 'We could have gone to Woodstock, to the Gem or the Palace for a matinee, and bought takeaway to bring back with us after. We could have had a day.'

I didn't expect Rose to understand that I didn't want to talk about it and I minded that Alf had told her. It was as if he'd taken away something private that belonged to me that I didn't want to share.

'Why is it such a secret?' Rose wanted to know.

'Because Mrs Margolis is entitled to a private life, that's why, and if Alf's got nothing better to do than pass on all his passengers' comings and goings I'm surprised he's ever managed to keep his customers.'

'Sorry I spoke,' Rose said.

I didn't like to have words with my sister and at least there was one thing she was right about. It would have been better if I hadn't gone to the Jewish cemetery with Mrs Margolis. It put ideas in my head and made me think about things that didn't really have anything to do with me.

I can't exactly say why it is that I go but I do. No one will turn you away from a cemetery. I'm not the only person there although there are never very many. I used to worry that someone would stop me and ask my business but they never have because the people who come here know enough to leave each other in privacy with the people that they've come to see.

It isn't my place and there are some things you can do for others and other things that are too private, but even so I go. Shirley and Susannah are Mr Silver's wife and daughter. I know that if he'd wanted me to know their names he would have told me but he never did. There are not very many stones on the graves and so I bend down and I pick up one for each. I don't do it disrespectfully. I don't do it for myself and I don't claim to do it on behalf of anyone else. I just stand for a while and think how much they were loved and how lucky they were and then I put my stones down and I walk with my head down to the gate.

A WEDDING AND A FUNERAL

I am twenty-five, Rose is not yet twenty-two and too young to be married.

'Our life has to change some time, Ruby,' she says. 'You keep saying Alf's too old for me but we've waited so long already I feel like I'm catching up with him.'

I know that Rose is only waiting to please me because I asked her to, to give her time to think it over, but by the time I asked her she'd already made her mind up.

'We can't keep on "going out" for ever,' she says. 'We want to be together, you know that and it's high time. It was high time a long time ago.'

Being married to Alf will make a big change in Rose's life. She'll have a house of her own, Alf's house in Observatory Estate where he used to live with his late mother. There'll be no more kitchen work and she'll have

Alf to take care of. I know that Alf loves Rose and I can see he makes her happy. The only thing that stands in their way is me and I can't change. Two years or three years or even ten years isn't going to make it any better.

'We've talked to Father Basil,' she says and I don't say anything. 'I told him that a church wedding was out of the question. So we'll get married in magistrates' court and Father Basil will give us a blessing, for Alf's late mother's sake and the sake of his family, and I hope you have no objection to that. You needn't be there if you don't want to be.'

What I want is to tell Rose some of the things you don't read in *People* magazine. I want to talk some sense into her.

'Mixed marriages are allowed now,' she says.

I'm sure Alf's told her so dozens of times. Mixed marriages have been allowed for five years now. That law fell away a year after Godfrey died. I wonder what was said in Steenbras Street when they saw that in the news-paper but I suppose they just let it pass. I wonder what they'll say in Steenbras Street when they hear about Rose.

'I'm twenty-one now,' she says, as if she has to tell me what age she is and we're in our room on the roof together and my side's tidy and hers is a mess like it always is.

'I hope you won't be against it,' she says. 'I don't know what I'll do if you are.'

All our lives I've looked out for my sister and this is as far as I've managed to come and I know some things and one of them is that I couldn't stand in Rose's way, not even if I wanted to. I know that she won't go against me and she'll say it doesn't matter. She's waited so long, she can wait a little bit longer but in the end she'll mind. In the long run it might turn her against me and something between us will be broken.

'I won't stand in your way,' I say.

I can see just by looking at her that for her it's like the sun coming out because she just stands in front of me looking at me as if she can't believe what I've just said and then she bursts into tears.

'I don't know what I'd have done if you'd said no,' she says.

'You'd have gone ahead and married him anyway,' I say.

'No, I wouldn't,' she says. 'Not if you were really against it.'

'Then you would have been a fool.'

I can get used to Alf. I can get used to anyone my sister chooses to make a life with. Ordinary girls may marry princes but only in *People* magazine. People like us make the best choices we can and get on with it, at least as far as I know and what would I know anyway? Marriage is for other people and so is love, or that's how it seems to me.

'Your turn will come soon,' Rose says.

'No thank you,' I say. 'You do what you feel you want to do but don't include me.'

I'm twenty-five years old and my bloom's still there. If I were to walk through the door in Steenbras Street tomorrow Auntie Olive could take one look at me and rub just as hard as she liked, she'd soon see for herself.

* * *

I'm surprised that Rose wants to go with me to Mrs Margolis's funeral and not just because it's something I can easily do on my own but because she and I had a difference of opinion about Mrs Margolis which led to strong words and a fall-out. It happened when I got my Office Management correspondence course diploma. Rose thought that when that happened I'd have my diploma in one hand and my notice to Mrs Margolis in the other, but I'd never do that.

'I thought you wanted to improve yourself,' Rose said, and I did but the time wasn't right yet.

'I don't understand you, Ruby,' Rose said. 'It's not just a new job we're talking about. You know that, don't you? What we're talking about is a new life.'

I told her that she was getting us mixed up. She was the one who was so keen to set out on a new life, not me. As far as I was concerned, I was happy to wait my time.

'You work for wages,' Rose said.

'I know that,' I said.

'She can pay someone else to look after her,' she said. 'The world won't fall apart if you finish up with Mrs Margolis and get on with your life.'

I knew my sister when she got cross like this; I knew better than anyone the way she could be when something made her angry.

'You fancy yourself, Ruby,' she said. 'That's the trouble. You think you're so wonderful that no one but you can do the work you do but I've got news for you. Yours isn't such a wonderful job. Anyone can do it, you're not so special. Mrs Margolis is so far gone now that half the time she doesn't even know it's you that's with her.'

She never did it intentionally. I think most of the time she didn't even know that she was doing it but Rose could be cruel sometimes.

'If it's all the same to you,' I said, 'I'll finish my time with Mrs Margolis.'

'I was only saying,' she said.

'I know you were "only saying",' I said, but it was too late for her to say that she was only saying and try to make it better.

Mrs Margolis doesn't die like she thought she would, in the night. She died in daylight on a sunny day just after morning wash and medicine and she was clean and tidy in her bed and Olga and I were there. There were flowers in her room and she could see them from where she lay. Classic FM was on the radio and it was just a little murmur in the room and some time before news headlines at eleven Olga told me that her time was coming close.

We sat with her and it was nothing new to us because we'd sat together like this, the three of us, before with Olga and me on either side of her bed and in that way she passed.

Olga stood up and went into the lounge and stopped the big clock and then she phoned down to the infirmary to send for a doctor and I went to the linen cupboard to fetch sheets to cover up the mirrors and I don't need very many. Some people have mirrors all over the place for decoration or so that a nice room can admire itself. The only mirrors in Mrs Margolis's flat are the one in the bathroom and the one on her dressing table.

It's funny covering Mrs Margolis's dressing-table mirror even before the doctor arrives with her still in her bed as if she's sleeping, before the arrangements are made to take her away. I hold the sheet up and I can see her and I can see myself in my blue dress with my dark bony face and my hair rolled up the back of my head a bit high on the top and held in with pins and kept down with gel.

I drape the sheet and it spills down over everything and there's just white in front of me and Mrs Margolis is lying dead in her bed and I'm gone too and it's a strange feeling.

I'm happy to do this business of the clocks and mirrors. Olga told me long ago that when the time came for Mrs Margolis this was what I must do. I've been used to serving the living and I see now that it's nice to do these last things for the dead. It's better than being pushed in the kitchen with Rose and told to stay there until our mother's been taken away like I was that other time. Someone should have been there to tell me these things then because I would have liked to do these things for my mother; it would have meant something to me.

It's quiet without the tick of the big clock in the lounge. You get so used to it that you don't even notice it any more, but now that it's silent, I notice. Five minutes to eleven o'clock. When she was still in the world Mrs Margolis liked the news. She liked radio and TV and the newspapers and she liked a person who knew how to tell a story well because she was a good storyteller herself.

I don't know what was on the news that day. It's 1990 and I'm twenty-four years old. When I was at the Queen's the people coming in and out of the kitchen had said we'd all live to see big changes in our lifetime and I thought that would be nice but I didn't pin my dreams on it and I'm still waiting.

Mr Mandela has been released and apartheid will soon be over and we'll be able to hold our heads up again with no one to stand in our way. I'm not so sure that I believe it. When I was a child my mother used to tell me that I'd be the 'Star of the Morning' and I used to believe that too but it never happened.

If you stay in a place for long enough, you get used to things and don't see them any more. I don't know how many times I've washed the ornaments. The Royal Doultons, 'Sweet Seventeen' and 'Jennifer', 'Clarissa' and 'Kate' and the little shepherdess and the shepherd with his painted blue eyes and the little girl on tiptoe reaching up towards the bird in the tree and never touching him.

I don't know how many times I've dusted all Mrs Margolis's framed photographs or polished the silver frames and cleaned the last white bits of Silvo out with the old soft toothbrush. I don't know how many times I've looked down at young Mr Silver and he's looked back at me. I can remember that picture better than I can remember how Mr Silver looked in real life in that time I knew him. I won't be able to look at it much longer and so I look at it long and hard now while I still can and try to know it really well so I can keep it exactly as it is inside my head. I'll be leaving one of these days and it will be left behind. It doesn't belong to me and I can't take it with me.

I had got used to the big painting over the mantelpiece but I see it again now. I stand in front of it and I look. It's not like staring at a live person and when people did look at Mrs Zelda Margolis in her day she never minded. I'd forgotten how big the painting was and so beautifully done you'd think that if you touched the red paint of her dress you'd feel real satin and not paint at all, and today it looks different to me in a way it never did before. I think it's the way the sun lights up the room or perhaps the shock of Mrs Margolis being gone out of this life for ever has just hit me. I feel Mrs Margolis's painted eyes looking down at me. She had long pale hair and there are pieces of light caught in it and you'd never know if it were today's light or another light altogether. I can't move and I can't breathe and Olga once told me that although you can feel a person's pulse stop and write down the time of death you never really know the exact moment that a soul passes but she's wrong, you do know. I can feel it and it's as if the room's shimmering. I feel the flap of butterflies floating light inside my stomach. The red colour of the dress is so bright and so filled with life it's dazzling and I can hardly bear to look at it and then it's over and she's gone.

'I'll go with you to the funeral,' Rose says. 'Alf and I will both go.' It's funny to be going somewhere with Rose and

Alf in the taxi. I could go with them any time I liked, Rose often asks me, but I don't think it's right and so I always say no, thank you and let them get on with their life and keep myself to myself.

'I thought Mrs Margolis knew a lot of people,' Rose says when we take our place at the funeral and she begins looking around and I say to be quiet. She's only come to the funeral because she knows she hurt my feelings during our argument and wants to make up for it.

Mrs Margolis did know a lot of people but she was old and almost all of them are in Pinelands now.

'And one day I'll be joining them,' she used to say. 'I don't mind. We had good days together and it's hard to be the last one left.'

You would think that every Saturday Pinelands would be full with children visiting late parents but Mrs Margolis told me that it's not like that, not any more. She never had children herself but in the end it didn't seem to make all that much difference. All those children are grown-up now and out of the country, making new lives for their own families in some colour-blind place where they can sleep secure in their beds every night. I can understand that. If I was blessed with children I think I might even feel that way myself. You can have enough of listening to people talking revolution and saying that if things don't change, one of these days the streets will be running red with blood and no one will be safe. When Mrs Margolis's friends want to visit their children they have to jump on an aeroplane. That's what it comes to and you have to take out an atlas to see where some of them have landed up, Perth and Sydney, London and San Diego, Toronto and Champagne, Texas. You don't know your own grandchildren and you can hardly understand a word that comes out of your own child's mouth. They talk American now or Australian or put-on English. That's the world that Mrs Margolis has left. It's a world of photos and making telephone calls in the middle of the night when one half of the world is asleep and the other half is just waking up.

'Can you imagine how sad that is?' Mrs Margolis once said to me. 'People my age standing by the phone in their nineties in the middle of the night talking baby talk to a great-grandchild who they'll be lucky if they ever see?'

It is sad and there's something else that's sad as well. Who will come and see them in Pinelands? I suppose that after what happened to my mother and father, which I haven't even told Rose, I should feel a bit better but I don't. I see now that even when there's a grave to go to, it isn't always possible to go. I suppose that should comfort me but it doesn't and I'm sure that sometimes when the mood takes me I will still go to Pinelands even now that Mrs Margolis has gone.

Rose and Alf and I are the odd ones out here. We stand at the back. Mrs Margolis is not the first Pleasant Ways resident to die. In that way Pleasant Ways is like Sacred Heart. When your time comes to leave there are always people queuing up to take your place.

The caregivers are always at the funeral and people come up to them afterwards and thank them for their care. 'We don't know how she could have managed without you,' they say. 'This was Auntie Lizzie's treasure.' 'Don't you know Sweetness? Surely you remember? It's been so many years now, she's almost like one of the family.'

I don't think anyone will say that about me because I'm not that kind of person. I think that I'm like the ornaments and the photographs. Once someone gets used to me being there, it's easy enough not to see me any more and I don't mind that. I don't like pushy people myself. So I stand at the back and afterwards some of the people come over and greet me and some do say thank you for what I did.

'You could have told them that you were just doing your job that you were paid to do,' Rose says but I couldn't have done that.

'You should have taken your diploma and held it out so they could see,' Rose says. 'I just wish you'd told them that you only stayed on till the end out of the goodness of your heart and that you have other, better things to go on to now.'

Rose has her mouth open to say more but she can see on my face that I don't want to hear whatever she has to say, not here, not right this moment. She's afraid that I'll go straight back to Pleasant Ways and start asking around to see if I can get another caregiver's job. Caregiving isn't skilled work, plenty of girls say they're willing to do it but it isn't everyone's cup of tea, especially towards the end. The more care a person needs the more the caregivers come and go. Rose is afraid I'll be a caregiver all my life but she needn't worry. She'll get married and be Mrs de Gouveia and have Alf to see that she's well looked after. Mrs Margolis needs no one now to tend her worldly needs, and as for me I will go on looking out for myself just as I've always done but I don't want to think about it right now.

'Where are you going?' Rose says.

'I forgot something,' I say and I go quickly before she can ask me what and I have to be very quick when Rose is looking after me but not even Rose needs to know everything.

'What?' she says.

'Something,' I say and I'm gone before she can stop me. I know where to go, a little way back the way we came and down a side path and I can't be here without going.

'We haven't got all day, Ruby,' Rose calls loudly after me. 'Alf has to get back to work.'

Why do I have to be the one who has a small, fat sister who stands shouting after me in a cemetery but I can't worry about that now. I will be very quick and they are where they always are. Nothing changes for the dead and that's just how I like things to be, but today it's different. There's been another visitor. There's a smooth flat stone right up close beside each headstone. There's someone else who remembers them, someone who has never forgotten and would never forget and something in my heart tells me that he's been here.

YOU CAN COUNT ON AUNTIE
OLIVE

I'm not in the mood for Rose's colour-blind wedding. It's out of hand and it will get worse. It started off as magistrates' court with a church blessing and tea in the church hall prepared by Rose's friends who she met doing tea after services. I was happy with that but that was only the beginning and I suppose I started it.

'We must at least tell the Steenbras Street family,' I say. 'They'll hold it against us if we don't.'

Changed law or no changed law concerning mixed marriage, I don't want to be the one to tell the Steenbras Street family. Athlone has always been more than good enough for them and it goes without saying that what's good enough for them is more than good enough for us. If Rose thinks Auntie Olive's going to be giving out any prizes to the first girl in our family to marry a white man, law or no law, then she's got a big surprise coming. If the government changes the law one way then it can always change it back again if it suits them, but there is one good thing about it though.

'Auntie Olive will never come to the wedding,' I say.

'Yes, she will,' says Rose. 'She'll go anywhere there's free tea and cake. Wild horses wouldn't keep her away, she'll be far too nosy.'

It's then that I begin to have my doubts.

'I would have had you for a bridesmaid,' Rose says. 'And I still will if you'd change your mind.'

'You don't have bridesmaids in a magistrates' court,' I say. 'Magistrates' court's very quick. It'll be over in five minutes.'

Magistrates' court doesn't worry Rose. She's going to have bridesmaids and she's going to have a wedding dress and a proper cake with a plastic bride and groom on the top and I'm going to be there because I can't miss my own sister's wedding and I'm going to die of embarrassment.

'I can if I want to,' Rose says and there's nothing you can do with her when she gets like this and that is only the start. Now magistrates' court and a blessing at Our Lady of Good Hope and tea in the church hall aren't enough either. Rose is going to have an evening reception at the Portuguese Community Hall in Mountain Road, Observatory.

'With dancing,' she says. 'And we'll ask all Alf's family and I'll have a going-away outfit, lavender slacks and a jacket with yellow touches, and a proper send-off.'

'Why?' I say. 'You're not going very far. The only place you're going is just down the road to Alf's house.'

'Because I want to,' she says.

'And where, might I ask, is the money going to come from for all this?'

'On the six-month-to-pay account,' Rose says.

Make debt and pay off is how Rose likes to live. I don't know where she gets this from because we were never like that in our family. If we couldn't afford something we didn't have it and it didn't do us any harm. It worries me so much that I lie awake at night and wonder how it can possibly end. Whatever way I look at it, all I can see is that there is only one way it can end and that is badly.

'You can't have everything your eye sees,' I say. I should save my breath but I can't stop myself. There's a terrible greed inside my sister. She shops like she eats and it's never enough and it frightens me sometimes because I think it will get her into debt and into trouble and into enormous fatness so that in the end people will look at her on the street and laugh.

If Rose wants a wedding with a proper wedding dress and four of Alf's cousins dressed in yellow with crowns of flowers on their heads for bridesmaids and tea in one place and dancing halfway across town in the Portuguese Community Hall, Mountain Road, Observatory, then she will have it.

'Auntie Olive will never come to the Portuguese Community Hall,' I say. 'You've told her the magistrates' court and the blessing and tea. You can leave it at that.'

'She'll never miss out on the party at the Community Hall,' Rose says. 'That's the best part.'

Perhaps Rose has forgotten about Godfrey but I haven't. She knows as well as I do why Auntie Olive won't have much time for the Portuguese community.

'It won't worry her,' Rose says, and that's too much even for me. I don't like to have words with my sister but sometimes I run out of patience and Rose isn't always as thoughtful as she could be.

'If you think that then you must be a fool,' I say and she stops where she is and she looks at me.

Rose is my own sister and I've seen her almost every day of her life so I suppose that I don't really see her any more, but lately I've been taking another look and I see now that she's a pretty girl. She has the same eyes as my mother. I think that's why over the years I haven't ticked her off nearly as much as I should have. Rose isn't some-one who'd ever pick a fight herself and although she has flashes of temper sometimes she doesn't fight back and it can be hard when you're trying to tell her something for her own good, to keep her going in the right direction. Then there are my mother's eyes looking out from my sister's face and my mother knows how I am and why I sometimes speak sharply to my sister but it puts me in the wrong, where I belong, and I always feel bad about it afterwards.

'Not everyone's like you, Ruby,' Rose says. 'You hold things inside you and can't let them go. Auntie Olive isn't like that. She never has been and she's not going to change now. If something happens that doesn't fit in with her plan, she'll push it to one side as if it never happened at all.'

I would like to say that it's not true, except it is.

'She does that with big things, Ruby,' Rose says. 'Not just with something small. Auntie Olive can twist big things around so if she told them today you'd wonder if she was telling the same story as the one you remember, and you know just as well as I do that it's true.'

I remember how Auntie Olive couldn't have us and how what we got in the end was Sacred Heart and last Sundays. We both know that and I minded, all those years I minded because I thought she could have done it differently, but I never said anything.

And she's done worse than that because it was Auntie Olive who took our mother away from us and put her in a pauper's grave where we could never find her again. I minded that even more but Rose doesn't know that or how I feel about it and she doesn't need to know.

I don't know how she makes it right about Godfrey. Perhaps she pretends that he's playing in the big football team in the sky. 'Doing very well.' That's how she always used to talk about him when he was still with us. 'He's got so many friends he hardly has time for his own family these days.' She used to say that too. 'That's Godfrey, he has a life of his own.'

I suppose that in a way Rose is right. Auntie Olive could do that and put it behind her and that's one way of dealing with it.

'You can count on Auntie Olive,' Rose says. 'We'll ask

her and she'll come. She'll make quite sure that she's not left out of anything.'

I think about it for a long time afterwards. Perhaps it's because I'm feeling sad about Mrs Margolis, perhaps I'm not myself as change is coming and I don't like change and when I feel like this I like to take the old times out and think about them again.

I think about my life and my sister's. I think about our parents and about Godfrey and Mr Silver and how he was that night when we were just the two of us in the dining room at the Queen's. I think of my life so far and what I've learned from it and what I choose to remember and how I remember it and I think about what it pleases me to forget and I can see now that I am no better than or different from Auntie Olive. I can also hide things when they hurt me and I see also that I have misjudged my sister and that I will have to watch out for her because she also knows more than she says.

A NICE LITTLE NEST EGG

Mr Leonard Green has taken care of Mrs Margolis's money over these last years since she wasn't able to manage by herself. He came to the flat once or twice a month and we exchanged a few words. He isn't like some of the others who stopped coming because after the stroke when Mrs Margolis couldn't talk properly it was just too hard. Mr Green was never like that. He would always stay and keep her company after the business talk was over. When she was still well you could sometimes hear him laugh and even though she couldn't join in the laughter any more she could still make a half-smile and she understood everything he said. It was nice to hear because when she had been herself Mrs Margolis liked to laugh. Later, even after she'd signed a paper in front of her lawyer for him to handle the business without having to come and ask her every five minutes, he still came to see her. Even when she was in bed all the time and couldn't speak he still came and he read to her out of the newspaper. 'She had a life, you know, Ruby,' he used to say to me after her death while we were going through the business of getting her things sorted out. 'She used to organize concert parties and entertain the troops during the war, but that was a long time ago.'

The painting is going to the Theatre on the Bay to be put up in the foyer with her name, birth and death on a brass plate underneath. I would like one day to see it there with Mrs Margolis, as she was then, looking down over her shoulder like she is in the painting at all those people who've paid their money for entertainment and are waiting for the show to begin.

'What will you do now, Ruby?' Mr Green says and I tell him. It's strange to be in Mrs Margolis's flat with half-packed boxes all over the floor. It's strange to be just Mr Green and me and the auctioneer's people coming and going and the Pleasant Ways manager bringing people to look round and murmuring about views of the sea and prices and 'fully serviced' and 'totally secure' and 'frail care if needed'. Mrs Margolis is gone from this place and life is moving on and I don't like it even though I will not be going empty-handed. This doesn't often happen but it's happened to me. Mrs Margolis has left me money. It's a fortune of money. I never thought I'd see so much money in all my life, no matter how many luxuries I went without or how hard I saved.

'It's not a "fortune", Ruby,' Mr Green says. 'It's a

sensible sum and if you look after it, it can be a nice little nest egg and that's exactly what she wanted for you.'

I don't care what Mr Green says. What Mrs Margolis has left me is a fortune to me and I can't really believe it. When he's gone I sit down on a chair with the flat half packed up all round me and I think what this will mean to me. I can almost laugh out loud because of the shock of it.

I sit there in my blue work dress with my hands over my mouth and my heart light, brimming over. The future shines in front of me – and then I put my hands down in my lap and realize that this is no laughing matter because I can't tell Rose. First of all because Rose will tell the whole world and in a place like Pleasant Ways you have to be careful. Not everyone is generous like Mrs Margolis has been and if it gets out what she did for me it can only cause resentment. That's one reason but there's another reason too. I've always shared everything with Rose and I will always share with her. I've given her food off my own plate when she's been hungry but I can't share this. Not the way Rose is now. This is our nest egg for our future and we're still young and it could come in useful but if I tell her now and give her her share it will be gone in five minutes. That's what will happen and I know it but I've never kept anything good like this from her before and I can see now that sometimes a thing can be too big and that this is such a thing and I can't tell her this. Half of this money will always be Rose's. That's the way we are and the way we've always been and it's safe with me. If I give it to her as a nice surprise one day when she needs it I'm sure she'll understand why I'm doing what I'm doing and not hold it against me.

I have three months' wages and my room until the next person moves in and Mr Green says I can take something for a memory, anything that I like because he's giving me his permission to do that and he's sure that Mrs Margolis wouldn't have minded.

I say if it's all right I'd like to take one of the photographs and I can see that he didn't expect that.

'Which one?' he says.

I think he expects me to choose one of the silver frames but that's not what I want. I want one right at the back in a plain dark-wood frame. My hand knows exactly where it is and I lift it up and show it to him.

'You didn't know Monty Margolis, did you?' he says and I shake my head and point. 'Mr Saul Silver got me my job here,' I say but that was before Mr Green's time.

'Did he?' he says. He seems surprised but Mr Green can work out his own story because he won't hear my story from me.

'That was a terrible thing that happened to him,' he says. 'All the same, life goes on. I hear that he's had some good fortune. He's met someone and he's getting married again.'

I don't believe it.

'One can really only wish him nothing but the best. Don't you think so? He always had a soft spot for Zelda, you know. She and Monty were very good to him. He was out here visiting just the other day and he called me and I told him it was near the end and too late for a visit.'

The photograph, my one thing I asked for as a memory, is in my hands and I make myself not look at it. My heart is beating thick and slow and I feel small and a fool while Mr Green tells me things that I don't know, because what am I after all but the caregiver and such things can hardly concern the caregiver.

'Want to change your mind?' Mr Green says. He thinks now that I have what I asked for in my hand that I think I've made a mistake.

'He wasn't at the funeral,' I say.

'No,' he says. 'He would already have been out of the country by then.'

'Is she a nice woman?' I ask. It isn't my place to ask. I should bite my tongue off because I have asked something that has nothing to do with me but I have held back and held on to certain things for a very long time and I can't stop myself.

'Very nice,' he says. 'At least I believe she is. Everyone who knows him and has met her seems to like her. I don't know her myself.'

I say that I'm glad for his sake and I will be glad. It's not what I expected, that's all, and this is one of the ways Rose is right about me. I always think I know everything but there are some things I don't know and I see now that Mr Silver and I are different in more ways than one and that I was wrong about him. I hold things inside me and once I have them I have them for ever, but he's not like that. He can let go and take hold of life again and it's shocking to me because I hadn't expected it. I'm angry

241

and I would like to blame him and hold it against him but I'm not such a fool. I know that I can't but all the same I can't be joyful.

'You can still change your mind,' Mr Green says. He means about the photograph and I say yes, I think I would like to.

'I'll take the ornament of the shepherd instead,' I say. 'I wouldn't like to trust it to just anyone. You have to be very careful when you wash it because it's so fragile it could easily break.'

'You should take the shepherdess too then,' Mr Green says. 'After all, they're a pair and it would be a pity to break them up now.'

TIMES HAVE CHANGED

I have a new outfit for Rose's wedding, a dress and jacket, new shoes and bag and a flower-petal hat with a veil that hangs over my forehead. I try it on when I'm alone in our roof-room and turn round and round again so I can see it from all sides and I'm more than satisfied with what I see. At least there will be one person at this wedding who isn't all decked out like a Christmas tree.

Rose is the wrong shape for a dress with a full skirt. You can keep on telling her this and making other suggestions but it doesn't help. She likes the dress she's chosen and it's her wedding and she'll have her own way.

'If I don't care why should you?' she says.

I don't think the bridesmaids will all fit into the magistrates' office and I wouldn't have chosen orange sashes with the yellow dresses but Rose likes it. I don't know much about weddings. I've never been to one before so I can't say how it's done. There's one thing that I do know though and I know it for sure. If the day should ever come when I get married it won't be like this.

Rose doesn't like the one-two-three and it's over business of the magistrates' court. It's no good telling her that it only feels like one-two-three and that she'll have the rest of her life to think about what she's been so busy promising.

There'll be an organist in the church to play before and after the blessing and Father Basil is happy if rose petals are thrown outside on the steps after the service.

'And Auntie Olive's coming,' Rose says. 'And Uncle Bertie and Patsy, so on our side we'll be full house and we're sending a taxi to fetch them.'

'That's nice,' I say.

'Yes, isn't it?' Rose says. 'It'll give them something to talk about for the next couple of months.'

The only thing wrong with Rose's big day is me. She doesn't say so but I know and it's not just the church business. That was all argued out at the beginning.

'My sister won't go into a church any more and so neither will I,' Rose said and she was brave. You have to be very brave to say that to a Portuguese family who are going to be your in-laws and be ready to stand by what you've said, but Rose is brave.

The more Rose goes on about it and the more out of hand the wedding plans get, the worse I feel. I think Rose doesn't tell me everything because out of the blue I hear that a second cousin's child is going to be flower girl. I want to know why and Rose says it's because she didn't know how to say no but that the child will go straight to the church because she could begin to get restless in the magistrates' office.

'A magistrates' court and a blessing after is as good as,' she keeps saying, although it isn't 'as good as' at all, no matter what way you look at it. What it is is second best and she knows it. We both do but even so she won't budge and it doesn't make me very popular with the de Gouveias. To them I must be the peculiar sister, the bossy one, the one who's been organizing Rose's life all these years and convent-educated but now godless on top of everything else. I can just imagine how many rosaries are being counted and how many prayers are being said for the wellbeing of my soul and they'd be surprised to know that I don't mind at all. They can pray their heads off on my behalf if they like. I have prayed hard enough myself in my time not to hold out too much hope for what their prayers may achieve.

Rose gets dressed for her wedding at Alf's sister's house. They set aside the main bedroom for her and all her wedding finery is laid out on the bed and her dress hung up outside the wardrobe door.

The photographer is waiting outside the door to be called in when the bride is ready and he's a friend of the family and doing the photos as a wedding present so there are plenty of pictures. There are some of Rose standing and some of her sitting in front of the dressing table holding her bouquet up to her face and looking at herself in the mirror. A de Gouveia cousin who's a florist made the bouquet. There's frangipani in it and maidenhair fern and the smell of it fills the room. There are pictures of the bride in her white dress with her bouquet in front of her standing in the middle of a sea of de Gouveia women and I'm in that one because I got pulled in and they insisted. There's a picture of Rose and me together and it's the first photograph ever of just the two of us and I wonder why we never had one taken before.

'Luxuries,' says Rose. 'You said it was a luxury and we needed our money for other things and so we never got around to it.'

I would like to say that I never said such a thing but I'm sure that I did and so I keep quiet. When all the posing is done Rose starts giving the photographer instructions about what she wants during the service, outside the church and at the reception as well. Whatever happens, she says, she wants to get together with our auntie and uncle and cousin from Athlone so that we can have a photograph taken of just our family together.

'I'm going to send Auntie Olive one for a memento,' Rose says sweet as pie. 'So she'll always have something to remind her of me on my wedding day.'

She can do that if she likes but I can tell her something for nothing, a photograph of Rose's wedding won't ever find a place on the sideboard in Steenbras Street. There are plenty of de Gouveias and they're all very nice, cheerful people who know how to enjoy themselves but when you get right down to it they're not Athlone people and they're all much too white for Auntie Olive to really have any time for them.

Before the wedding there was a little talk I had to have with my sister. Rose always makes it sound as if all of life is easy sailing but it isn't and there were things that I wanted her to think about because marriage is a serious business.

I told her that there was no more Mixed Marriages Act because that suited the government. They dropped it because they hoped it would make them look better to the outside world, but anyone who actually lived here knew that it didn't really change anything.

'It doesn't just suit the government,' Rose said. 'Just for a change what suits the government suits me too.'

'That's good,' I said. 'Just be sure and remember that it may not suit your neighbours because there's still Group Areas, in case you didn't know. When you move in with Alf in Observatory Estate they can come and take you away, married or not.'

I hated myself when I talked like that but someone had to say it and if it wasn't me then who was it going to be? Rose kept saying that she understood but I don't think she really did. Governments can make laws; they don't have to make sense. I didn't think Rose realized what it was really going to be like. She and Alf couldn't go and see a film together and they couldn't go to the beach. They couldn't hold hands in public and thank goodness he had a car because if they ever went anywhere on a bus or a train together they'd have to sit in separate sections.

'That's the life you're choosing,' I told her. 'If no one else takes the trouble to mention it to you then let me be the one with the bad news.'

'Life's how you make it,' she said. 'I like to look on the bright side.'

I love my sister but sometimes she was so much on 'the bright side' and seeing just what she wanted to see that she frightened me, and I was so worried for her that I could have shaken her because I didn't know what else there was I could do.

'Have you thought about children?' I asked. The words just jumped out of my mouth.

'We've thought about it,' she said, 'and you don't have to worry on that score. There won't be any children.'

I thought for a moment that I must have heard wrong.

'Don't look like that,' she said. 'You heard me. Alf's not getting younger and there are plenty of nieces and nephews and cousins to go round. We don't need children.'

I felt as if she'd slapped me in the face. I had no right to feel that and I knew it but that was exactly how I did feel. I didn't own Rose; she could do as she pleased. I knew that in my head but my heart just couldn't understand it.

'I'm going to be an old man's darling,' she said. 'That's what Alf says and I don't mind. And you needn't look like that, Ruby, it's going to be just fine.'

I don't know how I looked.

'It wasn't as if we had such a wonderful childhood. I know you did your best but we both have to face it. If we had the chance to have it all over again we'd say no, thanks very much, and run away just as fast as we could.'

I felt as if all the air was being sucked out of my body.

'It's my time now,' she said. 'It will still be you and me like it's always been, only now I'll have Alf and it suits us like this. We both want to go ahead, just the two of us without any children, and get the best out of life.'

It was out and she'd made up her mind and what was there to say? I looked at my sister, the soon-to-be bride, and thought about her husband-to-be who thought it was good enough for his wife to be 'an old man's darling'. It wouldn't be two minutes before Rose turned into a spoiled child herself if she didn't watch out. I looked away but it was too late because the thought had already come into my head. What I saw was two selfish people in a sad empty place and I had my own thoughts about that and about what marriage was intended for in the first place but I didn't say anything.

I was awake for half the night before Rose's wedding day. She'd had plenty of invitations from Alf's family to spend her last night as a single girl under their roof but she didn't.

'Why don't you?' I said.

'Because I don't want to,' she said. 'For my last night as a single girl I'd like it if it's just us because after I'm married I don't suppose it will be the same.'

'No, I don't suppose so,' I said, as if it was something I'd only just thought about that very minute.

* * *

249

Alf's family has taken to Rose in a big way. After all the years of being a good son to his mother, a good brother and cousin and a good friend, they were glad that Alf had found a good girl to make a life with.

As far as Alf's family was concerned, Rose was a girl who'd come young and fresh into his life and he could take care of her and be the one to show her the ways of the world. Rose is a girl with no secrets and no past that could really interest anyone. She was just the kind of girl they would have chosen themselves to be their new sister, their cousin and their aunt. The children were already calling her Auntie Rose as if they'd known her all their lives.

Alf's eldest sister was so happy to see Alf so happy that she decided that Rose was God's gift to their family and she thanked Him for it every day of her life. That was her business and I think half the time she said things like that for my benefit because in all this great happiness there was only one drawback and that was me. I was 'the sister who fell out with God' and what could I say about that? I would have liked things to be perfect and if there had been things I could have changed I would have, but that was one thing I could do nothing about. If I was to be 'peculiar' then that was what I'd be and they would have to take me as I was because I wasn't going to change.

Auntie Olive and Uncle Bertie and Patsy wouldn't be going to the magistrates' court and I would not be going into the church. The church porch was as far as I'd go and from there I could still hear the service and be part of it and I was willing to do that for my sister.

This is what I lay awake thinking about on the last morning my sister and I would wake up in the same room. Not about how I would be losing my sister but how I would have to go back and face God.

I thought back to how I got my gold stars in Sunday school and how I went to St Agnes's with my mother and father and how Rose had been far too young at the time to remember any of this.

I thought about how I used to jump in and out of God's house as if I was a child of that house as well as my own and it was understood that I could come and go as I pleased just as long as I behaved myself.

I thought about my mother asking me to sing 'Star of the Morning' and how she turned her full attention on me and listened to me as if what she heard was a full choir of angels singing and not just one little girl. There was a time when I did believe. I believed a lot. I believed as much as anyone possibly could believe and then, piece by piece, every bit of faith I had was taken from me.

'I want to look back and see you standing there,' Rose says.

'I said I would be and I will,' I say and I find a corner of the church porch under the notices and next to the hymnbook table and I tuck myself into it and the memory of it will be with me all my life.

Rose's dress is wrong for her but she looks beautiful and I make myself as small as I can in my corner and my heart is full. I feel as if I have run a race as hard and fast and straight as I could with all the strength I had and everything has gone right with me and brought me to this place where I am now and it is time to let go.

This church isn't like Good Shepherd or St Agnes's, it's much grander but it smells of prayer books and candle wax and dust and someone tends to it well. The brass is polished so that it gleams, the flowers are fresh and a smell of Mr Min comes from the pews. The altar cloth is crisp with starch and gleaming white and God, I think, would have no cause for complaint, although you can never be sure with God.

Looking out for Rose is over. It will be Alf's job now. Rose will be a married woman with a husband and a complete family who have already opened their arms and their hearts to her and I should be glad for her and I am. I will have my place just as I've always had but I will have to learn how to share and I had not thought of it that way before.

My sister is a fidgety bride. She keeps looking behind her. Right after she says 'I do' she looks behind her as if she's checking that the congregation are still in their places so that afterwards there will be no one who could say they can't remember the day Rose Jacobs became Mrs Alf de Gouveia. I want to step out from the little corner in the porch where I stand behind the prayer-book table and signal her to look forward because people might think she was thinking about changing her mind and it was far too late for that now. Whether she had second thoughts or not she was already married and what she had to do now was to be dignified and keep her eyes forward and act like a bride.

Then it's over. The music swells up, Rose and Alf make their way back up the aisle and there's a whole church filled with de Gouveias behind them and I make myself even smaller against the wall and let them pass. One thing about the de Gouveias is that they're not a quiet family. When the service is over everyone seems to be jostling and talking and laughing at the same time. The little cousins carrying baskets of rose petals are pushed to the front. The photographer is calling for people to come together to have their pictures taken and people who've had to hold back during the service are lighting up cigarettes. I'm not quite sure exactly where I'm supposed to fit in so I stay where I am in my new dress with the petal hat on my head and the last of the music thundering out behind me.

'Where have you got to, Ruby?' says a voice and it's Alf. 'Rose has been looking everywhere for you. She wants more photos taken. She wants a photo of the three of us together.'

I feel him take my arm and lead me into the push of the crowd and I put my head down and hold on to my hat and hang on to my new handbag and Alf takes me straight through the crowd to my sister.

'Where were you?' she says. 'I wanted to see you and I couldn't. I kept looking back and I still couldn't see you.'

'I was there,' I say.

'Well, I couldn't see you,' she says. 'I kept looking and I couldn't understand it because I know if you say you'll be somewhere, then you'll be there.'

'I was there,' I say and she shakes her head and takes

hold of my arm and keeps me against her as if she thinks that I'm about to go off somewhere. But I was there, just like I always am, just like I'll always be, because that's my place and there's really nothing that can ever change that.

HAVING ALF FOR A FRIEND

I am twenty-seven years old, living in the back room behind the kitchen at Rose and Alf's house. There was a big fight before I got there because when they first made me the offer I didn't want to take them up on it.

'Thank you, Rose,' I said. 'Thank you, Alf. It's very kind of you but I can look after myself.'

'How would you do that?' Rose asked.

'I could find a room,' I said.

'I'm offering you a room,' Rose said.

'I'm not one to impose,' I said. 'If anyone should know that, you should.'

'If you were imposing, I'd be the first one to say so,' she said.

'I don't think it's the right thing to start off a married life with a sister in the back room,' I said.

'It's my married life,' Rose said. 'Mine and Alf's and we're inviting you. We want you to come and live with us because we have room for you and it would make us happy and surely that's up to us to say?'

I said again that I could look after myself but Rose wasn't in a mood to listen to me.

'Why should you?' she said. 'You looked after me all these years and now it's my turn.'

'You've got Alf to worry about now,' I said.

'Alf thinks it's a good idea,' Rose said. 'It's almost like it was meant to be. Alf said so. It's a lovely big room for a spare room and we won't be having any other use for it and he works shifts and he doesn't want a wife who's always wondering what her sister's doing and if she's all right and taking care of herself. He knows I'll be happy if I have you there with me.'

My life had moved on. I couldn't stay in my roof-room at Pleasant Ways for ever. Often when a person loses her place because of death there'll be someone else who'll need her but I had other plans and a diploma in Office Management that I got by correspondence. It must be worth something because although you pay high fees for the pleasure you still have to work hard and pass your exams. They don't just take your money and reach into a drawer and hand over a diploma like something you buy over the counter at the OK Bazaar. It doesn't work like that but there's something else. I may have my diploma, which Rose thinks will open any door for me, but there's something I don't have and that's experience. If you look in the *Cape Times* classified under 'Jobs Offered' it always says experience and what they're looking for isn't the experience of life I had at Sacred Heart or with Mrs Margolis and the Pleasant Ways old people and it won't count in my favour that I've never done office work before.

I tried to give myself courage. I put on my outfit I bought for Rose's wedding and I stood in front of the mirror and I breathed. I took deep breaths, I closed my eyes and then I opened them again and looked at myself and to my own eyes I didn't look too bad. I thought that if I worked in an office anyone who employed me wouldn't have any cause to be ashamed of me and when they knew me better they'd know that I was prepared to work hard.

'How's it going?' That was every second sentence Rose said to me.

'Fine,' I'd say but it wasn't fine at all. I spent most of my time sitting all dressed up in my new room in my sister's house with my whole world turned upside down. Rose was married, Mrs Margolis had become the late Mrs Margolis and I had an Office Management diploma that I got by correspondence and I wasn't brave enough to use it, and then Alf came up with an answer.

'Didn't your mother used to work at Pescanova Fisheries?' he asked.

I didn't like it when Alf talked about my mother. I think it was because he was a newcomer in our lives. He never knew my mother and my mother was precious to me. I didn't have so many memories of her that I felt I could be generous about sharing them.

'I just don't like it,' I told Rose, when perhaps I should have kept quiet.

'But Alf isn't "other people",' Rose said and it was right but he was her husband, not mine, and it made me sorry that I'd ever told her how I felt because it wasn't a thing that she understood. If Alf minded that I said that then he never said so to me and I felt bad about it because I knew he was only trying to help me.

'If you like, I'll take a drive down past Pescanova,' he said. 'I'll ask around. Maybe there are still people who remember your mother from the old days. Maybe they need someone. You never know. It doesn't hurt to ask.'

'You see, Ruby,' said Rose, and I did see and what I saw was that Rose was going to be very smug now that she was Mrs de Gouveia but I saw something else too. Rose was always the one who asked how I was getting on and 'fine' was good enough for my sister, but I don't think that 'fine' was good enough for her husband. He knew by then that Rose and I were very different.

'Would you like me to do that?' he said and I said yes, I would. 'I'd be grateful to you.' I said that too and I meant it.

I think it's because of Alf going down in his taxi to Pescanova Fisheries and putting in a good word for me that I got the job.

'I think your diploma and how you are as a person may have helped,' Alf says.

'If you listened to me and weren't so shy and always looking back instead of forward you could have got an even better job,' Rose says and it's easy to say. She's not the one who has to go out and be among strangers.

'You should tell them that our mother once worked for them. Tell them you know the docks and fishing people from your days at the Queen's.'

'I didn't really know the docks,' I say. 'I kept myself to myself in those days.'

My life changed again but some things didn't change. If it were up to me I would have kept myself out of sight while Alf was in the house but Rose wouldn't have that. It was always Rose who called me to come out of my room and sit with them and watch TV. It was Rose who listened for me when I came home from work. It was Rose who called out before I was even halfway through the front door to ask how my day had been and if I would like tea and to tell me that we were having fish cakes for supper. Lucky Star minced pilchards and it was only after she'd cooked them that she thought about how I must see enough tins of fish every day to put me off them for life.

Being an old man's darling suited Rose.

'I was never going to be like you,' she said. 'But that's all right. Things always turn out as they should and for the best.'

'What do you think, Ruby?' Alf would ask me. 'Wouldn't you say that she was a girl worth waiting for?'

'Your turn next,' Rose says but I don't think so.

I think that I can work my way up in the office at

Pescanova and when I get home I can close my door in the back room of my sister's house and be in no one's way. When I'm asked to join in, I do and Alf's family and the people in Rose's new life accept me as I am and that's a good arrangement for me.

I have a new life among the living and my days with the dead are over. Rose and my mother and father and I will never be a family again, in this or any other life, and I accept that. I think that I should be like Mr Silver and move on and I hope that wherever he is he's happy and I wonder what it was that happened between us. I'm sure that there was something because if there wasn't then why can't I forget?

When Alf drives me to work in the morning, when we go on to the freeway towards the industrial area, if I look to the left I can see the Queen's, but I don't look to the left. I look straight in front of me because I don't want to see. I think that if I turn my head I will see straight through the walls and doors and windows right into the heart of the hotel and they will all still be there. Ruby and Mr Silver, she standing in front of him in her black waitress uniform with the name tag that she always hated pinned on her lapel. He at his same table with his head bent down. The lights in the kitchen are switched off for the night and they are in the half-light and what passed between them stays with them and whatever it was is not for us to know.

MR JACK JULIES

I look at Mr Jack Julies; he doesn't look at me. He's a big man but he's not what you'd call handsome. He has pockmarks on his face and it looks as if the salt from his life out on the sea has eaten right into him. Life has done what it's done to his face but you can see that even before that he didn't get off to a very good start. It looks as if his nose has been broken more than once and he has dark eyebrows that look like they're made out of wire.

I've walked past him in reception and once or twice in the passage when he was on his way to see one of the da Costas but I keep my eyes down and don't greet and he doesn't greet either, but I feel him.

'What do you mean, you "feel him"?' Rose says and it's hard to explain things like this to Rose.

'I don't know,' I say and I'm sorry now I spoke. It isn't

every day that I mention a man's name and when I do Rose pounces and wants to know more. She wants to know everything. She wants to know things that don't even exist. I think if I made up a big pack of nonsense and lies it would make her happy and if she was going to be happy that's exactly what I'd have to do. What she wants to know is that there's some man out there who's interested in me or who I'm interested in but it isn't like that, with Mr Jack Julies or with anyone else for that matter. It's just that Mr Jack Julies isn't like any man I've ever met before and that's the reason I can't help but notice him.

We have half an hour for lunch. In return we go home at half past four and miss the big rush when the sirens go for the factory workers to finish off at five. It suits us but half an hour isn't very much for lunch, especially if you stand in the queues at the food kiosks. I've found a little place of my own at the side of the building near the car park and when the weather's good I sit on the wall and I eat my lunch there and my lunch is always the same. A white bread sandwich, a piece of fruit and proper tea from home in a flask because I don't like the ice-cold canteen tea because it always tastes bitter.

'Old maid's lunch,' Rose calls it but that's all right. Anyone who knows me knows that once I'm set in a pattern and comfortable I don't like change. I'm happy in my same place on the wall by the parking lot eating my same lunch.

I'm not sitting there waiting for Mr Jack Julies to find

me, and in any case you can't find something if you're not looking for it in the first place. Mr Jack Julies isn't looking for anything at all except maybe his car parked in the parking lot but all the same he finds me and I'm glad I've spent all that time before that minute having my own little looks at him. Someone who didn't know that he wasn't the handsomest man in the world and wasn't prepared for it might have let it show on her face.

'Don't they give the staff lunch?' he says and he indicates with his head towards the Pescanova building and I tell him, no.

'They should,' he says and maybe they should but if they did I wouldn't have it because it would probably be fish every day and Friday fish, white fish and potato and rice at Sacred Heart, was more than enough to put me off fish for life. Never mind my sister's love affair with Lucky Star minced pilchards.

'I've seen you,' he says. 'Working in the office.'

I'm not going to tell him that I've seen him because in the first place he's such a big man it would be hard not to see him, and in the second place I think he knows I have although I've never seen him so close up before. He has light green eyes, which means white blood somewhere. His mother must have had a gentleman visitor in the night when her husband wasn't home. That's what people say about people with that colouring but I wouldn't like to be the person who says that to him.

'What's your name?' he says.

'What's yours?' I say, acting smart like my sister.

'I think you already know that,' he says and I've

learned my first lesson, which is that it is no good trying to act smart with Mr Jack Julies.

I told Rose that if she started spreading the story that Mr Jack Julies is my 'boyfriend' I'd kill her and I don't usually talk like that but I don't know of any other way to say it that she'll understand.

'What is he then?' she says.

'He's my friend,' I say. It's only three words but if Rose has ever understood any three words in her life I wish that she'd understand these. People who have any sense don't want to get on the wrong side of Jack Julies and that includes me. It's true that he's singled me out and that's one thing, but if one day I am to be what he would call his 'girlfriend' that would be for him to say. Also, he would have to ask me first and he hasn't because that's not the way things are between us.

I was happy how we started off, with him spending my half-hour lunch break with me after he'd finished his business with the da Costas. He only comes in on a Friday and I never thought after that first time when he stopped to pass the time of day with me that it would become regular. Rose says I lie, I must have known all the time because a woman always knows something like that, but I didn't.

'I could have told you before you told me,' she says. 'I knew it when it was new clothes and best dress every Friday and nails painted Thursday night when you used to do them Saturday after you finished cleaning your room.'

'What difference does it make when I paint my nails?'
I say.

'Because if Saturday's your day for painting nails then
that's how it will be for ever because that's how you are
and you know it.'

I am like that and I did change my nail-painting day
in hopes, but I still say that I didn't expect Jack Julies to
come looking out for me the way he did.

'You did,' Rose says but she's wrong. I didn't 'expect'
it but I'd 'hoped' and after 'hoped' came 'looked forward'.
Then I began saving up things to tell him and looking at
my watch in case he was late and the next thing, before I
even knew what was happening, we had an 'arrangement'.

It's early days with Jack Julies if it's 'days' at all and I
don't want everything to be spoiled and Rose could spoil
things if she wanted to. I should have been more careful
when he asked me if there was somewhere he could come
and call on me properly that wasn't a car park with half
the factory looking at us and wondering what we were
talking about. If I had somewhere else I could have
invited him to I would have but I didn't, so in the end I
said that if he wanted to he could call on me in
Observatory Estate at my sister's house where I live.

I'm not used to a man, especially a man older than I am
who's made his way in life and earned people's respect,
paying attention to me and I would have liked to do
things in my own way and my way isn't my sister's.

When Rose first laid eyes on Jack Julies you could see
she thought he was the ugliest man she'd ever seen in her

life. He must have seen that and I'm sure it hurt him and he's learned not to show it, but Rose isn't eight years old any more and she could have tried harder.

'If you don't like him,' I said, 'you could have tried a little harder not to show it.'

'It's not what I like, it's what you like that counts,' Rose said and there was a big question mark that came after that.

'It's early days,' I said.

'Does that mean we'll be seeing more of him?' she said.

'Perhaps,' I said. 'That is if he feels like coming back here after the way you were today.'

'Oh, he'll feel like coming back here,' Rose said and she was right and I knew it.

RUBY IN BLOOM

Ruby always thought I was jealous of Jack Julies because he was the first man in her life but she was wrong. I knew there was a man. I knew the way a sister knows or one woman knows about another but I didn't ask.

'She'll tell you in her own time, when she's good and ready,' Alf said. 'That's if there's anything to tell.'

Alf's a good husband, he's a good man but he's a man after all. You couldn't really expect him to pick up something that any woman would be able to tell you in two seconds flat. Our auntie Olive always said that God reveals things in his own good time. All I can say is that waiting for God to reveal things is one thing and waiting for my sister, Ruby, to tell you what it was she was so set on keeping to herself is another thing altogether. If there's something you would like to know from Ruby, the only way to do it is to ask out straight, otherwise you could wait for ever. You could stop thinking about time passing and start to think how life on earth is short and if it's all the same to everyone there are some things that you'd like to know while you're still above ground.

I held myself in until I couldn't hold in for another second and then I asked her.

'So?' I said.

'So?' she said, in that way she had which meant that if you're hoping for an argument then watch out because if you say one more word your wish will very likely come true.

You could never say anything nice to Ruby about herself. She always brushed it away and said it was a lot of nonsense and please could we talk about something else but whether she liked it or not, Ruby was a pretty girl. She had beautiful clear skin that was very smooth when you touched it. She was vain about her hands although she didn't like people to know it. That came from her hotel days when her hands didn't look so wonderful and she kept putting them behind her or sitting on them or not taking her gloves off until the very last minute on Sundays. Later on people could look at her hands just as much as they liked. She was born with beautiful slim long-fingered hands and she looked after them. On Saturday when there was no rush and she could have the bathroom to herself for the whole morning if she liked she manicured her nails and rubbed Pond's hand cream into her hands. Then it was Sunsilk shampoo for her hair and when everything was done the final touch was Cutex

Really Red nail polish. In summer she sat outside in the yard and towelled her hair dry in the sun. You can't say such a thing to your own sister but my sister Ruby was beautiful with her hair half dry and all over the place down to her shoulders. I can see her now with her face pink from the rubbing and the sun falling down all around us and the freshly washed smell of her all around in the air.

'What are you looking at?' she'd say, putting the towel over her shoulders.

'I'm looking at you,' I'd say.

'You see me every day of your life. I don't know what's left to see.'

I never knew what to say when Ruby said that and so I kept quiet and Ruby got on with rubbing her hair till it was just about dry and we didn't say anything to each other but I sat with her anyway because I didn't want to leave.

If I could stop my time with my sister then that's where I'd like to stop it, with her in her bare feet and summer dressing gown sitting on my back-yard step and me in my house overall and slippers. The back yard wasn't grand. It was just some grass and a few daisy bushes and a trellis of sweet peas and a few branches that hung over from next door. There were wash lines at the side and three old wicker chairs half coming apart and a table on the back stoep where we sat out sometimes on hot nights and looked down over our neighbours' roofs to the bay. I could look at my sister then and she wouldn't even know I was looking, much less what I was thinking about. What I was thinking about was my married life and before that the orphanage and all the long way that we'd come. I was thinking that inside my house in Observatory Estate, inside my own married life, I had somehow managed to make a safe place for us and I was grateful and I was relieved. I did what Ruby used to do when she was a girl. I held my breath and then, when I couldn't hold it one second longer, just for the pleasure of the relief that it brings I exhaled and I didn't need a church and I didn't need it to be Sunday. I sat where I was in my slippers in my own back yard and gave thanks.

I think I did it because I knew things were about to change. Ruby was different. I don't know if she thought she could walk into the house right past me with a Truworth's dress shop carrier bag in her hand and I wouldn't notice. If you buy something new the whole road will know it before you even get to your front gate. Ruby was neat and tidy but she didn't have many clothes. She always wore the same clothes over and over again and tarted them up with little pieces of costume jewellery and scarves. When she needed something she'd go to OK Bazaar or Ackermans. Auntie Olive always used to go on at her and say that now she had a steady, well-paid job she ought to open a Truworth's account like Patsy did. What Auntie Olive didn't say was that when the letters about 'arrears' arrived at Steenbras Street, she was the one who had to get on the bus and go to town to put things right so that they could all hold their heads up again. Ruby would rather go without luxuries than have that happen to her. She would put newspaper in her shoes in winter if she really had to but she would never get into debt. It was cash or nothing with Ruby, so before she started buying herself new things she must have gone to Good Hope Savings Bank and drawn on her savings account and that's not a thing she did every day and it nearly killed me but I didn't ask.

'I bought a few frocks,' she'd say and I was sitting on her bed watching as she snipped off the price tags quickly with a pair of nail scissors and I watched while she hung up her new frocks, one by one, neat in her cupboard.

'And the rest?' I said because there were bras and panties too and petticoats and pantyhose.

'In case I'm in an accident,' she said and I never said a word.

'You know about people landing up in hospital because of accidents. You read about it every day.'

I knew about a lot of things. What I didn't know was about my sister Ruby spending money on a bottle of Apple Blossom perfume. She didn't have to hide it away from me. I could smell it on her when she came through the door on a Friday, and then later, when we sat down at the kitchen table to have our before-supper cup of tea. I used to put my cup down and get up and stand next to her and bend down a little bit and run my finger up and down her arm as if I was looking for dust.

'What's the matter with you?' she said.

'Nothing,' I said. 'I'm just checking to see if your bloom's still there.'

* * *

'I don't know what's got into you,' she said, but Ruby was never a good liar and she went red in the face when she said it.

'There's a man involved, isn't there?' I said and watched as she went even redder in the face while I waited for her to come up with some answer but she didn't have to say anything. I knew just by looking at her that if there wasn't a man involved there very soon would be. I knew enough about life by then to know at least that much and I'd wait for it and it would surely come, that moment when Ruby put her teacup down and told me the same old story that I could have told her.

'It's nothing,' she said.

'Tell me about "nothing",' I said and I waited.

'He's nice to talk to,' Ruby said, not looking straight in my face. 'And he's a good listener. You don't often find that.'

'I see,' I said and I thought to myself that if he's such a good listener then my sister Ruby must have been doing some talking and just as a beginning that would make a nice change.

'He's got fishing boats on the West Coast down Lambert's Bay way. He only comes to town on a Friday for business.'

'I see.'

'It's not what you think,' she said, giving me a look.

'What do you think I think?' I asked.

'You know how people are,' she said and I said that I

do and I know something else too. I know that there's no smoke without a fire.

'Where do you meet your friend?' I asked and she told me in the Pescanova car park during the lunch hour. 'And for how long?' I asked and she told me that it had been going on for quite a few weeks and I could see then what she'd been waiting for me to say since the conversation started.

'Don't you think it's time you brought him home so that we can have a look at him?' I said. 'This is your home too, you know. Your friends are always welcome here. There's no need to meet on street corners.'

'I don't know if he'll come,' she said.

She may not know but I do and I told her to ask if he'd like to come and have supper with us and she said she didn't think so, at least not yet because it was still early days.

'Maybe tea on Saturday?' she said.

Saturday is my afternoon at the community hall and Ruby knew better than anyone how much I looked forward to it. Sometimes we did karaoke, sometimes we played bingo or put on records and danced and sometimes Mr Fernandez played his accordion.

'There's no need for you to give up your Saturday,' Ruby said. 'I wouldn't expect that.'

'I see,' I said.

'Of course I wouldn't,' she said. 'I know how much you look forward to it.'

'Am I at least allowed to have a look at him?' I said. 'Or do you want to keep me hidden away?'

'Don't be silly,' she said. 'I haven't even asked him yet and I don't even know if he'll come.'

'He'll come,' I said and my sister looked away and asked how I could be sure and I didn't answer her but I was just as sure as anybody could be.

Ruby was a girl men would look at and if she gave them any encouragement once they'd looked at her they would be sure to come back for another look, but that's never been her way. Ruby was shy and she kept herself to herself and away from men but I could see that had changed. Ruby had looked at a man and he'd looked back and it came to me that Ruby would never again look quite as she did then, right then that minute, and silly things came into my head. I looked at my sister and knew that at last she was blooming and all I could hope for was that this man, whoever he was, was going to be good to her.

When the moment came that I did meet him he wasn't at all what I'd expected. In the first place he was the biggest man I'd ever seen in my life. That was the first thing I thought. The second thing was that even through the eyes of love no one could call him an oil painting, and the third thing was that I wouldn't like him to come up to me if I were out alone on the street on a dark night.

'Get away from the window,' Ruby said and I don't think I've ever seen her so dressed up or so nervous in her life.

'I'm just looking,' I said and I don't know what she was so agitated about. She must have known that when a strange man came driving up to our house in a Mercedes Benz motor car the rest of our road would be looking as well.

We all knew each other and where we fitted in. We knew the comers and goers and no one had ever seen a man like Jack Julies step out of a silver Mercedes Benz motor car in front of our gate or any gate in the street before, at least not so far as I knew. And he was an out-of-towner. His car had a West Coast registration number. The whole road will have known that long before he got to our gate.

'Rose,' Ruby said. 'I'm asking you nicely.'

I don't know if she slept at all during the night but I do know that she was up with the sun getting the house tidy. I could hear her in the lounge and in the kitchen and it never mattered how many doors you closed, you'd have to be a very peculiar woman not to hear your own kitchen tap running on and off and then on again. Even if you're in your nice big bed, half asleep against your husband's back.

When I got up and into my dressing gown and into the kitchen there was a tray all ready on the table. It had two cups and saucers and a plate of Ouma rusks set out on it and Ruby was in her overall with a guilty expression on her face and the whole place was smelling of Jik and Sunlight soap.

'I made coffee,' she said.

'I know,' I said. 'I could smell it.'

'With hot milk,' she said and I could see the milk pot

on the stove and she put down her scrubbing brush and picked up a dishcloth to take hold of the milk-pot handle.

'You can take some to Alf,' she said. 'It might be nice for him to have coffee in bed for a change.'

'What's this?' I asked.

'Nothing,' she said. 'I was in the mood and I thought I'd give the kitchen a little "go over", that's all. You do it every day. I don't see why I shouldn't take my turn once in a while.'

I took an Ouma rusk and dipped it in my coffee and put it in my mouth and sucked all the milky coffee out of it and it was delicious. I can close my eyes and taste it now.

The lino under my bare feet was still damp from the scrubbing.

'You don't have to eat off the floors, you know,' I said. 'We have plates.'

'I know,' she said. 'It makes me feel better, that's all.'

That was fine for Ruby. As for me, I didn't know how I should feel. I'd be a fool to be ashamed that in my sister's opinion my floors were not up to her new friend's high standards, or perhaps it was Ruby who should have been ashamed that she didn't think our house was good enough for him. It didn't matter. I took another rusk and said that it was nice of her to do a tidy-up and get up early to make coffee for Alf and me, and I said it nicely so that there would be no quarrel. My sister always liked things perfect and I wouldn't stand in her way if on that day, just for a change, things weren't just 'good enough'

to turn a blind eye to but more than good enough to
welcome a friend.

He was so tall that I thought he would have to bend his
head to get through the door but he did manage to get in
and once he was in he filled up the whole hallway.

'Mr Julies,' Ruby said. 'This is my sister, Rose.'

'Pleased to meet you,' I said and I sounded as if I was
back in Sacred Heart again and for a terrible minute I
thought I might curtsy as if he was royalty, and he just
stood there and he didn't say anything.

'Come in,' Ruby said and he was in and she moved to
one side to show him with her hand where the lounge was
and behind his big back I looked at my sister and raised
up my eyebrows and she gave me a look.

'Come in and sit down,' she said and I thought that he
surely was the biggest, ugliest man I'd ever seen and I
just hoped that Miss Ruby Apple Blossom Jacobs knew
what she might be letting herself in for.

I was never a big girl myself. I'm what you might call
'comfortably padded' but I can tell you one thing and
that is that even a girl like me who isn't slim like my
sister would know all about it if a man like Jack Julies
rolled over her in the night. I wondered if Ruby had
thought about that but I didn't think so. She was too
busy being polite. There she was in her new Truworth's
dress and the sandals that showed off her legs and there
was a smell of 'new' all over her and I might just as well
not have been there at all, but I knew something that she
didn't know. Ruby may not have been quite sure how

things would turn out between her and Jack Julies but Jack Julies knew. He'd made up his mind about Ruby a long time ago. I'd go so far as to say that he made his mind up the first moment he laid eyes on her.

ANOTHER MAN, THE RIGHT MAN

'You're a funny girl, Ruby,' he says. 'Why do you find it so hard to call me Jack? It's my name after all.'

I can't call him Jack. I think that the kind of woman who'd call him Jack and be easy with it would not be a woman like me. I call him Jack Julies and that's as far as I'll go, and at first it was hard but if you do something enough you can say it lots of different ways and it gets easier and I'm happy with it because it's friendly without being disrespectful.

Because of the kind of man he is, Jack Julies isn't someone who's going to make life easy for you. I knew it that first time when he came over and talked to me and I made out that I didn't know who he was. Jack Julies isn't a man who plays games and because I know that, I know that the way he keeps looking out for me and coming over to talk to me means that there's something about me that he likes.

I thought about maybe making an extra sandwich for him and asking him if he'd like to share but that would be forward, as though we had a firm arrangement and if he didn't come I'd have a right to feel let down, and it isn't like that. I just sit on the wall and take my sandwich out of the brown paper bag and unwrap it out of its greaseproof paper and then I take out my paper serviette and cover my lap with it. I eat in front of him, neat like I always do, and he watches me eat. He stands in front of me big as a wall between me and the rest of the world and we talk and I wonder what we'll do when winter comes and the weather gets too bad for sitting out.

He knows that I was in Sacred Heart and that I worked at the Queen's and for Mrs Margolis. He knows that I live with my sister, Mrs Rose de Gouveia, in Observatory Estate. I know he lives in Elands Bay and that he owns three fleets of fishing boats and has interests in a fish-canning factory.

I talk out of my turn and say what the da Costas say behind his back, which is that when the government changes and coloured people can own their own businesses and all his under-the-counter interests come to light people will see that he's a very rich man.

'Is that what's important to you?' he says. 'What you hear about me being rich?'

I would like to think that he knew enough about me to know that 'rich' isn't important to me. In fact, if I hadn't offended him, I would have liked to ask him if he could perhaps tell me exactly what being 'rich' is. For some people being rich is having a piece of bread and a bowl of soup for their supper. For someone else it may be to have a person who is truly their own, like the way I felt about Rose and why I clung on to her the way I did when we were in Sacred Heart. Maybe for him it's having three fishing fleets and an interest in a canning factory and goodness knows how many other businesses to do with fish.

If I was a person of words I could tell him that for me, being rich is sitting on a wall in the sunshine, taking your lunchtime sandwich out of a brown paper packet and knowing that an important man like him is going to come looking for you.

He says he likes me because I'm a good listener and a person who doesn't ask too many questions and I could say the same about him. I could also say that I like him because of his being such a big man. People would think twice about calling out to a girl or teasing her or making remarks when she's in the company of such a big man. I don't mind how he looks. He's not film star material but what would I care about that? When you spend time with another person you don't see them the same way the rest of the world sees them. You see them with your heart, not just with your eyes. I can't speak for Jack Julies but I know what I see when I look at him because this is not the first time this has happened to me but this is another time and another man.

* * *

'My sister and men,' Rose says but she never really did understand how it was between Mr Silver and me and she certainly doesn't understand about Jack Julies. Rose was the one who wanted to be an old man's darling and stand in the centre of someone's world and have her own house to do what she liked in and whatever she did would be right. I'm not like that and I'm sorry now that I told Rose what the da Costas said about Jack Julies being king of West Coast fishing and a man with plenty of money in his pocket. If a person has money, Rose is the kind of person who likes to see it, especially as far as I'm concerned.

'Don't give yourself away cheap, Ruby,' she says.

I tell her that I'm not 'giving myself away' at all and that I haven't been asked to but she doesn't want to listen.

'A man would have to go a very long way to find a woman like you.'

It's a surprise to me, hearing this coming out of my sister's mouth, and it's funny. How 'hard to get' can I be if all it took for Jack Julies to find me was to come up to the wall where I was sitting eating my sandwich?

'What are you looking at?' Rose says. 'If you weren't so hard to get to know and if you didn't put people off you the way you do, you could have had men queuing up for you.'

'What's this all about?' I say and she says it's nothing, just something she's wanted to say for a long time, only she's never said it before because all these years I've never really had a man interested in me.

She forgets or maybe she never really knew but I remember.

'And he'd better be good to you,' Rose says. 'Otherwise he'll have to answer to me.'

'What is it?' I say, acting as if I'm cross and running out of patience.

'I don't always say so,' she says, and tears come into her eyes and spill down her face, 'but I just want so much for you.'

I look at my sister and think that she may just as well stop crying. I know that she loves me and wants only the best for me. I don't need to see her tears to know that.

Jack Julies sees me Friday lunchtime in Pescanova's car park and on Saturdays he drives through from Elands Bay and visits me at my sister's house and I make lunch and we talk.

'Granny and Grandpa,' Rose says. 'You're like an old married couple who've been together for twenty-five years. He's got the money, ask him to show you the bright lights.'

I could have told her if I wanted to that Jack Julies has seen enough of the kind of 'bright lights' Rose is talking about to last him the rest of his life. At one time he took to drinking in a big way and then one day there was a terrible fight and something really bad happened that made him put it to one side and he's never touched a drop again. He won't tell me what and I don't want to know. He's known a lot of women, good ones and bad, and he hasn't always been good to them. He's been known to raise his hand to a woman but he would never do that to me. He's told me all these things because he says he wants everything straight between us and I've listened and I believe him.

'I am not what you would call a good Christian man,' he says. 'There are enough people who'll be happy to tell you that about me but I'll be happy to tell you myself. So listen carefully. I'm not a good Christian man. I say so myself, so when other people tell you, you ought to listen to them.'

There are some things about me that Jack Julies knows but I see that there is one big thing that he still has to learn, which is that I prefer to make up my own mind about people, and I already have my own thoughts about him.

Jack Julies hasn't taken to Rose. He's too big for her house and her house is too full of Rose and too untidy for him to be comfortable there.

In Rose's house you always have to clear a place before you can sit down. I don't know where half the things come from and every time I look there seem to be more. Every second thing she sees, she buys and takes home and she can never throw anything away. Alf never cleared out any of his late mother's things when she passed away and when Rose moved in she left things just as they were and added things of her own.

'You don't need all these things,' I said the first time I came to the house. 'We can pack them in boxes and put them in Alf's taxi and take them down to the Parade and you can sell them one price for the lot.'

'It's nice for Alf to have his mother's things,' Rose said. 'I don't mind and I'd never take it on myself just to throw them out as if they were rubbish.'

To most people this is exactly what they would be, but if Rose sees it differently it's not up to me to say, though there's one thing I do know. You can't keep such a place properly clean. There are old copies of *People* magazine piled up everywhere because Rose hasn't got the heart to throw them away. There are bits of material, all colours, just what takes Rose's fancy down at the remnant stalls, thrown over late Mrs de Gouveia's three-piece floral lounge suite because Rose says it's still good enough to use.

I've given up for myself but all the same I'm really sorry when the time comes to take Jack Julies to my sister's house where he can see for himself how she lives. We weren't brought up like this. In our mother's house there was a place for everything and everything in its place. You could smell the clean when you stepped through the front door but I'm sorry to say you can't say the same for my sister.

'Take him to your room then,' Rose says. 'You needn't look at me like that. We all know you don't have men into your bedroom but if the rest of the house doesn't suit you, what are you going to do? Entertain him outside in the street?'

Rose likes to make jokes about the room that I have at the back of the house, out of everyone's way.

'She should charge people to go in and see how tidy she is.' She always tells people that. 'Show them, Ruby,' she says. 'Let them see for themselves that I'm not making it up.'

I can shrug it off and say Rose likes to make a lot out of a little. I like things neat and tidy, I'm not going to apologize for that. I put things away and I tidy up after myself and I like everything in its place and the place must always be the same place and I like everything to be spotless because that's how I am.

I have two easy chairs and a table with an embroidered cloth over it in my room. I have a cupboard with a photo of Rose and me on her wedding day, framed, on top of it. There's the old photograph of us with our Steenbras Street so-called family and the little shepherd and his shepherdess friend that I got for a remembrance of Mrs Margolis and I still wash them and dry them and I take special care of them just like I always did.

Rose wanted me to put at least one of them in the lounge with her ornaments instead of stuck away where no one could see them, but I said no because they're a pair and should stay together. Also because neither of them would last five minutes in Rose's house.

I thought it would be funny spending Saturday with Jack Julies just the two of us in my room, but it isn't funny, it's nice and I like him being there even if he's too big in such a small room, which is always the case with him. I like it because my room is out of the way of the front of the house and we can be quiet there and just in case Rose gets any ideas I always make sure that the door stays wide open.

You can get used to things and I can get used to these

Saturdays and Jack Julies visiting me this way. Alf works most Saturdays and Rose does karaoke or plays cards at the Portuguese Community Hall and we are just we two and the house is very quiet and we can sit quietly together and talk.

I was sad about my sister when I brought Jack Julies to the house for the first time and she drew away from him because of his being so big and his looks. It's not something I will easily talk about but one day I would like to say it because I think that he would like to hear that you get used to his looks very quickly and he has a nice voice. It's a very soft voice for such a big man and his laugh is a nice surprise, I suppose because we have to get to know each other better and be comfortable before we get to the laughing stage and that takes time, but when it happens it's nice. It's my same feeling I used to have when I took a deep breath and held it for as long as I could and then let it all out, just for the pleasure of feeling the weight of the world roll off my shoulders. It's a strange and new feeling for me to have a friend who comes to look for me because I'm a person he would want to be with. I think that as long as Jack Julies is with me no one will come near me, nothing can hurt me and I will be safe.

My sister says that I'm a very peculiar woman and that if this is a courtship then it's the funniest courtship she's ever seen. She asks me what Jack Julies gives me and it's not a question I could ever answer in a way she would understand. I don't want to speak badly of Rose but Rose knows about taking. She takes everything anyone will give her. Whenever Alf walks through the door there's always a present for Rose and she expects it.

'I know you've got something for me,' she says. 'What is it?'

It's a game to them and there's always a chocolate or another stuffed toy, as if she's not far too old for them and doesn't have far too many already. It's easy to buy presents for Rose because Rose likes everything. Alf buys her cheap beads from the street vendors and takeaway chips from the fish shop on the way home even though he knows that Rose has already eaten and she eats far too much anyway.

'How do you expect me to say no?' she says. 'After all, they're a present.'

Rose is like a little girl the way she wants things and gets so excited with every new thing for a whole ten minutes, then puts it away because she's already bored with it and waiting for the next thing. Alf thinks it's wonderful and I think he should put a stop to it but I know he won't, and she's an old man's darling like she said she wanted to be and she's happy, but I'm not like that and it's not a life that would suit me.

'You can spend the rest of your life sitting Saturdays having nice little talks in a back room in Observatory,' she says. 'Some time you have to move on. You know that and he knows that and you've made it plain enough that it's none of my business but if I were you I'd say that Saturday's all well and good but now you'd like to know what he does with the rest of the week.'

I like Saturdays and I like my life how it is now with

Jack Julies in it. I'm happy not to talk about the rest of the week because I've learned a hard lesson and it's that you may just as well be happy with what life's seen fit to give you. If you ask for more you could find that you end up being given nothing at all, which would take you right back where you started, and if there's one thing I don't want, I don't want that.

People don't really know what Jack Julies is like but I do because he's like me. He spends his whole life wanting to see what trick life has up its sleeve for him and wondering if he'll be strong enough just to get from one end of it to the other whatever it is, and I understand that. There's something else I can say too and I am not ashamed to say it. Many bad things have happened to Jack Julies in his life but I am not one of them.

I had all sorts of stories ready about why I was asking him if he didn't mind if we did our visiting in my room at the back of the house but when the time came I didn't need any of them.

'I like it here,' he says.

'So do I,' I say. 'I'm sorry to say that my sister's not a very good housekeeper.'

'No, she's not,' he says and he says it for a fact, like it is, and it's funny for both of us and no one's hurt because there's no one there to hear it and it puts us on the same side of the fence.

Jack Julies says that since he's met me he lives from Saturday to Saturday. He thinks about it all week while he's working his man's life down on the West Coast and in Elands Bay.

'If the sea's what you choose, then you have to give everything to the sea,' he says. 'It makes you tough though, I can tell you that. That's how it is, how it's been with my life.'

He drinks tea out of my teacups, not my sister's. The teacups that I bought and put aside as the first thing I would have if I ever had a home of my own, and they look very small in his hands.

'What about you, Ruby?' he says.

'Nothing,' I say.

Sacred Heart, the Queen's, Pescanova Fisheries. He knows all those things and it's a very small life when you put it down like that and I would rather listen to him and he tells me that one of the reasons he likes me is because I'm such a good listener.

'A good girl,' he says. That's what he thought when he first saw me at the Pescanova offices. 'And a lady, not like the others.'

I don't know who 'the others' are and I don't ask. Jack Julies is older than I am, he's a man and men will be what they are. When you meet a man like him you expect that he'd have some hard living behind him and it's where he is now, at my sister's house every Saturday, that's important to me.

He likes a woman who lives quietly and keeps herself to herself. He's not interested in girls who are too painted up and have too many opinions that they like to express. He's not interested in people who only want dances and parties and having a good time. He wouldn't want a woman who made herself cheap and flaunted herself in front of other men and he wouldn't want a woman who drank.

'You know what I mean?' he says and I say I do but I'm not really sure I do. I've seen a few things in my life down at the Queen's but I think when he talks to me, the way he looks at me with his green eyes, that he's seen a great many more things than I have.

He's nice the way he touches things. He picks up the little shepherd and the shepherdess but he's careful and he must think they're funny because they make him smile and I ask him what it is that he finds to smile about when he looks at them.

'They're just the kind of thing I'd imagine you'd have,' he says. Then he points to Clarence-next-door's photograph of us taken in Steenbras Street and asks if that's my family and I say yes and he looks away from the picture and he doesn't ask any questions.

What I like about him is that he's always the same. He never seems to feel the heat or the cold. Once he's in the house and we're settled he always sits in his same chair and he takes off his sports coat and rolls up his shirt-sleeves and he has a tattoo of an anchor in blue on his arm.

I would like to touch it. I think he knows that and I think he knows how much.

'I'm not the right kind of man for you,' he says.

He says it more than once but every Friday he comes to Pescanova and looks at me eating my lunch out of the brown paper bag and every Saturday he's back and I'm neat and tidy in my best clothes waiting.

I shouldn't have told Rose what he said about not being a good Christian man but I did because I wanted to talk about him and when the words came out that was all I could think of to say.

'I could have told you that,' Rose says, 'and saved him the trouble and if that's the case, what is it he's looking for here?'

I should have kept my mouth shut and I have my own idea why Jack Julies comes here the way he does, sitting in the back room of my sister's house, drinking tea out of my small cups, touching my things, looking at me.

I have an idea about his hard life and his three fleets of boats being battered by the sea and the men who go out in them who look up to him. You can't work in a place like Pescanova Fisheries and not know about fishermen's lives and how it goes with them when the fish are running and how it goes with them when they're not.

I think that if I told Jack Julies about my life growing up in Sacred Heart, brought up by the nuns, to him it would be like it is for Rose and the people she reads about in *People* magazine. You can see all the pictures and know all the facts but even so you can't really imagine it because it's too different.

I think Jack Julies knows things that can't be spoken in a convent girl's bedroom at the back of her sister's house. We talk nicely to each other but it isn't what we say that counts and I have never been one who minds what passes between people in silence but I have looked in the silence and I can't find Jack Julies. He's too far away from me and my life is too different from his but his Saturday visits have made me brave and so I ask him.

'What do you want to know?' he says.

We're sitting in the back room like we always are and he's sitting in his chair and I'm sitting in mine. Through the open door is the kitchen and it has a back door out on to the yard and beyond the kitchen is the rest of the house and there's nobody here, except us.

'I grew up poor,' he says. 'It's not a new story. My father drank, my mother had too many children and sometimes there wasn't enough to eat and very often there was the back of the hand or the strap. Nothing new, I told you. You ask about me and there's nothing to say.'

I won't accept that because that's not all of it and we've come a little distance together, he and I, and he must let me in now or keep me out altogether and he knows it and I know it too. It's there in the air between us and it's hard because he's not a man that words come to easily.

'All right,' he says and he bends and takes off his shoes and because he's big he moves slowly, unlacing, loosening and then easing his foot out, and he's neat like me. He puts his shoes down by the side of the chair and then one by one he takes off his socks and rolls them into a ball and puts them in the heel of his left shoe, which is closest to him, and they are like giant's shoes. I could put my foot in one and it would be swallowed up and gone.

'Come, kneel down in front of me,' he says and I go and that's how we are with me on my knees in front of him and him sitting in the chair.

I can feel the ground under my knees. I close my eyes.

I am kneeling at the communion rail, blood of Christ, body of Christ. You can push Christ out of your life and close him out of your heart and you can turn your back on God but you have to be careful because they always come back for you. They come when it pleases them, when you least expect it and you're not the one who chooses the time or the place.

Godfrey's with me. He's so close to me, I can feel him.

'I can make you laugh, Ruby. If you look at me, you'll laugh, just see if you don't.'

I don't want to laugh. I feel filled up with something and what I'm filled up with isn't laughter.

'See this,' Jack Julies says and he pulls up his trouser leg, right side, and he pulls it up slow and neat and holds it so that I can see his ankle. His ankle's big. My hands, thumbs together one side, forefingers together on the other, could make a band around it and some time it must have been terribly wounded because it's dreadfully scarred.

I reach out my two fingers and lay them down on the wound. The flesh is raw-looking and red and ugly. It looks like something you would turn your head away from if you saw it in a butcher's shop. I think that some time he must have had a terrible accident or that something must have gnawed away at his leg right down to the bone and I look up at him and he looks down at me.

'When I was a boy,' he says, 'my father sold me to a farmer for wine money. I was ten, eleven years old and a big boy for my age and I could work even then. I hated my father but I couldn't stay where I was taken, I hated what happened to me there, I wanted to get away . . .'

. . . and so they tied him to a stake with a rope as if he was a dog and he pulled and chafed against it, like an animal in a trap, and it was his will against theirs until in the end they let him go because his will was stronger and he just wasn't worth all that trouble.

It's done now between us and I have stood in this place before in another room with another man in another time and I was different then.

He bends down and takes my face between his two hands.

'I'm not the man for you,' he says. His face is so close to mine that I can feel his breath. I look up at him into his eyes and I think that I should be the one to decide that and I stand up in front of him and look down and there's something I want to do.

I'm glad it's Saturday and my sister's house is empty. I go into the kitchen and run warm water into the first bowl I lay my hands on. It's one of Rose's 'finds', an old enamel bowl no one else would want even if you tried to give it away. It has green edges and a decoration of brown autumn leaves and somewhere in another room is a water jug that goes with it.

I take a cake of Sunlight soap and a clean towel from my own laundry and I go back into my room carrying the bowl and my towel and I close the door behind me.

'Like this,' I say and I kneel down again and put the bowl down beside me. I take his bare foot and lift it and set it down into the warm water and I wipe around the scar and it is truly horrible and I touch it lightly with my fingers. I let the soap slide across my hand and then I put it down next to me on the floor and put my soapy hands on his leg. I see the water flow against the scars in that part where they're deepest, where they bite hard down towards the bone. When I look up his head is bent down as if he's ashamed and then he lifts his head and he looks at me and although I've been there every Saturday for all the time he's been coming here it's as though he sees me for the first time. He takes his foot out of the bowl and sets it down on the cloth that I've laid out for him and I move the bowl aside. He holds his hands out and I am on my knees in front of him with my head cupped in his hands.

He says again that he's not the man for me and I say that I'm the one who'll decide that. I'm a grown woman now and I've fully found myself and our Saturdays will be different from now on.

'You better not go near Auntie Olive,' Rose says and I know what she means. My bloom has gone but I don't discuss this with my sister and Rose knows something that I knew before her. She's the person I've travelled longest with, the person most dear to me, but she can't be fully a part of my life like she once was and I think she knows that.

Things are changed but our arrangement stands and I don't ask Jack Julies things. When he's ready and has something to say to me, he'll tell me then. Then and not a minute before then, and I can wait.

QUEEN OF THE WEST COAST

'I suppose you'll be moving out one of these days,' Rose
says.

'Why should I do that?' I say as if I don't know what
she's talking about.

'You know what I mean,' she says. 'I think there are a
few questions that you should be asking Mr Jack Julies.'

She says she wants to show me something and she takes
my arm and turns me round and shows me behind the
kitchen door.

'This is a calendar,' she says. 'Go on, I want you to have
a good look so I can be quite sure you know what I'm
talking about.'

'So?' I say and she runs her finger along one line.

'That is a week,' she says. 'It has seven days. If you
don't believe me count them for yourself and then go and

297

ask your friend Mr Jack Julies what exactly it is that's happened to the other six and a half days. Because if you aren't interested, I am.'

I want to tell her the kind of man he is and the kind of life he's had and how he'll do things in his own way and in his own time. I'd like to tell her that there are a lot of things not said between us but understood by both of us just the same, but I can see that this isn't what she wants to hear.

'You need a proper life, Ruby,' she says.

'I have a proper life,' I say.

'No, you don't,' she says. 'And, if you ask me, it's up to you to do something about it.'

'You sound just like Auntie Olive,' I say, trying to make a joke of it, but Rose isn't in a mood for jokes.

'What do you think people are saying now?' she says.

'I really wouldn't know,' I say. 'I suppose they're saying that I have a gentleman friend to tea on Saturday and it's hardly likely that will cause the end of the world.'

'Now I'm going to sound exactly like Auntie Olive,' Rose says and she doesn't mean it in a funny way. 'You know what she'd say. I don't even have to tell you. She's say, "Tea? Is that what they're calling it these days? Well, I suppose that's as good a name for it as any." '

I don't like what my sister's saying to me and more than that, I don't like that there's nothing I can say back to her to put her in her place. I'm the eldest and I know exactly what she means and I'm angry and I'm ashamed. I'm angry because she's talking about something private that means much more to me than she knows, something that she knows nothing about, that's not hers to have an opinion about, and I'm ashamed because she's right and even more ashamed because there's nothing I can do about it.

'Do something about it,' Rose says as if she's reading my mind. 'If you don't, it could go on like this for years.'

She's right and I know it but I'm like I always am and afraid of change but I have seen something now and it has made me think differently. I think that I can make another person happy. Jack Julies may not be the easiest man in the world but life has taken a hand in making him the way he is and what life can do in one way it can do in another.

I have never been to Elands Bay on the West Coast. I don't know as much as Jack Julies does about fishing and fishermen but I do know that a boat can come into harbour and be safe. At least I know that much because that's how I've been feeling lately on Saturday afternoons in the back room at my sister's house and I believe that Jack Julies feels it too.

'Soon, Ruby,' Rose says. 'Because every Saturday his car stands outside our gate you lose a little bit more of your good name. If it stands there much longer you'll have no good name left and what you'll have in its place is a reputation, that's what, but if that's how you want to live your life, who am I to stand in your way?'

Rose can be cruel when she wants to because in her heart she must know that it's not like that. I'd hoped that in her heart she'd be glad for me that I'd found someone of my own at last.

'I am glad for you,' she says. 'But I never wanted it like this and not in our house and not under our roof. How do you think it looks for Alf and me?'

I'm red to the roots of my hair I'm so ashamed of how she sees me.

'I'm sorry,' she says. 'I'm sorry and I know you don't mean it, but all the same it has to be said and you know that as well as I do.'

I do know it and I promise my sister that I will do something about it but it isn't as easy as that. Jack Julies isn't a man you can push and he's not an easy man to approach and then, all of a sudden, like sometimes happens, life takes a turn again and the matter is out of my hands. Now I have no choice but to speak to him and it isn't going to be the easiest thing I've ever had to do and funnily enough I think of Mrs Margolis. At least there's one thing that no one will ever be able to say about Jack Julies and me, and that is that ours was a union not blessed with children.

I wait until after because I'm a coward. He's always closest and nicest to me then and I like 'after' best. I like the big bones in his body. I like the feel of his skin and I like the strong way his heart beats. You would think that 'after' you could tell him anything and it would be all right but you can never be sure and in the end it's not so hard to tell as I thought because I just tell facts. Facts only, that's what I tell myself, and if that's the best way for me to manage what has happened, then I think it may be the best way for him too.

I look at myself in the mirror and I look the same. I put my hand over my stomach and it's the same but soon it's going to start changing. Those are the facts and all I can do is tell them to him. I am too afraid to think about what we've done, starting a new life the way we have. I didn't think such a big thing could happen so easily. I know what Rose would say if she knew. She'd say that I have been so stupid that all she can think is that I wasn't thinking at all.

'Is this what you want?' he says when I tell him and I say I don't know.

I could say that it is what I want but I didn't want it this way and I could go further. I could say that he's what I want but not in this way either.

I can see it's not what he expected but he's a man and maybe men think differently about such things. It's not a man's body that is offered a gift such as this and I'm busy with facts but my heart sings another song. I ask myself a question about the new life starting in me and my cup is full because the question I ask is if God would give such gifts to someone that He's turned His face from?

'Is it what you want?' Jack Julies says again and I tell him quite sharp that he's already asked me that and it comes as a surprise to both of us because I don't usually talk to him as if we are equals.

'You never answered,' he says.

'I think it's your turn,' I say and that's another surprise. He sits up in bed and pulls the pillows up behind him and I move myself around so that I can sit sideways with my back to the wall. I keep the sheet and a bit of the blanket up over myself because even though my bloom is well and truly gone, I'm still not a woman who likes too much of her body to show. I sit with my back against the wall and my shoulders hunched because the wall is cold after the hot bed and I sit so that I can see his face.

It isn't something he expected. I can see that. It isn't something I expected either and I can just imagine, if Rose knew, what fools she'd think we both are and where did we think babies get started in the first place?

I think he'll say that he thought I'd 'looked after it' and I surprise myself again because if he does say that I'm going to say that in case he hasn't noticed we are two of us involved. He could just as easily have 'looked after it' as me. Why didn't he raise the subject after that first time? We would have been all right after the first time. It wasn't the first time that it happened.

I'm not his first woman, he's made no bones about that, but he's the first man for me and he knows it. I didn't have time to think too much about precautions. I never knew a baby could be in such a hurry to come into the world. I never knew, after the first time, if he'd ever want to be with me again. I thought I'd disappointed him and that he'd think I'd turned out just the same as all the rest. If Rose knew she'd have said that now he'd got what he came for, we wouldn't be seeing him again in a hurry, but she would be wrong because if that's what he came for he keeps coming back for more and that gives me courage. There's not very much I can do now except wait and when he's ready he says what he has to say.

'I don't mind,' he says. 'It wasn't exactly what I bargained on but it's all right.' He looks at me and it's a nice look. 'You're a good girl,' he says. 'I know a good girl when I see one. You'll be a good mother.'

For the first time I feel that it's going to be all right and I can exhale and he smiles and then he laughs and it's unusual for him.

'Caught out at my age,' he says, shaking his head, and he seems to think it's funny because he laughs again. 'If someone had told me I wouldn't have believed it. If it was any other woman but you I wouldn't have believed it either.'

I'm not 'any other woman'. I'm me and I don't see what 'any other woman' has to do with us or with this.

'It's fine with me,' he says. 'But this isn't my first child, you know, I've been here before.'

I didn't know.

'What do you think?' he says. 'My first was when I was seventeen and there have been a few more since then. What did you think, Ruby?' he says, looking at me. 'I'm a man. I'm forty-five years old. You must have some idea what kind of life I've had. You're the one who grew up with the nuns, not me.'

'Don't look like that,' he says. 'I said I'd take care of you and I will.'

It comes to me, sitting where I am, a stranger in my own bed with my back against the wall, that he's already 'taken care of me' but not in the way he means. I've waited and waited and I thought he would say certain things that I see now I had no right to expect. I know that he's a hard man and peculiar but I know another side of him too. We've had our moments, like men and women do, and he knows I know that other, softer side of him as well because that's the side he's always shown me and at least he has the decency to turn his head away when next he speaks.

'Look, Ruby,' he says. 'I never said but you never asked and as far as that goes, I think that you should blame yourself, not me. You were never full of questions like most women are, not even when we got to know each other better.'

I'm not 'most women'. He's told me that often enough and he's right. I think I must be stupider than most women are. My sister has tried to tell me that often enough and I see now that I should have listened to her.

As far as Jack Julies is concerned I can have 'my' baby and I'll be 'looked after' and I've been stupid but other women, I'm sure, have been stupid in this way before me. I don't even ask if there's a Mrs Jack Julies because of course there will be and I think about how big a fool I've been. Then I think something else and I don't know how anything can be funny at a time like this but this is.

Next time my sister asks me I'll know what to tell her. Now, at least I know what Mr Jack Julies does on those other six and a half days of the week.

THE INVISIBLE WOMAN

My baby died. It came away and there was nothing I could do to stop it happening.

'How could you have let such a thing happen in the first place?' Rose says. 'He's never going to marry you. If you'd asked me I could have told you at least that much.'

If I'd wanted to be told I probably would have asked. It's much easier to let your sister break your world apart than to do it yourself. That way, at least you have someone else to blame for it.

Boy or girl, what would they prefer? Some people have the luxury of wishing. As for me, I will take whatever God sees fit to give me and be grateful for the rest of my life. People have dreams for their unborn children but I have always been afraid of dreams and so I hide in facts. At least you can depend on facts because they never change. Mothers wonder what the child inside them will look like but I can't do that. If I could see a face I think my heart would burst right open.

'Did you think that you could manage on your own?' Rose wants to know but I know I wouldn't have been on my own because Rose would always be there.

'What on earth got into you?' she says again. 'What could you have been thinking of?'

I thought that God had taken me back. I thought that He must have seen how things had been with me over these years. I thought that in His great mercy He'd chosen to shine the light of His countenance upon me and give me that thing I wanted most, someone I could give my love to who would love me in return, but that wasn't the way it turned out.

'It was early days,' Rose says, as if that makes a difference. 'They couldn't even have said whether it was a boy or girl. I asked because I knew you'd want to know.'

I lie on a hospital bed between clean sheets and wonder where this different kind of pain has come from and where it has been hiding while it's waited for me all these years.

The doctors say I'm young and healthy and when I'm ready I can try again but they don't know me and I know differently. I think that this small spark of life that could have been mine lost faith and left me; the power of my love wasn't strong enough to keep it safe.

'Perhaps it's better this way after all,' Rose says and puts her arms around me. 'It's all right to cry,' she says but I am in that place beyond tears and I know it because I have been there before.

I haven't been to Pinelands for a long time but here I am, no one's wife and no one's mother, on the train and back to my old ways before I met Jack Julies. There's no 'Whites Only' any more, you can sit where you like. It's Sunday and Rose is at a Portuguese-style lunch, fish and flame-grilled chicken and fried potato, down at the Portuguese Community Hall. Everyone has cars these days and people don't eat at home any more; they go out to lunch. Churches are empty and burger palaces are full and the Pinelands train that goes on to Bellville is empty but not as empty as I am inside.

I think about the Fredericks family. I think about myself at the lunch table, last Sunday of the month every month of my childhood, and Uncle Bertie looking at Godfrey with so much love in his face and me thinking that there was something wrong with me. I can see them all, Auntie Olive and Uncle Bertie and Godfrey and Patsy. I can see Rose with her sulky face because she didn't want to be there. I can even see the Sunday chicken on the table and Auntie Olive who offered mashed potato one week and roast potato the next and I wonder, if I can see it all so clearly, why it is that no one can see me? I think that perhaps I am invisible. I'm looking at Uncle Bertie, wondering at the radiance of so much love that comes out of him when he looks at Godfrey. I am so empty inside with wanting someone to notice me and love me like that that I look away because it's just too hard to bear. That was emptiness. That was what I thought then, but I see now that I knew nothing about emptiness at all until I came to this new place.

I remember how Uncle Bertie used to show off about Godfrey. 'He's got a wonderful right boot.' 'Fast as lightning.' 'Lots of friends, hardly got any time to spare for his family but that's all right.'

It's quiet here like it always is. The old part's just the same and when you reach the place you want to be they are still there like they always are, as if they have been patiently waiting for you to remember and come back. Shirley and Susannah are still there and they're the same but I am different. I'm not the same young woman who's stood here before.

I haven't thought about Mr Silver for a long time but even so he's never left me. Whenever I came here before I would come and go very quickly, as if I had no right at all. I never knew them and I never knew all the people that they knew in their lives. I only went because I was someone who knew what happened and remembered. Today I stand for a long time and anyone may go anywhere they please these days. I don't care who sees me, a woman in a place I don't belong. Today I remember them, a woman and a girl I never knew, but there's something else today and I am closer to them than I once was. I don't have to explain anything to anyone any more. I have a right to be here now and I have earned it because since the last time I came this way I too have lost someone.

MY SISTER RUBY ON HER TWENTY-NINTH BIRTHDAY

'I'm not in the mood,' Ruby said.

'Make yourself in the mood then,' I said.

'You go,' she said.

'I'd look a big fool sitting there by myself,' I said. 'After all, it's not my birthday.'

I was sad, sadder than I could say about Ruby's baby. I sometimes think now that we are four of us in our house, Alf and me and Ruby and the baby-that-might-have-been that seems so close to us and blames us that it wasn't welcomed in the way it should have been.

I don't know what Ruby feels in her heart. Perhaps she feels that this is one more thing that's been taken from her just to put her in her place, but that's not how I feel. If there's one thing I've learned so far it's that life goes on whether you want it to or not. We still go on doing the things we do every day and from time to time we still have our treats.

Ruby opened her mouth to say something but I held up my hand to show her that whatever it was she wanted to say I didn't want to hear it.

It wasn't as if I was planning to take over the community hall and ask the whole neighbourhood to join us for food and music and dancing with a firework display to follow.

'All I'm asking for is for you to sit down and have a cup of tea with your own sister on the occasion of your twenty-ninth birthday. Now tell me, is that too much to ask?'

When you roped Ruby into doing something she didn't really want to do, she always went very quiet. That's one thing and the other is that she always liked to be prepared for things, she never liked surprises, so when Alf drove us through the pillars and into the driveway of the Mount Nelson Hotel in his taxi, the inside of the car was dead quiet. The only thing you could hear was my heart beating.

I couldn't bring myself to turn sideways and look at Alf's face but I knew he was looking right in front of him because he couldn't bring himself to look in the rear-view mirror at Ruby, who was sitting in the back seat.

'I thought you said tea?' Ruby said, and I felt like I used to feel when I was a little girl and Ruby caught me out doing something that I shouldn't be doing, but what I was doing that day wasn't something I shouldn't be doing. It was something I should have done a long time ago.

The Mount Nelson Hotel is probably the grandest place in all of Cape Town. It's rose-coloured and there are big white pillars in front of it and a long avenue of palm trees. Table Mountain is big behind it and it looks so close you would think you could reach out your hand and touch it.

When we were at Sacred Heart a big thing was made out of treats. Ruby always looked forward to those treats and when they were disasters she put them behind her and didn't talk about them again. The truth is that Ruby didn't really know what a proper treat was. I didn't myself until I met Alf.

I put my hand on Alf's arm very quiet and nice and asked him if he could just for a minute pull the taxi to one side and switch off the engine and he did, and I turned round in my seat and looked at Ruby.

'Tell me,' I said to her, 'what do you see?'

'Don't be foolish,' she said and her face had gone just as bright a pink as the building. I knew that there were things she wanted to say to me that she'd say if we were alone but she'd never say them with Alf sitting there behind the wheel. Not even if all she could see of him was the back of his head and his eyes in the rear-view mirror.

'Did you see any lions or tigers hiding behind the bushes in the garden?' I asked. 'Did you see the police waiting to jump out and tell us that we aren't allowed here and turn us away?'

I saw myself, a child again, on those long walks from

Sacred Heart into town on our way to last Sundays with
Auntie Olive, but that was a long time ago. Things had
happened to both of us. Life had happened to both of us
and neither of us was a child any more.

'I'm taking you to tea, Ruby,' I said. I'd made up my
mind. I can't live with such sadness and the ghost of a
dead baby who, for all I know, was never destined to come
into the world in the first place, and it wasn't me who
thought about tea, it was Alf who suggested it.

I'd asked him what I should do and he said to take
Ruby out somewhere really smart for a nice cup of tea so
she could feel a bit of life around her again. Tea, after all,
is about the everyday things that remind us that life
always goes on whether we like it or not. Tea was just
exactly the thing that Ruby needed right that minute.

I wasn't going to have a sister who said no to tea and
would rather keep herself locked up in the back bedroom
with her heart breaking from wishing that her life had
turned out differently. Not in my house, not while she
still had Alf and me.

I think that's what gave me courage to talk to Ruby
how I did because no one in this world was sorrier for
what had happened to her than I was.

'Whether you like it or not, we're going to enjoy ourselves, and I for one am going to have a plate of
sandwiches and a slice of cake and maybe a scone with
jam.'

I turned round in my seat and gave Ruby a look. 'And
you better have something too. There's no share or eat off
your sister's plate here. They don't give this tea away for

nothing, you know, and you can eat as much as you like.'

The inside of the car was full of my voice. 'And you're going to sit in a chair like a lady today and be waited on hand and foot, and while that's happening you're to start thinking about going forward instead of always stopping to look back.'

There was a very big quiet inside the car that seemed to go on for a long time and I thought that maybe I'd said too much.

'Is that what you call a birthday treat?' Ruby said, and I said it was and that she'd be very brave if she then told me what I could do with my treat and asked Alf please to turn the car around so that we could go home, but she didn't say that.

'If this is the treat, I suppose we better have it and get it over with,' she said, taking a breath and sitting up very straight with her back not even touching the back of the seat and her handbag held in both hands in her lap.

'I just hope you're not planning to eat your way right through the menu in front of strange people,' she said, as if what's happening is nothing that special. 'Because if you do, I'll die of shame right there at the tea table.'

That was my sister, the same sister I knew, the sister I'd always known, and I knew that she was going to pick up her life again and make the best she could of it. I knew that after everything that had happened it was going to be all right.

'If you don't mind,' she said, 'could you ask your husband to take us right up to the front door? Unless you want us to get out and walk from here, that is.'

When Ruby and I were in the middle of a difference, Alf was always 'my husband', as if he was someone we hardly knew and we were just the two of us again.

'Don't just jump out of the car when we get there,' I said, because I was grown-up too by then and knew how things ought to be done. 'Let Alf stop right in front of the door and he'll get out of the car and open the door for me and then for you.'

'I'm not jumping anywhere,' she said. 'And I don't need you to tell me how to get out of a taxi.'

When she stepped out of the car she stepped out like a queen and we walked past a Mount Nelson Hotel car with the name on the side. There was a chauffeur holding the door open and a very smart man getting out. Ruby never 'looked' at people, she'd rather keep her eyes on the ground, but she took a quick look at him. She looked at him as if she might know him and then she looked away and it was hard to know what she was thinking.

'I hope you'll eat like a decently brought up person and not hoover up your food like a vacuum cleaner,' she said as we went through the swing door, five star, inter-national. Ruby was ahead of me walking with a very straight back and when we came to the main lounge where tea was being served before I could even open my mouth she was the one who spoke.

'We'd like a table for two,' she said, as if she'd been coming to places like this all her life, and I nearly fell right over.

The waitress was wearing a black uniform with a white apron. There was a white waitress cap on her head. On the black lapel of her dress was a white badge with her name on it and suddenly I realized where we were and what I'd done and I took hold of Ruby's hand.

'Don't be cross with me,' I said very quietly as if the whole room was listening.

'I'm not cross,' she said, and I think that maybe then she understood why I chose this place.

We were offered seats in big velvet armchairs and the coffee table was pulled away while we settled and then put back afterwards when everyone was satisfied that we were quite comfortable and it was just about as grand as you could get.

'Thank you, Ida,' Ruby said, smiling at the waitress and looking at her badge.

'How do you know her name?' I said before I could stop myself, and Ruby was sitting very straight in her chair as if she belonged there and she looked at me and went on looking at me for what seemed like a very long time.

LIVING TO SEE CHANGE

Change has been with us for over ten years now and I did, after all, live to see it. People can live anywhere they like and I live in a house right next door to Rose. So Auntie Olive was wrong and it's a cause for celebration but at the same time it's strange to me.

'It's nice for you,' the people round here say. Nice that I can live in what used to be a whites-only neighbourhood, nice to still be among our old Portuguese neighbours who had always made Rose and me welcome even in the old days. I know that they mean well but when I think about where I'd choose to live it would always be close to my sister, wherever she might be, and there's no law that I've ever heard of that decides something like that.

Jack Julies comes on Saturdays like he always did but

this is my house, not my sister's, and what I do in my house and who comes to visit me and when is my business, not my sister's.

'After what he did to you, you should have sent for the police and had him thrown out,' Rose says. 'You should have taken a gun and shot him dead and if you wouldn't do it then maybe I should have done it for you because he deserved it.'

I would never do anything like that and nor would my sister but it makes Rose feel better to say it.

'You should phone his wife,' Rose said. 'That would put him in his place.'

Rose talks the way she does because she's my sister. What she forgets, although I keep on reminding her, is that what happened to me happened to him too. We both played our part in it and if I'd really wanted to I could have worked out for myself that there must be a wife, that there must be children.

Rose doesn't know anything about Jack Julies's life but I believe him when he tells me that he likes to be with me because I'm so neat and quiet and never ask any questions. When he tells me that he's told me things about himself that he's never told any other person, I believe that too.

I don't know how Jack Julies is for the other six and a half days of the week but when he's with me he's a gentleman and I look at him sitting big and quiet in his chair and he'd be surprised if he knew what I was think-ing. I would like to take away the bad things that happened to the boy he was and give him a better, gentler life. I know what the world sees when it looks at Jack Julies and I know what my sister sees, but he has touched me gently and I have seen the goodness inside him. I wonder what he might have been if he'd had a kinder life and then the anger comes on me again. You'd look at me and never believe that I could hold so much anger inside me but I can. I'm not God. I'm not the one who hands people their lives and watches while they make the best that they can out of them.

Even after what happened I would still open my door to Jack Julies on a Saturday. Rose calls him my 'visitor' and she doesn't mean it very nicely but that doesn't matter. She wished me a different kind of life that didn't come to pass but there are things that my sister doesn't know and after all that's passed between Jack Julies and me, he is and always will be someone very important to me because he's my friend.

'It's an old maid's house.' That's Rose's opinion. 'A place for everything and everything in its place and Ruby forever dusting.' This is what she tells people. 'I know you, Ruby,' she says. 'I'm not even out of the door before the teacups are in the sink and the pillows on the sofa are back in place.'

My sister thinks I'm so peculiar that I would sleep on the floor just so as not to disturb my bed.

'Everyone knows no one can tuck in a sheet with envelope corners the way you do, Ruby, but you don't have to do it every day. No one's coming on inspection.'

I know that but I was once a maid and a bed-maker

and I'm not a person who can easily let go of old habits. Rose has given up on me as regards tidiness and she's given up on me in the matter of Jack Julies as well. He likes me, he likes to spend time with me and he treats me with respect. There are some things we talk about and some things we don't and perhaps, after all, that's the right thing to do with such things, to leave them safe where they belong, in the silence.

THE SCANDAL

I am thirty-eight years old and not the person most likely
to cause a scandal. I've worked my way up at Pescanova
from junior filing clerk to office manager in charge of dis-
patch, delivery, accounts, petty cash and staff problems. I
have my own glass office now and from one o'clock to half
past one I close my door and open up my lunch packet
and take out my serviette and unwrap my sandwiches.
Miss Jacobs is who I am now, office manager and the da
Costa brothers' right hand. You have to watch your p's
and q's around Miss Jacobs. As far as the people who work
here are concerned, this is the only life I have. No one
knows anything about me outside my half-past-eight to
half-past-four work life, and that's how it should be when
you're in charge and responsible.

Rose says that one day they'll put up a statue in my

honour in the courtyard outside the Pescanova building and call it Our Lady of Perpetual Everything in Its Place and she can joke about it as much as she likes, I'll still go on being how I am. I like arrangements and once an arrangement's been made I like it to be quite clear that's what I expect. I don't like loafing or chatting and I don't like excuses. On the da Costa brothers' side, if they want something done quickly and properly they 'give it to Ruby', and that's how I got to rise up and be where I am.

'And where exactly is that?' Rose says, and although happy isn't a place I suppose I could say that I'm happy because I am. People don't have to like you when you're the office manager and I would have liked to be liked in the way that my sister is but I'm not my sister.

The staff at Pescanova see me sitting in my glass office getting on with my work or checking theirs and sometimes when I sit with my head down I can imagine what they see when they look at me. I can understand why there's no office gossip or chit-chat or lots of talking that goes suddenly quiet when the person who's being talked about comes into the room and can hear what's being said. I think that in some way I've let them down because there's nothing very interesting they can say about me. There's something I think though and it's something I haven't said to anyone, not even Rose. I'm glad that I work at Pescanova Fisheries where my mother once worked, in those days when there weren't that many people like the da Costas who were willing to take on a coloured woman.

'There's always a job for me there,' my mother used to say. 'They said so when I left and they were sorry to see me go and they meant it, so, just as soon as I feel a little bit better, I'll be going back and it'll be fine. You just see if it isn't.'

No one remembers that now but I do and I think of it. I feel as if I've stepped into my mother's shoes and am finishing the job that she had to leave through sickness and no fault of her own. I think she would have liked that and been pleased I'd done it because she wasn't a person who would ever willingly have let anyone down.

I have a small life but I can organize it how I like and it's better that way and when Jack Julies comes Saturdays we have our lunch and we talk and sometimes in the after-noon we watch television.

'You're my own sister but I don't understand you, Ruby,' Rose says and she's right, she doesn't understand me and I know her feelings, I don't need to keep hearing them over and over again.

Every Saturday evening after Jack Julies has gone home, when Rose is back from the Portuguese Community Hall I lock up my house and go over to my sister. Sometimes Alf's there and sometimes he's working and whatever way it is we'll finish the day together. We make something to eat and maybe watch the news on television or play a hand or two of cards and she doesn't ask how my day was or what I did and if she waits for me to say she'll wait a very long time. She knows I haven't had that much in my life that belonged only to me and that when I do I like to keep it to myself.

If she gives me a look as if she'd like to start something up, I give her a look back and she keeps quiet.

She used to say that she minded that Jack Julies came into her house, that she was surprised I'd allow it. She said that I'd be doing her a big favour if I asked him to park his silver Mercedes Benz round the corner where the neighbours couldn't see it.

'I don't want them to get ideas,' she says.

I suppose that if I was ever going to send Jack Julies away I would have done it after I lost my baby, but I didn't. Rose kept going to the Portuguese Community Hall on Saturdays and if Alf wasn't working he'd go along with her, so Jack Julies and I would always have the house to ourselves. But it wasn't the right thing. I never said anything but Jack Julies isn't a fool and he knew my sister and he knows what people are like and he must have thought about it like he thinks about everything and Jack Julies isn't a poor man, and that's how I got my house.

'I just hope he doesn't forget to mention it to his wife,' Rose says when I tell her about this change of arrangement. 'Because I can tell you something for nothing, if I was his wife I wouldn't be very happy about it.'

Rose doesn't understand but she doesn't have to. Some things are so deep inside a person that there's nothing in this world that will ever change them. I was a girl who wouldn't take a fifty-rand tip from a man because it was too much and because I thought that it would make things different between us and somehow make them less. Anyone with any sense would tell you it's very unlikely that a girl like this would ever grow into a woman who'd take a house from a man even if it was right next door to her sister and suited her down to the ground.

Rose may not think much of Jack Julies even though she doesn't really know him but in some ways Jack Julies knows me even better than my sister does. He knows me better than Mr Silver did in those long-ago days because he would never make me such an offer. He knows me too well for that.

'It's business,' I say. 'He's the landlord and I pay him rent.'

Every last Saturday of the month his rent money's in an envelope on the table in the hall. That's the arrangement and I don't mention it and neither does he but as he walks out the door he picks up the envelope and slides it into the inside pocket of his sports jacket.

'I wish I could make you feel different,' he says and I know he means it but that's how I am and it would take more than Jack Julies and all his good wishes to make me any different from how I am.

'In the beginning you thought he'd marry you,' Rose says. 'Don't lie and say you didn't because you did.'

I won't lie but I won't give an answer either. I look at Jack Julies and to me he's like a mountain that no one could ever bring down. He may be rough and nothing to look at if all you care to look at is on the outside. I know that he once kept things back from me. If I should ever forget, my sister will always be there and only too happy to remind me.

'A man can't forget he's got a wife and a house full of children,' she says. 'I've heard about convenient but I must say, Ruby, that's just too convenient to be true, even you must see that?'

I know that there are other things too, things that he's too ashamed to tell anyone, things that he'd never tell me. I can see it in his eyes and the way he looks sometimes when his mind's a long way away. He's a man who's done things there's no forgiveness for. You can see that in a man if you know how to look, and our lives have been very different but even so I think he'd be surprised if he knew what I thought sometimes when I look at him. It may be for different reasons but that doesn't matter. Different roads have brought us to this same place and we've found each other here. The world can see us any way it likes but we are the same, he and I. As far as grace and forgiveness is concerned, we stand on the same side.

I wear glasses for reading.

'Get contact lenses,' Rose says. I don't want contact lenses. Glasses suit me just fine. 'Granny Ruby,' Rose says. 'If you really want to be old before your time just hang a pair of glasses over your nose. I'll come with you to the optometrist,' she says. 'If you want to wear glasses, at least try on a few pairs and see if you don't change your mind to contacts. You'll see if I'm not right.'

Right or wrong, Rose will always be right and there'll never be anyone to tell her any different. The people

around her all like her far too much ever to point out that
no one in this world can ever be right all the time, not
even Mrs Rose de Gouveia, but this time she's wrong
about one thing. I will never be 'Granny Ruby'. I will
never be anyone's wife or mother or granny or aunt. I have
been a daughter, a sister, a niece and a cousin and that's
all I'm ever going to be.

No one talks about my lost baby because there's
nothing to say. I could say that my body remembers the
little time it spent with me but I'm not even sure about
that. When Rose and I were in Sacred Heart and things
were bad we used to play 'imagine' to try and make
things better. We used to try and imagine how it would
have been if things had turned out differently. I never
play 'imagine' any more. I used to but I stopped it and it
was the hardest thing I ever had to do in my life. I can't
imagine if my baby would have been a girl or boy, if it
might have looked like me or like its father. I will not
allow a face to form in my mind in case it has my
mother's eyes. I will not imagine a life outside my own
life in which I could have loved and been loved and been
happy. If I dreamed any dreams in that small dream-time
before it went along its way I don't remember them and
Rose is the only other person growing up quick behind
me that I will ever know now.

'You can, you can imagine, you just don't want to,'
Rose used to say to me when she was a little girl and she
was right then and she's right now. I can, I just don't
want to and I do it out of selfishness. I think that I can
bear many things but I don't think I could bear that.

* * *

I don't know Jack Julies's wife and as far as I know she doesn't know about me and she doesn't have to know, which is not to say that I'm not interested in what his life is like in Elands Bay. You won't believe it unless you know him like I do but if you didn't ask him out straight he'd be too shy to tell.

'Why do you want to know?' he says.

'I'm interested, that's all,' I say.

'Different,' he says but that's not an answer. 'Not like it is here with you,' he says but you can take that up in lots of ways and there are lots of things I don't push about but I push about this until one day he shows me a snap.

I don't know what I expected to see. It's just a snap like the one Clarence-next-door took of Rose and me with the Fredericks family and Jack Julies's family is just a family like any other family and he isn't in the picture. Perhaps he's the one who took the photograph. His wife is just a woman, older than I am, old enough to have had me for a daughter, a woman that I might have been if my life had been different.

There are six children, four boys and two girls, and they are just country boys and girls posing for a snap. One girl looks shy and one of the young boys is striking a cheeky pose and has a look about him as if he'll grow up to be trouble. The bigger girl is very much in the fashion and the mother has her arm round the shoulders of the youngest boy even though he's nearly as tall as she is and she holds him as if she would like to keep him back from something.

I'm glad Jack Julies doesn't do what some people do and come and stand next to me and point each one out to me and tell me their names and little stories about them because I wouldn't like that. I don't know why. I like them just where they are in that minute that the picture was taken and I see now that for all our sakes they must keep in their place and I must keep in mine.

'Before you've turned around you'll be looking middle age in the face and what will you have to show for it?'

My sister's opinion is that my youth has already gone down the drain and the rest of my life is on its way after it.

'You'll have nothing,' she says. 'But what's the point talking to you about it? You'll act like you're listening, you'll say, 'Yes, Rose,' and 'Thank you, Rose,' and then you'll go ahead and do what you've always done.'

Rose shouldn't have been quite so sure of herself because nothing stays how it is for ever and if there's anyone who should have known it, it should have been me. I'm the one who's always so quick to say that the minute you think an arrangement is well and truly in place and that nothing in this world can change it, that's when life comes along and puts you back where you belong.

I don't know what people think Jack Julies and I get up to when he comes to my house. If you listen to Rose you'd think I do those kinds of things women do who step out with another woman's husband looking for nothing but good times, draped in diamonds and rubies paid for with his money.

I was never a person who looked for good times. If I had been it would have been like Sister Angelica looking for God. I wouldn't even know where to begin and if I did begin I'd be sure and look in all the wrong places and knowing me all I'd find would be the not-so-good that's always bound to go along wherever a good time's going on. I just take what comes my way day by day and if it's not bad then I count it as good and more than good enough for me.

Jack Julies and I are like any other two ordinary people who have walked a distance together. We say what needs to be said but neither of us is very comfortable with words. People who give words can just as easily take them back again. We both know at least that much and we have our own ways of making known what needs to be known and it suits us.

'Like an old married couple,' Rose says about Jack Julies and me. 'Lunch and rugby on the TV and teatime and "Good afternoon, Ruby, and thank you" and that's him on his way.'

Jack Julies has got heavier over the years, though not fat from too much food like Rose. His bones have got tired and heavy inside him and he moves slowly but I don't mind. I slow down so that we match and we sit down at the table together and I give him bread and uncover the butter.

'I've put salt on already,' I say when I hand him his

food. That's what I always say and he always takes the salt cellar and sprinkles more, a whole plateful because he's partial to salt.

It's a winter day and the late morning sun shines down. He knocks on the door, eleven o'clock, just like he always does. He has a key, but he doesn't use it. He never has, even in the early days, and he fills up the doorway like he always does and the sun shines all around him and it's a Saturday just like any other.

We have our lunch. The tea tray's set for later and there's shortbread on a plate and there's a chiffon cover over it with red and blue flowers embroidered in the corners.

He likes to watch the rugby on TV. He has a leather La-Z-Boy chair and he likes to settle on it and then tip it back and I put the remote control in his hand and he smiles up at me when he takes it. His eyebrows look like grey wire these days. They used to be dark, like his hair, and his eyes always half closed against bright light, against the sun reflecting off the sea, against the world, the things he's seen, the things he always half expects, the things that have happened to him in his life. The things he can't change now.

He likes to turn up the sound when the rugby's on. You can see it, you can hear it and you can feel it vibrating all around you, the cheering, the remarks and the referee who's never right. Equal at half time and Breyton Paulse running fast as the wind, looking for a gap in the line but today Jack Julies isn't looking at Breyton Paulse, he's looking at me.

'Ruby,' he says. He wants to get up but he can't and when I turn round to look for myself I can see that something's very wrong with him. His lips are blue and his face is puffed out and he's purple with the effort of trying to breathe. He's trying to get up and I'm already up out of my chair and next to him wondering what's the matter. All the little veins on his face are standing out and he's gasping and his eyes are rolling back in his head. I have his arm to help him but he has to do his share because I can't move him by myself and I don't know him like this. There's the shrill of the whistle, the cheer, Breyton Paulse must have made his touchdown and the conversion kick's over but that's in another world where such things are important. Jack Julies is gasping for air and a horrible rasping sound is coming out of him and I know that he's beyond me. 'Please try,' I say. 'Oh, Jack, please try.' And I've never called him by his first name in all our time together but it's too late and he slumps back awkward, heavy, a deadweight in the chair and I'm ahead of myself. I know but I don't want to know.

I think that if I say that's enough, Jack Julies, and say it sharp so that he'll know I got a fright, he'll sit up and be himself again and there may be people who make pretend-dead jokes but Jack Julies isn't one of them. If he hadn't fallen half out of the chair with one hand hanging down and his head far back and skew you could say he was asleep, but people don't sleep with their eyes open and I've never been alone with a dead person before. Funny sounds are coming up my throat, sounds I've never made before but they must have been inside me ready all the time, ready to come out, because now they're right there and I have to stop them. I put my hand up to my mouth. If the world's to end then it would be better if it could go back five minutes and take me along with it. Five minutes isn't a long time if you think about it but I stand where I am, shaking, in the front room of my house and Jack Julies lies in his La-Z-Boy flip-back arm-chair and the referee is calling for a scrum and life goes on. The world doesn't stop to suit Ruby Jacobs. It never has and it never will.

I don't know what to do with a dead person, so I phone Rose and I tell her that she and Alf must come over. I'm at the door in my winter slacks and jersey with lace-up shoes on my feet.

'What's going on?' says Rose and the TV's blaring and Alf's the one who goes ahead into the front room between the La-Z-Boy and the TV and he looks down and stands still and then he reaches out to touch Jack Julies. He lets his hand rest on his shoulder, two fingers to the pulse point of his throat. It's strange to me how the TV howls in the background when the rest of the room is silent and my brother-in-law bending down beside Jack Julies turns his head round very slow to face me and shakes his head, no, it's done and he's gone.

'Looks like heart,' Alf says. 'It was probably over before he even knew what was happening.'

I wish it had been me. I would have taken that cup from him if I could and borne it myself because I knew him and no one but he knew how dear he had become to me.

'What now?' Rose says.

'We'd better call the police,' says Alf.

'Someone will have to tell the family,' Rose says as if it's been something she's been saving up to say for a very long time and Alf gives her a look. 'We'll leave that to the police,' he says. 'That's their job.'

'The family will want to know where he died,' Rose says. 'I mean it isn't as if he dropped down in the street or anything like that.'

I would like to ask what difference that can make but I don't say it because I know she's right. They will want to know. I would want to know if it were me.

'Sit down,' Rose says and she puts her arm round me and helps me to my chair. I don't think that I could have gone on standing even if my life depended on it because my legs won't hold me. 'I'm going to get you some sugar water,' Rose says. 'And Alf will do the necessary.'

I'm glad to have Rose there. I'm glad now she's got a little bit quieter in her own married life and isn't doing karaoke down at the Portuguese Community Hall and is sometimes at home with her husband on a Saturday afternoon when he's not working.

Someone has turned off the TV. I have a cup of sugar water in my hand but I don't need one hand, I need two because I can't hold the cup steady.

'The police are coming,' Alf says and there's nothing to do now but wait. Jack Julies lies in his chair just in the way that he left this life and now there's nothing left for us to do and we're not quite sure what we should say to each other.

It's a strange thing to sit in your own chair in your own house on a Saturday afternoon with a cup of sugar water in your hands and feel your whole life changing around you. It feels to me as if something outside myself and much bigger than I am is making the earth move. It feels as if the whole house is rocking and I want to find something, anything that's still standing steady in its place where it was twenty minutes before so that I can hold on to it and be safe.

'The police are going to have to tell his family, you know,' Rose says just like she's said twice before. 'So, if they didn't know already, they'll know now, especially when it comes out that he owns this house.'

I know that. I don't need to hear it now. Since the day Jack Julies told me that he'd been keeping an eye open and put a word out that he was in the market for a property in this area and bought this house next to my sister and rented it out to me I've been happy here.

I like my house. It's my pride and joy to keep it clean and I'm fussy. Everyone who knows me knows that.

'You can eat off her floors, you know,' Rose says and she makes a joke of it but the truth is that you probably could and if you couldn't it wouldn't be my fault. I like clean floors and curtains and linen. I beat out my loose rugs at least once a week. I wash windows and I scrub floors. If I suddenly stopped cleaning the way I do I'd put the rubber glove factories out of business, Rose says, because I'm fussy about that too. I don't put my hands anywhere near water unless I have gloves on and when I do the floors I use Cobra liquid floor polish with a special applicator that you hold by a handle. Another joke Rose talks about is how I don't believe in luxuries but you can look in my broom cupboard any day you like and you'll find the latest top-of-the-range vacuum cleaner and polisher.

Jack Julies never said that he noticed how vain I was about my hands. Even after rubber glove washing-up with extra-gentle Sunlight liquid in the wash-up water I liked to sit in my seat next to his and rub cream into my hands. He never said it out loud but I know that he liked to watch me and I never used cheap hand cream. Woolworth's Magnolia, that's what I like, and we could sit there quite happily, the two of us together, with the sweet smell of magnolia between us.

THE JOYRIDE

I'd never taken a day off work since the first day I started down at Pescanova but after Jack Julies died in the house where I live I had to put in for sick leave. Rose could see that I was very far from myself. I knew this because of her silence. I knew that there were things she'd have liked to say, none of them very nice things, but she didn't say them because she could see how sick I was feeling. If she could, Rose would have said that it was ridiculous to be as sick as I was about a man I only saw six hours a week on Saturday, and in the last years most of those six hours had been spent watching sport on the TV.

All the same, I was sick. I've never been a person who likes change and I always knew where I stood with Jack Julies but all that was over and finished with the day he died, and then there was the matter of the house. I loved my house and I did think of it as mine although perhaps that was wrong of me. When Jack Julies died I had to look at it differently and face up to what I'd known all along, which was that this was not and never had been my house. The house belonged to Jack Julies. When he died his rent money was in an envelope on the table in the hall with his name on it and the date, same as every end of the month, so he could always keep track and know that I was up to date. I always put the envelope down for him to pick up and he always took it but I knew that would change. What I didn't know is how change would happen or how it would be and I was sick to my heart with worry and then the terrible thing happened to us and if we'd been expecting anything at all, we certainly hadn't been expecting something like this.

After the police came and the district surgeon to confirm cause of death and sign the death certificate, an ambulance came to take the body away. People came out like they always do and Rose said for me to stay in the house because people would be interested enough already without my going out in the street for a last look at my regular gentleman caller who dropped dead in my house.

I started to cry then and Rose said it was stupid. She gave me a tissue and said it was a fine time to start crying now because we'd sat with a dead body for nearly two hours and we knew he was definitely gone and there was no point in tears. There was nothing that we could do or could have done about it. Heart attacks are like that and we're grown-up people and she's sorry for mentioning it

but someone has to and so it may as well be her. Jack
Julies was older than we are. He wasn't exactly a spring
chicken and he'd had a hard life.

Jack Julies was such a big man and so heavy that Alf
had to help the ambulance men with the stretcher.
Alf isn't exactly Arnold Schwarzenegger, so he went outside and called for two of the neighbours to give a hand
and they came in and I didn't like it. My neighbours had
never been in my house before because I'm not a person
who wants neighbours coming in and out of my house. I
had my sister next door and that was more than good
enough for me.

I suppose that helping to carry a dead man out of the
house of a woman who always keeps herself respectable
makes a person look at that woman differently. It's not
how anyone would have liked it but there was nothing
that I could do about it.

Everyone's different, they come and go differently and
it's never how you expect. I'd been remembering how I
met Jack Julies. In those days when I was sitting on the
wall outside Pescanova Fisheries and he was a big shadow
in front of me that fell across my lunch, I was glad he was
a big man with big hands because he made me feel safe.

I've seen the snap of Jack Julies's West Coast family. I
knew that he'd become an important man who the
government liked, who had plenty of interests and even
more on the horizon. I knew that at last he'd made more
than enough money to buy him as much respect as he had
ever longed for in his life. On that score, at least, he could
leave this world satisfied.

I was glad for what he had told me about how his life was and if I had our time over I would have it again and never do it differently, but I never felt his soul pass. One minute he was there and the next minute he was doubled up as if he had stomach ache and he had a look of surprise on his face and the life just got jerked out of him and I didn't know that it could be like that. I thought about it afterwards, after Rose had gone next door to get her Alf some supper, after Jack Julies had been carried down the front steps through the gate for the last time. I thought about it when I was alone in my house that wasn't really my house, with the rent money in the envelope on the table in the passage.

I wondered if this is the way life works in the end but I don't suppose I'll ever know. I didn't know if there was anyone who had the answers and if there was, it wasn't anyone I knew who I could perhaps have asked. Then I remembered Mrs Margolis and how it felt standing in front of her picture on the day that she died and I suppose people go in the way that they've lived and Jack Julies was a hard, strong, quiet kind of man. He worked hard to make his money, to earn people's respect and get where he landed up in life. Once he laid claim to something he would never have given up without a battle and if you took on Jack Julies then you'd know you were in for some fight. The only way to get something away from him was to wait for that moment when he wasn't on his guard and pull it away quickly before he'd even realized what was happening. He'd have smiled if he could have heard me but that's how he was and he knew he was like that. We have our ways but life knows how we are and when our time comes life will have its own way and then we find out, as if we hadn't known, that life was always out there one step ahead of us all along.

As if there wasn't already enough scandal, as if the neighbours hadn't already had more than their fair share for one day, at nine o'clock that night there was a bang on the front door. I am not a woman who opens my front door at nine o'clock at night. Not when I'm already in my pyjamas and slippers, but the banging didn't stop and I thought I ought to phone Alf because whoever it was wasn't taking 'not in' for an answer and the banging went on and on. I thought perhaps it was the police back again but the police always say who they are. As if my nerves weren't bad enough or I didn't have enough on my mind after all that had gone on, I now had this new thing and so I phoned Alf and five minutes later the banging stopped.

I was on one side of the door and Alf was outside. I could hear he was talking very nicely and politely and there were two other voices talking back not quite so nicely, not to each other and not to Alf either, and then there was quiet. Then there was more talking and Alf called me through the door.

'Ruby, you better open up.'

Alf sounded scared. For all I knew he could have been standing on the other side of the door with two men and one of them holding a gun to his head.

'Open up, Ruby,' he said and by then I could imagine lights going on up and down the street and people who'd known me for years as a respectable woman wondering what this new thing was that had suddenly started going on at my house.

I couldn't imagine who it was or what it was about. What I did know was that I didn't need any more scandal and so I opened the door and Alf was outside on the doorstep. You could see that he'd got himself together in a hurry. You could see he'd pulled on a pair of jeans and a jersey over his pyjamas because the pyjama top was showing out of the top of the jersey and he had towelling pull-on slippers on his feet and there were two big men with him.

I didn't know them but I knew who they were. I didn't know because I'd once seen them in a photograph, which I could see when I saw them face to face was taken a long time ago. I knew who they were because of the size of them and because I could see their father in them. I'm not used to opening up my door in what is, to me, the middle of the night to let strangers in. I'm not used to men seeing me in my pyjamas and slippers with my hair already unpinned and brushed out for the night but I stood aside anyway and let them come in.

'That's our dad's car outside,' one of them, I think he was the younger one, said. 'We'd like the keys if you don't mind.'

'Do you mind?' said the other one and he held out his hand as if he thought I had Jack Julies's big bunch of car keys in my dressing-gown pocket, as if I would even remember, after all that had happened, where he might have put them.

'They weren't on him when the police came to take him away,' the first one said. 'We asked.'

'And if there's anything else of our father's here, then we'd like to take that back too,' said the other one and I could see that he was the bigger one and almost certainly the elder and so I looked at his brother.

It had been a very strange day. It will always stand out from other days and when I remembered it I would remember Jack Julies's two big boys with so much of their father in them standing inside the doorway of my house, filling it up with how big they were. I'd remember that and something else too, something I'd already begun telling myself that I must never forget, which was that it wasn't my house at all. The house belonged to their father and it was almost certain that they had more right to be there than I did.

'We want our father's things that you're keeping,' the second one said. 'The police said we could come and get them.'

'You have no right to anything of his,' the first one said. 'We asked at the police station and they told us.'

They seemed so sure, but as far as I knew I didn't have anything of his and so I didn't know what to say to them.

'He didn't have his sports jacket with him when they took him away,' the second one said. 'We checked at the police station.'

Jack Julies was always a neat man. He never wore jerseys or a vest. He would have gone barefoot and been happy but once you've worn shoes that you worked for yourself you would be proud to wear shoes even if you weren't really very comfortable in them. He never felt the cold and he never owned a suit but he always had a good sports jacket and flannels just for smart and I had a special wooden hanger for him that I bought at Markham's because in that way Jack Julies was like me. He liked to look after his things and in the time we were together it was my pleasure to take his jacket from him and hang it up neat outside the cupboard door in my bedroom.

I didn't want these boys in my bedroom but I showed them where it was even though they didn't really need me to show them because they were already on their way there while I just stood looking at them. They were in and out and they came back with the jacket and so they must have seen my double bed with its gold satin cover and my dressing table with my pictures and my women's things on it. I suppose they saw the enamel basin with the green edges and the pattern of brown leaves all around it and the matching water jug that stands inside it that I asked my sister for.

'Why on earth would anyone want to have that?' Rose said, even though she was the one who'd bought it in the first place.

'I just want it,' I said.

'Suit yourself,' she said and she gave it to me.

Old-fashioned, ugly, a plain woman in a plain house in a plain pair of pyjamas and a dressing gown who keeps a pair of folded spectacles on the table next to her bed so that when she gets up in the morning she can see. That's what they'll think. I was surprised they could even bring themselves to look at me. Miss Saturday afternoon. The woman their father had chosen. I suppose they must have had their own thoughts about what went on over the years in that room in the bed with the gold satin bedspread over it, and they were still very young when you looked at them from where I stood. Young men in their prime and I suppose they saw a woman my age in pyjamas and slippers and thought they knew it all but what could they know? They knew nothing at all.

'We found it,' the first one said as though they'd found something that had been stolen, hidden away in the back of a cupboard.

'You better check if the wallet's still there,' said the second one but he could have saved his breath because his brother was already busy checking.

'Take this,' his brother said and handed the jacket over all bundled up as if it was on its way to a second-hand shop. Their father had stood where they were standing many times during our time together and I knew, without ever having had to be told, that they wouldn't have acted like that if he'd been there. They wouldn't have dared and I felt sad for Jack Julies and ashamed because of these children.

'I think it's all right,' the first one said after he'd counted the money and put the wallet in his own pants back pocket. 'It looks as if it's all there but how can we know?'

He was looking me up and down but there was a great

calmness in me and I could look back at him and hold his gaze.

'I've got the keys,' called the second one. 'They're right here on the table.'

Alf and I stood and watched as they walked backwards and forwards past the chair where their father had died that afternoon, where his body had lain while we waited for the ambulance to come. Now that they'd started, once they were finished taking their father's things back I thought they'd probably help themselves to mine and if they did there was nothing very much I could do about it.

'What's this?' the second one said, holding up the envelope with their father's name on it and the date.

'Money,' I said and he nodded and put it in the pocket of his shirt. He didn't even ask any questions.

'We're done here then,' said his brother. 'Unless there's anything else?'

I didn't know how they knew, I suppose the police told them, but they knew about me and now they'd been in my house that more than likely wasn't going to be my house for very much longer. They'd been into my bedroom where no man but their father had ever been. If they'd ever wondered about me then their wondering days were over because now they'd seen everything that there was to see. I didn't think that they were young men who were given to wondering. I thought that they were more the kind of young men who were quick to jump to conclusions and accept what they thought it was that they'd seen and it didn't matter. My business was never with them; it was with their father. For my part they could have stayed in the out-of-date photograph where they belonged and I could see then why Jack Julies never talked about them or told me anything about them, not even their names. It wasn't because he was cutting me out, it was because there was nothing to say.

When they'd done they moved towards the door getting ready to go and Alf would have let them out but they were big and in a hurry and it seemed to me that they had already appointed themselves the masters here and poor Alf'd had quite enough for one night. He stood aside and let them pass.

Then the first one stopped and turned back and looked at me and his father's jacket was bundled anyhow over his arm and the keys of the car were in his hand and he looked at me for what felt like a very long time. He looked at me in the way you look at a person you know you'll never see again in your life.

'The joyride's over,' he said. 'I just hope you enjoyed it while it lasted because if you think you can come after us with threats or demands or with your hand out expecting money from us, then you better think again.'

He looked at me and he looked at Alf.

'Don't start anything with us,' he said. 'I'm telling you now and I'm only going to tell you this once. If you do, if you even think about it, you'll be sorry.'

Then they were gone and they closed the door very quietly behind them but there was a cold draught of winter night air in the room. It was strange but these men, these sons of Jack Julies coming as they did into that house, now I'd seen them for myself and I'd listened to the kind of men they were, I knew what I hadn't known before. Jack Julies had had a hard life and he'd gone from me but after I'd seen the kind of men his sons were I could be quite sure in my heart what had brought him to my door in the first place.

A CHILD'S PORTION

Every time I'm out on a street with not too many other people around me I get nervous. If a car slows down next to me, even if I know it's just slowing down because there's a traffic light ahead, my heart starts beating faster, I go weak at the knees and I think that my last moment has come.

'It isn't their money,' Rose says. 'It's your money. He left it to you.'

That's true but Rose has never seen Jack Julies's children. You only have to take one look at them to see that they're not the kind of children who'll be happy to see any of their father's money going in anyone else's direction.

'If they try anything funny they'll end up in jail,' Rose says.

'I think you should get a gun,' says Alf when we're alone together, just the two of us, and Rose can't hear. 'You needn't look at me like that, I've never said you should use it. All I'm saying is that it might be wise, just to be on the safe side.'

Alf keeps a gun in his taxi these new days 'just to be on the safe side' because you never know who your next fare might be, but I don't think a gun would be much good to me. The best thing I can do is to keep my eyes open and my wits about me and after that just hope for the best. I've already put a new lock and a chain on the front door. I've gone to the chemist to get pills to keep my nerves steady and I've made up my mind that if Jack Julies's sons do come after me, I'll tell them the truth. I have never taken anything from anyone in my life and I've never asked anyone for anything either. I don't think I would even know how to do it. I was sad when Jack Julies died in his La-Z-Boy armchair in my house. I'm sorry he's gone and that I won't see him any more. It's funny how people are. Your mind knows something but your heart is slow to catch up and on Saturdays I still get dressed up. It's stupid, I know that but I do it anyway because I can't stop myself and even without looking at my watch I know it's eleven o'clock and all those years when he called on me Jack Julies was always on time. We used to have a little joke about it, in the latter days, how he would sit the last few minutes in the car and wait so our arrangement would always be exact. On those Saturdays you could set your watch by him and I'm sure that there were quite a few people in my street who did because he knew how I was about arrangements and being on time and that was his way of teasing me. Rose says that my ways are set in concrete by now and I couldn't change them even if I wanted to and I think she's right.

It used to worry me the way Jack Julies died, one minute here and then gone. In our days together, I used to like to lie close to him and lay my hand on his chest where my fingers could feel his heart beat. He had a strong steady heartbeat that in many ways was just like he was. It was certain, you could depend on it and it made me feel safe. I never thought that one day that heart would stop beating but then he had his heart attack and it did and it was a shock. I kept remembering how he looked and what came into my mind then and I couldn't get it out of my head for a long time afterwards. I thought that this is how someone looks when the life is pulled out of him. So quick, like a fish with the hook firm in its mouth yanked up out of the sea, finished, thrown into the boat with the rest of the catch. Then, in a moment, the sea is back to itself again as if nothing has happened.

'You look terrible,' Rose says to me one day.

I know I look terrible, I don't need to hear it. I feel terrible about all of it and everyone who knows me knows how I hate change and this is a big change and I can't believe Jack Julies is gone from my life and I don't have anything to remember him by, not even a photograph.

'You look terrible in your face,' Rose says, trying to find some way to make it better when all she's doing is making it worse. 'I mean, you're neat and tidy like you always are, you just don't look good in your face, that's all.'

'Thank you,' I say because that's my sister.

The funeral was at Elands Bay and I didn't go. The da Costas went and some of the staff. They hired a minibus and I could have gone but I didn't because life goes on and someone has to stay and see that business carries on just like it always does.

It was a fine day, the day of the funeral. It was a late morning service and plenty of people drove up from town and there was a lunch at the house afterwards and half the West Coast went.

'He wasn't called king of the West Coast for nothing, you know,' Mr da Costa said.

No boats went out from Elands Bay on the day of the funeral so that everyone could have a chance to pay their respects. The cannery was closed so the factory workers and their families could also be part of it and there were government people as well, from the Department of Sea Fisheries.

'Quite a send-off.' That's how Mr da Costa put it. 'Are you sure you don't want to come along, Ruby?' he said. 'I could put someone in your place here to stand in for you.'

I didn't want someone put in my place to stand in for me. I wanted to be in my own place where I always was. That has always been more than good enough for me. I've seen plenty of staff coming and going at Pescanova and because I've always been the one who stayed, except for

Mr da Costa and his brother there was no one there who really knew me or anything about me. Mr da Costa had known me for a long time though. He was there in the days when Jack Julies first saw me, but if he knew more than he said he never mentioned it and if he had any thoughts about it then he certainly kept his opinions to himself.

It was a fine day in Paarden Eiland industrial area that day just like it was everywhere else and in its way, which was a very small way, it was a truly remarkable day because Miss Ruby Jacobs did something that no one could ever remember her doing before. She broke an arrangement.

At one o'clock I took the packet with my lunch in it and went into the courtyard. As I made my way I saw the faces of the people I passed and I knew that there were one or two who would have liked to make a remark but they thought twice about it. Everyone who knew me knew that I had my habits. I'm sure there were a few who joked about it behind my back but it didn't do anyone any harm to see that sometimes Miss Ruby Jacobs can also surprise people.

It was a fine day and I settled myself on the wall in the sun. My sister, Rose, who thinks she knows me backwards, forwards and sideways, would have had a big surprise if she knew what I was thinking. She thinks I spend too much time trying to hold on to the memory of people who have passed on instead of thinking about the future, but just for once in her life she would have been

wrong. Right that minute I wasn't thinking about something that was happening in a graveyard somewhere
down on the West Coast. What I was thinking was that
once there'd been a girl who sat on the very same wall
where I was sitting right that minute eating her lunch
just as I was eating mine. White bread sandwich, fruit
and a flask of tea and a man coming towards her, a man
big enough to stand between her and the world.

'What's your name?' he asked her and she asked him
his name and he said he thought she already knew that.

I never expected anything from Mr Jack Julies, not when
he was living and not after he died. What I expected was
my notice to leave my house next door to Rose that
wasn't my house at all.

'If that happens you should put up a fight for it,' Rose
said but I didn't want to fight for it. I couldn't stay in a
place where I had no right to be and where I wasn't
wanted. I'd seen two of Jack Julies's children and I could
see what they were like. You could see just by looking at
them that they were the kind of young men who wouldn't
rest until they'd had what was theirs and I couldn't blame
them for that and so all I could do was wait.

'If it comes to that you'll come back to us,' Rose said.

I don't know why she said 'if it comes to that' because
it would come to that, there were no two ways about it,
and if I did go back to Rose I would have liked to know
where she thought she was going to put me. The minute
I'd moved out and she got her back room to herself again
she'd started to fill it up with things. She started from the

bed and the floor and the chairs and things just piled up and the piles got higher and higher until you could just as well say that the room disappeared altogether. Besides which, I'd changed since those days when I lived with my sister. I knew what it was to have a home of my own and Rose could joke just as much as she liked about my dusting and cleaning. She could be generous like she always was and say that I ought to know by then that any home of hers would always be my home too and there'd always be a place for me there, but all the same I didn't see how I could do it.

I lay in bed at night and I thought about it. My spectacles were where they always were, on the table next to my bed, and Rose made jokes about that too but the truth was that in my own house I didn't need spectacles. I could walk through that house in pitch dark or even blindfold and still know where everything was and I minded that I would soon have to make other plans although I didn't show it.

I had a lawyer's letter after Jack Julies died and I was too scared to open it. I put it in my bag and every time I open my bag to take something out and see the letter still sitting there I get even more upset. I know that the letter's going to tell me that the 'joyride' is over. It's time to start packing my bags and looking for somewhere else to stay.

People always say there's a lesson in everything that happens to us and I suppose there was a lesson in all this as well although I'm not quite sure yet exactly what it was. I do know one thing though. If what had happened between Jack Julies and me was what his son called a 'joyride' then it came and went like a shooting star and before I could even take hold of it, it was gone.

I couldn't bring myself to open the letter and I couldn't stand seeing it lying unopened in my bag. In the end I had to tell Rose.

'What are you telling me?' she said. 'Are you telling me that you've been walking around for a week with a lawyer's letter in your bag but you're too scared to open it?'

It sounded very foolish when someone said it out loud like that and I wasn't a fool. I knew that I had to face what was coming my way but maybe I was a fool because not opening the letter wasn't going to change anything. It didn't make me enjoy my last days in my house any more. It didn't take me back to that time when Jack Julies was in my life and I felt safe.

'Give it to me,' Rose said and she held out her hand and I opened my bag and I took out the letter and gave it to her and she made such a performance of that you'd think that she was on the stage giving a show. She lifted herself out of the chair where she was sitting and went out of the room to fetch a knife from the kitchen so that she could open the letter with it and I sat there and I waited. She cleared a space on the dining-room table and put the letter down and she gave me a look and then she bent over and slit open the envelope and she gave me another look.

I would have liked to say, 'Thank you, Rose, I knew without the performance that I was being a fool,' but I didn't say anything. I just sat on the edge of the chair with my handbag still on my lap.

'Honestly, Ruby,' she said, 'I don't know about you. Truly, I give up. How do you think you can deal with a thing if you won't even look it in the face? Did you think one day you'd open up your bag and the letter would be gone, vanished into thin air, and all your problems would be over?'

I could have told her that was exactly what I would have liked even though I knew it wasn't possible.

'Here you are,' she said and she looked at the letter and then she gave it to me. 'Read it,' she said, 'and see what all the fuss and you working yourself up into such a terrible state was all about.'

It was a very short letter. It said that until the estate of the late Jack Julies was finalized I should pay the rent money directly into a bank account and it gave an account number. It said that when the estate had been finalized I could expect further contact from them.

'What do you think "further contact" means?' she said and I said that I had no idea and held my hand out to show that I wanted the envelope back. She gave me the envelope without saying anything else so I could put the letter back inside it because I'm fussy about things like that. I wouldn't like a loose letter just floating around inside my bag and I folded it neatly and put it back in my bag where it came from and all the time Rose watched me.

'All I can say is that if this is just the start of it and it's going to be like this for the next couple of months while all this blows over and everything gets settled, we're all going to be in for a very hard time.'

I don't know where Rose learned to be how she is, untidy, floating along in life, easy-going like she is and never afraid of anything. She certainly never learned it from me.

Everyone now knows that when Jack Julies's estate was finalized he'd left me the house and he'd left me some money but I have not yet decided whether I will accept this. I suppose I ought to have been thankful and happy but the truth is that instead I expected his children to come after me to tell me that I had no right to take what was rightfully theirs and say that they wanted it back. They must have known because there's no way you can keep a thing like that secret.

'If people never knew about you and him before, they'll certainly know now,' Rose says. 'You don't leave a woman a house and a nice little nest egg if all she did for you was give you tea on a Saturday.'

This isn't a thing you like to hear. I would have liked to say that it wasn't like that but I know that even if I explain till I'm blue in the face that's how it will look to other people even if it wasn't like that for me.

The da Costas surely know even if they don't say anything and if one person at Pescanova knows something it's not five minutes before the whole building knows. If it wasn't that I was so afraid that his children would come after me and make my life difficult I could have seen that there was a funny side to what happened to me.

It didn't matter any more like it would have done once but I can just imagine what Auntie Olive would say.

'I don't know how much he left you in money terms, Ruby,' she'd say. 'But I do know one thing and that is that there isn't enough money in this world can ever give a girl back her bloom and her good name.'

And what is there that I could say to that except yes, Auntie Olive, and thank you, Auntie Olive, and who would have thought in my Steenbras Street days that a woman like me would lose her bloom and her good name in quite the way I did.

If I felt that I had no right to something I could never talk myself into believing that I had. For a long time in my life if anyone offered me anything I always wanted to look over my shoulder to see who was standing behind me. I always thought there must be someone standing behind me and that would be the person that the offer was properly meant for. I think people who grow up the way I did are like that. Life will change; things will get better but once that is in you, you won't easily get it out again.

I'm not easy with what Jack Julies has seen fit to do for me. It's something that I have to think about and it's not just because I'm afraid that his family will blame me or that his children will come after me and find some way to take it out on me, although I did think that in the beginning. I have a great many things weighing on my mind because of this money that's coming my way.

When Rose gets really fed up with me she calls me

'my sister' as if there are three of us instead of just two.

'Only my sister would want to say no, thank you when something like this comes her way. I don't know of anyone else who would be so stupid or so ungrateful, do you, Alf?'

'I haven't said no, thank you,' I say. 'All I'm saying is that I'd like to think about it.'

'I give up, Ruby,' Rose says. 'I just give up. If this man didn't want you to have this he wouldn't have left it to you. If he wanted it to go to his children, then that's how he would have arranged it. How difficult can that be to understand? How much is there to think about in that?'

My sister sees a grown woman being offered long-term security by a man who was in a position to offer it. I see a girl who was offered a fifty-rand note by a man who should have known better.

'Goodness me, Ruby,' Rose says. 'It isn't as if the money won't be useful. Who are you all of a sudden? Oprah Winfrey with more money than you know how to spend? Any other person would be down on their knees thanking God for their good fortune.'

She should have known better than to say something like that but I don't make an issue of it and I don't answer at once. I just sit quiet and she's quiet too because she knows she's said too much and so she doesn't make it worse by saying anything else.

'The money isn't coming from God, Rose,' I say when I eventually decide that it's time to say something. 'It's being offered by Jack Julies and that's what I'm thinking about.'

* * *

We don't talk about love, Rose and me. When she married Alf she talked about being 'an old man's darling'. She didn't talk about love and they've lived together all these years and they're happy so perhaps that was love after all and she found it without even looking for it and I'd believe it if it were so because that's the kind of thing that happens to Rose.

I would like to keep my house but a house is only a house after all. If it takes Jack Julies's money for me to keep it maybe I can let it go and find somewhere else and not have to be grateful to anyone and be independent.

It's funny how two women, sisters like Rose and me, can be so different. Rose is how she is but I don't need worldly things in the same way that she does. She says that one day when I pass on, if I go before her, cleaning up after me will be the easiest job in the world. One packing case will be more than enough to take everything I possess. Knowing me, by the time she gets round to doing what has to be done she'll find that the packing case has already been packed by me, before I died so that I would die neat, a place for everything and everything in its place.

She's right but in the meantime, while I'm still alive, I don't really need Jack Julies's money. I have a nice job and it's not like the old days. These days there's a company pension to look forward to. I have the windfall from Mrs Margolis which I got for 'thank you' and appreciation for my hard work taking care of her, which I didn't tell Rose about for a very long time but which she knows about now.

'How could you take that and not take from Jack Julies?' she wants to know and that's a question I can't easily answer. I accepted from Mrs Margolis but I don't think that I can take from Jack Julies.

Then I make up my mind and I don't even tell Rose. I just phone up and make an appointment to see the lawyer who sent me the letter about Jack Julies's estate. I take time off to go through to the Palms Office Park in Sir Lowry Road on a Friday afternoon to speak to Mr Abdulrahman and he's very polite and he listens.

It isn't so easy as it sounds to give something back to an estate and I don't know what gets into me. There's been so much about the business of Jack Julies and his money that's been worrying me and pressing down on me and I want to get it off my chest and out of my life and so I tell the truth. I tell this man who I don't know how it was between Jack Julies and me and where I fitted into his life. I tell him that what I gave, I gave for nothing and I don't want this money. I tell him that there's something in Jack Julies's children that frightens me and how they came to my house on the day their father passed away and took it over and marched through it as if it was already theirs.

Mr Abdulrahman is a very smart man and his office is very neat and he's a good listener. I told Rose that afterwards and she said she'd be a good listener too if she was getting the kind of money he's more than likely getting for finalizing the estate of a rich man like Jack Julies.

I was never with Jack Julies because he was rich. I told
Mr Abdulrahman that. I also told him that although the
world may see me as a woman alone, if you look close
enough you can see that I'm not really alone at all. I have
a sister, I have a good job and I've got money in the bank
and more than enough for my needs.

I'm telling him this, getting it all off my chest and all
the time thinking that if Rose were right there in the
room and could hear me I'd definitely be 'my sister' and
I'd be more than that. I'd be 'my sister who always knows
better especially when she's thinking for other people'.

All the years I was with him, I would never take from
Jack Julies, not so much as a bunch of flowers, without
letting him know that I'd be happier if he didn't spend so
much money on me. It didn't matter if it was his money
and he thought he should at least be allowed to do what
he liked with it. I always told him that there were other
people in his life that came ahead of me and anyway, I
couldn't take things from a man because for me that was
like giving away my independence.

'I see now that a man has to die before he can do something nice for you,' Rose says. 'But I see now that even
that's not good enough. I see that you have to go further
than beyond the grave to get away from Miss Ruby
Jacobs when she wants to arrange other people's lives just
like she does her own.' For all I know, she may be
right.

Mr Abdulrahman says what Jack Julies set down in his
Will was what he wanted and he must have done what he
thought was right and fair, and then Mr Abdulrahman

says something to me that no one had ever said to me in regard to Jack Julies's estate before.

The Will is in front of him on the desk. It's a big document, big like Jack Julies was, and he turns over the pages one by one quite slowly, looking, I suppose, for the part that concerns me and because I'm only such a small part of it I'm not all that easy to find. I wonder if he does this so that I can see exactly where I fit into all the big business that the king of the West Coast was involved in and be properly put in my place.

'His family are all very well taken care of,' he says, 'if that's what's worrying you. I can't give you figures but if it makes you feel any better what I can tell you is that you get a child's portion. It's a nice little sum but not really so very much in relation to the whole estate.'

He looks at me as if he wants me to say something but what is there I can say?

'We talked about it and he specifically wanted it arranged that way. In fact, he wanted that exact wording.'

Jack Julies and I never talked about what happened to me. I never said how I felt and he never asked. It isn't something I can talk about, not even now. The baby was the biggest change in all my life and my greatest loss and I thought that although it was a great thing for me, it wasn't a great thing for him. I even thought that because it happened like it did, as far as he was concerned it might even have been a difficulty solved. I thought that he'd forgotten but I see now that I was wrong.

I say that I never played 'imagine', that I never look at

children on the street and think 'my child would be that age now'. I say that I can walk right past a dark-skinned, green-eyed child and not think that my child's father was not what you would call a good-looking man but he had eyes that any woman would look twice at. I say that I never play 'imagine' but I lie. Most of the time I lie only to myself but I see that I wasn't able to lie to Jack Julies and I see now that he isn't lost to me the way I thought he was and I see that I've been selfish.

I don't know what Mr Abdulrahman knows or how much. I suppose he knows enough and maybe I come as a surprise to him and he expected someone different. I think that I must look small and plain to him and there's nothing very much I can do about that. It's one thing being Miss Ruby Jacobs of Pescanova Fisheries, being Miss Jacobs in Mr Abdulrahman's office at the Palms Office Park is another thing altogether. I'm a private person and there are things that have been said here that I've never talked about to a stranger before and there are things I understand now which I never understood before. I think of all the years there had been things that Jack Julies would have had on his mind that he would have liked to speak out loud and although he was never a man who could easily find words, I think that he has said them now.

I get into the lift and go down to the ground, to the shopping mall level and I step out into noise and light and another world and I think about the small world Jack Julies and I made for each other. I wonder if there's anyone here who could imagine a whole world held together by tea and talk and shortbread and the quiet time when I lay beside him and put my two fingers against his chest because I liked to feel his heart beating because it made me feel safe.

I don't want to draw attention to myself but I can't stand any more. I must find somewhere to sit down. There are benches and I find one. No Whites Only any more and I'm glad today that I can sit anywhere I choose in any public place because I couldn't take another step even if my life depended on it. I feel as if I've walked a hundred thousand miles to get to where I am now and I must sit down because my knees feel as if they're giving way underneath me.

The tears come and they aren't tears that you can wipe away quickly with your hand. I am a small woman, sitting small with my handbag tucked under my elbow on my left-hand side. I take off my glasses and fold them in my lap. It's a funny life and someone who in his own way must have cared for me gives me a child's portion. I don't think I'm Oprah Winfrey like Rose once said about me but I'm a well-off woman now. I never really thought about being well off or what it would feel like if I was, but if I had I would never have thought it would feel like this.

GOD'S WAITING ROOM

For as long as I can remember Rose has been saying that I'm old before my time and I agree with her. My arrangements have got even smaller as I've got older. All the small corners of my life are properly arranged and that suits me. I like my supper tray set in a proper way. I pack my lunch packet the same every day just like I always did. I don't waste plastic bags that can be used over again and I save string. I work out in advance what TV programme I want to watch and I get ready the same way step-by-step every night. The only thing that ever changes is the hot-water bottle when the weather turns cold and no hot-water bottle and the extra blanket taken off the bed in the summer.

I think that I can go on like this for a very long time but, as is usual in my case, life has other plans for me and

I get sick. The young people in the Pescanova offices and the factory workers have a saying about getting older. They say that when old age comes after you it never comes alone. It brings all its children and grandchildren and other relatives along with it. They mean the aches and pains and all the little things that go wrong with the body.

I am forty years old now, not very old at all, four years older than my mother was when she died. As I grow older I'm leaving behind me all those who are gone. Godfrey, Mrs Margolis and even Shirley and Susannah and now even Jack Julies stay just where I left them and I see now that this is what getting older's all about. If those who knew me saw me now I don't think they'd even recognize me any more. I should let them go because I don't really have the strength to hold on to them but I can't do that because even after all this time I'm still not really strong enough to let them go.

There's such a lot of talk about health and looking after oneself. Worrying so much about health is the same as facing up to the fact that some time or other, no matter how often you go to the gym or how many vitamin pills you take, anyone can get sick and most people do.

Rose's bathroom is so full of things it's like a chemist's shop. You're always falling over all the latest health products at her house. Echinacea and milk thistle, everything the chemist recommends and every kind of herbal cure from the health shop, and that's not to mention the slimming medicine. She's got every wonder, quick-fix slimming formula that you see on TV between the soap operas. She has milk shakes you can drink instead of eating food. She has pills that swell up in your stomach and help you lose a whole dress size in two weeks. You name it and Rose has got it, but I don't think that among all those things there's anything to help me with the something that's happening inside me now. I can feel it inside me like a little visitor waiting its time to see how long before I realize it's there and take notice. I've felt change coming at me from all kinds of different directions by now but this is the first time I can feel it coming from inside myself. I know that if I ignore it long enough it will still make itself felt because that's its job but in the meantime, while I keep it complete inside me, before the whole world knows, these are special days and I'm happy.

'Ruby must be taking something,' Rose says but she's wrong, it isn't that, it's altogether the other way round.

Half the world gets in and out of Alf's taxi every day and taxi drivers are like I've sometimes felt myself to be, which is to say invisible. People talk out their whole lives in taxis and never think that anyone's listening, but Alf's listening and when he gets home when his shift's done he tells Rose. Young people take Ecstasy these days. It makes them feel that they're flying and fills them up with goodwill.

I'm not taking Ecstasy but I am filled up with life. I don't even mind the minibus taxi squash going to work in the morning like I do these days. Everyone half sitting on everyone else's lap and the taxi's hurtling along and the boy who works for the taxi driver calls where we're heading for out of the half-open side door and if someone calls back and tells him to stop we slow down and stop and the door is slid open to let in another passenger and that is only life going on after all, doing what it has to do, the way life always does.

I get in the taxis morning and evening. I used to hate it but I don't hate it any more because it's only a part of life and every part of life is precious to me now. I know that there's something inside me digging in and making itself at home but my little shadow needn't feel too pleased with itself. This thing will run its course and whatever way it goes, I will be the victor. I've made up my mind about that.

You never see young people going along the street in ones and twos any more. They move around in swarms these days but their confidence and energy don't frighten me the way they used to. They can go by me or they can drift around me. I'm not the orphan girl who moves aside to make way for the other, real people. I feel free to feel their joy. They have so much of it that I don't think they're going to begrudge me my small share. In fact, I don't think they will even miss it.

'What's got into you, Ruby?' Rose says and I could answer her but I don't. At long last, after all this time, life has got into me. All of life is going on around me and for all of my life I have stood to one side, too frightened to join in and be a part, but that time's past now. I never believed in luxuries. I've never learned the pleasure of accepting something given with love but each day with all its joys and all its imperfections is a gift to me now even though I know it can't last. Eventually I will have to tell her but then that was always the arrangement.

'You should have told me,' Rose says.

'I am telling you,' I say. 'I'm telling you now.'

'Well, it's not the end of the world,' she says.

If I hadn't already made my own peace or if I had a sharp side to my tongue the way my sister has, I suppose I could make a joke about it. After all, it's my world that we're talking about but just so long as it is my world and I can arrange it any way I like, I've had time to think and in my own mind my arrangements are already all in place.

When Rose finds it hard to look me in the eye and hard or not, she knows she has to do it, it means that she's afraid.

'You've got the money,' Rose says. 'And if you tell me that private doctors are a luxury and that you won't indulge yourself then, sick or not, I can't answer for myself, really I can't. Not this time. You hear what I'm telling you, Ruby?'

I'm sure they can hear what she's telling me two houses down the street. She doesn't understand but that's all right. I don't mind being in the cancer waiting room at the state hospital with all the other patients because I feel that I belong there. Some of them come from very far away with no money left, not knowing what will happen to them next, and there are all kinds of people, from all walks of life, men and women, old and young, and there are all colours too. My sister may not understand and that's all right but maybe Auntie Olive should come here and learn a lesson. You don't need a government or big books filled with laws to know that we are all the same. In that way God is one step ahead of us just like He always is and He has His own way of showing us, just like He always has.

What Rose doesn't seem to understand is that I don't mind. I'm grateful that, without my ever wishing for it, these days we have medical insurance and I have money in the bank.

I've now given up my job at Pescanova due to ill health and there's no one left who'll remember me now because old Mr da Costa, the da Costa brothers' father, died but this has happened once before. It happened to my mother and although there may be no one else now who remembers, I do.

'I'm very sorry, Ruby,' Mr da Costa says and he says other nice things about me and how hard I work and how I came up through the business and have been a credit to both Pescanova and myself.

'I'd like to think of this as temporary,' he says. 'You know that whenever you're ready, the minute you feel well enough you can come back. Your job will always be here waiting for you and we'll be glad to have you.'

I say thank you. I know he means it but I know better now than I did when I was a child and a job at Pescanova Fisheries was a lifeline and something I held on to. I know that and there's something different in me now and

I'm not the way I once was. I'm ready to let go now and go wherever life decides to take me and so much inside me has changed but there's one thing that hasn't. I don't take it as being 'Thy Will be Done'. I waited for God once but He never came. I minded then and I mind more now. It's wrong to make a fool out of a child who had such faith. I made my mind up then and I see no reason to change it now. I have not troubled God for very many years; I will not trouble him now.

Doctors don't like to give bad news. They don't like it any more than anyone else does and this tired, over-worked doctor in the state hospital is very young. He has my case notes on the desk in front of him. He knows my history and he's done his best for me. What he doesn't know is my heart or how I feel in my body. There are no tests or X-rays or examinations or medical textbooks that can tell him that.

He has his head bent down over his notes and he keeps it there for much longer than he needs to because he doesn't want to look at me. He reminds me of Mr Silver. I don't know why. I'm sitting on the other side of the desk with my handbag on my lap waiting for him to say what he knows he has to say and what I would like to do is put my handbag down, lean forward and reach out and touch him. Softly, the way his own mother would, and tell him that what my sister said was right. This isn't the end of the world. Worlds end, that's true, but they don't end in this way. He has his job to do and it's not the easiest job in the world and I've been careless with myself but it's not for him to carry all the worries of the world on his young shoulders. I know because I've tried.

I want to leave this life the way I want to leave it. I need no remarks from other people. 'You'll be just fine,' they'll say. 'It's amazing what they can do these days.' 'We know you, you're a fighter.' 'Day by day, one step at a time.' I don't want that. I've had a small quiet life and I want quiet now. I want my own house and my own things and I want to go this last way with my sister.

I never knew that Rose could be so gentle and so quiet but she can. I never know how much Rose knows or what she doesn't know. I suppose that's because I've spent so much of my own life speaking for her, even those times when I should have been quiet and let her speak for herself.

I tried so hard to make sure that she remembered that she was someone and not just 'someone' but someone who was important and had her own place in the world. That's what I promised my mother and I did my best.

I think perhaps in the end I told her things that had never happened at all and that all I gave her were my own dreams of how I wished things were and how I wanted them to be.

Rose stays in my house now just like Auntie Olive stayed with our mother but there are not two frightened little girls watching how it is. Those two girls are gone now and I feel as if the weight of the entire world has been taken from my shoulders because this is not a place for children.

All these years I've been so neat and tidy I could make my way around my own house blindfold or in the pitch dark. I hope Rose remembers it because I'm tired now. I don't have the strength to tell her but I think I know my sister and I think I know what she'll say.

'Ruby?' she'll say. 'No need to worry about Ruby. I know my sister. Eyes closed, blindfold, she'll always be able to find her way around her own house, no matter how dark it may be outside.'

FOR RUBY
ON THE OCCASION OF HER FIRST COMMUNION

The taxi business isn't what it was when Alf started out. These days you take your life in your hands if you let a stranger into your car. Springbok Taxis have seen better days. The kind of customer you want has his own car and doesn't need you. With the kind of customer you get you have to keep a gun where you can take hold of it in a hurry if you need it and that's no way to live. Who wants to send a husband out in the morning and not be sure that he'll come home at night or if you should expect the police at the door to say that they have news for you and you'd better sit down. This is the new South Africa and I'm not how I once was. I've just lost my sister and I can't spare my husband and I have another problem.

All of Ruby's business was in good order. We always said that about her, everything in its place and all the arrangements properly taken care of. That was Ruby in life and that's how she left things when she died and all that she has is coming to me. I'm well off now and 'well off' isn't like you think it will be when you have nothing. It worries me and that's not something my sister would have expected me to say. She would have thought that my only worry would be how quickly I could get down to the shops and how fast I could spend the money that she left me, but Ruby was wrong about me. I did go a little bit reckless in my young days and in my young married life but when you've never had anything and what you have is given to you and not always what you'd choose for yourself, you do like to have things. I never had more than I could pay off every month. That's a hard thing to explain to a sister who thinks that having a spare pair of shoes is a luxury.

Ruby was funny about money. I never thought she'd take the money from Jack Julies and not just because she thought that his children would come after her and ask for it back, which they never did. Maybe it was her gold star she got for Sunday school attendance at St Agnes's in those early days when our mother and father were still with us, when we were a family, as Ruby would say. She never could believe that something could come to a person so easily in life, something they hadn't worked for and had done nothing to deserve. She thought there was something wrong about money that came to you that way. She thought that if you weren't careful it could lead you into bad ways. It wasn't like her to take Jack Julies's money but she did, although I see now that she never spent one cent of it, which makes me a very comfortably off woman. But my sitting pretty with money in the bank is one thing. Being without my sister who I've been with all my life is another thing altogether.

Her whole life, whenever she could, my sister was always there standing between me and the rest of the world, trying to keep me safe. She tried to make it up to me for the things I never had. What she couldn't understand is that you can't miss what you never had and she was the one that minded so much, not because I always felt that I was given other things instead.

I was never the clever one but I never minded that. I got a good man to look after me and a house I can do what I like in and friends and a Portuguese family. So I could say that God was good to me and I can say it now without getting a look from my sister.

I've talked to Ruby all my life. I don't see why I should stop now. Death may be powerful but it's not as powerful as all that, not where my sister and I are concerned.

'Surely, now that she's gone, she deserves a bit of peace,' Alf says.

It's true that I'm a talker and Ruby wasn't and most of the time I probably talked enough for both of us but I don't think she ever minded. Ruby knew better than anyone else did that there were two things she wasn't good with. One was people that she hadn't got to know really well, and the other was words. My sister was a person who bottled things up and kept them close to her heart and I think that if I hadn't spoken up for her sometimes people would never have known how she felt about anything.

When I talk about God and say how blessed I am I say over my shoulder, 'I can talk about God now, Ruby, and there's nothing you can do to stop me.'

I think she would find it funny and that she wouldn't mind. She always said that she'd turned her back on God and that she had her reasons and that they were her business. I could do what suited me. Ruby always said so but she knew very well that she was always the one who led the way. What you do to keep your sister company and what you think in your heart are two different things and Ruby always had her 'reasons' and I had my reasons too. Ruby said that she could manage without God but she never said that she could manage without me and although she was older than me and more strong-willed, I would never have put her in that position. I loved her far too much and she was too important for me ever to have done that.

I was never sure about Ruby and God but it wasn't a subject that you could raise. I thought that all of her life she missed Him although in her own way she was too proud to say so and dying didn't change that but it worried me.

People say when someone dies and it's someone really close like Ruby was to me that you really can't believe they're gone but that's not true. I could feel Ruby leaving me and that's not how people say it's supposed to be either. It isn't always here one minute and gone the next like it was with Jack Julies. Ruby and I parted little by little and in that time we talked ourselves out and that was all right too. We talked about the old days and happier times and then she began to get more tired and her pills began to be stronger and she could get up less and less and in the end we were just quiet together. I would lie down on the bed next to her, like we used to do when we were little girls, and it was fine just the two of us in the quiet house in the half-dark waiting while time passed.

I haven't packed up Ruby's house yet. I'm going to wait for the house to be sold and until that happens I'll leave her things just where they are. I like to be there with her same things around me and the smell of her and her floor polish and her sparkling kitchen that always smelled of Jik and her Woolworth's Magnolia hand cream.

Her clothes still hang in the cupboard. The bed's made and covered with the gold satin bedspread that she liked so much. Her spectacles that I used to tease her about are still folded up on the table next to her bed. In the drawer of the bedside table is the missal she got from our mother and father on the day that she made her first communion. Inside it is written: 'For Ruby, on the occasion of her first communion – 8th March, 1973 – St Agnes's Church, Woodstock. With much love from Mommy and Daddy.'

It's very old now and falling apart but she'd never part with it because our mother wrote that message inside it for her. She liked to imagine our mother as she was then, young and well, sitting at the table with the brand new missal open in front of her.

'Can't you just see her?' Ruby would say. 'Writing in it while we were asleep in our room at the back, keeping it for a surprise for first communion Sunday?'

Ruby said she must have written carefully, there was no room for mistakes because your missal is something that you keep with you for life.

I hold my sister's missal in my hand and think of that now. Our mother wrote in ballpoint pen and I'm sure she wrote very carefully but there's a small ink blot on the 'R' of 'Ruby' and that's a part of it now and we wouldn't want it any other way and there's something else too. Something I know that I never asked Ruby about. She has a bookmark. At Sacred Heart we didn't have much but the nuns were forever giving us markers with pictures of saints or texts printed on them to give us courage to live our lives the way good Catholics should. 'Best friends' used to give cards to each other and Ruby's one came from a girl called Molly Small who took a shine to Ruby and she was a girl alone and asked Ruby for 'best friends' but Ruby couldn't because of me. I suppose she gave the text before Ruby had time to tell her and then she couldn't ask to have it back again and in the end Molly didn't make old bones. She was out playing on a building site where she shouldn't have been and she fell off some scaffolding and hit her head on the ground and died, and Ruby felt very bad about it, as if she had let her down, but she hadn't. Ruby still has the bookmark. It has purple pansies on it. It says 'May the Lord Bless You and Keep You' and there's a pattern in gold round the corners and it's lasted much better than the missal has. You have to be careful when you touch the missal because its binding's coming apart.

You do funny things sometimes when you're taking a trip down memory lane. We don't have many photographs. Ruby says we had a family snap album once when we were girls and she asked Auntie Olive about it but she said she didn't know. It must have got lost when they packed up our mother's house and that was the end of that. Ruby didn't lay the blame on anyone but in later years she minded very much and took it very badly. There are no pictures of our mother and father or us in our Sacred Heart days, except the one of us with our so-called Steenbras Street family that Clarence-next-door took that Ruby was so fond of that she kept it framed by her bed. Then there's Ruby and me on my wedding day but Ruby was never one who liked being pushed forward and she didn't like having her picture taken.

'I see you every day of your life,' she'd say to me. 'And you see me. You don't need a photo of me. You know what I look like.'

I'm sorry now that it worked out that way.

Sometimes, especially in the early days, I asked to see the missal and what my mother wrote in it because I didn't have one of my own because my father died and when my time came my mother was too sick to get me one. Ruby hung on to hers as if it was pure gold and I had to specially ask to see it. It didn't matter to me as much as I made out because I'd already begun to move away from the idea that I'd ever really had a mother and a father at all. The only thing I was really sure of was Ruby and she liked to be asked to show her missal. When she was feeling down or going through lonely times I'd ask to see it because it pleased her and that was when I noticed something funny. Every time I saw it Molly's bookmark was in a different place, moving on through the church year just like a bookmark in a missal is supposed to do. I never said anything because it was a subject you couldn't raise with my sister, but if Ruby wasn't moving it then it must have been divine intervention from the Holy Spirit. I'm not the one who got a star for attendance in St Agnes's Sunday school but I know enough to know at least that much.

Ruby thought things through before she made up her mind but when an arrangement had been put in its place if you wanted to stay on the right side of her that was the end of the story. Because I knew her and knew how she was and because for the most part I'm the easy-going one, whatever she wanted and however she wanted it was fine with me.

'Cremation,' she said. 'No notice in the newspaper, no flowers and if you've got any ideas about taking that photo of you and me on your wedding day and putting a black ribbon around it and clearing a place on your sideboard for it, you can put them out of your head.'

Those were Ruby's instructions.

'No Garden of Remembrance, no ashes scattered and I don't want people who don't know me coming back here poking around my house and drinking tea and eating sandwiches.

'Are you listening?' she said.

I was listening but I didn't want to hear.

'I don't want the whole laying-out business either,' she said. 'I suppose you'll have to tell Auntie Olive and that's just the kind of nonsense idea she'd put in your head. I don't want people looking at me when I'm dead. Are you listening to me, Rosie?'

She'd never called me Rosie in my whole life before and I was listening.

'That's how I want it, very quiet and you have to pay attention because you're the one who has to see that's the way it happens.'

I said, 'Yes, Ruby,' and she said, 'Look me in the eyes and mean it,' and I said, 'Yes, Ruby,' and I'd been saying, 'Yes, Ruby,' all my life to keep my sister happy and for the sake of peace. I couldn't have stopped even if I'd wanted to. I'd never let my sister down in life and I wouldn't have let her down now that she was coming to the end, although none of what she wanted was the way I would have wanted it.

Ruby didn't like the dark. She thought I didn't know that but I did. She could arrange herself so that she could find her way blindfold, eyes closed, through pitch dark in familiar places but that didn't mean she liked it. Ruby could put on a brave face when she had to and she was very brave when it came to me but she was always afraid of the dark although she'd rather have died than say so. Now she's dead and there's something I'd like to do for her to show her that, although there were things she thought I didn't know and some things she didn't want me to know, there was nothing about my sister that I didn't know.

THE LIGHT OF HIS
COUNTENANCE

If Ruby had been here she would have said that Auntie
Olive would never come. She said that when I got
married and I'd say again what I said then.

'Of course she'll come. Alf's going to fetch her and you
try and stop Auntie Olive getting into a taxi with all the
neighbours out to see. You couldn't keep her away even if
you wanted to and Patsy and poor old Uncle Bertie will
have to come too because she'll make them.'

I knew they'd never miss it for the world, no matter
what they said behind our backs, because they were far
too nosy for that. Then they'd go back to Athlone and
have their say about us poor relations but that doesn't
worry me. I never minded what they said and I didn't
mind now. Ruby was the one who minded and if we'd

wanted we could have said a few things too. Our cousin Patsy's got four children now and she's also got the first divorce in our family. She's back in her mother's house and maybe that's something Auntie Olive might have thought about before she had a lot to say to my sister and me but she won't because Auntie Olive's not like that, she never was and she's certainly not going to change now.

Woodstock wasn't a place I ever went back to after Ruby and I left as children but I go there very often now and can see for myself that Woodstock isn't and never can be Athlone. Auntie Olive would have been happy to point that out free of charge but it still wouldn't have mattered to me. I would have believed what Ruby told me above what my auntie Olive said any day. I spent a big part of my life imagining things the way my sister told them because what she was telling was not just about her and my mother and father, it was about my life too. I was too small to remember but she always told it as if I had played a big part in those Woodstock days. It was as if I was at the centre of everything and nothing could have happened without my being there but I don't think that was true. I think that she only told me the way she did because in those days, stories of our happier times were all she had to give and when Ruby loved someone she was a generous giver, even if it meant that she had to take less for herself.

Woodstock may not be Athlone but Woodstock is where we started out. Now I have this new business at St Agnes's that has taken me there quite often, I've been walking through the streets, seeing for myself, and it's not at all like I thought it would be. It's not like Ruby told me. It's a poor people's place and tumbledown. There's washing hanging out on the street and people sit outside on their front steps or even on old lounge chairs all coming to pieces, sagging, with their insides unravelling like string, just sitting out there greeting their neighbours and watching the world go by. There are small children looked out for by next-size-up children playing in the street and some cars and one with all its wheels off that looks as if it's been there for ever.

I always said hello to everyone because that's how I am and they soon got to know me. I'm the woman who gave the big donation to St Agnes's Church. I don't know what they expected me to be like. Maybe someone grand or someone white and all they got was me, but they wouldn't have been happy with someone grand or someone white walking their streets so in that way it's probably just as well.

Neighbourhoods are like people, I suppose. They can fall on hard times. Ruby was in the front of the queue in our family when imagination was handed out. She could imagine anything you like. All you had to do was ask her and in her mind she would see just how it was and how it could be and when I was small she used to do that for me. I'd ask her something and she'd tell me, sometimes in her ordinary voice as if she was telling me a story. Sometimes whispering when I went into the big girls' dormitory at night and crept in next to her when we were in Sacred Heart and things weren't so good for us.

I don't know what Clive Street was like when we were children and it was our street where we lived. I don't know if it's come down or come down very far or not come down at all, but some of the houses here are condemned now and rats scurry in the dark places on the street and over the years places change and that wasn't how Ruby remembered it.

I know that our parents liked to sit out on the pavement when the day's work was done. I know that children played out in the street, skipping rope and kicking the tin. I know the one-size-bigger children had to watch out for the small ones and I can't imagine very much but I can imagine Ruby as a little girl looking after me because that's what she did all of her life.

It's too late now to know if I've done the right thing. There have been builders on the site. There's a big hole knocked in the side wall of the church and people stop to look at it and ask what's going on and what happened to the Roof Appeal, so whatever happens next, I'm responsible for that much at least. I keep thinking about Ruby and how she would never waste money on luxuries but to me this isn't a luxury and I think St Agnes's is the right place. I don't think Ruby would mind coming back and ending up where she began. No matter what it was really like in those days, whether it was how Ruby remembered it or not, I think that time when she was a little girl in Clive Street was the one time she was really happy. It was after that she turned her back on God and I often think about that. Once she'd done that and told me what she'd done Ruby never set her foot inside a church again, and once I decided to set my course by hers, neither did I. I wouldn't go back on it, not even for Alf, or even so that I could have a proper wedding which was what I really wanted, instead of just a blessing in a church.

Our Lady of Good Hope is a beautiful church. Even from the back, standing in the church porch which was as far as Ruby would go, you can see that, and afterwards I asked Ruby what she thought.

'Very nice,' she said. 'It's very nice if you're the kind of person who needs to be reminded how great God is and how many victories He's had.'

I didn't know what she meant.

'The windows,' she had said. She asked me if all those times I was doing tea for Father Basil I'd been so busy saying 'Milk or sugar?' or 'Help yourself to a biscuit' that I never had time to look at the windows.

'Lazarus rises from the dead. David kills Goliath. The walls of Jericho fall down.'

I had looked at my sister because there was a funny sound in her voice that I didn't like.

'Don't look at me like that,' she said. 'All you have to do when you go there again is look around you and you'll see and if you don't get a proper look don't worry. God will bring the sun out for you and they'll fill up with light. He can do that, you know, if He puts his mind to it.'

Ruby always used to like church. She once said that God's house was like being in her own house. It isn't as if I had said that she should go back to God. I knew that was a forbidden subject and I'd never have told her what to do. It's just that I did teas at Our Lady of Good Hope every Sunday and she'd never seen inside it before and I had had my marriage blessed there and I was only saying.

'It was very nice, Rose,' she said because she never liked speaking sharply to me. 'Very nice, really it was and you should tell them that once they've had enough of God's great victories they should put in a window for me so that people will also remember that sometimes even God has failures.'

She knew I never liked it when she spoke like that. It was like some other person had got into her. When she was like that it upset me and made me unhappy and I couldn't even bring myself to look at her.

'It wouldn't have to be a very big window,' she said.

Then she had turned away from me and that was all she ever had to say on the subject.

Auntie Olive says that she's never heard of such foolishness or such a waste of money but all the same she'll come and see for herself.

'You should get the story straight, Rose,' she says. 'Ruby had her good points and bad points just like the rest of us but she was never a saint.'

I know that. I remember her saying that once about my mother. I know better than anyone that my sister was an ordinary woman and she lived a small and ordinary life. She'd be the first to say so. I walk past women like her every day out on the street. Ordinary women going about the ordinary business of life, but small lives when you look at them closely are more than big enough to hold all those things in life that are important.

I'm not my sister but even so, when I put my mind to something I can also make 'arrangements' and one thing I've discovered is that when you've got some money and want to spend it 'arrangements' can be very easy to make.

I am how I am and I'm not so interested in small if I can get something bigger and I like colour, lots of colour, really bright, that's what suits me and I'm putting a nice size stained-glass window in St Agnes's Church, Woodstock, in memory of my sister.

Woodstock is not the smartest suburb in the world. If you listen to Auntie Olive she'll tell you that it's a slum and always was and perhaps she's right but the sun shines there just the same, just like it does everywhere else.

'God can bring the sun out and fill the world up with light. He can do that if He wants to.'

That's what my sister had said to me and that's what I think of while I wait for my window. I think that I will have bright colours and when I'm ready I will ask God to bring out the sun and while He's at it, what I'd really like is the brightest sun that He can manage. I want it to shine through my window so that everyone can see what a bright light even the small life of an ordinary woman brings to the world.

When Ruby was a little girl my mother used to ask her to sing 'Star of the Morning'. It was my mother's favourite hymn and Ruby liked to sing it because it made her feel important. She told me that and in later years she used to sing it to me sometimes to remind me and to this day, if you ask me, I can still sing it myself.

When you have money you can ask for anything you like and I ask for silver stars, a sky full of them. You can have silver and you can have gold too if you like. I ask for bright colours, the brightest colours the glass man can find in all his boxes of glass. Ruby red, sky blue, fuchsia, marigold and plum, emerald green, purple, berry red and violet. I ask for a little girl, in a St Agnes pink uniform dress with the black check lines going across it and her hair in plaits tied with pink ribbon. I want a road but not like the roads around here. I want a road that goes through green fields and I want even more colours for the flowers and I want the girl walking confident and happy like little girls are who are full of themselves because they know what love is.

'That poor man at the stained-glass workshop must think you're mad.'

That's my husband's opinion but I don't care. It's my money and I can spend it how I like and I know exactly what I want.

I want the road to be very clear. I want anyone who sees it to be able to see that this little girl's on her way home and that she's quite certain of the way and there's one last thing I want. I want a nice scroll at the top with a name across it.

'Star of the Morning'. That's what I want. I want it for my sister.

All my life I've known my sister Ruby and I know things about her that she never even knew I knew. I knew that all her life the one thing she wanted most of all was to be loved and I knew how much she wanted it. In all the trials of her life I knew how much she missed not having God to turn to and how she longed for Him to find some way to take her back. Sometimes I would look at her when she didn't know I was looking and I'd think that if He really wanted to He could give her what she'd longed for. All He would have to do is let her see how much He loved her, which was something that was so easy for her once when she was a little girl and took His love for granted. I wanted Him to do what they say in church He does. I wanted him to lift up the light of His countenance on Ruby and when He did, I wanted it to shine so bright that it would light her way all the long way home.

There's no plaque with Ruby's name on it, not exactly, because she never wanted that but perhaps some day someone might pay a visit to St Agnes's and wonder at such brightness in such a poor place and about the person who had a life that was remembered this way.

In time there'll be no one left who'll remember the real story. I know that but it doesn't matter.

' "Star of the Morning", what does that mean?' they'll say. 'Who was she, do you think? She must have been someone but there's not even a name.' No name, no birth date, no death date but she was someone all the same, that's something they'd be right about.

When Ruby was feeling down she used to say all the things she never was and never would be in her life and it worried her. She'd tap them off on her fingers, as if she was counting, as if she thought she might forget something and she did forget, in the way you forget the things around you that you see every day. Close family was important to her, yet she was no longer anyone's child, she was no one's wife, and no one's mother. She'd never be a grandmother and she'd never be an aunt and that was my fault. If she could have had her choice it was not how she would have liked things to be.

I always liked to stay on the right side of Ruby but even so I don't think that I will have let her down if I don't do every single thing she told me right down to the very last letter. I have something, one last thing of my own now, that I would like to give my sister to take with her on her journey just for a memory and there's no one that can give her this but me and I don't think that she'll mind. She never wanted a plaque but the plaque's very small. I don't think that too many people will even notice it's there.

Beloved Sister

That's all and it's not very much but she was always that. It's not all she might have wished to be but it's something at least and I don't think it will be too heavy a burden for her to carry as she goes on her way.

THE END

PEOPLE LIKE OURSELVES
Pamela Jooste

'HER WRITING IS CLEAR, LIGHT AND SHARPLY OBSERVANT'
Barbara Trapido, *Spectator*

Julia belongs to the inner circle of Johannesburg high society. But in the New South Africa, things have changed – the days of tea on the lawn are over.

Julia's husband, Douglas, is a serial adulterer who is no longer prepared to pay for the small luxuries she has always enjoyed. Her daughter has rebelled herself right out of Julia's life. She doesn't seem to be able to manage the 'home workers' who seem to have developed a will of their own, and her best friend, Caroline, is quietly considering killing her husband.

Now Douglas's ex-wife, who is never spoken of, has announced her intention of coming to visit from London bringing, no doubt, her politically correct credentials along with her. She's coming to see Nelson Mandela, she says.

People Like Ourselves takes a wry look at the brave new world that is the 'African miracle' today, by the prize-winning author of *Frieda and Min*, *Like Water in Wild Places* and *Dance with a Poor Man's Daughter*.

'PERCEPTIVE AND SENSITIVE AND EXTREMELY FUNNY'
The Times

'JOOSTE IS A SIGNIFICANT VOICE IN SOUTH AFRICAN WRITING . . . SHE CHALLENGES US TO SEE THE HURT, THE ANXIETY, THE TRUTHS'
Cape Argus

'FEW NOVELISTS HAVE WRITTEN ABOUT THE NEW SOUTH AFRICA IN THIS ACCESSIBLE, HUMOROUS AND INSIGHTFUL WAY, TO REVEAL A DARING AND PROVOCATIVE VISION OF LIFE AFTER TRUTH AND RECONCILIATION'
The Cape Times

9780552998710

BLACK SWAN

LIKE WATER IN WILD PLACES
Pamela Jooste

FROM THE PRIZE-WINNING AUTHOR OF *DANCE WITH A POOR MAN'S DAUGHTER*

'A REMARKABLE NOVEL . . . OUGHT TO WIN PRIZES . . . A GREAT BOOK'
Jennifer Crocker, *Cape Times*

'JOOSTE IS A SENSITIVE WRITER AND A MASTER OF UNDERSTATEMENT'
Isobel Shepherd Smith, *The Times*

The stories and legends of the Bushmen were told to Conrad when he was twelve years old. He was on a hunting trip with his father, Jack Hartmann, a brutal but confused man who 'gave' Conrad an old Bushman to teach him the ways of the land. Bastiaan taught him not only about the beasts and plants and soil, but inculcated in Conrad a philosophy that would remain with him throughout his life.

But at home Conrad learns a different set of rules as he and Beeky, the young sister he adores, huddle together listening to the sound of his mother being beaten and told she is trash. Jack Hartmann, a senator and man of power in the community, hates his wife and daughter as much as he loves his son, and Conrad's mother impresses on him that he must always protect and guard his little sister.

As they achieve maturity, Conrad appears to conform to the vision his father has for him, But Beeky defies her father and the establishment, and goes her own way, yearning for a new South Africa, a new life, tenderness and kindness in place of hatred and derision.

The story of their fulfilment, tragedy and the return of hope is the portrayal of an ancient land fighting towards redemption.

'HER UNDERSTANDING OF CHARACTER AND MOTIVATION, OF THE WAY IN WHICH HUMANITY CAN SHINE THROUGH IN ONE AREA AND FAIL LAMENTABLY IN ANOTHER IS OUTSTANDING. UNRESERVEDLY RECOMMENDED'
James Mitchell, *The Star*, South Africa

9780552998673

BLACK SWAN

FRIEDA AND MIN
Pamela Jooste

FROM THE PRIZE-WINNING AUTHOR OF *DANCE WITH A POOR MAN'S DAUGHTER*

'ONE OF THE NEW BREED OF WOMEN WRITERS IN SOUTH AFRICA WHO ARE TELLING OUR STORY WITH SUCH POWER AND TALENT'
Cape Times

When Frieda first met Min, with her golden hair and ivory bones, what struck her most was that Min was wearing a pair of African sandals, the sort made out of old car tyres. She was a silent, unhappy girl, dumped on Frieda's exuberant family in Johannesburg for the summer of 1964 so that her mother could go off with her new husband. In a way, Min and Frieda were both outsiders – Min, raised in the bush by her idealistic doctor father, and Frieda, daughter of a poor Jewish saxophone player, who lived almost on top of a native neighbourhood. The two girls, thrown together – the 'white kaffir' and the poor Jewish girl – formed a strange but loyal friendship, a friendship that was to last through the terrible years of oppression and betrayal during the time of South Africa under Apartheid.

'A NOVEL THAT EVERYONE SHOULD READ . . . HAS THAT RARE ABILITY TO BE BOTH MOVING AND FUNNY . . . DESERVES ALL THE PRAISE THAT IT WILL SURELY GET'
Pamela Weaver, *Examiner*

'HAS A GOOD STORY TO TELL AND SHE TELLS IT WELL . . . HAS LOST NONE OF THE QUALITIES THAT MADE *DANCE WITH A POOR MAN'S DAUGHTER* SO CREDIBLE'
Isobel Shepherd-Smith, *The Times*

9780552997584

BLACK SWAN

DANCE WITH A POOR MAN'S DAUGHTER
Pamela Jooste

'IMMENSELY MOVING AND READABLE'
Isobel Shepherd Smith, *The Times*

'My name is Lily Daniels and I live in the Valley, in an old house at the top of a hill with a loquat tree in the garden. We are all women in our house. My grandmother, my Aunt Stella with her hopalong leg, and me. The men in our family are not worth much. They are the cross we have to bear. Some of us, like my mother, don't live here any more. People say she went on the Kimberley train to try for white and I mustn't blame her because she could get away with it even if we didn't believe she would.'

Through the sharp yet loving eyes of eleven-year-old Lily we see the whole exotic, vivid, vigorous culture of the Cape Coloured community at the time when apartheid threatened its destruction. As Lily's beautiful but angry mother returns to Cape Town, determined to fight for justice for her family, so the story of Lily's past – and future – erupts. *Dance with a Poor Man's Daughter* is a powerful and moving tribute to a richly individual people.

'HIGHLY READABLE, SENSITIVE AND INTENSLY MOVING . . .
A FINE ACHIEVEMENT'
Mail and Guardian, South Africa

'TOUGH, SMART AND VULNERABLE . . . EMBLEMATIC OF AN
ENTIRE PEOPLE'
Independent

'I COULD HARDLY PUT THIS BOOK DOWN'
Cape Times

WINNER OF THE COMMONWEALTH BEST FIRST BOOK
AWARD FOR THE AFRICAN REGION

WINNER OF THE SANLAM LITERARY AWARD

WINNER OF THE BOOK DATA'S SOUTH AFRICAN
BOOKSELLER'S CHOICE AWARD

9780552997577

BLACK SWAN